# Other Titles By

# Wanda Y. Thomas

ENCHANTED DESIRE

FOREVER LOVE

PASSION'S JOURNEY

SUBTLE SECRETS

TREASURED DREAMS
(HOMELAND HEROES AND HEROINES, VOL. 2 ANTHOLOGY)

TRULY INSEPARABLE

# A Request for Closure

Wanda Y. Thomas

Parker Publishing, LLC

**Noire Allure** is an imprint of Parker Publishing, LLC.

Copyright © 2007 by Wanda Y. Thomas

Published by Parker Publishing, LLC
12523 Limonite Avenue, Suite #440-438
Mira Loma, California 91752
www.parker-publishing.com

ISBN 978-1-60043-016-9

First Edition

Manufactured in the United States of America

# Dedication

*This book is dedicated to my son, Marcel. I wish you a long life filled with love, peace, health, happiness, and the blessing of life-long friendships.*

# Acknowledgements

To my new publishing family—Parker Publishing, particularly, Miriam, Angelique, Deatri, and Genice. Thanks for the faith y'all!

To my editor Sidney-thanks for knocking this one around with me and for the use of your skills…but I'm sending you some purple pens…I really hate that red!

To my fans—your feedback and enjoyment of my work inspires me to continue writing. Thank you for the love.

To my sister-authors—Angie Daniels, JM Jeffries, TT Henderson, Natalie Dunbar, Pamela Leigh Starr, Seressia Glass, Gwyneth Bolton, Dyanne Davis, and AC Arthur. Y'all are so talented and I am humbled to part of this illustrious group, as well as so pleased to be able to count each of you as my friend.

To all—if God has blessed you with friends, cultivate the relationship and cherish each one. Besides the love of your family, friendship is one of the greatest blessings you can receive.

I must acknowledge the real inspiration behind this book: Jacci, Lisa, Jack, Evans, Michael, Stanley, and everybody's baby: Shannan, and countless others, which makes the list too long to name here. Thanks for the years of friendship and for the love. To old and new friends–we've had a hell of a ride and a lot fun…but the ride's not over so let's keep it going!

And finally…to my first love…Alvin Jack…although they sometimes don't stay, God brings people into your life for a reason…our time together was filled with love, laughter, and tears, but the lessons I learned during our relationship have lasted for a lifetime.

THE PRESENT

COLORADO SPRINGS,
COLORADO

SUMMER, 1999

# Chapter 1

*Paige Michaels*

They say you never forget your first love. That one man who was the first to rock your world so tough, currents still ripple through you whenever you think about him. You might be married to this man right now or maybe you haven't seen him in years. But this man—your first love—is the one you'll never forget.

Paige Michaels stood on the small, cement patio outside her condo looking out into the distance. Her mind was not on the scenic view or the changes time had wrought on the Colorado landscape. She was thinking about her first love, and how much their time together had influenced her life. She often found herself thinking about the past and the things she'd experienced in becoming the woman she was today. So far, her choices had made her a wife and mother at the age of seventeen, a divorcée at eighteen, and the owner of a highly lucrative executive services firm at forty-four. Sometimes Paige couldn't help wondering how her life might have turned out if only she'd made a different set of choices—would her life have been better, worse, or pretty much the same?

The sun was setting when Paige looked to the west. She watched streaks of hot pink, golden-orange, and misty lavender commingle and follow the sinking sun behind the Colorado Rocky Mountain range. The sunsets in Colorado were always a glorious sight and reminded Paige of the seasons. In the spring, the colors were fresh and new, like the cycle of life that unfurled each year. In the summer, they were bright and warm, like the heat and laziness of the days. In the fall, they were sharp and crisp, as if reflecting the hues of the changing foliage, and in winter, they were ethereal and cool, as if encased in the snow crystals that filled the air. She liked summer the best, which was why she'd chosen the month of July for her wedding.

Paige took one last look at the resplendent horizon then entered the house. She went into the kitchen, opened the day planner lying on the counter, and called her office in Denver. Listening to the messages, she jotted down some notes on the executives scheduled to go through training courses over the next couple of months. Then she picked up the wineglasses and a bottle of Chardonnay she'd set out earlier.

In the living room, Paige stopped and surveyed the space through eyes that had drifted back in time. For years, she had felt a growing need to come back to this city and this apartment complex. After one of her clients, a real estate broker mentioned that his firm acquired the property, it had seemed fitting somehow that she purchase the condominium. Once the wedding was over, the condo would become one of several rental properties in her investment portfolio and she'd return the furniture and the cream and peach décor items she'd rented.

In retrospect, it had worked out perfectly. This was the place where the chaos of her life had brought her to a turning point and holding her wedding in Colorado Springs would bring her life full circle. The last few months had been hectic and there had been times when she'd questioned her sanity. It was in those moments she missed Jazmin and Arianna most.

Paige moved to a black soft leather couch, set the items in her hands on the glass-topped table, and popped the cork on the wine. She filled her crystal wineglass, drank it down, and refilled the glass. Lounging back, she closed her eyes, enjoying the cool breeze wafting in through the open patio doors as her thoughts turned back to the two women who were closer to her than family.

Her friendships with the two women had begun at different times, but it was in this three-story building that the three of them had come together and formed a bond that had endured the test of time. Paige had always thought their friendship had flourished because of the things they'd all shared in common. A year separated their ages; all had been born in the month of July, and all three had left households headed by mothers none wanted to emulate in life. Hers had died five years ago. Paige drank deeply from her glass. Damn, sometimes she missed the old witch.

She knew it wasn't so much what they had in common as much as it was the uniqueness each had brought into the friendship. She'd been the wild child blowing through drugs and men like a tornado winding through town. Arianna, though naïve in many ways, had always been willing to lend an ear. She wrote romance novels and lived on a farm in Kansas with her husband and three boys. As arbiter, Jazmin had a way of calming things down among the three of them. She could also cause a ruckus if riled. After years on the international modeling circuit, Jazmin had opened a string of exclusive beauty salons. She lived in New York City now and she was married to a doctor. Paige had long suspected and now knew for a fact that the union was not a happy one. What she couldn't understand was why Jazmin, of all people, would try to play it off as if it were.

Paige had been pushing for a reunion for years. Arianna and Jazmin had never been able to agree on a date that would work for both of them. She could understand that. Both of them led extremely busy lives. However, the chapters in your book of life opened, filled, and closed so fast it was hard to keep up with the passage of time, and for every choice made, other possibilities remained unexplored. Most people had something in their past they wished they'd handled differently. Usually, it was pride that prevented them from taking advantage of the opportunity to effect a positive change. She'd seized her opportunity and her restless spirit was calm. She just wanted the same thing for her friends.

She sipped from her glass. Now her girls wouldn't even return her calls, and to Paige, that was unacceptable. The three of them had been friends too long for her to let Arianna and Jazmin slip out of her life. Since they both seemed hell-bent on ignoring her, this time she'd sent each of them a telegram, hoping the short missive would get her friends back to Colorado. She'd know, in a few days at most, whether Jazmin and Arianna would come back and whether the reunion she longed for would take place.

## A *Request for Closure*

"Why are you sitting in the dark?"

Paige pushed herself up. "I was thinking."

"About what?"

"Arianna and Jazmin…and whether they'll come home this time."

"Well, all you can do now is wait and see."

"I know, but you know me, the *now* queen. I won't be able to calm down completely until I hear from them. But even if Arianna can't make it, I sure hope that Jazmin does. I'm worried about her."

"If they do come, do you want me here when they arrive?"

"No, at least not until I give you a call. I'd like to spend some time alone with my girls."

"I understand."

She tilted her head, her eyes loving as they roamed his face. "Do you really?"

He sighed. "Yeah, I do." He picked up the book on the table. "You ready?"

"Yes," she said, and reaching out, Paige turned on the peach-colored lamp sitting on the corner table as he came to join her on the couch.

# Chapter 2

*Arianna Jackson-Lane*

Frederick Lane, Freddie to his family and friends, reached into his pocket and pulled out a five-dollar bill. He handed the money to the pimply-faced teenager at his front door.

The boy grinned. "Thank you, sir, and you have a nice day!"

"Thanks," Freddie said, closing the door. He stared at the yellow envelope addressed to his wife and an inexplicable feeling of unease washed over him. Though tempted, he quelled the urge to open the telegram. Besides, once Arianna read the message, he would know what it said. He and his wife didn't keep secrets from each another.

Freddie ran a hand over his unshaven face and turned for the kitchen where his wife and three boisterous sons had already assembled for breakfast. He arrived just in time to see ten-year-old Brett flick a wet corn flake off his spoon at his seven-year-old brother, Robert, who then repaid his brother in kind. Arianna, busy wiping the face of their eighteen-month-old toddler, James, presumably hadn't witnessed the commotion going on between their sons.

Freddie stopped in the doorway. Sunlight streaming through the kitchen window brought out the highlights in her shoulder-length, auburn hair and formed a halo around Arianna. Her creamy brown skin seemed to glow in the sunshine. The blue chenille robe hid a figure of curves so luscious Freddie got excited just thinking about them, and when she looked at him, her caramel-colored eyes were so full of love they touched his soul. Satisfied with his wife and his life, he walked into the kitchen.

A smile lit up Arianna's face, as it always did whenever Freddie came into her view. His sable skin had a natural sheen. Jet-black curls blanketed his well-shaped head. His chin was square and strong, and topped with a set of generous lips and a thin black mustache. His chiseled jaw and high cheekbones drew attention away from his wide nose to thickly fringed hazel eyes that always showed the depth of his feelings for her. Broad shoulders tapered down to arms that rippled with muscles and a powerful physique honed from years of hard work. Freddie's six-foot, six-inch frame and imposing size belied his gentle nature.

"Morning, baby. Who was at the door?"

"A telegram...for you." Freddie leaned down for her brief kiss before handing over the envelope and taking his seat at the head of the table.

"For me?" Arianna dropped the washcloth. "I wonder who would be sending a telegram to me."

"Why don't you open it and find out who sent it." Freddie tried to appear disinterested as he reached for the platter of sausage and eggs sitting in the middle of the table. Had Arianna been observing him, she would have seen the anxiety in his eyes when she ripped open the envelope and read the message.

Without comment, she slid the telegram back inside and laid the envelope beside her plate. "Brett and Robert, if the two of you don't stop throwing cereal at this table, you'll both go to time out."

"But Mommy," Robert wailed, "Brett started it."

"And I'm ending it. Now, both of you eat. When you're done, I want the two of you to clean up that junkyard you call a bedroom."

"Mom, I have a game today. I don't have time to clean my room."

"You'll clean your room before you go to your game or you won't be going."

"I have to go," Brett responded. "The team needs me! Tell her, Dad."

Brett was the star pitcher on his little league team. His father was the coach. "You heard what I said, Son. I told you and Bobby to clean that room yesterday. The two of you decided to play. Today, you get to live with the consequences of that decision."

"Awww," Brett responded.

Arianna eyed her oldest, a miniature version of his father with her skin tone. "Awww, nothing. Now eat and then get busy on that room."

Freddie heard and processed the conversation without really listening to a thing. His gaze strayed to the envelope, then up to his wife's face.

"Baby, your parents want to ride with us to the game, so we'll need to leave a little early."

"Yes," he said quietly. "Mom called last night while you were taking your bath."

"Oh, then you already knew."

"Yeah, honey. I already knew." What he didn't know was what that telegram said, and he wanted to know why Arianna hadn't yet told him. Maybe he should ask to see it, but a gut feeling told Freddie it was something he'd be better off not knowing.

He reached for the toast. "Are you boys finished?"

"Yes, sir," they both answered immediately.

"Then take your bowls to the sink and go and get started on your bedroom. The game doesn't begin until three, so you have plenty of time to get it into tip-top shape for your mother."

He winked at his wife and Arianna rewarded him with a soft stroke of her hand along his cheek. When she pulled back, the envelope fell to the floor. Arianna picked it up and stuffed it into a pocket of her robe before standing to lift James from his high chair. She cuddled her baby against her chest. "Come on, Boo, its time for your bath."

At the doorway, she turned back. "Baby, do you need anything before I go upstairs?"

His eyes roamed her face. "No, honey. I have everything I need. When I'm finished with breakfast, I'll get the kitchen in order while you're giving James his bath."

"Thank you, baby. You are always so good to me, and the best man any woman could have."

Freddie pushed his mouth into a lopsided grin. "I'll check on the boys' progress in that room before I head out to the barn."

"I love you."

Do you really? The unbidden question rocked Freddie to his core. He hadn't questioned his wife's love for him during the entire time of his marriage. Why now, when Arianna had not given him any reason to doubt her feelings for him? He forced the negative thoughts from his mind and dug into the food on his plate. His wife did love him; he was sure of it and in the end that was all that really mattered.

—··—

The farther Arianna moved away from her husband, the more guilt weighed down her steps. She should have immediately shown the telegram to Freddie She'd seen his confusion and the change in his eye color, from gray to green—their color whenever he was anxious or upset. However, she was also sure that not showing Freddie the telegram was the best thing to do, at least until she thought of a way to make him understand how she felt about it. The message inside was too volatile and would hurt her husband too much. She'd done that once in their relationship and had promised herself that she would never hurt Frederick Lane in that manner again.

Freddie was a good man, and one that she would be a fool to take a chance on losing. However, for one time stopping second, that's exactly what Arianna had wanted to do. Now all she wanted was to go back to her husband and assure him that everything was okay.

Instead, she climbed the stairs. In the nursery, she gently set her son inside a colorful playpen, and then went into the boys' bathroom. She prepared his bath, stopping on her way out of the room when she caught sight of herself in the mirror. Arianna pulled the envelope from her pocket and reread the telegram.

*Ari,*

*I know that I've been asking for years, but you have to come now. It has taken me years to find the right man and I am finally getting married. The wedding will be small; and I want you and Jazz to be my matrons of honor. Please come and share my joy on the happiest day of my life. Call me when you get this message and let me know when you can get to Colorado.*

*I love you, girl,*

*Oh, there is one more thing that you should know. Jace has agreed to stand up for my intended and he told me to let you know that he is looking forward to seeing you again.*

*Paige*

The mirror reflected Arianna's agitation and confusion. Why now? Why now, when she had waited so long to hear even one word from him? Why now, when she had three wonderful sons and a loving and supportive husband who had provided her with a better life than any she could have dreamed?

"Honey, are you all right?"

Arianna tensed. Freddie was so sensitive to her and to her needs; it was useless to try to hide anything from him. He already knew something was wrong.

His arms curved around her waist. "Arianna?"

She rested against his frame and let his warmth comfort her. "I'm fine, baby."

Freddie rubbed his cheek against the softness of her locks. Arianna turned in his arms and met his lips when he angled his head and sought her mouth.

The kiss they shared felt intoxicating and packed so much heat Freddie had to drag his mouth away to catch his breath. Arianna pressed against him. In response, his manhood began to rise and thicken and Freddie groaned as he took her lips and made love to her mouth again. Only Arianna had the power to do this to him, to make him so needy that he could think of nothing else except tossing her on their bed and driving himself into her until she milked him of his essence.

Because of that, it took everything Freddie had within him to drop his arms and step away from his wife. Arianna moaned in protest. Her eyes fluttered open and she moved toward him, seeking the warmth of his arms again.

Freddie held up his hand. "No, Ari."

She grabbed his hand and pulled him to her until their bodies were flush. Freddie fought to bring his body back under submission, tipping his wife's chin with one of his hands while the other anchored her waist and stopped her sensual movements.

He waited until her eyes opened, kissed her softly, and held her gaze. "Arianna Lane, is there something you need to tell me?"

# Chapter 3

*Jazmin Reed-Miller*

Jazmin Reed-Miller pulled the metal grate across the front of the door. She attached three locks, and then gave the grate a fierce shake to make sure they would hold before turning to the stylist who'd stood guard as she secured her salon for the night.

"Goodnight, Brandy."

"Night, Jazz. Take care and be sure to tell that handsome husband of yours that I said hello."

Jazmin twisted her lips to keep from blurting out the truth. Yes, William was handsome, and all of her female employees and clients thought she was so lucky to have landed him. Jazmin knew all too well that their envy was misplaced. Of course, she would never tell them that. In public, she and William presented themselves as the perfect couple, a guise quickly discarded inside the walls of their home. Not even Arianna and Paige knew the true state of her marriage to William Arthur Miller, one of New York City's most preeminent and highly respected pediatricians.

Jazmin hurried over to the black Lexus sitting in a reserved spot behind her shop. She tucked herself into the soft, champagne-colored seat and stuck her key into the ignition. Then she sat back into the seat. She had no reason to hurry home, and if William was there, she wanted to be somewhere else, anywhere else.

Quicker than a blink, her mind turned to Vincent Marks. Lately, he'd been occupying a place in her thoughts, but Jazmin had put it down to the promo she'd seen last week advertising a new daytime series with Vincent in a lead role. Her heart increased its rhythmic beat.

## A *Request for Closure*

Twenty years ago when she'd decided to resume her modeling career, she'd had every intention of returning to marry Vincent. For two years, they had fought to hold on to their relationship, but daily conversations combined with infrequent visits had taken their toll. By tacit agreement, both had let their relationship drift away.

She knew that after eleven years in the NBA, he had cut and released two R&B singles that went platinum. He'd also spent a few years as a sports broadcaster before setting his sights on Hollywood. Jazmin couldn't remember the name of the woman he'd married ten years ago. She could only remember how devastated she'd been by the news. She had wed William two months later, only to learn through a mutual acquaintance that Brick had ended his marriage after six months. But as with everything else he'd done in his professional life, she knew that Vincent's career as an actor would be successful, too.

Jazmin was happy for him. At least that's what she told herself as she started her car and headed onto the busy street. Pride framed her face when she saw the large, white light bulbs spelling out the name of her salon, Exotica. The one salon she'd dreamed of owning had morphed into five, four of which she'd strategically located in European cities where the rich and the beautiful indulged their passions. The look of pride faded from her face when she thought about her life with William Miller again.

She needed a drink, and with that thought, Jazmin pulled into a side lot. She parked her car in front of a hole-in-the-wall lounge, only one of many she frequented in a bid to keep herself away from her own house.

It was eleven o'clock when Jazmin left the bar sailing in the glow of five vodka tonics, and after midnight when she parked in a garage next to William's black Porsche, his silver Mercedes-Benz, and his pride and joy, a custom-built, 1992 red Lamborghini Diablo he'd picked up at an auction. Her husband had an obsession for acquiring beautiful and expensive things, and as with anything that held his attention, William took it to the extreme.

Turning away, Jazmin entered through the side door, grateful for the recessed lighting lining the shiny hardwood as she passed by the Italian-tiled island in the middle of the kitchen. She paused when she saw the light under the door to William's study, and then she headed for the stairs. Halfway up, she heard the door open.

"Jazmin, may I have a minute of your time…in the study, if you don't mind?"

He turned away, but not before Jazmin saw him sway and catch himself. William had been drinking, which meant that the only thing awaiting her in that study was another confrontation.

Silently praying for strength, Jazmin stood in the doorway of a large, cozily decorated room; William was sitting behind his cherry wood desk. He had a glass in his hand, filled with what she knew to be Hennessey, his drink of choice. William was an attractive man…no, make that classically handsome. Everything about his looks bespoke of William's carefully planned lineage, from his light-toned skin and gray eyes to the wavy brown hair on his head.

For Jazmin, character traits such as his domineering nature and uncontrolled temper had destroyed any feelings she'd had for him long ago.

William almost groaned aloud when Jazmin wet her lips with her tongue. He loved his wife and wanting the woman he'd married back in his arms, he'd come home early, determined to end their estrangement. He'd ordered in her favorite Italian dinner and had just finished arranging a large bouquet of orange roses on the romantically set table when a messenger arrived at his door. At first, he'd laid the telegram on the hallway table where he knew that Jazmin would see it. A couple of hours later, unable to allay his curiosity, he'd opened and read the message.

Malevolence colored William's gaze when he thought about his ruined plans. "Did you have a good time this evening?"

She'd heard the ominous tone that filled his voice but Jazmin entered the room anyway. "No more than any other evening. Why, did you miss me?"

William snorted and sipped from his glass. The first time he'd seen Jazmin had been in Central Park. Normally, he would have never approached a stranger on the streets of New York. However, the tears on her face had compelled him to take a seat next to her and ascertain the reason why a gorgeous woman would sit in a park on a sunny day crying. Learning that she'd just attended her mother's funeral had prompted William to let Jazmin use his chest as a handkerchief. Then he'd taken her across the street for a bite to eat and had ended the meal by getting her phone number.

Jazmin had been a model then and preparing to leave for an extended stay in Europe. They had a whirlwind, three-week courtship, at the end of which William had asked Jazmin to be his wife. Once she'd left on the tour, he'd done what was necessary during her absence to make sure their marriage took place as soon as she returned.

They had taken their vows at his family's cottage in Oak Bluffs, Massachusetts—for several generations, a summer stomping ground of affluent African-Americans. They had spent the first week of their honeymoon at the cottage before leaving for Jamaica, where for William, their relationship had changed. From the male waiters and staff at their hotel to unknown men on the beach, Jazmin had attracted attention wherever they went. In his heart, William knew he couldn't blame her. Jazmin was an extraordinarily beautiful woman. But it was then that he'd known that, as with his first, he would have to contain his gorgeous, socially prone wife.

On rare occasions, like tonight when she pinned her vacant stare on him or when a telling bruise marked her flawless skin, the things William had done to get Jazmin nagged at his conscience. Not enough for him to experience any regret, but enough for him to question what he could have done differently.

He set his glass on the desk. "No more than any other evening. Why, are you feeling guilty?"

"What do you want, William?"

"What I want is to know where my wife has been for the past six hours."

"If you really wanted to know, then you would have called the shop."

"I did call the shop, which closed at six. It is now after midnight."

Jazmin turned for the door. "I'm going to bed."

"Aren't you even curious as to why I wanted to see you this evening?"

"Not really. Goodnight, William."

"Then perhaps you'd be interested in seeing this!"

The thunderous sound of his voice stopped Jazmin in her tracks. When she turned back, William was on his feet and he held a yellow envelope in his outstretched hand. Taking her time, she walked over and took the envelope. His eyes narrowed to slits as she removed and read the message. The last sentence caught and held Jazmin's attention.

*...Oh, there is one more thing that you should know. Brick has agreed to sing at the wedding and he told me to let you know that he is looking forward to seeing you again.*

*Paige*

Her heart pounded so furiously, Jazmin thought it would explode. She looked up, encountered her husband's cold stare, and quickly tempered her expression. Over the years, she'd learned the wisdom of keeping her feelings hidden lest she give William another weapon with which to irritate the hell out of her.

"Is this Brick person one of the men you've been seeing behind my back?"

Jazmin didn't bother with a response. William's constant accusations were funny in a perverse sort of way because while he had a string of mistresses across the city, she hadn't stepped out on him once, and not because she hadn't had ample opportunities.

A long time ago, Jazmin had promised herself the one and only time she married would not end in divorce, and since she'd pledged her life to the bastard, she felt duty bound to stick by that vow. At least she had until she'd read the message in her hands.

William walked over to her. "Are you going to answer me, Jazmin, or are you thinking up another lie to convince me that you have always been true to our marriage?"

She stuffed the telegram into her purse. "What's the point of this discussion, William? You don't really care if another man has an interest in me. You don't care about me at all. If you did you wouldn't leave this house every night to go and fuck one of your many mistresses."

When he backhanded her, Jazmin didn't cringe and she didn't cry. She simply moved her hand to her mouth and wiped away the blood that trickled from her lip. "Nice one, William. Maybe next time you won't be so drunk and you can really do some damage."

Jazmin knew she shouldn't provoke William, especially when he had been drinking, but she couldn't seem to stop herself, not when she knew that Vincent Marks wanted to see her again. Knowing that brought back a little of the woman she'd once been and heightened her contempt for the man she called her husband.

William lifted his hand again; Jazmin tensed and closed her eyes, but opened them a few moments later to find that he'd left the room. With a sigh, Jazmin exited the study just as the door to the garage slammed closed. Despite the throb in her lip, Jazmin smiled as she climbed the stairs to her bedroom.

# THE REUNION

# COLORADO SPRINGS, COLORADO

# SUMMER, 1999

# Chapter 4

*Arianna*

Nothing could have prepared her for the sight of the white, three-story building or for the memories that came along with it. The last time she'd come to Colorado had been for her mother's funeral eight years earlier. She'd flown in on the day of the interment and left for the airport immediately after the services, and she hadn't told anyone outside of her family that she was coming. On the plane this morning, Arianna had told herself that she was ready, that she could handle whatever lay in store for her that weekend.

She drew in a deep breath and then blew it out. This was going to be harder than she'd thought. It was okay, she told herself. After all, it was only one weekend out of her life and a really old building that held memories but no power over her. She could get through this and then return home to her family.

When she'd shown Freddie the telegram, she'd waited for him to tell her that she couldn't go. She'd wanted him to say that he didn't want her seeing the man who'd caused the only real dissension in their relationship. Freddie hadn't done that. He'd told her to pack her bags and had used the farm and the boys as reasons for him to remain at home.

Using her hand to shield her eyes from the bright sun, Arianna looked up at the building again. For years, Paige had been pushing for a reunion, but her reasons had always been a confusing muddle of thoughts and Arianna had always found excuses to not come.

With her husband's blessing, Arianna was back in Colorado Springs. She told herself that she wanted to see her friends again. That it would be great to hang out for the weekend, to reunite, to reacquaint, and to reaffirm their friendship. While that was true, there was another reason Arianna was still not ready to acknowledge.

Lifting her suitcase, she crossed the parking lot, but instead of going to Paige's condo, Arianna climbed the seven wooden steps on the side of the building to the second floor. She walked down the carpeted hallway and stopped in front of the door marked 12B.

A lot of things had happened to her behind that door. She'd lost her virginity, fallen in love, and had her heart broken all in the span of a few years. When the memories assailed her, Arianna set her suitcase on the floor as the meaning behind what Paige had been saying finally became clear to her.

For seventeen years, she had felt sheltered and protected in the bosom of her family and in thinking she'd put Jace Barnes behind her, Arianna had unknowingly let more than miles separate her from her friends. Jace had been the first man she'd ever loved and it took Arianna a long time to get over him. She had gotten over him, but Jace had always been there in the back of her mind, lurking and surfacing on rare occasions when she'd wonder what had happened to him. Arianna had always known that Jace would come back. Now that he had, she would get the answers she'd so desperately sought before Frederick Lane came into her life.

Arianna reached into her purse for her cell phone, dialing the number as she sat on top of her large, brown suitcase.

"Brett," she said when her son answered. "It's Mom."

"Mom! I miss you. When are you coming home?"

"Soon, my darling, real soon. Is your Dad there?"

"He's in the kitchen fixing a bottle for James."

"Go, and tell him that I'm on the phone."

While waiting for her husband, Arianna heard her baby crying in the background and spoke to Robert, who reiterated how much her family loved and missed her.

"Honey, did you make it all right?"

The resonant timbre of her husband's voice washed over Arianna like a warm spring shower, pulling her back to where she belonged, and where she should have stayed. "I'm fine, baby. I called to let you know that I arrived safely and—" When her baby cried out again, Arianna switched gears. "Freddie, what's wrong with James? He's been crying since I called. He's probably missing me. I'm coming home."

"James is fine. He just woke up from his nap and you are not coming home. Paige expects you to be in her wedding and you have something you need to resolve. I don't want that man coming between us ever again."

"He's not coming between us, Freddie. I love you. You know that."

"Arianna, you once told me that you would always love Jace Barnes and when he sent for you, you would go to him. Well, now you have your chance."

Everything in her world stopped. "W-what are you saying, baby?"

"I'm saying that I'm not willing to share you anymore, Arianna. I'm saying that I want my wife to be whole and I want her to want and to love only me, and if you can't do that…then I'm saying that I don't want you to come back to me."

"Freddie." The word left her mouth in a rush of air. "You can't possibly mean that. I don't care about Jace Barnes. I love you and I thought that you loved me."

"I do love you, Ari, and I pray that when this weekend is over you will have chosen me and the life we've built together. I have to go; the boys need me."

'Freddie, wait! Freddie, please don't…!"

The line had already gone dead. Arianna furiously dialed her number again. The line rang and rang, but no one picked up the phone.

———∽∿∾———

*Jazmin*

When the yellow cab rolled to a stop, Jazmin handed the driver a twenty and waved away his offer of change. So what if the ride from the airport only cost five dollars. She was in the mood to be generous today.

## A *Request for Closure*

The driver left the car to retrieve her luggage from the trunk. Staring up at the building, Jazmin blinked back tears that came unbidden to her eyes with the memories of the time she'd lived in the Pikes Peak Avenue Apartments, particularly the months she'd shared with Vincent Marks.

Jazmin ran a hand through her hair and then down her cheek, grimacing when she felt the dull ache along her jaw line. When she'd told William of her plans to leave for Paige's wedding, the fight had been bad, worse than any they'd had in the ten years of their marriage. She'd never seen her husband so enraged, and after his fist had connected with her jaw, Jazmin could remember nothing that happened immediately afterward. She could only recall awakening in her bedroom and finding William on his knees with his head on her stomach, sobbing and babbling like an idiot.

When he sensed that she was awake, he'd gathered her battered torso in his arms and whispered fervent words of an apology, while at the same time blaming her for inciting his rage. If only she wouldn't challenge him. If only she would do as he asked, things could be different between them. He would change, he'd promised, and he would never put his hands on her again.

Jazmin had listened as she had so many times during their marriage, sure that William would not change and he would put his hands on her again. It was always the same, the same empty words, and the same empty promises.

For the first five years of her marriage, Jazmin had acquiesced to every one of William's demands. She'd changed the way she dressed, the way she spoke, and toned down her penchant for befriending those she did not know, and she had lost a little of herself with each alteration. She'd told herself that her husband did love her as she compromised, complied, and consented in an effort to mold herself into the woman William had wanted her to be. She'd given in and given up so much until Jazmin could find in herself no part of the woman that she'd once been.

William's so-called love was like poison, a slow moving toxin that tormented her mind and shattered her spirit a little more with each

24

passing day. This time she'd survived his wrath, but the next time she might not be so lucky, and Jazmin Reed-Miller was not ready to die. Nor would she end up like her mother: man-less, friend-less, and talking to her dogs about her six failed marriages until the day she died.

The morning after the fight, Jazmin had packed her bags and moved into a hotel. She'd filed for a divorce, and three weeks later, left Brandy in charge of the salon and caught a flight to Colorado. Life didn't often offer do-overs, and if it turned out that Vincent Marks still wanted her, Jazmin made a new vow that this time she'd get it right.

She sniffled again and pulled a tissue out of her purse. What in the world was the matter with her? Dabbing at her eyes and nose, she wondered when she'd turned into such a runny-nosed wimp. She used to be so strong. That had been then—so many years ago. Now, she was softer, a little more beat down, and not so apt to fly off the handle to prove how tough she was.

"Ma'am, are you getting out here?"

Jazmin blinked at the cab driver who stood there waiting for her to make a move. She quickly gathered her purse and stepped from the car.

The apartment building looked different now, as did the entire street and block. Academy Boulevard encompassed six lanes and was a major intersection, and there were homes and apartment buildings on what had once been empty land. Everything had changed, and yet she felt the same and she could almost make herself believe that it had all happened yesterday.

With a sigh, Jazmin lifted her suitcase and turned toward the first floor, corner condo—Paige's old apartment. It would be good to see her girls again.

Paige took a deep breath and opened the front door. For a few hazy moments, all she could do was stare at her friend. In the lavender pantsuit, it was hard to tell that Jazmin had gained a few pounds. Her black hair was styled into an elegant twist and her beautifully made up face appeared fuller. Her smile was bright, but it wasn't enough to erase the bleak shadows in the depths of her black eyes.

## A Request for Closure

"Well, am I coming inside or am I supposed to park my ass out here on the floor?"

A heartbeat later, Paige was in the hallway rocking her friend in a tight embrace. Jazmin grimaced, but did her best to return the hug of welcome.

Paige stepped back. "Come in, come in. I'm so glad to see you and so happy that you could come for my wedding." She set Jazmin's luggage by the door and led her over to the couch. "How was your trip out? Good?"

"The trip was fine, P. Is Ari here?"

"Not yet, which is surprising since her flight landed over an hour ago." She shrugged, unconcerned. "But I'm sure she'll find her way here soon enough."

Jazmin examined Paige. Gold highlights no longer tipped the ends of her hair and the short curly style suited her oval-shaped face. Paige had not gained an ounce on her svelte figure and her copper brown eyes radiated happiness.

Paige opened a teakwood box on the table and extracted a cigarette. "When did you start smoking?"

"When I gave up weed." Paige crossed one slender leg over the other. "Some of those executives I coach are hardheaded and cause a lot of stress, which is why their HR departments send them to me in the first place. Smoking helps me relax at the end of the day." Paige lit the cigarette and inhaled. "But I don't smoke nearly as much since I got engaged." She waved her left hand in the air.

Jazmin inspected the five-carat marquise diamond ring. "It's beautiful, P."

"Thanks. It took a long time but I finally figured out where my love lay."

"You've been awfully secretive about this man. Where is he? What's his name? Tell me something, girl."

Paige's mouth curved upward. "You'll know everything you need to know soon enough."

26

Jazmin tsked her tongue in impatience. "Whateva, P. Keep your damn secrets."

Paige left the sofa, crossing to the stereo where she loaded several CDs. A few moments later, Anita Baker's sultry-sounding voice floated out into the space. "I can hardly believe it has been twenty years since the three of us lived here."

Jazmin chuckled. "I know, girl. The years passed so fast, I hardly noticed until the crow's feet and wrinkles around my mouth showed up in the mirror. But you look fantastic."

Paige returned to the couch and picked up her cigarette. "Thanks, but I have just as many wrinkles. Life's been rough at times, though lately mine's been good, but that youthful face of the girl you met is long gone, never to return."

Jazmin kicked off her shoes and made herself comfortable on the sofa cushions. "How did we meet anyway?"

"My stepdad of the moment introduced us. Being an insurance rep, a new black family meant money to him."

"Now, I remember," Jazmin said. "We had just met and when I pulled a joint out of my purse, I thought you were going to wet your pants from the shock of seeing an illegal drug in the hands of a normal person."

"There has never been anything normal about you, Jazmin Reed, not from the moment we met."

"And I thought you were boring."

"I wasn't boring! I was sixteen, pregnant, and trying to hold it together until my fiancé returned home from basic training."

"You were boring! You didn't smoke, you didn't drink, and you certainly didn't do drugs. You were a goody-two shoes, whose only apparent vice was getting laid."

"Well, maybe I was a little boring. But I wanted a healthy baby so I had to be good."

"Then you had Jessie, sent Thomas packing, and discarded your Suzy Homemaker duds for party girl gear."

"That's because I knew that marriage was doomed from the start."

## A Request for Closure

"Now there we are on the same wavelength, girlfriend. I sure wish I'd rethought my decision to marry William Miller. Girl, talk about a huge mistake."

"What! You've always told me that you were happy with your husband."

"Then you heard wrong, but I don't want talk about my marriage. I want to know where Arianna is. Are you sure her flight arrived on time?"

# Chapter 5

*Arianna*

"A re you okay, Miss?"

Arianna turned away from the man's inquisitive stare. "I'm fine."

"Are you sure?"

"Yes, I'm sure."

"Well, if you're sure."

"I'm sure. Thank you for your concern."

She waited until he moved away, and then surveyed the area. It was a familiar place because she'd come here once before when her heart had taken a blow that almost leveled her, only this time the park didn't have the same effect. She had found no peace and Arianna wasn't sure she ever would again now that she knew her husband didn't want her anymore. Sharp, aching pains stabbed at her chest and Arianna folded her arms over her heart as her thoughts took her back in time…

———*✦✦✦*———

Frederick Lane had come into her life at a time when she'd been at her lowest. She'd moved in with Paige in Denver, and after nine months of missing Jace, she'd flown to New York to see him. Jace hadn't even attempted to accommodate her visit. Utterly despondent, Arianna had returned home and waited for him to call and explain. Jace never called.

Several weeks later, she had come out of her bedroom and found a dark and strikingly handsome man sitting in the living room. He was a tall man who took up a lot space on the couch. He looked trapped and was obviously uncomfortable with the personal questions seven-year-old Jessica Michaels, Paige's daughter, thought it her place to ask.

Jessie had always been precocious. Knowing that, Arianna charged to the rescue and immediately forgot what she was going to say when their gazes met. Before she knew it, Arianna was sitting next to Frederick Lane having a conversation, and a few minutes later, feeling strangely disappointed when Paige and her date interrupted. The three of them were going to the club and Freddie's sudden hug and kiss on her cheek at the door, as well as their chat, had accompanied Arianna into a fitful sleep.

The following night, he'd come back and Arianna still couldn't recall how Freddie had coaxed her into talking about Jace or how he'd ended up in her bed. All she knew was that by the time the sun rose the next morning, Frederick Allen Lane had torn a rent in the veil covering her eyes.

Arianna hadn't planned to see Freddie again, but over the next six months, they somehow fell into a casual routine that was confined to her bedroom. When she needed Freddie, he came with the understanding that while she shared her body with him, her heart was in New York with Jace Barnes. She hadn't known that Freddie had a problem with their arrangement until the night he'd shown up unexpectedly and witnessed the hug that she'd given to one of her neighbors.

In the bedroom, Freddie had stripped off her clothes, removed his own, and positioned Arianna on the bed. He pinned her arms above her head, entered her body, and stopped. "You want this real bad, don't you?"

She humped her body. "Please, Freddie."

"Who was that man and what is he to you?"

The man was a neighbor who'd carried a large box up three flights of stairs to her apartment. "A neighbor and he's married."

Freddie released her arms and wrapped his hands around her calves. "Are you sleeping with him, Arianna?"

She tried to move and get him started, but Freddie refused to cooperate. "No," she finally answered.

Still holding her legs, Freddie moved his hips like pistons, his long strokes deep and straining. To her, it felt as if he were trying to punish or prove something to Arianna. When it was over, they sat side by side on the bed.

"What was that about, Freddie?"

"Nothing," he said, a little on the morose side.

"It didn't feel like nothing. It felt like you were trying to hurt me. Was this about my neighbor?"

"This is not about your neighbor, Arianna! This is about the man in your heart! Why can't you let him go? Jace Barnes is not coming back and he won't send for you. I don't care what he said!"

"Jace *will* send for me," she said through trembling lips. "He needs to straighten out a few things before we can be together."

"And you still believe that?"

"Yes!"

"Why?"

"Because he said so!"

"Well, according to you, he hasn't said so lately. And he doesn't appear to miss you very much. Otherwise he'd be here or you'd be there with him!" Freddie drew in a deep breath and swiped his hands down his face. "You're a fool, Arianna Jackson! And you're throwing away something that's standing right in front of you for something that will never be."

For a moment, Freddie's words left her speechless, because Arianna knew that he was right. Jace hadn't called or kept his promise, and by now, he had to have gotten his divorce. Was it possible that he had forgotten about her? Then she pushed the negative thoughts from her mind. Jace would call and he would explain. She needed to be more patient.

She leveled a glare at Freddie. He had a lot of nerve talking to her like that. They used each other for sex and they didn't pretend to themselves or to other people that they were involved on any other level. "That was a cruel thing to say to me, Frederick Lane, when you knew about Jace before any of this ever started. I will always love Jace and when he sends for me, I'm going to him. I don't care how many years it takes!"

## A Request for Closure

The wound she'd inflicted opened before her eyes and Arianna almost regretted her outburst. Freddie apologized and left; Arianna knew it was over between the two of them. Three weeks later, he called and asked her to dinner. She declined and invited him over and was somewhat dismayed when Freddie told her he wouldn't see her again until she agreed to go out with him; Arianna reluctantly agreed.

Compatibility was not even a question; romance and fun were the words that came to her mind when she thought about their dates. Freddie was a great listener and actually cared about what she thought. He knew how to make her laugh and the burning passion they shared in bed seemed to grow every time he took Arianna in his arms. It took another year for Arianna realized that in the process of bringing the joy back into her life, Frederick Lane had also won her heart.

A few weeks later, Freddie kissed Arianna awake and mounted her. His first stroke was so long and so deep, she felt every inch of him. Moving with relentless surety, Freddie used his body to try to convey the depth of his feelings for her. Arianna bucked and rocked under Freddie's passionate assault and cried out her pleasure several times.

"I tried to make you forget him," Freddie whispered near her ear as he thrust his hips forward one last time and rode the wave of pleasure that washed over him.

When their breathing returned to normal, Freddie cradled Arianna in her arms and guided her head to his chest.

"I'm leaving."

"I know. You usually do."

"No, honey. I mean, I'm leaving Colorado...today."

That got her attention and Arianna sat up. "Where are you going?"

"Home. To Kansas."

"When will you be back?"

Freddie sighed and sat up, too. "I'm not coming back."

"Why, Freddie?"

"My family is having problems and they need me to come home. I have to go."

"Why are you telling me this now, on the day you're planning to leave?"

Freddie exhaled. "I didn't know how to tell you, Ari. I wasn't sure how you'd react."

She was alarmed, which she carefully kept hidden. "How did you expect me to react?"

"Well, I kind of hoped you'd ask me to stay."

"Why would I do that? Your family should come before me. If they need you, then you should go."

Freddie opened his arms, holding Arianna close when she snuggled into his strong embrace. "You're upset, aren't you?" She shook her head no. "Yes, you are, but it's going to be okay."

"I know. It's just that...it just seems as if I've been through this before."

"Not with me, you haven't. And if it will make you feel any better, I don't want to leave you."

"But you will," she murmured.

"What do you want from me, Arianna! We've been seeing each other for two years and in all that time, you've never indicated that you needed anything more from me than the use of my body." He lifted her arm and pointed to the bracelet that glinted in the light. "And if you do care for me why are you still wearing Jace's bracelet? I don't understand what you want."

She wanted him to stay, but Arianna locked the words away in her heart. Another man she loved was leaving her life and there wasn't thing one she could do about it. "I don't want anything, Freddie. We make love, but we are not in love. So, there isn't going to be any big crying scene. It's been fun while it lasted and I'll miss you when you're gone."

"That's where you're wrong, honey. I know you don't want to hear this, but I have to say it at least once before I go. I love you, Arianna Jackson. I have for a while now. But you're not ready to accept my love and I can't stay here and continue to watch you pine for a man who doesn't deserve it. I also want you to be happy and I hope that he sends for you and that it works out the way you want." Freddie flopped back on the pillows. "So, I'm going home and I'm going to try to forget and try to stop loving you."

Frightened by the thought of never seeing Freddie again, Arianna sat up on the bed. With great deliberation, she removed the bracelet from her wrist. She showed it to Freddie, then leaned over his body, and dropped the jewelry into the trashcan by the bed. "I love you, Frederick Allan Lane, and I'm sorry I didn't tell you sooner. When you go and leave me here, I'm not going to stop loving you."

One week later, they wed at the courthouse. Freddie had warned Arianna that Delphos, Kansas, was a small farming community, but she hadn't realized that he'd meant a town of less than two hundred people. Delphos had one library inside the town's only bank, one movie house, one general store, and a one-room, historical museum.

Freddie's parents lived thirty miles from town in a two-level, two-bedroom house painted white with blue shutters. It had a wraparound, screened-in porch and swing. A yellow tractor sat off to the side next to a barn painted rusty red, and a white post fence surrounded the grassy yard. Looking outward, she saw acres and acres of land filled with tall, green corn and golden stalks of wheat swaying in the breeze of a hot, mid-summer afternoon. And when Freddie's mother, Madeline, pulled her into an embrace and immediately accepted her as the daughter she'd never had, all Arianna could think was that as much as she loved Frederick Allan Lane, she could never, ever live here.

Months later, Arianna still hadn't adjusted to her new life. She hadn't wanted to meet their neighbors, even though his parents had organized an outdoor barbecue to celebrate their marriage. She had no interest in the farm, or the animals in the barn, or the corn in the field, and she had flat out refused to go fishing with her husband. With each passing day, Arianna had grown sadder, thinner, and more depressed, and she'd rebuffed every attempt Freddie made to get to her to talk. He'd turned to his mother for help. Madeline had encouraged Arianna to get involved in some of the local organizations so she would feel a sense of belonging.

Taking that advice, Arianna had become a member of the domestic arts club, the historical society, and the Rotary Club. Each time the town formed a new committee, Arianna had been the first to volunteer, but she still felt displaced. Then she'd joined the library board and with Freddie's love for her as her blanket, reading had become a balm to her soul; and when she started penning her own stories, her salvation...

Delphos, Kansas, was Freddie's hometown but it had become her hometown, too. Frederick Allan Lane was the rock she depended on and their sons were the beats of her heart. She needed her husband the way the sun needed the sky and the way the birds needed the trees. They'd been through too much for Freddie to throw it all away as if their time together meant nothing. Distressed by the thoughts running through her head, Arianna pulled her plane ticket and cell phone out of her purse. She'd returned to Colorado to bring closure to her past. Because of that decision, her future was in jeopardy, and it was a future Arianna had no intention of losing.

# THE PAST

# SUMMER, 1979

# IT'S ALL ABOUT THE PARTY

# Chapter 6

*Arianna*

I was thinking about my life when, out of the blue, an unreal feeling hit me. Feeling faint and a little dizzy, I pressed my fingers to my temple. Then I observed the gyrating bodies packed like sardines on the overcrowded dance floor. What we were doing in this sweatbox?

The moment passed and I chalked my state up to the booze I'd consumed, and the mix of stale perfume, offending cologne, and sweaty body funk. What did it matter anyway since tonight was no different from any other Friday night?

I'd left my job at five and headed for the club where I'd tipped several seven and sevens and gotten my party groove on. When the club closed, I paid my two dollars at the door to attend this after-hours party. For the last two hours, I've been wondering why, when there had to be something else I could be doing. Only I didn't know what that something else was.

All I knew was that experiencing the moment was important to me. I savored it, enjoyed it, and when it ended, I moved on to the next, and since this was the start of Memorial Day weekend, I could look forward to three days of continuous movement.

Like most of the residents in this town, I landed here because I am the daughter of a career military man, air force. Because his military pay was not enough to support the people living under his roof, my father had to take a second job, which meant that he wasn't home a lot. When he was, he and my mother engaged in screaming, name-calling, and physical fights. Mostly, I remember always being afraid that something would spark and my parents would go after each other and of being terrified when they did. Then my mother found religion and life, as I'd known it, got worse.

At church, she listened attentively to sermons that taught the bible's principles of peace and love. At home, she turned our house into even more of a war zone, only now she focused most of her anger on us kids. She made it her mission to strip what little enjoyment I did have from my life. I could no longer listen to the radio, go to the movies, or watch any of the popular shows on television. My mother did not allow dating. I could not wear makeup, or any of the latest styles, and I certainly couldn't bring any of those sinners from school to our house.

Attending church became the focal point of my rigidly controlled world. If I wasn't actually in church, then I was at a bible study talking about church. Holidays, including birthdays, also became a thing of the past. We did continue to celebrate Thanksgiving, however, but only because my father, who'd hadn't joined what I now believe was a cult, liked his turkey and stuffing and refused to bend to my mother's evil nature on that issue.

As a young girl, I couldn't understand what was happening. Now I think my mother was pissed off with the way her life turned out. I guess I'd be pissed, too, if I had seven kids, no money, and a roving husband.

My biggest problem with that sect was their belief that God was going to destroy the world, and the year they had chosen for this disastrous event was the year that I was to graduate from high school. I spent that year watching the sky for a hail of fire to rain down and take out mankind. The following year, the sect changed the date and I enrolled in business school.

Since then, religion has dropped to the bottom of my priority list. I believe in the Almighty and that Jesus died on the cross for the forgiveness of our sins. However, I also believe that God meant for life to be lived, and that's exactly what I've decided to do.

My six siblings and I are not close. It's not that I don't love them. I do, but when you grow up with parents who view each other as the enemy, it's hard to cultivate those kindred bonds. The closest people to me are Paige Michaels and Jazmin Reed—two women with soft hearts who, like me, grew up with crazy, control-freak mothers. With her golden skin, gold-tipped brown hair, and svelte figure, Paige reminds me of a lioness. Her roar is not all that threatening, but all of those vain 'all about me' characteristics associated with the sign of Leo are markedly apparent in Paige.

Jazmin is one of those in-your- face people. She has black hair, black eyes, light brown skin, and a personality so vibrant that when I met her, it had scared the hell of out me. Jazmin is tough and not afraid to go after what she wants, and she'll cuss you out in a heartbeat, so you really don't want to piss her off. Underneath it all, though, Jazmin is a gentle soul and a loyal friend. You just have to get closer to her to know that.

I met Paige first, in business school. Actually, it was more like two ships passing in the night. I'd enter the building on my way to class as she was leaving on her way to cut class. We'd say hi and go on about our business. I graduated and accepted a manager level position in the finance department of an air force defense contractor. I had lost track of Paige until the day I stopped by the executive wing and saw her sitting in one of the conference rooms. There still were no sparks of friendship, but we continued our hi-and-bye routine.

Shortly after starting that job, I leased an apartment on Pikes Peak Avenue. It had one bedroom, white walls, and rust brown carpet. I added navy blue furniture, a bunch of cutesy decorator items, and lots of green plants. The thing I enjoyed most was the quiet—no fighting, no shouting, and no one calling my name.

I'd moved across town ready to be hip and cool. However, I was from the suburbs and didn't know a soul until one day I met this darling, chocolate brown baby who invited me to her house for dinner. Her name was Jessica, and for some reason, she thought it was cool to hang out in my second floor, middle of the hallway apartment. A few weeks later, I met her mother.

That's when I decided, "Okay, Lord. You want Paige and me to be friends, then so be it." We've been cool ever since.

Getting shoved from behind jarred me back into the present. I swung around to locate the offender and a solid chest clad in black filled my view. I lifted my head until my eyes encountered a devilishly hand-some, ebony face. I stopped moving and I know my mouth dropped open.

He was so fine!

"Excuse me," he mouthed with a wink.

It was one of those moments. Had I not been so tipsy, I might have recognized it for what it was—something to covet and remember. I did notice the way the brotha was checking me out and something in his gaze was so disturbing, I turned away from him.

He bumped me several more times. It was not accidental, but instead of acknowledging the man trying to gain my attention, I maneu-vered around my dance partner. A minute or two later, that same guy was bumping up against me again. I concentrated on moving to the music until the song ended, then I pushed through the crowd and left the floor.

I did a quick visual for Jazmin or Paige, but didn't spot either of my girls. Pulling the coat check stub from the pocket of the black miniskirt I'd worn with a matching vest and a turquoise blouse, I went to get my coat and purse.

"Would you like to dance?"

I glanced over my shoulder, saw the black clad chest, and turned away. "I'm leaving."

"But the party's just starting."

I took my things from the woman and dropped a dollar into the glass bowl on the shelf. "Sorry, maybe next time."

He didn't follow me, but I felt his eyes on me all the way out the door.

---

*Paige*

I'm at this party to keep my eye on Pierce Reynolds and his flirtatious always-out-there behind. I've been trying to figure out his game all night. At the club, he ignored me. At this party, he's been doing the same thing.

We're supposed to be a couple. So why is he across the room pushing up on another woman while I sit here pissed and wanting so badly to kick his ass? Before walking off, Pierce had claimed the woman was a friend from his hometown, but my name is not Stupid. Put simply, Pierce Reynolds is a dog. I've been with him too long not to know that, but out of all the dogs that have passed through my life, Pierce is the one who's stayed the longest. Lately, he's been hinting that he's about to wrap my finger in gold. I am not about to risk losing that hard-earned piece of metal.

With the air thickening around me, I was having a hard time breathing, and knowing how close I was to going off, I surveyed the room for my girls. I needed one of them to help me put this shit in perspective. I didn't see Jazmin or Arianna, and I was tired of thinking about Pierce Reynolds. So for the benefit of the women in that room, I pasted a smile on my lips and played my role like an actress stalking an Oscar. Inside, my heart wasn't in it because even if Pierce did marry me, I knew that no matter what I did, I would never be enough to satisfy him.

I knew that because I'd already been down that road with my mother, my ex-husband, and too many other men not worth remembering. I was tired of feeling as if I wasn't enough, but I couldn't seem to find the path that would lead me off that painful highway.

I met Thomas, my ex, when I was a junior in high school and I truly thought it was love at first sight when he began showing an interest in me. He was a jock and a senior, with a light, almost white skin tone, dark 'good' hair, and brown eyes.

Now I think my attraction had a lot to do with the fact that while my mother had always had a man around, none had ever stayed long enough for me to learn anything about them or they me. Or, as a counselor my mother dragged me to when I was eight once told me, all that Oedipus parental syndrome crap. I have never seen my father, a man who didn't marry my mother, and by the time I was in high school, she had divorced three men and had had a string of boyfriends between each one.

Four months into my relationship with Thomas, I learned that I was carrying his child. I had cleaned the house every day, cooked dinner every night, and made sure everyone's clothes were clean and pressed. I was president of my sophomore and junior classes, had made the cheerleading squad and honor roll list for the last four years. Despite all of my achievements, when my mother found out that I was pregnant, she called me a whore. Then she marched me over to Thomas's house, confronted his parents, and demanded they make their son marry me.

Bending under the pressure, Thomas graduated from high school, and instead of going to college, he joined the army for the paycheck. When he left for basic training in Texas, my mother got busy planning our wedding and by the time Christmas rolled around, we were married. When Thomas left for his first assignment in Monterey, California, I was too far along to go and, per 'their' agreement, I was to join him after I had the baby. However, I had plans of my own.

All through my pregnancy, I had continued to earn my high school credits, and when Jessica was born, I enrolled in an accelerated program. Thomas didn't seem to care whether I came to California or not. Jessie was six months old when he called and said that he didn't want to be married to me. Since I didn't want to be married to him either, our divorce was amicable with Thomas receiving visitation rights he's never exercised, and I, monthly child support checks courtesy of Uncle Sam.

I never talk about Thomas, and I haven't heard from him since our divorce conversation. Thinking about him, though, naturally brought on thoughts of my daughter. Like me, Jessica has never seen her father and I ripped up every picture I had of Thomas after the divorce. I probably shouldn't have done that. Jessie is young now, but one day she might want to know who her father is, and then what am I supposed to do?

Most of the time my daughter calls me Paige, which I don't have a problem with because it irritates my mother. I figure it's her problem. Jessie knows that I'm the mother, and as long as we understand each other, what difference does it make what she calls me? I am trying to raise my daughter to be strong, and to make sure Jessie knows that no matter what she does, I will always love her. More than anything, I want my daughter to grow up with a father and I'm doing all that I can to rectify that situation.

I watched Pierce's hand slide down the front of the woman's blouse. My heart began to pound and I dropped my eyes. Why was I putting myself through this? It couldn't possibly be worth it. Then I thought about Jessie and I knew that it was. I could feel the pressure building again, so I sat up. I needed something else to focus on besides Pierce and my daughter.

Seeing all those fine 'GQ' looking brothas, and more than a few of them checking me out, was reassuring. Colorado Springs was a town full of handsome men. The military shipped them in and shipped them out on a regular basis. I have to admit that I've sampled more than my share. I know my girls think that I am way too free with my affections, but I can't help the way I feel about men. To me, a gorgeous black man is like a fine wine, full-bodied, robust, and bursting with flavor. I love every-thing about them: their features, their build, their confidence, and their rhythm of movement, in and out of bed. And when I'm on my back listening to one of them groan in pleasure, I feel powerful, as if I can do any and everything. It is only afterward, when the euphoria wears off, that another kind of feeling attacks and tries to take over.

"Paige Michaels! Girl, you are a sight for sore eyes."

Marshall Stokes was one of those gorgeous black men. "Hey," I said.

"Hay is for horses and I don't see any barns in here, girl."

I laughed. "How are you, Marshall?"

"Better now that I've seen you. Get up off that couch and come dance with me."

He lifted my hand. I glanced at the corner. Pierce was staring at me and though, for the most part, I've been faithful to him, Marshall was a recent indiscretion I'd committed when my resistance was low. Then again, Pierce had his nerve when he had some other heffa hugged up in a corner. However, the thought of that ring on my finger kept me centered.

"Not tonight, Marshall. Maybe another time."

"Ooh, Paige. Why'd you go and stab a brotha in the heart and take away all my hopes and dreams? It's cool, though. I'll pull out the knife and catch up with you another time."

## A Request for Closure

"See ya."

Marshall walked away and immediately started making moves on another more available candidate for his bed. He wasn't any better than the rest of them, but there wasn't a doubt in my mind that, if not for Pierce, I would have been the one wiggling under him tonight.

Oh well. Such is life. When I received my divorce papers, I decided that I was free. So far, dumping Thomas Michaels has proven to be one of the few good decisions I've made in my life. It motivated me to find a job and move out of my mother's house. Living on my own hasn't always easy, but I've managed to squeeze out a lot of fun, *and* I have a man. Pierce may not be perfect, but he loves me enough to walk me down the aisle again and to take care of my daughter. Before that can happen, though, I need to figure out a way to get my man out of that damn corner.

——⟡——

### Jazmin

It's time for me to go home because I've had it with this sad excuse for a party. It isn't that I don't want to be here, necessarily. It's that I don't want to be in Colorado Springs, period. I want to go home—to New York City—a place I think about and miss so much at times it makes my head hurt. I miss its heart, its pace, and its beat. I miss the people, driven people. People with goals, and dreams, and the backbone to reach them. I have dreams and goals and yet here I am stuck in a one-horse town with one-dimensional people who seem satisfied with their lot in life. But my mother is here and so is my sister, so at least I have some family, if you can call them that.

My sister and I rarely talk, and growing up with my mother, or the General as I called her under my breath, had been a hellish nightmare. Mommy was so mean and so critical of everything we did that I used to think she'd never had any dreams. That was before my sister let me know that the General used to be a dancer and that she'd once landed a part in the chorus line of a Broadway play. The kicker was that Mommy had given up her dream to marry my father, who after five years and three kids had packed his bags and run for the door.

On the other side of that door was another woman, of course, and I can understand how that could make my mother lose her grip on reality, temporarily. But what I don't understand was why she blamed his desertion on us kids, especially since she's been married four times since my father left. I once heard her say that a sweet woman could always attract a good man. For the General, attraction was as far as it went. As soon as a man slipped a ring on her finger, she immediately transformed into the bitch from hell. My back still bears faint scars as evidence of her skills with an electric cord.

To avoid tangling with her, I became adept at sneaking out of the house. I spent my time in the streets, hanging out with the wrong people, getting high, and generally being a pain in the ass to anyone who crossed my path. That ended the night one of the girls in my crew threw a brick through the window of Macy's and the police hauled all our asses to jail.

The next morning, Mommy picked me up at the police station and drove me to a pink house that looked as if it was a hundred years old. The roof was a patchwork of missing shingles. There was a board in one of the windows where a pane should have been and the only thing saving the screen door was the rusty screw that still held the bottom in place. The yard was dirt and puddles of mud. Right next to the house sat another smaller, pink structure. Other than appearing to list to the right, it looked to be in much better condition than the house. Coming from inside, I could hear the loud talk and laughter of women.

And that's how I wound up working in Mrs. Coleman's beauty shop, which was nothing more than the garage off her kitchen.

I paid off my debt to Macy's and continued to work for Mrs. Coleman. By the time I turned sixteen, I could style hair better than Mrs. Coleman. I also knew that I had found my calling, only what I had in mind went way beyond anything I'd seen in Mrs. Coleman's dilapidated garage.

## A Request for Closure

One day, I planned to own a real beauty salon, one that treated the whole woman, from the top of her head to the tip of her toes. To keep myself motivated, I kept the vision of my salon firmly planted in my mind. Not a day passed when I didn't envision mint green and white draped over golden rods, tropical palm trees, and piles of large pillows scattered about for lounging. I saw young men with bulging muscles and wide chests giving total massages, wrapping seaweed, and applying mud. I saw these same men serving herbal tea in porcelain cups and handing out crystal flutes filled with champagne.

If not for the accident, I would already have my salon, but shit happens and you gotta find a way to move forward in spite of the obstacles of life. Thinking about the accident soured my mood even more and I turned to the barkeep for the night and ordered another vodka tonic.

Facing the room, I sipped at my drink, observed the people on the dance floor, and tried to keep my thoughts from trippin' down memory lane. It was wasted effort since my mind had already taken off on the unplanned tour.

My modeling career began when a Ford rep spotted me doing my thing at a hair show in Chicago and told me that my place was not behind the stage, but out front where people could see me. I took his card, which read, Michael Peters, Ford Modeling Agency, and returned to New York and Mrs. Coleman's garage. Thinking about what Michael had said, I studied that card for three weeks before I finally picked up the phone and dialed the number.

Mostly I worked the walk in local fashion shows, but my face did appear on a few fashion magazine covers. My career ended during a show in which one of the designers decided that the glittery baubles on the bodice of her dresses needed more sparkle and felt that a lone spotlight would produce the desired effect. That last minute change cost me my career. Blinded by the spotlight, and not quite sure where the catwalk ended, I slipped off the edge and three other models landed in a heap on top of me, breaking my right leg in three places and my left ankle.

When the doctor told me, I wanted to find and kill that heffa. Although gigs had come my way pretty steadily, I had been too young and too stupid to purchase medical insurance. The multiple operations and hospital stays wiped out every dime I had saved for my salon. By then, the General had married her fifth husband, a career army soldier, and had moved to Colorado Springs. I didn't want to leave New York, but I had no choice. I was unemployed, broke, and had no prospects for the future.

Until the General moved here, I never knew black people lived in the state of Colorado, and if you discount the soldiers on Fort Carson Army Base, there really aren't that many of them here. Except for the mountains sitting way off to the west, compared to New York, this place is a desert, covered with flat land with nothing on it except horses, cows, and trees. Leaving the airport, Mommy drove down Academy Boulevard, a two-lane road that she said was a major route through the city. There were no buildings and hardly any traffic. I wondered when I'd died and gone to hell.

My rehabilitation was a long and painful process that took months and depressed me even more. There I was, stuck in a cow town with absolutely nothing to do. I hadn't met anybody, I couldn't go anywhere, and I couldn't find a radio station that played anything resembling black music.

Country tunes for a country town. Perfect!

I scanned the room, searching for Karen Brown, a woman who ran her mouth way too much and generally got on my nerves. She wanted to be my friend, and since my Pinto was in the shop, I'd called and asked Karen if she wanted to hang. I would rather have ridden with one of my girls, but Paige was hangin' with her man tonight and Arianna had already hit the streets by the time I called her. I couldn't locate Karen, but I did spot Paige sitting on a sofa, looking like somebody had stolen her golden ticket. I shifted my eyes in the direction she was glaring.

I'd been telling Paige since she met him that Pierce was a dog. However, my girl was hardheaded and hoping for the brass ring. It wasn't gonna happen, because Pierce Reynolds was a prime example of what was wrong with the men in this town. All they required was a warm bed and a willing body. With the ratio of men to women being what it was, even an ugly chick could have men promising her the moon if it meant rocking on top of her at night.

That's why I never took any of these Negroes or anything they said seriously. I had my own plans and the only person who was going to make my dreams come true was me.

I looked over at Paige again. Girlfriend was doing her best to play it off like what was going on in that corner hadn't jacked up her world, but I knew she was hurting.

I downed the rest of my drink. God, I really hate this fucking town, I thought as I went over to try to raise my girl out of her funky mood.

# Chapter 7

*Paige*

W ho stuck a bug up your ass?"

Leave it to Jazmin to get right to the heart of things. "A dog that goes by the name of Pierce Reynolds."

I saw the almost imperceptible shake of her head and knew I had erred. Those women sitting beside me had perked up at my words. Jazmin glared at one of them who pretended not to see it until my girl confronted the matter head-on.

"You wanna move your ass by yourself or get thrown off this couch?"

The girl's loud gasp preceded her quick departure, as well as that of her friends. Jazmin plopped down next to me.

I laughed. "You've got to be one of the craziest people I know, scaring off those women like that."

Jazmin pulled a joint and a lighter out of the pocket of her dress. "Heffa should've just moved. She knew I wanted to sit down." She lit the joint and passed it to me. "Here, girl. You need this more than I do."

"Thanks. Seen Ari around anywhere?"

Jazmin Reed can roll her eyes like no one else I've ever seen. "Now you know that Ari is shaking her ass out on that floor. Last time I saw her, she had some salivating jerk rubbing up against her like he was hoping to fuck her brains out tonight."

"Well, we both know that ain't gonna happen. Arianna don't put her stuff out there like that, but must you *always* be so crude, Jazmin?"

"Girl, please! You want crude, then let me tell you about this boy I met last week. His name is Marcus, and girl, the boy tongued the surface of both of my titties before he took one of my nipples into his mouth and sucked on it so hard I screamed. Or I could tell you how I thrashed on the bed when his fingers played in the hairy patch between my legs. Girl, that boy had the longest, hardest—"

I almost choked on the smoke I'd inhaled into my lungs when my laughter burst out of my mouth. "Knock it off, Jazz! We're really good friends, but even I don't want to know you or any of the men you screw that well!"

"Well, at least you're laughing now."

I sobered immediately and my gaze returned to Pierce. "I just don't understand what's wrong with me and why I can't hold on to a man."

"Girl, there ain't a thing wrong with you. You're a beautiful woman and you can have any man you want. It's just that you keep bringing home stray dogs."

"Yeah, but why is that?"

"I don't know, P. It could be this city or it could be that we're hangin' in the wrong spots. I've been here for years and you've lived here all your life. Neither of us has found a man that makes us break out in a cold sweat. Arianna either. I'm thinking about moving back home. I can barely stand it here anymore."

I sat up, stunned. I knew that Jazmin had never liked Colorado Springs. By her standards, it was a marginal cow town at best. But if she moved away, what was I supposed to do? We'd been through so much together. She'd been in the delivery room when I had Jessie and I'd cried on her shoulder when Thomas and I divorced. She couldn't move; she was my best friend in the whole world.

"You can't move! You have to stay here because…well, I don't know why right now, but I love you and I need you here."

"Chill, P," she said, with her eyes focused on something or someone across the room. "I didn't say I was moving. I said I was thinking about it. By the way, Jace is here."

I sat up, craning my neck so that I could get a closer peek. "Where?"

She pointed. "Over by the door."

When I spotted Jace, I had to catch my breath. Dressed in black pants, an open neck, black shirt, and a royal blue jacket, the boy was too clean. I dropped back to the couch, feeling a little silly and wondering what I was trying so hard to see. We'd had a brief fling, but I wasn't interested in Jace Barnes.

Playing it off, I slanted Jazmin a look of boredom. "So?"

She exhaled. "So, why don't you go over and say hello."

"Girl, I ain't thinkin' 'bout Jace Barnes. That was over a long time ago."

"Paige, sometimes you are so dense I want to smack you. I'm not telling you to sleep with the man, but if you want to get Pierce out of that corner, then I suggest you get off this couch."

It took me a while to consider what she'd said and to conclude that Jazmin was right, but by the time I left the couch, Jace was nowhere to be found. I moved to the edge of the floor and exhaled in frustration. Pierce was still in that corner and I was hunting for Marshall when my eyes landed on a handsome face. He was sitting all by himself on the other side of the room and I quickly pushed my way through the crowd. Jermaine Lewis would do just fine.

He stood as I approached. "Hey, Lewis."

"Hi," he said, before hastily shifting his eyes away.

The boy was so shy, it bordered on pathetic. I started to pop my fingers and sway my hips. "Will you dance with me?"

He swallowed. "S-sure."

We walked to the edge of the dance floor. By then, the music had changed and the soft strands of a slow jam drifted out over the crowd. Lewis rubbed his hands on the back of his jeans before carefully placing them on the top of my hips. His eyes stared at something over my shoulder. I don't know why the boy was so nervous, acting as if we didn't already know each other. He was Pierce's best friend and he was at my house almost more than Pierce.

"Lewis."

"Huh," he said.

## A Request for Closure

"We're supposed to be slow dancing. You're holding me like a fragile piece of china you're afraid you might break."

He smiled—a wide, beautiful smile that brightened his entire face. Why hadn't I noticed that before?

"Sorry," he said, pulling me closer.

I laid my head on his chest. His heart began to race and then he abruptly dropped his arms.

I looked up at him. "What's wrong?"

Lewis was breathing as if he'd run a marathon. "Nothing, but maybe we shouldn't be dancing like this."

"Why not?"

"Paige, you're Pierce's woman. Maybe you should get him to dance with you."

I stepped closer. "If I wanted to dance with Pierce, I wouldn't be here with you."

What looked like an expression of pain crossed his face. "Don't do this, Paige. I don't want to be used as some kind of pawn in a fight you're having with your man."

"Lewis, if you don't want to dance with me, say so and I'll be on my way."

"I don't want to dance with you."

The man had to be crazy. I was wearing a midnight blue, strapless dress that showed my assets. My shit was tight and any man in the room would have happily taken his place. "Cool, see ya around."

Highly insulted, I spun on my heel and was about to step off when I heard him say softly, "Paige, wait." He took several deep breaths as if gathering his courage to say something monumental. "Paige, I like you, all right. I really, really like you, but I never intended to tell you because Pierce *is* my main man. But I happen to know that he's shipping out in two days and something tells me that he hasn't said anything to you. And I also wanted to say…well, I-I wanted you to know that if you ever need a friend that you can call on me."

Pins and needles pinged at my brain and I stared at Lewis as if he'd lost his mind. "You don't know what you're talking about, Lewis. Pierce would never leave without saying something to me. I'm his woman, for God sakes! Why would you say something like that to me?"

Lewis grabbed my arms and bent down in my face. "Paige, I didn't tell you about Pierce to cause a scene, but I don't like the way he's planning to disrespect you. Come with me, because there are some things you need to know."

He sheltered me from the onlookers and led me toward the front door. Outside, I stopped. "I'm going back in there."

"No, Paige. I won't let you do that, and besides, Pierce just left. He's on his way to your crib to get his things."

"What?" I practically screamed the word.

"Paige, listen to me! Pierce is leaving. He's not taking you with him and he's not interested in hearing anything you have to say about it. His plan was to leave you stranded at this party while he went to your apartment and packed his gear. He wanted to be gone before you found a ride home."

This was not happening. I knew Pierce Reynolds was a dog, but the man also had to be a fiend to do something like this to get rid of a woman. On the other hand, what kind of woman was I if I was capable of driving a man to this extreme? I didn't know. I wasn't sure that I wanted to know. All I could do was hang my head as tears the size of big, fat raindrops dripped from my eyes.

Lewis took my hand. "Come on, I'm getting you out of here."

Two times one is two, I thought as Lewis packed me into a sky blue TransAm. Two times two is four. Two times three is six. Reciting the multiplication tables I'd learned in elementary school usually helped to calm me down. This time it wasn't working and when Lewis entered the car, I was back to bawling. He handed me a white handkerchief.

"Thank you," I murmured, using it to dry my face.

"You're welcome. My mother taught me to always have a clean one on hand, because you never know who might need one."

I stared into the night, my heart numb and my mind in a daze. Several minutes passed before Lewis brushed a lock of my hair back from my face.

## A Request for Closure

"Do you love him?"

I had to think about that for a minute. Honestly, what hurt the most was the blow to my ego. "No," I finally answered.

He shifted in his seat and turned the key in the ignition. "That's good," he said over the roar of the engine.

# Chapter 8

*Jazmin*

My feet were kicking my ass and I really needed to find Karen. It was three o'clock in the morning and there was nothing in the room that interested me, not even the commotion that broke out by the door or the people rushing over to see what was happening. That was when I finally spotted Karen and I was heading her way when the crowd suddenly parted. I stopped dead in my tracks.

He was absolutely gorgeous, tall, dark, and fine with straight black hair that I saw he wore in a ponytail that hung to his shoulders when he turned to speak to someone behind him. His face looked angular, but full enough to feel good under my fingers. His nose was slender, his mouth smooth and plump, and his eyes round and spaced perfectly apart. A fire burned in their depths that I could see from where I stood not more than ten feet from him. His body looked long and lithe, his build accentuated by the silver jumpsuit he wore over a long-sleeved black shirt. He stood heads above the large gathering, oozing confidence and blatantly aware that his charm and personality were enough to drive his fans wild.

I ran over to Karen and tugged on her arm. "Who is that?"

"That," she said with a sigh, "is Brick. Vincent Bernard Marks, actually, and the man is a celebrity in this town."

"Celebrity?"

"Not celebrity as in movie star. Brick was a jock in high school. He played basketball, baseball, and ran track. He was a superstar." She paused to take a breath. "He played ball at the University of New Mexico and I heard yesterday he signed with the NBA."

## A Request for Closure

That said, Karen rose on her toes and added her shouts to those of the entourage swarming around Vincent Marks.

I was standing there pretending I wasn't interested when the man's dark gaze centered on me. When Brick excused himself and moved in my direction, my heart quivered in my chest. I tried to look away. I couldn't. His eyes were like magnets, drawing me in against my will.

His stride was one of leisure, clearly stating that he was in no hurry. It was as if he knew that I wasn't going anywhere and that he could get to me in the next few minutes, the next few days, or next week and I would still be standing there waiting on him. What made the moment even more pathetic was that the brotha was right. I wasn't going anywhere.

That's when my inner child decided it was time to speak up. Her name was Magnolia; I called her Mags. Mags hailed from New York City, and she was one tough chick.

*Why are you standing here like you ain't never seen a man before?*

Her voice was loud and resounded in my head. Ignoring Mags, I focused on the man moving my way.

*Girl please! That man should be standing here waiting on you.*

I glanced at Brick again and decided that Mags was right; he was going to have to wait on me. I turned and then walked away from that excited crowd, away from the shouts of adoration, and away from Vincent Marks, the man everybody called Brick.

I was standing at the bar when a large hand swept across my backside and settled on the cushion of my butt. A tremor of delight ran down my spine. "If you want to keep that hand then you might want to move it."

"I don't think I can," he breathed into my ear. "Forest green is my favorite color and in this dress your luscious behind is calling out to me like a precious jewel begging for my touch."

I drew in a deep breath and exhaled. His voice was so deep and so syrupy I wanted to eat this man up with a spoon. "But the jewel is mine. It's expensive and I don't think you can afford it."

He slid his hand across my backside again. "Baby doll," he whispered, "I'll do whatever it takes to afford this jewel."

I turned then, and his black eyes shimmered with amusement. "Come and dance for me, baby doll." He took my hand, tugged me away from the bar, and the crowd parted as Brick led me to the center of the floor. "Now," he said. "Dance for me."

I felt the stares of everyone in the room as Brick crossed his arms over his chest and focused his eyes on me.

"Dance for him," a deep voice shouted. "Show the man what you got, girl."

"No," I said after a minute or two of silence had passed. "I want *you* to dance for me."

A murmur ran through the crowd. Surprise tightened Brick's features. Then he dropped his arms. "Okay, baby doll. We'll dance this one together."

His hand felt hot when he pulled me into his arms. His lips brushed across my cheek. I thought it was a kiss, but Brick was aiming for my ear.

"Where did you come from, Jazmin?"

My head snapped back. "H-how did you know my name?"

"I'm a psychic," he said with a grin.

I stifled the urge to giggle. "How do you really know my name, Brick?"

His shoulders moved in a shrug beneath my hands. "I asked Karen Brown and it seems as if you did, too."

"What do you mean by that?"

"You called me Brick."

"Oh." It was all I could think to say considering the embarrassed warmth flooding my cheeks.

"Are you a friend of Karen's?"

"Sort of. Why?"

"Well…she wouldn't tell me your last name and I wasn't sure whether she knew it or if she didn't want to give up the info."

"Reed," I said.

"Reed," he whispered near my ear. "Jazmin Reed. Jaz-min Reed." My name sounded like a song and I wondered if this was his way of remembering it. "Jaz-min. J-J-J-J. Jazzy. I like it. I'm calling you Jazzy."

## A *Request for Closure*

Everyone called me Jazz, but when Brick said Jazzy, I definitely heard music. After dancing several sets, we walked to an empty table that had suddenly appeared against the wall. Sizzling heat swirled around us, and most of it flared from the female eyes following us as we left the floor.

As if sensing the hostility, Brick squeezed my hand tighter. He seated me and then cupped my cheek in his hand. "Relax, Jazzy," he said in a soft velvet voice. "You're the woman I'm with. I'll be right back."

He walked away, his stride limber and loose, until he stopped near some guys at the bar. My heart skipped a beat when I saw Marcus running his mouth and pointing in my direction. Now, I knew that the Negro was not talking about me, but I didn't get a chance to go any further with that thought because a hand clamped down on my shoulder.

"What do you think you're doing?"

She'd appeared out of nowhere, and brown eyes flashing daggers and lips thinned by anger backed up the hostility she directed at me.

"I'm minding my own business."

Karen sat down. "Don't you see these women staring at you, Jazmin? Why do you think that is?"

"Frankly, I don't give a good Goddamn."

Karen exhaled. "Look, Jazmin. I like you and I want to be your friend, but you're an outsider, and there is no way these women are going to let you walk off with one of their men."

The girl had to be nuts, coming over here trying to warn somebody. "Are you talking for yourself or for all the other women up in here?"

She tsked her tongue. "Personally, I ain't studdin' no Vincent Marks. The boy's way too flashy for my taste."

Karen was a liar and I started to call her on it, but I engaged her eyes instead. "In that case, Karen, you can go and tell all those other heffas that I said that they can go straight to hell! If I want Vincent Marks, I'm going to have Vincent Marks, and there ain't thing one any of them can do about it."

Brick arrived at the table, cutting off her response.

"Hey, Karen."

She fluttered her lashes up at him. "Hey Brick."

Since Karen didn't leave his chair, Brick grabbed another one and joined us at the table. Karen then settled in for the long haul, monopolizing the conversation and deliberately trying to distract Brick's attention from me by bringing up memories of their school days, shit I knew nothing about. However, it made my heart glad to see that although he conversed with her, Brick's eyes never left mine.

—⁓⁓—

"Will you have breakfast with me, Jazzy?" The party had finally wound down and we were gathering our things to leave.

Before I could open my mouth, Karen grabbed my arm and pulled me aside. "Jazmin, you can't go with him. You don't even know this man. You came with me. You leave with me!"

I already had a mother and I knew then that a friendship with Karen Brown was out of the question. However, as much as I hated to admit it, she was right. I couldn't go off with Brick. Paige was the queen of one-night stands. I had to get to know the man first, at least go on a couple of dates. Besides, I didn't want the boy to think I was that easy.

He broke the silent tension. "I'll understand if you can't go, Jazzy." Then, as if from thin air, he produced an ink pen. "But you can't leave without giving me your number."

I grabbed a napkin and scribbled down his number. He reached for the paper and deliberately slid his fingers over my hand. My heart jumped into overdrive. We stared some more until Karen pulled me in the direction of the door.

"Bye," I said.

"Later, Jazzy," he said.

We had almost reached the exit when a set of long fingers tangled with mine. Brick squeezed my hand, took the lead, and navigated a path through the women who'd gathered at the door. At Karen's car, he stepped in front of me and my whole world became Vincent Bernard Marks, his natural male scent, his cologne, his body, and his lips. He pressed his mouth against mine in a kiss that brimmed with underlying passion. Lifting up, he stepped aside and helped me into the seat.

Karen started the engine before the door closed. She was backing out of the space as I rolled down the window.

"Bye, Brick," I called as she hit the gas.

If he responded, I never heard it because by that time, Karen was heading for the street.

I sat back in the seat. "He's really fine."

Karen sucked her teeth. "Girl, please. Don't be getting all hooked up with him. He's a smooth talkin' player and nothing but a ladies man."

In the dark, I smirked a little. "Well, I think I'm a lady."

"Vincent Marks ain't no good, girl. In high school, all the girls ran after him and he sampled every one of them."

*Except you,* I thought, *or this shit wouldn't bother you so much.* "Whateva, Karen."

"You need to listen, Jazmin. Brick Marks ain't no damn good! Today, it'll be you. Tomorrow, he'll be with somebody else. Believe me, I know what I'm talking about."

*At least you think you do.* I didn't care what Karen thought about me or about Brick. I had something else on my mind and that was how I was going to catch that man.

At home, I readied myself for bed. I flipped back the mint green, white striped spread and climbed under the covers. My phone rang before my head hit the pillow. I reached for the receiver, hoping it was who I thought it was.

"Jaz…min. J-J-J-J. Jazmin Reed. Jazzy."

It was, and he was singing my name. I sat up. "Hey," I said.

"Hey," he said.

That one word made my heart jump. It had sounded so rich and arousing. I inhaled deeply and stopped breathing. I could think of nothing to say.

"What are you doing this morning, girl?"

"Nothing," I said.

"Nothing?"

"Actually, I'm laying here in my bed about to go to sleep."

Brick chuckled. "I thought you'd be laying in your bed thinking about me, 'cause I'm sure laying here thinking about you. What kind of plans you got today, Jazmin?"

"None, why?"

"Because now you've got some. I'm coming to get you, Jazzy-girl."

"How you gonna do that when you don't know where I live?"

"Oh, I'll find you, Jazzy. But I know you need to catch some Z's, and I do, too. Goodnight, Jazmin Reed, I'll see you later this morning."

"Goodnight," I said, totally amazed at the brazenness of this man.

"Oh, there is one more thing, my Jazzy."

"What's that," I whispered.

"When you snuggle under your covers and close your eyes...dream about me, 'cause I'm sure gonna dream about you!"

Damn, I thought. I hung up the telephone and floated down to my pillows. The man was too much.

—~~~—

*Paige*

Lewis didn't take me straight home. He said it was because he didn't want me to see Pierce clearing out his stuff. I think it was more about him not being a witness to a violent confrontation or becoming an accomplice in a murder investigation.

We stopped by a restaurant and after the hostess showed us to our booth, he did his best to lighten the mood. His jokes were stupid, but I cracked up anyway. "It's a good thing you aren't trying to make it as a comedian, because your jokes are so lame."

"Lame maybe, but they've put you in a better mood."

"Know something, Lewis? You been coming over to my house with Pierce for a long time and I hardly know anything about you. Where are you from?"

"California."

## A Request for Closure

I crinkled my nose. I'd never left the state of Colorado, but I'd heard about those California boys. "You're not gay or one of those surfer dudes, are you?"

Lewis sighed in exasperation. "Paige, people who live in California are the same as those in any other state. People of that particular persuasion live everywhere and not everyone owns a surfboard. To answer your question, I am neither. Right now, I'm under contract to Uncle Sam for another year and a half. When this hitch is up, I plan to return to Los Angeles and enroll in school using my GI bill to finance my education as a future lawyer. However, tonight, I'm simply Jermaine Jacob Lewis, a man who's grateful to finally have the privilege of sharing a meal with a woman he finds beautiful."

Whoa...even by my standards, this brotha was moving way too fast. I picked up my menu. "Um...maybe we should decide what we want to eat before the waitress gets here."

Lewis slid around the table until he was right next to me. He removed the menu from my hands. "Do I make you nervous, Paige Michaels?"

"N-No."

He captured my mouth beneath his. The tip of his tongue flicked out, plying the seam of my mouth with soft touches as I sat in an unresponsive stupor.

He pulled back. "What about now?"

I lowered my gaze and licked my lips, tasting his kiss, tasting him. I looked at him again. Amusement tinged his eyes. This man was toying with me. "Actually, that was kind of nice."

Lewis chuckled. "If you liked that, then you're sure to love this."

I slapped my hands against his chest. "What do you think you're doing? Just because you let me cry on your shoulder doesn't mean that I'm going to sleep with you tonight."

He slouched back. "Paige, what's going on here has nothing to do with Pierce. This has to do with you and me, and the feelings I've had for you since the moment we met. I know my timing is off and that I shouldn't have made any moves on you tonight, but I couldn't help myself. I apologize if you feel that I've disrespected you or that I'm trying to take advantage of you in any way."

Yeah, right. Men are all the same—dogs every last one of them! I picked up my menu and when the waitress came, ordered a burrito and coke. Lewis ordered a hamburger and fries. When the food arrived, we stared at each other, but the camaraderie we'd shared earlier was gone and I was ready to go home.

On the ride to my apartment, we didn't speak. Despite his remorse, I was simmering. While the impression of his kiss still lingered on my lips, I did feel that he had overstepped his bounds, especially after what had happened to me tonight.

Entering my apartment, I switched on a lamp and surveyed the room. Though Pierce had cleared out his stuff, nothing had really changed. The same brown and beige furniture filled the space. The same grouping of large, straw fans hung on the wall over the couch, and the same metal étagère held my television and stereo system.

A couple of things were different though. Pierce had taken most of the albums and a picture of Jessie that had been sitting on the étagère was missing. Why he'd taken that was a mystery, since he'd hardly spent any time with my daughter.

I heard the door close and Lewis walked up behind me. "Pierce is gone, and you shouldn't waste any more time crying over him. The brotha is a real jackass!"

"How can you say that? Pierce is supposed to be your friend."

"He is my friend. That's why I can say these things about him. Pierce doesn't care about anyone except Pierce. I don't like the way he treated you or Jessie. I knew about the other women and I did try to rap with him about it. He said that you were his and what he did with you was his business. Until now, I had to stay out of it because Pierce was right. You were his woman."

"I always suspected there were other women, but until you confirmed it I didn't know for sure."

"You're kidding," Lewis said, as if he couldn't believe I was that asinine.

## A Request for Closure

"No," I said, as anger seethed. "Until tonight, I honestly believed that Pierce loved me." Knowing that he hadn't hurt, but at least Jessie had never warmed up to him and that was one less thing for me to worry about. "It's late, Lewis, and I'm tired. You've been so good to me tonight, why don't you stay here and head out to the barracks in the morning."

He surveyed the living room. "Okay, but I'm a little too long for the couch. If you'll toss me a couple of pillows and a blanket, I can bunk in here on the floor."

I looked at Lewis...I mean, I really looked at Lewis, and something fluttered in my chest. "Yeah, you could do that, but wouldn't you be more comfortable sleeping in a bed?"

His head snapped up. "What?"

I turned for the hallway. "Lewis, I'm going to bed and you're welcome to join me if you're so inclined."

Thirty minutes later, I came out of the bathroom. Though I had condemned him earlier, I was glad that I had taken the time to shower, perfume my body, and slip into a sexy nightgown when I saw the covered lump in my bed. I slipped beneath the lacy peach coverlet and sheets.

Scooting down, I reached to caress his cheek. My hand encountered a long, large object. I continued searching and found that there was not one, but two of them and they were covered with socks. I reached down further and touched a pair of pants.

I flopped back on the pillows. Here I'd been hoping for a night of loving and the man I'd invited into my bed had fallen asleep. And he hadn't bothered to remove his clothes. Talk about another blow to my already tattered ego.

I rose up on my elbows. Well, I had accomplished one of my goals. Lewis was in my bed. I nudged his thigh with my foot. "Lewis." He groaned and rolled over, but he didn't wake up. So, I did it again. "Lewis."

His hand rubbed his nose. "What?"

"Lewis, wake up!"

His eyes barely opened. "What?"

"What are you doing?"

"Sleeping." He adjusted his pillows and closed his eyes again.

"Lewis!"

"What is it, Paige?"

"You're at the wrong end of the bed. And if you're going to stay in this bed, your head needs to be up here with mine, and lose those clothes, too."

"Yeah?"

I wet my lips with my tongue. "Yeah." He crawled to the head of the bed. "What about your pillows?"

His deep brown eyes shimmered and their message made my heart beat faster. Lewis wanted me as much as I wanted him.

"Don't need no stinkin' pillows," he said in a low growl. "You'll do fine."

His arms surrounded me, but instead of the beginning of a passionate encounter, Lewis began to rock, a slow and gentle sway that reminded me of cradling Jessie in my arms when she was a baby. At first, I lay stiffly, trying to figure out what he was doing, but as the time lengthened from five minutes to ten, I relaxed. After the turmoil of the evening, the quiet was peaceful, fortifying and I closed my eyes.

I was drifting in and out of a half sleep when Lewis left the bed. A feeling of coldness crept over me. Already I missed the warmth he'd provided. I lifted my head, beckoning him with my eyes.

"Roll over."

I hesitated, but did as he'd asked.

Lewis lifted my nightgown, straddled my body, and slid his hands over my skin. He rubbed the kinks and tension from my back and shoulders. The total body massage ended with his fingers gently kneading my scalp. I lay there feeling serenely fluid and loose, but the blood rushing through my veins felt hot and feverish.

Thirty minutes had passed since Lewis began plying my body with his hands. He was still dressed, my nightgown was still on, and all of my erotic zones were pulsing. He left the bed and undressed. A rush of excitement ran through me when I saw what his clothes had hidden from view.

## A *Request for Closure*

Lewis had the physique of a god, tall and golden. Long, sturdy arms hung down, ending at his powerfully built hips that led to muscular thighs and even longer legs. My eyes focused on one area of his body. It stood out prominently, hard and straight from a thatch of dark hair, and all I could think about was how much I wanted him inside me.

I examined his face, expecting to see the bashful demeanor he displayed whenever he was anywhere near me. Instead, I saw a man whose face openly expressed his desire for me, and one who was completely in control of his emotions.

He removed my nightgown and guided me downward. "I can't wait to make you mine," he whispered, right before his first thrust sank into my body. I groaned and squeezed my eyes closed on a tremor of exquisite pleasure. Lewis immediately set a very slow rhythm and each time he entered and withdrew, he observed my face. I felt as if I was drowning, not with pleasure but with impatience. I had waited too long for this; I needed to feel the friction.

"Faster," I whimpered, digging my nails into his buttocks in an effort to force him down. "Please, Lewis. I need to feel you faster."

He groaned. "Sweet girl, in a minute I'm going to give you what you want. Right now, I'm trying to get to know you inside and out."

To please me, he gave me several very fast strokes, and then his quest to acquaint himself with my body began again. It hit me then what he was doing. Lewis was not having sex with me; he was making love, and for the first time in my life, I knew and felt the difference.

His manhood sank into me again. Then the speed of his thrusts increased. I wrapped my legs around his waist and lifted my hips to meet each of his powerful strokes. A few minutes later, a divine explosion ripped through my body.

Hours later, I stretched languidly. Lewis had fallen asleep. He'd always been so quiet, so seemingly uninterested in what was going on around him. The image he projected was not the man I now knew. Lewis had taken me on a heavenly trip more incredible than any I'd ever experienced, and I couldn't wait to go again.

# Chapter 9

*Jazmin*

My eyes opened to sunshine and pounding on my front door. I looked at the clock, saw that it was seven, and groaned. I'd only been asleep for two hours. The pounding on my door started again in direct correlation with the thumping in my head, only the door was louder. I really needed to stop drinking.

I staggered from the bed and pulled on my robe. If it was Paige, I was gonna kill the girl; she was way too happy in the morning. I left my bedroom and almost stumbled to the floor when I banged my thigh against the chair in my living room.

My furniture was white, the carpet pale gray, and I'd filled my étagère with those little crystal figurines that sold three for ten dollars in the mall. I liked light colors because it made the room appear bigger, and a lot of glass and brass, and pillows. Rubbing my leg, I made it the rest of the way without further mishap and turned the locks.

"Good morning, Jazzy." Brick wore jeans, a lightweight pullover, and a grin from ear to ear. "It sure took you long enough to open this door."

He walked by me and into my apartment; I glanced down at my attire.

The hem had fallen on the back of the red robe and my elbows poked through the threadbare material. The thing was older than the hills and the colors in the Bronco football jersey I wore underneath had faded many washings ago. There was a hole in the middle where my stomach showed through, and my hair had to be standing up all over my head because I hadn't bothered to tie it down before I went to bed. I glanced up, found him staring, and I wanted to die. This was not how I wanted this man to see me.

"You're looking lovely this morning, Jazzy-girl."

I waited for the punch line because surely the man was joking. I pulled my tatty robe around my body. "Wh-what are you doing here, Brick?"

He walked toward me. "I told you that I was coming to get you, Jazmin Reed."

I backed up a step. "But...but that was only two hours ago."

Tenderness softened his face. "Yeah."

When he stopped in front of me, I tried to look everywhere except at that man. Brick moved closer and grabbed one of my hands. He lifted my arm in the air and twirled me around.

"Mmm," he toned. "My Jazzy is beautiful in anything."

God, I was so embarrassed, but I didn't have time to think about that because a second later, I was in his arms. Breathing harshly, he gazed deep into my eyes, and then cupped the back of my head. I closed my eyes in anticipation of another spine tingling kiss, but felt instead the touch of one of his fingers on my lips, slowly sliding along their outline. It felt so sensual and so soft, almost like the light touch of a feather.

Then I felt something wet and I opened my eyes. Brick was using the tip of his tongue to trace the same path as his finger. Our gazes connected again and our lips came together in a leisurely excursion that seemed to last an eternity. A tremor of pleasure had just begun to work its way through my chest when Brick released me and stepped back.

I brought my hands up to my warm cheeks and tried to slow my breathing.

"It's time for you to get dressed, Jazzy. We have a lot on our agenda today."

—❧—

*Arianna*

Persistent knocking on my front door roused me from a deep party-induced sleep. I squinted at the clock. At eight o'clock on a Saturday morning, whoever was at that door had better be prepared to die. "All right," I mumbled, shrugging into my robe when the knocking started again.

"Good morning!"

I loved Paige Michaels, I really did, but the girl was one of those happy-get-on-my-nerves morning people. "Girl, please. It is way too early for this."

"Ooh, I can see that someone's in a bad mood this morning."

"It ain't about a bad mood. It's about a hangover."

"If you'd do what I told you and pop two aspirins before you go to bed, you wouldn't have a hangover."

"Yeah, yeah, Doctor Quack, whateva. What's got your butt up so bright and early anyway?"

"Love, girlfriend."

"Love?" I rolled my eyes. "P, it's a little early to hear about you and Pierce Reynolds this morning. Maybe you could come back a later."

She flopped down on the couch. "Pierce?" she said as if spitting a bug out of her mouth. "I'm talking about Lewis."

The name sounded familiar, but the pounding in my head made it hard to concentrate. However, the name finally clicked. "P, are you talking about Jermaine Lewis, Pierce's friend?" She nodded. "Paige, you can't be serious! You slept with Jermaine Lewis last night?"

"Yeah girl, and he was good, too."

I don't think I'll ever understand Paige Michaels or any woman who could let so many men stick their organ inside their body without even a hint of there being any kind of relationship. Or maybe I'm just prudish in my thinking. "What about Pierce? Aren't you worried that he's going to find out that you slept with his friend?"

Her expression changed into one so evil I held my breath. "I don't care what that Negro finds out. If I ever see his trifling ass again, I'll tell him myself!"

"*If* you ever see him again?" When a tear rolled down her cheek, I sat beside her on the sofa. "What happened last night, P?"

## A *Request for Closure*

"Pierce left, Ari. Lewis told me that he's shipping out in two days. Last night, he left me stranded at that party, went to my house and packed his stuff and left. He didn't say goodbye to me or to Jessie." She huffed out a breath and dried her eyes. "But it's okay, because Lewis stepped in to take his place. He says he'll be here another eighteen months before he heads back to LA. Who knows, maybe he'll take me and Jessie with him."

Paige was shopping for a husband. The problem: Colorado Springs was a shallow pond stocked with low class parasites. I'd never said anything to her about it, but I thought that for her to keep casting her net and dragging out leeches was not only a waste of time, but also stupid. She wasn't gonna find any love in that pond because there's not a man alive who can even say the word commitment without spitting all over himself.

Oh, I'd had the fantasy once, just like every other little girl who ever played dress up and forced a dirty, gap-toothed boy into the role of playground groom. Then one night, I saw my father slap my mother across the mouth in front of company during an argument that had ignited over a wrong play she'd made in a silly-ass card game—and so ended that childhood dream.

"All you've done is sleep with this man, Paige. Don't you think it's a little early to start making wedding plans?"

"All I'm saying is, who knows?" She stood up. "I'd better get back downstairs. Lewis is supposed to be taking me to breakfast."

That comment put a frown on my face. "I just know that you did not leave Jessie alone in your apartment with a man."

"I'm not that stupid. Jessie's outside somewhere playing."

"Well, that's good to know," I said, walking Paige to the door. "I'm going back to bed. If you need me, you know where I am. Otherwise, I'll hook up with ya later."

She turned back to me. "Oh, the reason I came up was to ask you about Chad's party. It starts at ten. Wanna ride over together?"

"Aren't you riding with Lewis?"

"He's pulling guard duty tonight. We might hook up there, but it will be late."

"Is Jazz riding with us?"

"Don't know. I talked to her last night at the party, but then she disappeared. I'll call and ask her later."

"Just let me know."

"I will, see ya later." Paige moved into the hallway. "You should take those aspirin before you go back to bed. You'll feel better when you get up."

"Yeah, yeah," I said, closing the door.

In my bedroom, I removed my robe and slipped under the lavender spread on my bed. Another day—another heartbreak—another party. One man had left Paige's life and she'd immediately replaced him with another and had plans to hit the streets that evening. Easy come, easy go. A few tears and move on. That was the way we rolled. We were young. We had jobs, and we partied six nights out of the week. I didn't have many good memories living in my mother's house and I was looking to fill my fun quotient as much as possible. Paige wanted a husband. Jazmin wanted a salon, and all I wanted was a good time.

I turned on my back and closed my eyes, but didn't anticipate the question that suddenly popped into my mind: Is this all there is to life?

—–𝒶𝓋𝓋𝓇—–

*Jazmin*

There is nothing that a model likes more than clothes, except maybe chocolate and a forbidden slice of pizza every now and then. I stood in front of the full-length mirror in a deep violet gown made of the finest crepe topped by gossamer chiffon. I looked great and I slink-walked over to where Brick sat in a chair, the same chair he'd occupied in the exclusive boutique for the last hour and a half.

He twisted his lips and shook his head no.

73

## A *Request for Closure*

I shrugged and headed back into the dressing room. At my apartment, I'd showered and donned a black halter-top and wraparound cotton skirt. He'd taken me to breakfast and as I sat in the booth across from him, something in his eyes kept drawing me to him. I felt a connection, something that was almost spiritual and rare. Whatever that something was, it felt right and went much deeper than anything I had felt with any other man.

Ten minutes later, I stepped out into the viewing area again, this time wearing a dark green, jersey matte with a muted gold leaf design on the front and back. It was clingy and molded my curves.

Brick flashed a thumbs-up.

I returned to the dressing room, replaced the gown on the padded hanger, and hung it with the other dresses Brick indicated that he liked. They included a jaunty jet-black, knee length dress made of raw china silk, and a deep peach, twenties-style flapper dress accented with tiny clear glass beads. I had one more dress to try on and I quickly slipped it over my head. This time when I stepped out, Brick came to his feet.

"That's the one, Jazzy," he said.

The dress was a deep, vibrant coral, made entirely of Alençon lace with a see-through midriff designed in a floral motif.

"I want to see you in this one tonight."

I went back into the dressing room to put on my street duds and get the rest of my dresses. We next stopped for lingerie and shoes. By the time we left the mall and walked outside into the warm sunshine, I couldn't even fathom the amount of cash Vincent Marks had left behind, and couldn't help wondering what I'd have to do in payment for all of these wonderful clothes.

"I want you to meet my mom," he said, handing me into a brand new white Continental Mark V with a rich cranberry interior. He'd received it as part of his signing bonus.

I settled into my seat, turning to him when he entered the car. "Why?"

"Why what, Jazzy?"

74

"Why do you want me to meet your mother? I only met you last night, and while I've had a wonderful day with you so far, we don't know each other."

"I know everything that I need to know." Then he reached into the backseat of the car. When he turned back, he dropped two magazines into my lap. My eyes widened in astonishment and I sought his eyes.

"You're my dream girl, Jazzy," he said. "I've been staring at those covers for years and I promised myself that if God was good and I ever in this life got to meet you again, I'd do everything in my power to make you mine."

I didn't know whether to be flattered or to jump out of the car. The boy had been faking me out from the moment we met, and something about this was spooky.

*Real spooky*, Mags reiterated.

"I-I don't understand."

"There are some things we don't need to understand. But I'll tell you a story while we grab a bite to eat. Then I'm taking you to meet my mother."

Brick found an Italian restaurant and requested a dark corner in the back. I started to tell him that Italian food was my favorite, but then I glanced at the magazines in my hands. One of them had published an in-depth interview. Anything Vincent Marks wanted to know about me was there in black and white. He seated me and moved around the table to his chair. After ordering two glasses of water with a lime twist, he turned to me.

"The first time I saw you, I was seventeen," he said. "I'd come to New York with my mother to check out some colleges that had offered me a basketball scholarship. We were on our way to eat when you came barreling around the corner and collided with my chest." Brick reached across the table and ran a finger tenderly down my face. "You stroked my cheek, flashed one of the most beautiful smiles I'd ever seen, and said you were sorry. Then off you went again, head down, coat flapping in the wind behind you. I knew you'd already forgotten about me. I ran after you and my mother and the school rep found me in an alleyway standing in front of a door. The sign said, 'Models enter here.'

"When I asked, the rep said that there was a fashion show going on inside, and since college sports reps will do or give you anything to induce you to go to their school, instead of going to eat, we attended your show."

I sat back in my chair, absolutely amazed. Fortunately, the waiter came to our table. Brick ordered lasagna with extra cheese, a Caesar salad, and French bread, buttered but without the garlic. Again, I glanced at the magazines on the table.

"But how did you know that I was in Colorado Springs?"

"I'm telling this tale, Jazzy-girl. However, since I know patience isn't one of your stronger personality traits, I'll tell you now that it was my mother. But back to my story... After the show, I told the rep that I wanted to meet you. He arranged for me to go backstage. It was the most memorable experience of my life."

When the waiter returned with our food, I picked up my fork and dug in. I hadn't eaten since lunch yesterday. I had polished off my salad and had started on my lasagna when I paused with my fork midway to my mouth. "Now I remember you. You're that really tall, skinny kid who wore his hair in this gigantic Afro."

Brick grinned. "Yeah, that was me. I was going for the biggest 'fro in the school. I thought I was such hot stuff back then."

"Think you are now, too, Mr. Jock, but you're not."

"You mean to tell me that you weren't impressed with all that dough I dropped on you this morning?"

"Boy, get real. As much as I like shopping, what I want in a man has nothing to do with his money. I want to know what's in his mind and what's in his heart. If we can connect in those two places, then everything else will be a breeze."

He nodded. "That's deep."

I cocked my brow. "Yes. It is."

Brick reached for my hand. "Jazmin, I'm sorry that you had that accident and that it ended your modeling career. You were one of the best, and I know in my heart that you were headed for superstardom."

"Thank you. It's been tough, but life goes on so don't go gettin' all maudlin on me. And you still haven't told me how you knew that I was in Colorado Springs."

"I told you, my mother."

"And?"

"And she saw you in the grocery store a couple of weeks ago and couldn't believe her eyes. She left her cart in the middle of the floor and called me at school."

"Oh," I said.

"She told me that you seemed to be walking fine, but that you looked really unhappy. I was ready to drop everything and come home right then, but it was finals week, and I had to get that piece of paper because no one knows how long this basketball thing is going to last."

Not many jocks think beyond their last paycheck and I was glad to hear that Brick had a plan for the future. "Okay. That explains how you knew I was in Colorado Springs. But how did you know that I would be at that party last night?"

"I didn't. I was out cruisin' with some of my homeboys and we just happened to drop in on that party. I think you know one of them…Marcus Hillman."

"Damn," I said under my breath.

He squeezed my fingers. "It's okay, Jazmin. I know the score, but starting right this minute, the game we're playing is one on one. From now on, no more creepin' because I'm the only cat who'll be sharing your sheets at night."

While I sat in that chair unable to think up a smart-ass comeback, Brick took out his wallet and laid money in the little brown tray. Then he stood and held out his hand. "Unless you have a problem with that."

I took his hand. "I don't have a problem with that."

"Good, then let's jet. My mother is waiting on us."

# THE PAST

# SUMMER, 1979

# THE SHIFTING WINDS
# OF CHANGE

# Chapter 10

*Arianna*

Chandler Houston had a laid out crib, from the crystal chandelier hanging in the foyer to the fabric-covered walls in the great room. Paige and I stood on lush white carpet in a vast space filled with expensive black and white furnishings, and every electronic device known to man.

"Glad you gals could make it," Chandler said as he walked towards them. He took us individually into his arms for a quick squeeze.

"Thanks for having us," Paige said.

He continued to stare at me. "How you doing, sugar?"

Chandler, with his curly black hair and hazel eyes, had it going on in the looks department. He was also a genius and a mathematician working for NORAD. At twenty-five, Chandler was a charmer with a claim that he was ready to live the married life with me as his lady. Six months into our relationship, he'd put a three-carat rock on my finger. I liked Chandler a lot, but love was never in the picture. I returned his ring after three months but we've remained very close friends. "I'm fine, Chad."

He landed a quick kiss on the side of my mouth. "Yes you are, sugar, and I'm still waiting for you to change your mind."

"You are not. And I know Stacy Chapman would not be happy to know her man is over here flirting with me."

"Ari, you know I'm doing time with Stacy until I can convince you to put my ring back on your finger. I am and will always be your man."

He pulled me into his arms and was doing a pretty persuasive job of stating his case when the doorbell pealed and Paige cleared her throat simultaneously.

## A *Request for Closure*

Chandler released me and caressed my cheek with the back of his hand. "Sugar, don't leave until I've had a chance to talk to you. All right?"

I was still recovering from the invigorating sensations of his kiss and could only nod. Chad went to the door and Jazmin walked in on the arm of one of the finest brothas I have ever seen in my life. Chandler announced that the guest of honor had arrived. Jazmin stayed by Vincent Marks' side, preening in his glory as Chad introduced them to the VIPs. Then she headed in our direction.

"When did you hook up with him?" Paige's voice was a mix of curiosity and yearning.

"Last night, girl, and have I got news for the two of you.

Although my slinky black number was very classy and Paige's mahogany silk pantsuit was lovely, the dress Jazmin Reed had on was divine. She wore her hair brushed back and off to the side in a sleek thick mane that curled under at the ends. Her nails matched the coral in her shoes and dress and the jewelry on her neck and wrist sparkled like diamonds.

"What's up," I said.

"Love," Jazmin said.

I tsked my tongue. "Not you, too."

Her hand landed on her waist. "And what is that supposed to mean, Arianna Jackson?"

"Ask, P."

"She's talking about Lewis. He and I hooked up last night."

Jazmin's eyes went wide. "Hooked up! With Lewis? What happened to Pierce?"

"Girl, that Negro left last night, and all I can say is good riddance to rotten trash!"

I listened as they related their stories. It appeared that while I was sleeping, my friends had found love during the night. Paige, I wasn't so sure about; after all, another man she'd hoped to marry had dumped her without notice. Sometimes love did strike like lightening, but I suspected that for her, Lewis was more of a rebound thing. Jazmin, on the other hand, might have found the real deal. She was gushing with pride over a man—something I'd never heard her do before. I glanced over at Vincent Marks. The man was definitely something to gush about.

When we parted, I sipped on a drink and rapped with a few people before deciding that this was not where I wanted to be. I went to locate Paige. She was on the couch with a group of people bent over the table snorting lines of coke, and she was sitting next to one of the finest men in the room. I waved my hand in front of her face.

"I'm ready to jet."

Paige, looking glassy-eyed and toasted, frowned at me. "Why?"

"Let's just say that I'm ready to do something else."

"Well, I'm not ready to go."

"Let's not have a fight here, ladies."

Paige seemed to snap to then. "Arianna Jackson, Jermaine Lewis. Lewis, Arianna."

"So, you're the Lewis that Paige has been raving about all day. I'm glad to meet you."

"And you're Arianna. I'm glad to meet you, too."

"You've being hangin' for a while. I'm surprised we haven't been introduced before."

"No, we haven't been formally introduced, but I've seen you at Paige's. You're as beautiful as she is."

I glanced at Paige. "I like him."

She smoothed her hand down the back of his head. "I do, too."

"Did you happen to drive over here?"

"Yeah, and before you ask, I'll make sure Paige gets home."

"Thanks," I said, giving her a quick hug. "I'll see you tomorrow. Don't do anything I wouldn't do. Oh, what am I saying? You will anyway."

"That's so true, but you be cool out there."

"I will. See ya."

I checked the room for Chandler before I left the party. I didn't know what he wanted to speak to me about, but he had my number so I didn't worry about it. As I drove out of Chandler's circular driveway, home didn't seem like such a good place to go. Instead, I decided to pop by my friend Monica Wells' crib to see if I could get her to hang with me for a minute.

Since Chandler lived in Broadmoor with the ritzy folks, I had about a forty-minute drive back into the city, which left plenty of time to exercise my mind. I guess the reason Chandler immediately clogged my thoughts was that I had just left his house. Honestly, I'd never really given him a chance, which was kind of dumb since the man had plenty of moola, looks, and a secure future, which I'd heard somewhere were the basic mainstays of any successful relationship.

My girls thought I was stupidest thing walking for letting a man like Chandler Houston slip out of my grasp. They said had he proposed to them, they would've sopped up that man like he was the last biscuit on a plate with sausage gravy. Chad was a biscuit and he came with a lot of sausage in his gravy, but I didn't feel anything for him other than friendship.

I stopped at a red light on Circle and watched the traffic rolling through the intersection. I don't know why I didn't feel more for Chad. I guess I was waiting for something more or better. Only I had no idea what that more or better was. I knew what I didn't want, and that was to be like my mother who'd given seven babies to a man who couldn't find his own bed at night. The light turned green and I made a left turn, heading back into the city and toward Monica's house.

—◦◦◦—

*Paige*

Five minutes after Arianna left, I knew that I should have gone with her. I was in the middle of a heart-stopping kiss when Lewis suddenly went statue still in my arms. I turned my head and encountered the frigid black eyes of Pierce Reynolds. When he started in our direction, Lewis grabbed my hand and gave it a reassuring squeeze.

"Stay calm," he said.

"I am calm," I said.

"You don't have to worry about anything."

"I'm not worried."

"I won't let him hurt you."

I pressed myself into his side. "I know."

"Now ain't this the shit! My big, black boots ain't even crossed the state line and my woman done already got herself a replacement in the form of my dawg. Whadup, Nigga?"

"Reynolds," Lewis said, rising to his feet.

Pierce reared back, and then he chuckled under his breath. "Reynolds? What happened to my main man? Here I been thinkin' you and me were boys, and all this time you been creepin' behind my back, bonin' my bitch."

"Pierce!" I was about to tell Pierce Reynolds where he could stick his bitch when Lewis' grip on my hand tightened.

Pierce slanted his gaze at me. Hate sizzled in his eyes and I grew instantly afraid. I stepped closer to Lewis.

"Then again, I suppose it doesn't really matter since she's screwed just about every dick on the base."

Lewis quickly surveyed the room. "Not in here, man. You wanna rap, then let's you and me step outside."

Pierce waved his arm toward the door. "Let's do this thing then."

I stood frozen as Lewis walked by Pierce. Then the enormity of what was about to happen hit me. I didn't give a damn about Pierce Reynolds, but both of those men were soldiers—soldiers trained to kill!

"Hey y'all," someone shouted. "There's a fight going down outside."

I watched in horror as everyone in the room rushed for the door; then snapping to, I quickly followed. I had almost reached the door when someone grabbed my arm and yanked me back.

"Stay here, P."

I pulled at my arm. "No, I have to stop this!"

"You can't stop it. It's gone too far."

Something inside me sagged and I turned around to find Jazmin holding out a glass filled with a clear brown liquid.

## A Request for Closure

"Drink this."

"I don't want a drink. I have to help Lewis. He's out there because of me."

"And what is it that you think you're going to be able to do? That fight ain't about you. It's about respect and there's nothing you can do to stop it."

I took the glass and downed the contents. Jazmin was right. That fight had nothing to do with me, at least not from Pierce's slant. The man had tried to blow town without a color-me-gone, so he couldn't care less if I dropped off the face of the earth. The fact that Lewis, his boy, had taken the lease on a space he'd abandoned had tapped his ego. I rubbed my stomach where the mix of cocaine and whiskey had started to burn and slowly walked back to the couch. I plopped down and sent up a prayer for an end to the nightmare my life had become.

A short while later the front door opened and people spilled back into the room. I jumped up from the couch frantically searching for Lewis, and then I saw him, standing tall and proud. As the crowd gradually thinned, I saw him more clearly. Dirt and grass covered his clothes, blood trickled from his bottom lip, and a cut had opened over his right eye. The other one was already turning purple. Lewis threw out his arms and I ran to him as fast as my feet could get me there.

"Here you go, my knight in shining armor." I handed Lewis a cold, rib eye steak.

He snatched it out of my hand and slapped it on his left eye. "It's not funny, Paige."

I sat on the couch beside him. "But you are my knight; you proved it tonight by fighting for my honor."

"Oh, now you got jokes?" He leaned toward me and gently pinched the nipple of my left breast. "But so you know, that fight was not about your honor. I was fighting for the privilege of getting inside that luscious body of yours again."

"So, now you got the jokes—not. Let me say again that comedy is not in your future."

Lewis stared into the room. "That's probably true...but are you?"

I wanted so much to say yes, but a lot had happened to me in the last twenty-four hours. A man, only one of countless many, had dumped me and before his scent had even left my house, I'd taken another into my bed.

Yes, I wanted to get married, but I knew that I couldn't keep dropping my drawers for these army boys that came sniffing around in the hopes that one of them would put a ring on my finger. I was twenty-two, and still a young woman and Jessie was a very young child. What was the rush? I had plenty of time to snag a husband before Jessica grew up.

I thought about Arianna. Everywhere we went she had men tripping over themselves trying to get to her. In the last year, two had proposed and another she'd met when she first moved here had been so persistent that Arianna had threatened to put a hit out on him. Chandler Houston had been the most successful; she'd actually worn his ring. Obviously, my girl knew something that I didn't know. Maybe it was time that I learned her secret.

Lewis was waiting expectantly for my answer. I cupped his face and tenderly kissed the cut over his eye. "Perhaps, but why don't we wait and see."

—◦◦◦—

*Arianna*

"Thanks," I said to my partner when the slow jam ended.

He escorted me back to my table and as soon as he left, I knew that something was wrong. I scanned the dance floor and when I didn't see Monica or Jamie Knight, who we'd also convinced to come with us, I made several passes through the club. Monica had insisted on driving so the girl couldn't have forgotten that I'd left my car parked in her driveway. I was on my way around again when a man stepped in front of me, blocking my path.

"Is something wrong?"

Still telling myself that I was mistaken, I glanced up at him. "I don't want to believe this, but I think my girlfriends left me here."

"Don't worry, sweetheart. Hang with me and I'll make sure you get home." He grabbed my hand and led me to the dance floor where he molded me snugly against his frame. "I'm Jace Barnes."

"Arianna, and thanks for offering the ride."

He hugged me closer. "I'll never leave you stranded, Arianna."

When the dance ended, he took me to his booth. He seemed a bit agitated as he shifted his eyes away from me and exhaled as one might when they had finally reached a goal. I rose slightly in the seat to survey the area over by the door of the club.

"What are you looking for, sweetheart?"

I sat back down. "My friends. I was hoping they might have remembered by now and come back for me."

Jace swallowed and looked away from me again. "Um...would you like a drink?"

Before I could respond, he'd signaled for a waitress and placed the order.

"How'd you know?"

"How'd I know what?"

"That I like Seagram 7 and 7-Up."

"I have a habit of noticing things...especially beautiful things that interest me."

His lips spread into an alluring smile. I ducked my head, somewhat perplexed, and tried to slow the rushed beating of my heart. Yeah, I thought I was hip and cool all right, but Jace Barnes was hipper and cooler. He towered over my five-foot-six inches by almost a foot. His build was not particularly large, but the muscles he had felt firmly packed and hard, and while he had a young face, his eyes held a wisdom that had only come from living. Jace knew things I didn't know.

For the remainder of the night, I was the total focus of his attention. Jace stared at me a lot and kept dipping his head in front of my face as though to limit my view to only him. With his eyes, he seemed to be trying to communicate something to me. I guess I wasn't on the same wavelength.

He picked up one of my hands and began rubbing my fingers and caressing my palm. "Are you going to tell me your last name?"

My club name was Sheila—no last name—just Sheila. It was one of those clubbing rules Paige and Jazmin had taught me, and mainly for the jerks who wouldn't take no for an answer. "Jackson," I told him.

"What's your middle name?"

"What's *your* middle name?"

"Jace."

My brow rose. "Isn't Jace your first name?"

"No." He cleared his throat. "My first name is, and don't you dare laugh, Alvin."

"Al-vin." I cracked up.

"I asked you not to laugh," he said, smiling, too. "It's a family name and when you call my mother's house, you should ask for Alvin."

That sobered me up quick. "You live with your mother?"

"No. I live in the barracks. My mother lives in New York. That's where I'm from. When you call her house, you should ask for Alvin, though."

New York? I tried to figure out why he had mentioned this to me, about his mother, I mean. It seemed to imply more than one night, but that was impossible. This was going to be a one-night stand. Wasn't it?

"Hey Arianna. Long time, no see."

I looked up and into the black eyes of a man I'd known for years. Grant Hamilton and I had grown up in church together, and he, like me, had fled that den of charlatans as soon as our birth certificates endorsed our right to do so. "Grant," I said. "How are you?"

He took a seat in the booth and nodded at Jace. "Been doing okay."

Because of the loud music, we tilted our heads closer and proceeded to chat about nothing for a minute before he rose from the booth.

"Nice seeing you, Arianna."

"You too," I said. "Bye, Grant."

## A Request for Closure

Jace released an impatient breath of air, the same impatience he'd displayed toward any man who'd spoken to me. All night, he'd been rubbing up against me, shooing away predators, bestowing compliments meant to heighten my sensual awareness, and his unwavering concentration and immersing gaze had done their job.

Jace Barnes made me nervous. Not scared nervous, but the kind of nervous that paired itself with expectation. I knew what he wanted. Jace was a player in the game, and while I wasn't a virgin, what I knew about sex would take up no more than three lines on a one-page, one-sided pamphlet. I was equally sure that if I let him, Jace would show me the things he knew. In his eyes, I saw a sea churning with desire. Looking deeper, I saw a hint of vulnerability that made me wonder if the boy was really all that. For once in my life, I was going to throw caution to the wind and find out.

A waitress arrived at our table to announce last call and Jace ordered another round of drinks. When they came, he picked his up and sipped from the glass.

"How old are you, Arianna?"

"Why do you need to know?"

His dark, bedroom eyes locked on mine, and then he shrugged. "I don't."

An uneasy quiet settled over our table. Uneasy because I knew we both felt the sexually charged heat that had encased us all night long. Leaving the club, Jace held my hand. I never knew handholding could be a sexual experience, but the way he rubbed my fingers and caressed my palm as if he were testing the softness of silk had tingles running up my spine.

As we approached his car, a shiny black Firebird, I noticed that there were people inside and my sex meter dropped to sub zero. "Who are they?"

He looped a pair of long arms around my body from behind. "Nobody important, but they're with me." His hands swept my hair back over my shoulders. "Don't be mad, sweetheart. Actually, I don't even know those guys. I was getting dressed and they were sitting on their bunks looking sad, so I asked if they wanted to tag along. I'm gonna drop 'em at the base. Then it's you and me," he murmured right before he fastened his lips on mine. Shock held me immobile until he took my hand again and continued to the car.

"Hit the back, man," Jace ordered when we arrived. "Arianna's riding up front with me."

"I ain't moving, Barnes. Let's go."

The next thing I knew, Jace had the man's throat trapped inside his hand. "Unless you're planning on hitchin' a ride back to the barracks, I suggest you move."

The man moved and Jace helped me into the car. I couldn't help thinking about how quickly his temper had flared, and when he folded himself into the car, I hugged my door, my apprehension growing as I realized the predicament I'd placed myself in. Here I was at two in the morning, sitting in a car with four strangers. Could I have been any stupider?

"You going somewhere, baby girl?"

His voice reached out to me in the dark easing some of my trepidation. I didn't know a lot about Jace Barnes, but I had a feeling that I could trust this man. "No."

"I was wondering why you're sitting all the way over there...when you should be over here next to me." He tugged me across the seat.

"Will you drop me off first?" I whispered.

Several silent heartbeats passed before he placed his mouth at my ear. "Arianna...c-can I come back?"

He sounded hesitant and that boosted my confidence. It would seem that Mr. I'm-all-that-and-a bag-of-chips had a chink in his armor after all. "You'd better or I'll be real disappointed."

A short while later, Jace parked in front of my building and walked me up. He took my key and opened the door.

"Twenty minutes and don't you dare go to sleep."

"Okay," I said, and saw him out.

## A *Request for Closure*

A quick shower, some candles, and when the knock came twenty minutes later, I was dressed in a sheer white, lacy nightgown. I grabbed my robe and went to the door

"Alvin Jace Barnes, reporting for duty as requested."

"Arianna Yevette Jackson," I replied. "You're right on time, Mr. Barnes. And that's Y-E-V-E-T-T-E not Y-V."

He smiled that enthralling smile again and walked into my apartment. I looked heavenward and silently said thanks.

# Chapter 11

*Jazmin*

I waited nervously while Brick unlocked the door to my apartment. In the car, he'd responded whenever I said anything, but mostly he'd been quiet. I tried to convince myself that he was tired. We'd put in a long day after what had essentially been a two-hour nap. More likely the reason was tied to the five men he'd huddled with at the party—two specifically that I had slept with in the past—and the conversation they'd shared.

Inside, I headed for my bedroom to change into something more comfortable. I wasn't aware that Brick had followed until his tongue stroked side of my neck. "You're beautiful, Jazzy," he whispered in my ear. "And I love the taste of your skin."

A shiver coursed through my body.

He placed his mouth at my ear. "Those men at the party told me they knew you."

My heart froze in my chest. "I, um, I do know a couple of them."

Brick kissed the corner of my mouth. "I don't think you understand what I'm trying to tell you, Jazmin. Those men at the party…we grew up together, lived in the same neighborhood, attended the same schools. I've known those men my entire life and we are not in the habit of keeping secrets from each other."

My heart raced as my imagination took flight. What did those men say?

Brick stepped back. "Come to me when you've changed, and wear the lilac nightgown." Then he walked out of my bedroom.

For a moment, I stood there wondering what those men told Brick and just how detailed their conversation had been. Then I heard the front door open and close. I ran into the living room. Vincent Marks had left my apartment.

I stayed where I was, waiting, hoping that the door would open again. Five minutes later, I returned to my bedroom. I sat on the bed and folded my hands in my lap.

"I am not going to cry," I told myself, right before I bowed my head and burst into tears.

*See...that's what your ass gets for messin' around with those pretty boys.*

Ignoring Mags, I inhaled a deep breath and let it out slowly.

*Why are you sitting here bawling? That man ain't the be all, end all. You can have any man you want.*

I sucked up my sniffles and dried my face with my hands.

*Fuck the son of bitch! He ain't no goddamn saint either!*

Shut up, Mags, I thought, snapping off the necklace and bracelet and flinging them both across the room. I rose and kicked off my coral shoes, sending them flying. Then I reached behind my back, trying to get to the zipper on the dress so I could take it off and fling it somewhere, too. I was twisting, and turning, and bending over, and I couldn't get my fingers to touch the thing. I stood up ready to locate a pair of scissors when the zipper suddenly whizzed down.

The rhinestone necklace flipped over my shoulder. I closed my eyes when it began moving backward and slowly wound its way around the base of my neck. I swung around. Brick was there, sipping from a red straw stuck in the middle of a Coca-Cola Icee. The rhinestone necklace dangled from his fingers.

He lowered the cup, flipped the necklace into his hand, and dropped it into the pocket of his suit. "Since you don't like that piece, Jazzy-girl," he said, reaching his fingers inside the front pocket of the brocade vest he wore, "maybe you'll like this one better."

He pulled out a blue velvet box, flipped the lid, and my mouth dropped open. Somehow, I found my senses and the ability to speak. "Y-you...you have to be kidding."

Brick shook his head no.

"B-but, I thought you'd left."

He shook his head no again.

I shrieked and when we collided, the Icee and the velvet box hit the floor as Brick gathered me into his arms. A shower of tiny pecks rained down on my face, and when our mouths connected, I returned Brick's kiss like a woman possessed.

A short while later, I cleaned up the mess from the Icee while he searched for my ring, finally spotting it in the corner behind the door. We sat side-by-side on the bed. I was grinning like an idiot, but the expression on his face was more serious than that of a college professor about to flunk an entire class of students.

"This ring comes with a couple of contingencies, Jazmin."

"What," I asked, staring at the five-carat diamond sparkling on my left hand.

"One, you don't get it tonight."

"Why not?" I didn't even try to hide my disappointment.

"Because the two of us just came together yesterday, and while I can state definitively that I love you and you're the girl I'm gonna marry, can you say the same about me?"

I twisted my lips. The day we'd shared had certainly turned my head and centered the focus of my attention on Brick. But love? Now that was something to consider. "You're the girl I'm gonna marry," I quipped.

"Funny, Jazzy, not exactly what I want to hear, though. So, until you can look me in the eye and say that you love me more than life itself, and you *will* love me more than life itself, the ring stays in the box on the dresser."

I reared back. "On whose dresser?"

"Yours." Brick leaned in and gave me a peck on the lips. "Two, being the wife of a player, and I mean that in its truest form, is not easy, Jazzy. I'm a first-round draft choice. Once we publicly announce our engagement, the media is going to hound you, and even when that dies down, you're going hear rumors about me that I'm telling you right now won't be true. The jealousy you faced last night and tonight is only the beginning.

## A Request for Closure

"You'll have to get used to me being on the road for days at a time, for a lot of days of the year, and know in your heart that I'm going to be true to our marriage vows. And all of that is only the beginning, so I want you to think about everything I've told you and take as much time as you need to decide if you can live that kind of life with me."

Brick exhaled and his eyes shifted away. It was the first time he seemed nervous. He walked to the dresser and picked up the blue velvet box. "Jazzy, tonight when those men told me that they'd been in your bed, I felt like I'd been slit open and gutted. They were supposed to be my boys and they'd had something I'd been dreaming about for the last five years." Brick turned around. "But they are my boys and they had no idea that I was in love with the most beautiful woman in the world."

"Brick," I said on a breath. "I didn't—"

"Wait," he said, quickly returning to the bed. He lifted my hand and fingered the ring, pushing it back and forth on my finger. "You're like a fine mare, Jazmin Reed—sleek, gorgeous, and seductive. I told myself that it didn't matter because had I had the opportunity to bed you, I would have done the same thing. So...where does that leave us?"

"I don't know."

"It leaves us right here and right now, and the only things that matter are those that have happened since I saw you last night. Nothing that happened before that minute, that second, except our first meeting in New York, is important to me."

He slipped the ring off my finger, placed it back in the box, and took it over to the dresser. Already I felt as if something important was missing.

"Now for the last contingency. I've had it in my head for five years, that I would be your first lover." He laughed softly. "A silly boyhood fantasy that I've held as a reality only in my heart. I knew you'd had a string of lovers and that you could probably teach me a thing or two or three," he said with a shrug. "But Jazzy, the fact that you're here with me proves that dreams can and do come true, and I want to make that boyhood fantasy come as close to being a reality as possible."

I swallowed, unsure where the man was going with this line of thought.

Brick pulled off his jacket and laid it across the back of a chair. "So, tonight I'm going to take you to bed because I think I'll explode if I don't, and I'm going to make you mine. After that, there will be no more sex until our wedding night."

"What!" My voice was only slightly softer than a shout.

"You heard what I said, Jazmin. Why don't you take a hot bath? When you get out, I'll be waiting to see you in that lilac nightgown."

He left again and I sat there unable to believe, let alone process, everything Brick had told me. It was too much to take in all at one time.

However, before I could even begin to wrap my mind around any of Brick's contingencies, Mags popped up and asked, *Is he freakin' serious?*

An hour or so later, I entered a candlelit bedroom heavily scented with jasmine. Herbie Hancock played on the stereo and candles of every shape and size sat on the dresser where my ring twinkled like a star. Brick, dressed in black silk pajamas with the top fully unbuttoned, lay prone on the bed, his eyes so full of heat my skin pebbled with bumps. I walked to the edge of my bed, which he had remade with white silk sheets and covered from top to bottom with red and pink rose petals.

Brick left the bed. "You look gorgeous, Jazmin."

"Thank you. You look nice, too."

He tipped my chin. "You'd have to be looking at me to know that. Touch me, Jazzy."

I sucked in a fortifying breath and streaked my hand through his hair. It fell freely about his shoulders and felt soft and silky, and I did it again, letting my hand drift down to the solid mass of his chest where firm muscles rippled beneath my touch. Leaning forward, I wet one of his nipples with my tongue and heard his intake of air right before he lifted me off my feet. Brick deposited me in the middle of a fragrant garden where he quickly joined me. His head dipped and our mouths fused together in an urgent coupling that left me dizzy.

Brick moaned into my mouth and touched our foreheads together for a few moments to catch his breath. "Okay, Jazzy-girl. That's two you've won. Show me what else you got."

## A Request for Closure

I squirmed from under him and stood by the side of the bed. Dipping and swaying to the music, I shimmied my shoulders until the purple kimono slithered down my back and flowed to the floor.

"Turn around, Jazzy." His voice sounded raspy, as if he were struggling for air.

I peeked at him over my shoulder, then reached back to unhook the matching lace bra. I tugged it off and tossed it over my head. Then I turned, stepped from the pool of material, and put my hands on my waist. Brick was on his feet and he no longer wore his pajamas.

I had to catch my breath. African king was all I could think of, and one who only needed a golden crown to sit atop his silky black strands. His manhood throbbed against my back when Brick lifted me in his arms and placed me on the bed. His hands felt like soft flint as they caressed my skin, sparking tingles with every touch. His lips left a trail of heat my intoxicated senses struggled to handle. When Brick finally entered me, for a timeless moment everything stopped. And then I was bumping and moaning, and lifting my hips, and straining to meet his deep, hard thrusts. Brick was riding the waves of ecstasy, too, burning his scent and touch into my pores, assaulting my ears with words of slurred passion, commanding me to tell him that I would never want another lover.

Two hours later, I turned my head and found him smiling at me. His hands skirted the surface of my stomach in a circular, feathery movement.

"About contingency number three," he said.

"Yes," I said

"I just tossed it out."

—◦◦◦—

*Arianna*

Jace hung his suit in the closet and then ran both hands over his black wavy hair. He was tall and lean and dark, dark brown; his stance was that of an African warrior, proudly confident, his body magnificently toned, his eyes blazing heat and clearly broadcasting his intentions. The male part of him claimed my attention. My nerves tingled and pulsed. It looked long; it looked thick; it looked ready.

He crossed to the bed. I let him pull me up into his arms. His breath touched my cheek.

"Jace," I whispered. "I want you to know that I don't normally pick up men in clubs."

"I know," he said. His mouth covered mine for a couple of seconds, and then we both stretched out on the bed. Jace propped his head on his hand, leaned forward, and stroked his thumb across my cheek. He came whisper close. I closed my eyes.

"How old are you, Arianna?"

I moaned in disappointment and blinked my eyes open. "What?"

"How old are you?"

You never give up, do you?"

"No, so give up the info."

"Twenty-three," I said.

"Hmmm," he said. "Old enough to drink. Old enough for love. Old enough for me." He sat up and placed pillows behind his back. "Where did you grow up?"

He had to be kidding. Here I was ready to get it on and this man wanted my bio. "I'm a military brat...air force," I added when his brows rose with interest. "My dad retired a technical sergeant. I've lived in lots of places."

"Like where?"

"Well, I was born in Springfield, Massachusetts. I have also lived in New York—"

"City?"

"No, state. And in North Carolina—that's where my mother's people are from."

"Where are your father's people?"

"Virginia. Anyway, I've also lived in Bermuda, Dover, Delaware, and Omaha, Nebraska. My dad's next tour would have been somewhere in

Europe, but after my mother said he'd be going alone, he decided to retire."

"You're a gypsy," Jace commented. "They must have really loved each other for him to do that...your parents, I mean."

"I don't know...I guess."

"Which place did you like best?"

This was way too much chitchat for me. I wanted this man to teach me something and I wanted the lessons to begin now. "Jace, can we talk about this later," I said, trying to kiss him.

He held me by the shoulders, his eyes steady, and his voice stern. "No. I wanna talk about it now."

I sighed in defeat. "Probably, Bermuda...but maybe here."

"Why here?"

"Because here is where I met you."

Desire flared in his eyes. I was hoping that now things would get started, but Jace sat back and made himself comfortable on his pillows again.

"How many boyfriends have you had?"

Jeez, I thought. Can we skip the dialogue and get to the main event? I needed to get this man interested in making love, only I didn't know how to do it. I inched my hand into his lap. Jace picked it up and dropped it back into mine. Then he crossed his hands behind his head and his feet at the ankles. I guess that meant we weren't supposed to touch either.

"How many boyfriends?" he insisted.

"All of them?"

"All of them, starting with the very first."

I quickly made a count in my head. "Six," I said.

His brow rose. "Only six?"

"Yes," I said.

"How many have taken you to bed?"

My cheeks heated. This was getting downright embarrassing. "Why are you asking these questions?"

One of his hands skimmed the underside of my right breast. "How many have seen these?"

Now I was getting mad.

"Arianna?"

"Three," I muttered.

Jace tipped my chin up with his finger. "Sweetheart, I wanted to know because from now on, I'm the only one who has that privilege." He kissed my cheek. "Goodnight."

"Good…night," I repeated, stunned.

"Yeah." He stood, flipped back the covers, and got into bed. "I'll see you in the morning."

"Jace? What do you mean by…goodnight?"

"Arianna, how many times have you invited a man you've just met into your bed?"

I didn't respond.

"Never," he said. "You don't sleep around, baby girl, and any relationship you've had was probably long-term. That's not going to change with me. Now, goodnight, Arianna Yevette Jackson."

I sat for a minute, shaking my head in disbelief. Jace Barnes had to be joking. He wouldn't set me up like this and then not come through when he knew why I'd invited him up. My confusion mounted as I waited for him to take me in his arms and give me the loving his eyes and hands had promised all night. A few more minutes passed. I rose, blew out the candles, and climbed back into bed.

Jace did pull me close. He went to sleep. I lay there most of the night trying to figure out this strange, strange, very nice man.

I must have fallen asleep because when I woke up Jace was suckling at my right breast. I smoothed my hand over his head.

"Morning, baby girl."

"Good morning. What are you doing?"

"Having breakfast."

"Really," I said.

"Yeah. That's what folks usually do in the morning."

"But I thought you said—"

## A *Request for Closure*

"That was last night, Arianna." His gaze seemed to darken and smolder. "It's no longer night and I'm ready for love."

We reached for each other, ending further conversation. His hands massaged my breasts and his lips cruised over my mouth. He kissed a trail down my body and his hands found the area between my thighs. I was lost and writhing in the fire when his mouth replaced his hand. I tensed, and for a few uncomprehending moments, I lay there with my eyes wide open. Then a wonderful feeling stole over me, intense and so pleasurable my hips arched of their own accord. I felt Jace's hands on my legs, pushing them down, and he centered his tongue on the core of my body, applying a constant pressure.

A weight pressed down on my chest. I tried to suck in air. The more I tried to breathe, the heavier the weight became. I was wiggling and moaning and he was flicking his tongue back and forth when something snapped in my brain and I exploded in an ecstasy of light.

Our gazes fused when he lifted his head. His lips curved up knowingly. "That was your first time, wasn't it?"

The current flowing between us was powerful; I could only nod. Jace placed me back on the pillows. His kiss on my lips was tender as he positioned his pulsing manhood. His first stroke took my breath away, and sank so deep I thought he'd touched the back of my womb. His second one and the third took me to a place I'd never been before. It was a glorious place; a utopia of pleasure that I couldn't get enough of. The intense warmth started low in my belly and was quickly spreading upward when Jace suddenly grasped me tightly against his chest, thrust one last time, and I shattered into a million pieces.

Much later that morning, I lay completely awestruck in the shelter of his arms. Nothing in my experience had prepared me for his kind of lovemaking or left my sensitized body craving more. I felt whole, complete, as if I found the missing piece. I looked over at Jace. His eyes held a promise to fulfill all of my needs, but...hunger called.

We left the bed, showered and dressed. Jace turned on the television. I inspected my almost empty refrigerator for something to eat.

He answered the knock at the door and I heard him say, "Hi, Jessie."

My brows rose in surprise. Not because Jessie was at the door, she usually came up to watch cartoons on Saturday, but because Jace knew her by name, but I pushed off the thoughts forming in the back of my mind.

"Come on in," he said.

"What are you doing up here?"

"Visiting," Jace said.

"Are you visiting Auntie Ari?"

"Yep."

I left the kitchen. "Hi, baby," I said, kissing Jessica's cheek. "Where's Paige this morning?"

"Her and Lewis are still in bed."

"Jace, I need to run downstairs. I'll be right back. Come on, Jessie."

She took my hand and skipped along as we made our way down the hallway and the stairs. I went directly to the kitchen to raid Paige's refrigerator. She came around the corner.

"Do you have any bacon?"

"In the back. You making breakfast?"

"Yes, but not for you."

"Oh, you have company?"

I rose up and grinned. "Yep."

"It's Jace," Jessica said.

Paige frowned. "Jace? Jace who?"

"Barnes," I supplied, sticking my head back into her refrigerator. I found the bacon and headed for the door as Lewis came around the corner. "Morning, Lewis. Thanks, Paige. Later."

# Chapter 12

*Paige*

Lewis planted a wet kiss on the back of my neck. He tried for another and I shrugged out of his arms.

"What's wrong with you?"

"Nothing," I snapped, slamming a pot on the stove. In the thirty minutes since Arianna had breezed out my door, I'd done nothing but stomp around my kitchen and bang pots and pans. I was so mad I wanted to scream and keep screaming until everything changed back to the way that it was supposed to be.

"Are you planning on cooking something in that pot or are you just going to keep banging it on the stove?"

"Why don't you go and find something to do and leave me alone."

Lewis turned to Jessica and lifted her in his arms. "Good morning, sunshine." He smirked at me when she kissed him on the cheek. "At least somebody in this house is glad to have me around."

I stomped from the room. What in the hell was going on around here? I flopped down on my bed. Three times one is three. What was Jace Barnes doing in Arianna's apartment? Three times two is six. Her face had been so radiant when she said his name that I had almost believed she was as pure and innocent as she seemed.

Three times three is nine! Shit!

Arianna had to know that Jace Barnes was my man...okay, so maybe that wasn't true. Jace and I had never really dated and we stopped sleeping together when I hooked up with Pierce. He'd attended a couple of the weekend parties I used to throw, and then Jace stopped coming around. You can call me a silly-ass fool if you want, but I truly believed that when a man parked his head on my pillow, he was mine for life! The bruise on my ego was getting bigger and bigger and if this crap didn't stop and soon, I was gonna hurt somebody.

Lewis poked his head into the room. "I'm taking Jessie to breakfast. You want us to bring you something back?"

"What? I'm not invited to go with you?"

He entered then. "Paige, your daughter says she's hungry and you seem a bit edgy this morning. I thought we'd give you a little time to yourself, but you're welcome to come along if you want."

I was wrong to take my anger out on Lewis and if I didn't watch my step, he might fly the coop, too. "That's okay. You two go and have a good time."

I glanced at the clock and picked up the telephone anyway. Jazmin was going to be really pissed, but I needed to vent how I felt to someone and I needed to do it right now.

I waited through seven rings before Jazmin finally picked up the phone and mumbled, "Hello."

"Girl, you will not believe what that heffa is doing!"

"What heffa?"

"The one who lives upstairs. Do you know she actually had the audacity to come up my house and take my bacon to feed that bastard after she fucked him last night?"

I heard the yawn she tried to muffle. "What heffa and what bastard, P?"

My intake of air must have sounded like a wind machine. "Arianna and that damn Jace Barnes!"

"No," she said. The tone of her voice had dropped, indicating her disbelief.

"Yes!"

"What are you going to do?"

What was I going to do? What I felt like doing was snatching her devious ass bald and painting her cheek with a good right cross. "I don't know," I said. "Cuss her out, I guess."

"I think I'd be doing a little more than cussing her out. I'd be kicking me some ass, both of 'em." There was a pregnant pause before Jazmin continued. "Then again, maybe Ari doesn't know about the two of you."

"How could she *not* know?"

"P, you and I have been hangin' for years; Ari hasn't been around that long. I bet she has no idea that Jace was once your man."

"Jace Barnes was never my man…we just slept together occasionally."

"Whateva, Paige. But the fact is that you and Jace did have a thing once, and I don't think you want to be comparing notes with Arianna about what happened in your beds. In any case, you need to talk to her and straighten out things. Once she knows, she'll probably drop Jace like a hot brick."

I knew Jazmin was trying to get me to see the situation from Arianna's point of view. I couldn't because the only point that mattered was mine and Jazmin had better not be taking Arianna's side in this because she was my friend first. Then again, Arianna was supposed to be my friend, too. She was a little unschooled as far as life was concerned but that wasn't her fault, so perhaps a crash course in acceptable conduct among girlfriends and their men was in order for her.

"You're right," I said after a couple of minutes.

"I know," she said a little too smugly for my taste. "Arianna is good people, P. I don't think you want to lose her friendship over a simple misunderstanding. Talk to her and hopefully she'll listen."

I sighed. "I think I'm going to need some backup on this one."

"No problem."

"Cool. So, got any plans today?"

"Yes, and he's in my bed. So goodbye."

*Arianna*

Jace needed clothes so we drove to the base. I sat on the hood of his car (the barracks did not allow women inside) waiting and shooing away a constant stream of desperate men looking to hook up with anything without a beard. I was sitting there happy as a flea on a dog when one of the men who'd been in the car last night stopped in front of me.

"Hi," he said.

"Hi," I said.

"You waiting on Barnes?"

"Mmm hmmm."

"Didn't see him around yesterday. Guess you two hit it off, huh?"

I stared at him, wondering what the man expected me to say. "I guess."

"You plannin' on being his lady?"

"Plannin' on it."

He lifted his hand toward my face. I pushed it away.

"Too bad, but when you feel the need to knock boots with a real man, look me up. The name's Anthony Williams, in case you forgot." He winked. "For you, I'll be Tony the Tiger."

That's when I saw Jace. He was smiling and whistling as he walked out of the barracks. That stopped when he saw Tony.

"You'd better book it on outta here," I said.

Tony glanced over his shoulder. "Baby, don't trip. Ain't nothing over there I can't handle."

"Williams! Need to rap with you, man."

Tony sauntered over, and a few seconds later couldn't seem to get inside the barracks fast enough. When Jace turned for the car, he was smiling again. I observed his easy stride and wondered how a man could go from anger to calmness so quickly.

"What did you say to him, Jace?"

He lifted me from the hood. "Nothing you need to worry your pretty head about."

## A Request for Closure

In the car, I got out my lipstick and flipped down the mirror. "I'd really like to know what you said to Tony."

He started the engine. "Don't you see it?"

"See what?"

"Look in the mirror again."

I did. "I don't get it," I said, sitting back.

He chuckled. "Baby girl, you mean to tell me that you didn't see that sign?"

"Jace, what in the world are you talking about?"

He traced his finger across my forehead before turning his attention back to the road. "Jace's Property."

—✥—

Cooking dinner that night, I had a funny feeling that I couldn't shake. After leaving the base, we'd visited a couple of Jace's friends, gone grocery shopping, and he'd taken me to get my car. Though I'd seen Monica's car parked in her driveway, she hadn't answered her door, which struck me as weird because I'd also seen the curtains flutter as if somebody were standing behind them watching me.

After dinner, Jace sent me to the couch while he cleaned the kitchen. He joined me when he finished and I settled my head on his thigh until the movie ended.

"I guess you're about ready to hit the bed."

"Pretty much. Work day tomorrow."

"I know," he said, standing. He clinked off the TV. "Come here."

I came and Jace enfolded me in his arms. "Sweetheart, I have to go."

"Go where?"

"Back to the base. My unit will be out on bivouac this week. I won't be able to see you 'til I get back."

"I beg your pardon," I said, as a chill settled over me. I knew what was coming. Jace had gotten what he wanted and I'd made a huge mistake.

"I said, my unit's been assigned to the field and I won't be able to see you for a week."

He could have said something else. Something like, "I had a good time screwing you and I hope you have a wonderful life." That would have been honest—no regrets and no future expectations. Instead, he'd fed me a line and I was mad.

"Then go, and when you leave, don't bother coming back."

I left him standing there. In my room, I sat on the bed and began the process of putting Jace Barnes behind me. In only two days together, he had opened a well of feelings I had never before experienced with a man. I had thought that what we shared was the beginning of something good, but he'd ruined it.

I heard movement. Jace was standing in the doorway looking so pathetic I almost went over to him. I willed myself to stay put. I was trying to show him that I didn't care.

"Baby girl, I *am* coming back."

"Alvin, if you're leaving, then leave."

He came over to me. "Sweetheart, you aren't listening. I said I'll be back."

"Alvin, it's been a great weekend, but I have to go to work in the morning. So, if you don't mind…"

He tried to take me in his arms, then picked up my hand when I resisted. "Sweetheart, I'll see you in a week."

"Goodbye, Alvin."

He looked as if he wanted to say something, and then he walked out of the room. As soon as the door closed behind him, I wanted to throw it open and go after him. I tried to tell myself that being in the field wasn't dangerous, that it was like going camping. However, growing up in the military, I knew that wasn't true. Bivouac wasn't a big campout on a military base. It was training for battle, training for war. They used real ammunition and sometimes the men did get hurt, even killed.

I stared at the door and willed him back to me. Jace didn't come and I went to bed. I didn't know why Jace's leaving had affected me so much.

## A Request for Closure

It shouldn't have been that big of a deal. Jace had been my first one-night stand and instead of one great night, we'd had two.

I was lying in the dark telling myself to be satisfied with that when someone rapped on my front door. I crept into the living room and peeped through the hole, then threw open the door and myself into his arms.

"Told you I'd be back," he said, solemnly.

"I'm sorry."

"No, I'm the one who's sorry. I should have schooled you better."

"It's okay, Jace. I'm a military brat, remember?"

He took off his clothes and climbed into bed. "You're a brat, all right, but I don't think the military had anything to do with it. Come here, baby girl."

At three in the morning, Jace gently shook me awake. "Ari, I have to leave. My unit moves out in a couple of hours. Walk me to the door."

Half asleep, I did as he'd requested. "I promise, I'll see you in a week, Arianna."

"Okay," I mumbled.

He kissed me, then touched his finger to my nose. "Lock this door after me. I won't leave until I hear the locks."

"Okay," I mumbled again. Then I opened my eyes. "Jace, I...take care of yourself."

"I will. I already told you, I'm coming back."

---

*Jazmin*

The alarm clock on my nightstand buzzed. I pounded the thing off and turned to my side, peeking at the silver bucket where empty champagne bottles sat floating in water. Two of them, which Brick and I had polished off the night before, and that was after attending another party thrown in his honor. Instead of running the streets with Brick for the last four days, I should have been studying for my exam and using Paige and Arianna to practice the fine art of manicuring nails.

Not that I cared anything about nails. My forté was hair, but if I wanted my salon, I needed a state license, and that was something Mrs. Coleman hadn't been able to help me with since she hadn't been licensed either. Nor had her cousin who'd done nails or her mother who'd washed hair in the sink. To avoid the taxman, Mrs. Coleman had run her business on a cash only basis. Her philosophy was, "What Uncle Sam don't see, he don't need to know."

In my salon, my stuff was going to be straight, which was why for the last year, I've been hauling my behind off to cosmetology school every Monday, Wednesday, and Friday, and working part-time at a department store in the afternoons, evenings, and on the weekends.

I had already completed the general cosmetology courses because they were the easiest for me. Once I passed this manicuring course, I had only two more to go: esthetician, which consisted of classes on the proper care and treatment of skin, and the instructors' sessions. I didn't have to take all of those courses, but in my salon, I wanted to be able to advise my clients on any problem they might have. To do that, I needed to be knowledgeable about every aspect of the business and I sure didn't want my staff to have more education than I did.

I glanced at those champagne bottles again. I was getting too old for this shit, especially when I knew that today I had to be at the top of my game. Miss Knudsen, our instructor, could ferret out a speck on a flea and she'd been riding my ass a lot tougher than the rest of the class. Of course, that might have had something to do with the respectful cussing out I gave her when she flunked me for leaving a used nail file on my station. Cosmetology school was too expensive to keep doing this shit over and over again.

Feeling as if I'd crawled out from under a rock, I went into the bathroom and splashed cold water on my face. Then I fought through the urge to get back in my bed and went to the kitchen where I quickly brewed a pot of coffee. I filled my cup, grabbed my textbook, and sat at the kitchen table. I needed to cram a little before I had to head out the door for school.

"Jazzy. Jaaa-zy. Jazmin!"

I yawned and looked up at Brick.

"Is there some particular reason why you are sleeping at the kitchen table?"

*Sleeping?* "What time is it, Brick?"

"Eight thirty-eight. Why?"

"Oh no! I gotta go!" I jumped up and ran into the bedroom.

"Jazzy, where are you going?"

I was already in the bathroom, doing a quick wash up, brushing my teeth, and spitting out mouthwash. Then I ran into the closet and grabbed the first thing I saw. I was jumping into those too tight jeans when Brick walked into the room.

"Jazmin, where are you going?"

I popped my head through the top of a turtleneck shirt. "School," I said, grabbing my manicure kit and running for the door.

—◁∕∿∕▷—

Later that night, I slammed into the house. Not only had Knudsen failed me, but I had flunked the exam, too! I was so mad I almost missed seeing Brick perched on the couch. He rose to his feet and his expression told me that he was not a happy man.

I dropped my stuff on the table. "Don't start with me. I've already had a fucked-up day." Then I stalked to my bedroom.

I was standing at the dresser staring at that ring when his arms circled my waist. "I flunked my test today."

"I'm sorry," he said

"For the second time."

"Then I'm doubly sorry…but Jazzy, what are we talking about?"

"Cosmetology school. I flunked my course on manicuring today."

"Oh," he said, releasing me. He picked up the ring box, stared at it for a minute, and then set the box back down. Brick chuckled softly. "Know something, Jazzy? Outside of that years-old magazine interview, I don't know thing one about you; and not once during the last few days did it occur to me that you had a life before I found you. I figured I'd come in here, overwhelm you with my charm and money, and we'd trip down happily-ever-after together. I don't know anything about the woman you are today. What you want; what you need; what you dream about."

"I know. Other than basketball, I don't know anything about you either."

Brick stared at me for what seemed like a long time. "Okay, Jazzy. We're going to do something about that starting now."

"I need to study."

He nodded. "Then I'm going to get out of your hair. I know how distracting it can be to have someone buzzing around when you need to concentrate."

"Thank you."

"Come see me out, Jazzy-girl."

At the door, Brick ran his finger down my cheek. "When you're taking a break from the books, Jazzy, think about me, 'cause I'm sure gonna be thinking about you. Later, beautiful one."

He left and I went back my bedroom. For a few moments, I stared at my ring. It looked kind of ethereal, almost unreal. In the back of my mind—so far back, I could hardly call it a memory—I remembered the General reading the story of Cinderella to me. It was a tale about a young girl whose life had taken a turn for the worse, but a prince had rescued and married her. Like that story, the past few days had been totally unreal and I could hardly believe that they had happened to me. With that in mind, I snatched up my ring, and headed for Paige's apartment.

# Chapter 13

*Paige*

"You've got to be kidding me," I said, snatching the blue velvet box out of Jazmin's hand and gave her ring a close inspection.

"Nope," she said.

"You just met this man, Jazmin. How did you go from Chad's party to getting engaged to Vincent Marks so fast?"

"Actually, I met Brick years ago when he was only seventeen. I was still modeling then, and he says that he saw one of my shows and fell in love."

Jazmin launched into her story of what had happened after she left the party. I did my best to hide my envy and be happy for my friend, but inside I was screaming again. Three men had proposed to Arianna and she didn't even want to get married. Brick had asked Jazmin to marry him after one day together, even if she couldn't wear the ring yet. First, Arianna and now Jazmin. Why didn't any of these men want to marry me?

So, when Arianna walked into my kitchen looking all happy and sexually satisfied, that only added to my ire. She'd spent the entire weekend screwing a man who had once been in my bed and she didn't seem to give a damn what I thought about it.

I just kept thinking she had to know after seeing my reaction on Sunday. I hadn't gone anywhere near her apartment since then, and we hadn't ridden to work or gone to lunch together yesterday or today, which, if she hadn't gotten it on Sunday, should have been an indication that I had a problem with what she was doing.

"Hey P. Hey Jazz," she said, sitting at the kitchen table.

"Hey," Jazmin said. She held out her ring. "Look!"

I didn't say anything as Arianna inspected the ring. "Brick asked you to marry him already? And you said yes! My Lord, didn't the two of you meet this weekend?"

Jazmin leaned back in her chair with a smirk. "Let's just say I got it like that."

Arianna got up and hugged Jazmin. "Congratulations, Jazz. That man is too fine and you deserve it." Then she returned to her chair. "Tell me everything!"

I turned away as Jazmin told her story for the second time, getting more and more agitated with every word. I was happy for Jazmin and I should have been happy for Arianna, too, when she related her weekend with Jace, but I wasn't and I couldn't understand why since I'd had a wonderful time with Lewis.

I faced them again and propped a hand on my waist. "You know, Arianna, among girlfriends, there is one rule we all must honor. We do not fuck around with the same men. If you're going to do things like that, then you can't be friends with Jazz and me anymore."

Her brows rose and I almost believed the bafflement and skepticism in her face.

"P, what are you talking about?"

"Jace," I said, then watched Arianna breathe in air. So much air I thought she'd pass out. She looked up at me with cringing, glistening eyes, eyes that did not want to accept the obvious.

"Jace w-who?" Her voice quivered.

Jazmin touched her arm. "Barnes."

Arianna sat there for a minute, her body still as she absorbed the news. My throat tightened in sympathy for her, but I was determined to stand my ground. "I can't believe you didn't know."

Her eyes filled with distress. "How would I know?"

"Haven't you seen him down here, Ari?" Jazmin asked.

"The only man I've ever seen down here is Pierce Reynolds." Then she suddenly leaped to her feet. "I have to g-go," she said, her voice breaking.

"Arianna," Jazmin said, following her. "Is it serious?"

"I don't know," I heard her say, and then the door opened and closed.

Jazmin returned to the kitchen. "I'm not sure we should have done that, Paige."

—◈—

Later that night, Lewis kissed me and swung his feet over the side of the bed. "I have to go. I need to get back to the base."

"I thought you were going to spend the night."

"No can do. I have a barracks inspection at oh five hundred hours and a weapons check before that. I gotta check in and get my stuff in order. Don't worry, I'll be back tomorrow. It'll be late though."

I rubbed my hand over his back. I knew that I should think about what I was about to say before I opened my mouth, but I said it anyway. "Lewis, why don't you move in with me? You're here so much anyway and that way you won't have to leave every night."

He eyeballed me over his shoulder. "You sure you want me to do that, Paige?"

The tinges of jealousy I still felt over Jazmin and Arianna fluttered. "I'm sure."

"Okaaay, but why don't we start this off slow. I'll bring a few of my things on Saturday and we'll see how it goes from there."

He dressed and I walked him to the door.

"See you tomorrow."

"Bye," I said, then headed back to my bedroom.

I climbed under the covers and pulled them up to my chin. Jessie was spending the night with her grandmother, at my mother's request. It was part of her weekly agenda to pump my daughter for information on what was going down in my house. I knew she'd lecture me on whatever she found out later, but I didn't care. I was a grown woman. What went on in my house where I paid the rent was my own business, and it provided me with a break from my motherly duties.

I lay there in the dark, thinking about Lewis and wondering why I'd asked him to move in with me. I couldn't figure out why it bothered me so much, since it was no different from what I'd done with any other man I'd ever been involved with, including Pierce.

Jazmin had never let any of the men she'd been involved with move in with her; neither had Arianna. They seemed perfectly satisfied living by themselves. In that respect, I guess I was less like the two of them and more like my mother.

Married or single, she had always had a man in the house. She said that if a woman took care of her man, he was more appreciative of her and less likely to leave. She also told me that once a man moved in and established his space, it was easier to marry her than to pack his bags and move on. On that score, she might be right, since a couple of my mother's boyfriends had actually married her.

Besides, what did Arianna and Jazmin do in their apartments with nothing but a mirror for company? I had a hard enough time figuring out how to keep Jessie entertained and off my nerves without having to find a way to amuse myself, too. Having a man around provided a diversion and gave me something to focus on. I wasn't really into housework, but I did know how to cook, and I knew how to clean, and I knew how to keep a man satisfied in bed—I had never heard any complaints in that department.

My thoughts turned to Arianna. While I felt a great deal better for having gotten it off my chest, I knew that I had deeply hurt my friend. Jazmin had advised me to talk to Arianna again. She felt that Jace and Arianna could have shared the beginning of something real, and since I'd never really been interested in the man that I should tell Arianna and give her my blessing, so to speak.

Whatever those two had done to get Jace and Brick twisted up like that, I couldn't understand. I lay there in the dark some more and tried to put it all out of my mind. The house was so quiet that I should have been able to fall asleep. Lord knows, I was mentally tired and after the workout I'd had with Lewis, I should have been physically tired as well. I turned to my side and closed my eyes, but the agitation I'd felt over that last few days still flowed through my body meeting at the juncture of my thighs where it pulsated with the stirring of desire. I tried to ignore the feeling and the urges that accompanied it by squeezing my thighs and rubbing my feet together.

Ten minutes later, I sat up and reached for the telephone.

"Can I come over?"

"Sure," he said.

"I'll be there in thirty minutes."

———⧕⧔———

*Arianna*

I sat in the dark in my apartment wiping away more of the tears that had been falling all night. Earlier that evening, I'd gone shopping. It was what I usually did when I was upset. Two hours and three hundred dollars later, I'd returned home disgusted with myself. Instead of stupidly spending that money, I should have been paying some of those bills sitting on my dresser, most of which were already late.

I was a foolish idiot, and I sure as hell had no business messing with these men. With all that religion and not being allowed to date, I was an unskilled ingénue, too inexperienced to know what I wanted and too proud to confess that I didn't know what I was doing.

Paige and Jazmin thought that I was being selective, that I was waiting for the right guy for me. The truth was, I didn't have a clue about men. My only example had been my father, a liar, a wife beater, and a cheat. I knew I didn't want a man like my father, but I didn't know how to look beyond the enticing smile and twinkling eyes and delve into what lay underneath, something I wish I'd done with Jace.

I heaved a calming breath. Alvin Barnes was a lying bastard and I didn't want to think about him anymore.

I got up and put on some music, then went to the kitchen for a glass of iced tea. I stood in the open refrigerator door staring at all the food that

Jace had bought. That made me angry and I slammed the door closed and leaned against the counter, drumming my fingers on the tile.

*You like him.*

My mind was not finished with Jace Barnes.

No, I'ma kill the bastard.

*Right. He'll show up here and you'll be in his arms.*

No, I stressed. I'm gonna kill the bastard. My only problem is what to use; I don't own a gun.

Determined not to think about Jace anymore, I spent the rest of my evening baking a cake for Jessie and after indulging myself in a long, hot bubble bath, I went to bed.

———

On Thursday, the base in Greenland threatened to strike in violation of the contract with the Air Force. I spent the day doling out money and sending people off to the airport. Around eight-thirty that night, I arrived home with a briefcase full of petty cash forms that I had to reconcile before morning, but all I could do was sit and kick off my shoes. I stretched out on the couch, not intending to sleep, but to rest awhile before tackling those receipts.

The ringing telephone pulled me from my slumber. I picked up the receiver and mumbled a barely audible, "Hello."

"Is Alvin there?" The female voice sounded soft and seductive.

"No," I replied a little testily. "Who is this?"

"Alvin left this number for me to call if I needed to talk to him and couldn't reach him on the base."

Did he now? I thought. "I don't know why Jace gave you this number. He doesn't live here and he never has."

"But Alvin said he'd met a wonderful—"

"Who is this?" I repeated louder and ruder this time.

"His mother."

## A Request for Closure

My eyes snapped open and my brain flipped on. "I'm sorry, Mrs. Barnes, but Alvin isn't here. His unit is out on bivouac this week."

"Oh, that's right. I remember, he did tell me that, too. I'm sorry to have bothered you, Arianna."

"It's all right, Mrs. Barnes. Would you like to leave a message for Alvin?"

"No-no. It can wait 'til he gets back. Thank you and goodbye."

"Goodbye."

I hung up the telephone. What was I going to do with Alvin Jace Barnes? He'd given out my telephone number to his family, hadn't bothered to tell me, and I'd just acted like a jackass with his mother.

I was going kill that man if I ever saw him again.

I exchanged my work clothes for a gown and robe and I had just organized my paperwork when a knock sounded on my door. I looked through the peephole and groaned. It was Russell Cunningham, a man who asked me to marry him at least once a month. Russell wanted a wife and a mother for his two kids. I wanted Russell to leave me alone. He'd seen my car in the parking lot, so I knew he wouldn't leave until I talked to him. I opened the door and blocked his entrance. "What do you want?"

Russell stood there, dressed in fatigues, nervously twisting his cap in his hands. "I needed to see you."

"Why?"

"Arianna, can I come inside?"

"No."

"Ari, please, I won't stay long. I need to talk to you."

I turned for the couch. He closed the door and sat beside me.

I picked up a pile of papers. "Mind if I work while you...talk?" Not waiting for his answer, I pulled my calculator forward and starting running numbers.

"Ari?"

"Hmmm."

"Why don't you like me?"

"I like you, Russell," I said.

120

He sprang up from the couch. "But not enough to marry me!"

Russell's timing was way off tonight. After the last two days, I was not about to put up with any of his crap. "That's right, and I am way too busy to have this discussion with you again."

He pulled me up by the arm. "It's my kids, isn't it?"

"No, Russell. And let go of me!"

He released me. "Barnes can't do anything for you that I can't do better."

"How do you know about him?"

"I saw you leave the club with him the other night."

"And how do you figure that concerns you, Russell?"

"I want to marry you!" He pulled me into his arms. "Marry me, Arianna. I've got money and you won't have to work. I'll give you anything you want. You want a house, tell me and I'll buy you a house. Clothes, you'll have more clothes than you know what to do with. What about a car? Let me buy you a car."

This was my fault for being so damn nice. I'd met the Negro one night in the club, let him buy me a drink, and listened to his tale of woe. His wife had left him; he didn't know why, but he'd come home from work one day and found her gone, his two kids left behind. I knew why the sistah had booked. In one night, I'd gone from a friendly interlude in a club to the object of his obsession. The man was crazy. "I don't want anything from you, Russell."

"Marry me, Ari. I swear you'll never regret it," he murmured, slipping my robe from my shoulders.

I tried to push him away while fighting to hang on to my clothes. We fell to the floor with him landing on top of me. Before I could catch my breath, Russell had unzipped his pants and yanked my nightgown up around my waist.

"Russell!"

He froze, and then scrambled off my body. "I didn't mean to do that," he moaned, holding his head in his hands. "I love you!" He scrubbed his face with his hands, stood, and zipped his pants before reaching down to help me to my feet. I slapped his hand away.

## A Request for Closure

"Don't touch me," I said getting up on my own.

"You hate me now, don't you?"

I wanted to hate him. What he'd done was a serious violation and would have been worse if he hadn't come to his senses. But I looked at Russell and actually felt sorry for him. I sighed deeply and plopped down on the couch. "No, Russell. I don't hate you, but you do know that you can never come here again."

"Please don't say that, Arianna." He brushed away the tears on my cheeks. "If you want Barnes, then have him. I love you, so I can't say I won't care. But I promise I won't say anything, and when it's over, I'll be waiting for you."

"Don't wait for me, because I'm not coming." I was about to break down, and I knew it. I hugged myself to stop the trembles. "Goodbye, Russell."

His shoulders slumped as he slunk to the door. "Not goodbye, Arianna. Until later."

Shaking like a leaf in the wind, I got up to lock the door. I went into the bedroom and pulled my journal from one of the drawers in my dresser. It was only one of many I'd been writing in since childhood. Mostly I'd filled them with dark thoughts, emotions I needed to express when I was hurting or needed to escape the sounds of the battles constantly waged around me.

Tonight, I wrote down how I felt about Jace, and what an imbecile I was for letting him use me. I lashed out at Russell and cursed my mother, and then I started crying because what I really wanted was for her to hold me and tell me that everything would be all right. I wrote about Paige and Jazmin, and how I felt they had attacked me when I didn't understand what I'd done wrong.

Drained, I closed my journal and put it away. I returned to the living room, surveyed the mess, and couldn't make myself deal with it. I sat on the couch, wrapped my arms around my legs, and laid my head on my knees, and cried. I felt devastated, violated, and utterly sucked dry, and I desperately needed someone to talk to because at the age of twenty-three, I felt as if I'd just crashed and burned.

*Jazmin*

I entered the house on Friday in a much better mood than two nights earlier. That was partly because I'd gone to the dean of the school about Miss Knudsen. I would still have to make up the written exam, but he'd raised my live model grade to a B. Now I could get started on the skin care curriculum, due to start at the end of the month. The other reason I was happy was because Brick had called to say that he was on his way over to my apartment.

Twenty minutes later, I'd put Peabo Bryson on the stereo and I was lying on the sofa with my feet propped up thinking about my girls and Jace Barnes. I honestly had had no idea that Arianna would react the way she had when Paige dropped the news about Jace.

Focused on myself, I'd missed the flashing neon sign: Arianna and a man she'd picked up in a club. When I first met Arianna, I knew almost immediately that she and I could never be friends. The girl acted too goody-goody and standoffish for me, and if a man even approached her, she'd go all-rigid on the guy, as if someone had screwed her knees together.

Since Paige liked her, I'd decided that if girlfriend was gonna hang with me, that tight bun on her head had to go, along with her dowdy, Pollyanna clothes. So, I sat her down one day, untwisted all that glorious brown hair, slapped some makeup on her face, and dressed her in a black halter top and a red miniskirt. That night I took her to the club, sat back, and waited for the show. It took all of thirty seconds for the men in that club to stampede our table, and Arianna's been beating them back ever since.

This thing Arianna had for Jace Barnes was seriously real. Had I been paying attention, I would have squashed that conversation before Paige had a chance to get it started. I racked my brain for a way to smooth the path for those two because I had feeling that before it was over things were gonna get real ugly.

## A Request for Closure

I left the couch to answer the door. Brick grabbed me around the waist, bent me back, and laid a fierce smack on my mouth. He wiggled his eyebrows in jest. "Miss me?"

"You're a real nut case, did you know that?" He swung me back up. "And yes, I did miss you."

"Good. Now go and pack a bag; we have a flight to catch."

*Hold up*, I thought. "Pack a bag? What for?"

"We're spending the weekend in Vegas, Jazzy-girl."

Vegas! My eyes lit up like the Strip itself. Unlike the Strip, the lights went out just as quickly. "I can't go."

"Why not?"

Brick was bopping his head to the music as if he didn't have a care in the world, and he probably didn't. I, however, had bills to pay. "I have to go to work in the morning."

He stopped moving and his forehead crinkled in a frown. "Nooooo, you have to go to Vegas with me."

"Nooooo, I have to go to work."

"Come on, Jazzy. Wouldn't you rather hit the casinos and sit by the pool?"

"Of course I would, who wouldn't?"

"Then call in sick." Brick started moving to the music again.

I crossed to the sofa and sat down. Hanging swimsuits on a rack; wearing a swimsuit by the pool. Stacking cups on a shelf; stacking chips on a poker table. Watching television, watching a Vegas show. Oh yeah, Vegas had it all over standing on my feet for eight hours in a department store. "Okay," I said. "Only I can't call until tomorrow morning."

Brick clapped his hands. "No problem, Jazzy. Get a move on though, we need to get to the airport. Oh, and you need to pack a couple of those gowns."

"Why?"

"David's getting married while we're there."

"Who is David?"

"One of the players. The whole team is going, and they're bringing wives and girlfriends."

Brick didn't have to say any more. I went to my bedroom and picked up the phone. Paige and Arianna needed to know the deal so that they wouldn't worry about me over the weekend.

# Chapter 14

*Arianna*

About noon on Saturday, I opened my eyes to the thump of a pounding headache and the persistent ringing of the telephone. Too depressed to stay home last night, I'd gone out and had a whale of a time. Another shrill blasted my brain and I quickly reached for the receiver.

"I'm back!"

Anger increased the pain in my head. "I'm thrilled."

"You sound like you didn't miss me."

"I didn't," I said quietly.

"What?"

"Nothing. By the way, your mother called a couple of days ago. You should call her back."

Jace chuckled. "Oh yeah. I forgot to mention that I gave her your phone number."

"Yes, you did," I said. "And fuck you, Alvin Barnes!"

I hung up.

Less than thirty seconds later, the phone rang again. "What!"

"Girl, don't ever say those two words to me again. What's wrong with you, Arianna?"

"Nothing."

Jace sighed. "Baby girl, talk to me."

"I don't want to talk to you and I don't want you calling here ever again!"

I slammed down the telephone and headed for the bathroom. I had just finished dressing when pounding loud enough to wake the dead started on my door. I knew who it was.

"Go away, Jace!"

"Open this door!"

"No! I said for you to go away!"

"Woman, you got five seconds to open this door...then I'm coming in there."

I squinted through the peephole. Jace stood there dressed in his camouflage greens. I glanced at the telephone. He'd given me five seconds. I'd never make it. His boot hit the door.

"Jace! Please stop!"

"You want me to stop, then get this muthafucka open! Now!"

His foot hit the door again. "Okay," I yelled, and turned the locks.

The front door opened and I backed away when Jace stalked into the room. His eyes narrowed to pinpoints of light right before he jerked me into his arms and planted his lips on mine. He grabbed my arm when the kiss ended, led me to the couch, and pushed me down on it.

"Don't you move." He sat in the chair and crossed one long leg over the other, then trained his eyes on me. "Do you have any idea how much shit I just took in those barracks because of you?"

"No, and I don't care."

"Well, it was a lot. The guys think it's damn funny and are having a field day."

I stood up. "Why don't *you* tell your story to somebody who gives a damn?"

"Sit down!"

I sat, but my stare was assiduously hostile. His was too. Then his eyes suddenly shifted.

"Who gave those to you?"

I had received the large bouquet of red roses—Russell's useless attempt at an apology—last night on my way out the door and hadn't gotten around to tossing them yet. "Nobody you know."

Jace leaped to his feet, picked up the vase, and strode into the kitchen. When he returned, he slammed the empty vase on the table. "*You* don't know him either!"

I bristled with anger. "You have some nerve coming in here and tossing my things into the trash. Who the hell do you think you are?"

127

Jace exhaled. "Baby girl, what is this about?"

"Like you don't know," I muttered.

"I don't know...that's why I'm asking the question."

I planted my hands on my waist. "First floor, corner apartment...Paige Michaels. The woman you've been fucking!"

"So," he said after a minute. "Can I take it that you've condemned me without the benefit of a trial?"

"You can take it any damn way you please, you bastard."

I jumped when he moved and towered over me. It happened so fast, I didn't have a chance to go anywhere.

"I'm getting damn tired of hearing you speak to me like this. I don't like it and I won't stand for it!" He grabbed my hand. "Let's go!"

"Go where?"

"Downstairs!"

I jerked my hand back. "I'm not going anywhere with you! You want to go downstairs, you can go by yourself."

"Arianna, this is nuts. What happened between Paige and me happened long before I met you. How can you hold what happened in the past against me?"

I dropped to the couch. "She was my friend."

Jace sat beside me and steered my head to his chest. "And she's still your friend."

"No, she's not. She hates me."

"No she doesn't," he said soothingly.

"Yes she does."

"But why? You haven't done anything."

"I slept with you, and she told me I couldn't be her friend anymore. I didn't know about the two of you, Jace. I swear I didn't. What am I supposed to do now?"

"I'll be your friend," he said quietly. "Where are your keys?"

"On the dresser," I said, too tired to think.

When he came back, he took my hand. "I have to go," he said, leading me toward the door.

"B-but you can't take my keys."

"I'm not taking your keys." He reached into his pocket and placed his keys in my hand. "I'm taking your car. If you need to go somewhere, use mine."

He kissed me and left. I went into the kitchen. Petals, stems, and thorns were all over the floor. Jace hadn't thrown those roses away. He had destroyed them. I sighed and cleaned up the mess.

My front door opened and Jessica walked in. "Hi, Auntie Ari. Got anything to eat?"

"Under the plastic cover on the counter."

Jessie lifted the lid and turned to me with saucer eyes. "Can I have some?"

"It's may I, and yes, I baked it for you."

Two large dimples appeared in her cheeks. She ran to me and hugged my legs, then went back into the kitchen. She climbed up on the counter and took a plate and a glass out of the cabinet.

"Need help?"

"No, I can do it."

Jessie cut a large slab of cake, filled the glass with milk, and carried her food to the dining room table. I sat at the table with her.

"You weren't here this morning."

Chocolate already covered her mouth. "I know."

"Where'd ya go?"

"Out."

"Oh."

She finished eating, and then went into the bathroom to clean her face. She turned on the television when she came out and I joined her on the couch.

She laid her head on my arm. "Did he hit you?"

I glanced down at Jessie, who I now knew had heard Jace and me fighting. "No, baby. He didn't hit me."

"But he yelled at you."

"Yes, baby. He yelled."

"Why?"

"I guess I made him mad."

A Request for Closure

"Oh." She pressed closer and I felt her tremble. "Auntie Ari, I was scared."

I hugged her. "You wanna know a secret?" She nodded. "I was scared, too."

"Is he coming back?"

"Probably."

She frowned up at me. "You gonna let him in?"

"Probably." Then to get her off the subject, I sat her up. "Let's do your hair."

Jessica went to get the brush and hair grease, and then sat on the floor and I began brushing the espresso brown, naturally curly tresses.

She turned around. "I don't like boys that yell. It's scary. I think they're bad.

I caught her hair up in a rubber band, braided the end of the ponytail, and helped her up. "Jessie, sometimes adults get mad at each other and they yell. That doesn't make them bad people. Doesn't your mom yell at you sometimes?"

"Paige yells *all* the time."

"Does that make her a bad person?"

"No."

"Well, Jace is not a bad person either, and when he comes back, I bet he won't be mad anymore. Okay?"

She nodded. "Can I stay up here with you?"

"I think you should go outside and play."

Little brown arms hugged my neck. "I love you," she whispered.

"I love you, too." I took her hand and walked with her to the door. "See you later. Okay?"

"See you later."

I watched Jessie skip down the hall until she disappeared around the corner, then entered my apartment and went to clean up her mess. I was sure going to miss that little girl.

—ᴧᴧᴧ—

Sometime later, I woke up to the sound of jingling keys. I had taken aspirin to help combat the effects of the previous evening's hangover and lain down for a nap to ease the emotional distress caused by the argument with Jace. I glanced at the clock right before his lips settled over mine. He'd been gone for almost four hours.

He jingled the keys over me again. I reached up to take them. He pulled them back. "These are mine," he said with a grin.

I lifted up on my elbows. "What's that?" I nodded toward the two suitcases on the floor by the closet.

"My stuff. Get up and give me some space, woman."

"Jace," I said.

He held up his hand. "Arianna, we are not fighting about this."

He left the room and I sat there trying to figure out what had happened, and not exactly sure that I knew or liked it. I did know that Jace was way beyond my realm of experience. He was too confident and being from New York definitely carried that bad boy persona. He was overwhelming me and I wished again that I had somebody that I could talk to about this. Regardless of how I felt about any of it, Jace Barnes was moving in, and somehow I had to reconcile myself to the inevitable.

I felt a warm gaze on me. Jace was leaning against the door jam. His eyes seemed to glaze over as he walked into the room. When he reached me, he tangled his fingers in my hair and leaned down to kiss me. Then he pulled me into his arms and hugged me tight. I laid my head on his chest and tried to stop the tears filling my eyes.

"I know you don't like this, baby girl. Find a way to deal with it, though, because this is the way it's going to be."

"I don't get a say in the matter."

"Not in this. I've already made this decision."

He led me out of the bedroom. Then he stood behind me with his arms looped around my body. "You like?"

"I like," I said, still checking out the dining room table.

A glass vase sat in the middle, holding a large bouquet of yellow roses. One pink rose was on my plate, along with a white envelope. Jace seated me, then went into the kitchen and began dumping Chinese takeout into dishes. The flowers were a different color, but I knew they were replacements for the ones he'd destroyed. He was apologizing.

I first sniffed the pink rose, and then picked up the envelope. "What's this?"

"Open it."

I lifted the flap and counted the hundred dollar bills. I waited until he'd brought out the food, filled the wineglasses, and said a blessing. "Jace, I don't need or want this."

His brow arched. "So?

"So, take it back."

"It's yours."

"But I don't want it."

His jaw clenched. "Then burn it, Arianna, and on payday, you can make another fire. Or you can pay the rent and whatever else needs paying around here. Oh, and I took your car in today. That thing was long overdue for a tune up. It's been washed, waxed, and the tank's filled. Let me know when you're running low. I'll take it in and bring it back to you."

The last thing on my mind was that car. "Why are you doing this?"

He looked at me as if I was an imbecile to have asked. "You're my lady. Now eat. Your food's getting cold."

"Jace," I said.

"Eat," he said.

I left my chair and stood behind him hugging his neck. "Are you trying to make me fall in love with you?"

"Yes," he said simply.

That one threw me. I was joking. Clearly, he was not. I returned to my chair and stared at my plate. Jace stabbed a shrimp and raised his fork to my lips. I was chewing when I realized that I didn't know anything about this man who'd moved into my house. "Jace, where did this money come from?"

"My account."

"But there's a thousand dollars in that envelope."

"I know, Arianna, I put it in there."

I chewed and swallowed. "But Jace, you can't possibly afford to give me this much money."

He sighed as if already tired of the conversation. He picked up and placed my fork into my hand. "I can afford it, Ari, and you need to eat. I wanna go to the club later."

I set the fork down because it occurred to me that we had smoked a lot of weed during our first weekend together. I also knew that some of the military's finest supplemented their income selling the stuff.

"But *how* can you afford it, Jace? This is a lot of cash to just be handing somebody."

"I had my mother wire it to me. That's why she called; she wanted to know where to send it."

The boy was trying to give me his mother's money! "No, Alvin. You send this money back to your mother! I can't believe that you would ask her for it in the first place."

Jace stilled, and when he turned to me, his eyes blazed. "What kind of man do you think I am that I would take money from my own mother! That money is mine, Arianna, and I can do with it what I wish, and this is the last time I'm going to tell you to eat!"

I picked up my fork. I had so many questions but I wasn't sure whether the flames in his eyes had gone out. I stirred the rice around on my plate and decided to go for it. "Jace, how old are you?"

He chuckled. "Why? You think it's gonna make a difference?"

"I told you my age. It's only fair that you tell me yours."

"Twenty."

I slumped back in my chair. Twenty! He had to be kidding! I didn't have a man. I had a boy trying to take over my life! Okay, so there weren't that many years difference in our ages, but at least I was old enough to drink legally. He wasn't even supposed to be in the clubs. I examined his face. I knew he looked young, but I had assumed his age to be somewhere around mine. But twenty...! What the hell was I supposed to do with a baby?

# Chapter 15

*Paige*

By the time I arrived, the Black Stallion had already filled up with the usual Saturday night crowd. There were no empty tables and I stood at the railing wondering why I was there at all since this was not the way I had envisioned my evening.

In celebration of Lewis moving in and being my new man, I had planned a romantic night of intimacy. I had purchased candles, flowers, and a new nightgown. I had prepared a wonderful dinner and had even dropped Jessie off at my sister's for the night so that there would be no interruptions.

Two hours ago, Lewis had called to say that he would be later than he'd thought and for me not to wait up for him. Feeling sorry for myself, I'd put everything away, grabbed a glass and the wine chilling in the refrigerator, and headed for the couch. I drank glass after glass thinking about Arianna and Jazmin. Every man they met fell in love with them. What did they have or do that I didn't have or do? I would give anything to know the answer to that question.

My solo pity party lasted for over an hour and instead of doing the smart thing and going to bed, I decided that going out would cure my doldrums and take my mind off my friends. In my fuchsia mini dress and spiked heels, I looked sultry and sexy; and my slinky fine behind was ready to get my groove on.

Walking into the club and seeing Arianna and Jace instantly popped my party bubble.

It wasn't their presence that bothered me, since Colorado Springs only had two clubs that catered to black clientele. And I told myself that it wasn't the way they were so into each other, as if they were the only people on the planet. I think what got to me was that I now knew that Arianna had made her choice, and that she hadn't chosen our friendship.

With a huff, I spun on my heel and parked on a stool at the bar. I ordered a glass of white wine and when it came, I swiveled around and continued to observe the two of them.

Jace wore a black suit with a white shirt and red tie, Arianna, a red peasant blouse and a black flounce skirt. I couldn't deny that they made an impressive couple. Jace touched his lips to hers. My pulse quickened at the intimate gesture. It wasn't one of those long drawn-out kisses, or quick pecks on the lips, but one that had looked so delicate and so pleasurable that a shiver coursed through my body. His fingers tangled in her hair and tilted her head back; his lips trailed a tantalizingly slow path along her bare shoulders. The passion flowing between the two of them was all consuming, and so hot, it was a wonder they didn't burst into flames.

For short while, I had let Jace use my body, and while every encounter had been sexually gratifying, he'd never once looked at me or doled out any of the affection he was showering on Arianna. Jace had always come in the middle of the night. He'd climb into my bed and enter my body, and as soon as he'd satisfied his natural urges, he'd dress and leave my house. There had been no cuddling, or talk of a next time, and for him no reason to stay.

They exchanged another passionate kiss and I suddenly knew why I was so hot and bothered.

Jace Barnes had fucked me. He was making love to Arianna Jackson.

I pushed out a deep breath. The same way Jermaine Lewis had been making love to me all week. What was I doing in this club? Lewis was at my house, no doubt wondering where I was, and here I sat in a dark, smoke-filled room watching my best friend get what I should have been getting.

Two times one is two. Two times two is four. Two times three is six. Dammit, it just wasn't fair!

I ordered and nursed another glass of wine, seething over my thoughts. What I should have done was take my drunken ass home to bed. Instead of doing that, I got off my stool and with all the booze I'd consumed backing my bravado, crossed the room to where Jace and Arianna sat. Thoroughly disgusted when I saw them kissing again, I cleared my throat and waited impatiently for them to look up.

Arianna looked like a deer caught in headlights. Jace looked furious. I smiled at him anyway, too far in to back down now. "Hello," I said.

"Paige," he said quietly.

I slid into the booth next to him and laid my hand on his arm. "Long time no see."

Jace removed my hand and leaned toward Arianna. "Why are you here Paige?"

I scooted closer to him. "I was wondering why you don't drop by my crib anymore. We used to have so much fun together."

I was talking to Jace, but my eyes were on Arianna and her reaction to my presence. I watched her nose flare slightly and her eyes narrowed in annoyance. If Jace wasn't between us, I believe that Arianna would have tried to slap the shit out of me.

She opened her mouth, but whatever she was going to say, Jace squashed when he grabbed her hand. Then he fixed his glacial stare on me.

"Anything you and I did was over a long time ago, so I don't understand why you want to disrespect my lady by bringing it up now. To tell you the truth, I can't think of anything that was memorable about that time or important enough to me to tell Arianna. So, if there's nothing else, you can go back to wherever it is you were before you decided to come over here and bother us."

I gasped, but not out loud because then they would have known how much his words had cut into me. I gritted my teeth, rose to my feet, and without another word went back to my stool at the bar.

About five minutes had passed when I felt the heat of another body press close to mine.

"Hey, hot mama, you wanna dance?"

I glanced over my shoulder. The man was tall, brown, and fine. I swallowed the remainder of my wine and swung around to face him. "Sure," I said, giving him my hand as I hopped off the stool.

On the floor, I stepped into his embrace. I rubbed my hands over his back, feeling the tightness of his muscles and pressed myself against his bulky frame. Still feeling the sting of humiliation, I peeked over his shoulder at Arianna and Jace. They were kissing again and he had the back of her head cupped in one of his hands. I curved both of mine around my dance partner and brought his head down. His lips found mine and I closed my eyes, hoping to experience the same thrill of emotion I'd seen in Arianna's face.

It didn't even come close. When the kiss ended, all I felt was a keen sense of disappointment, and when I looked over at Arianna, she was watching me.

I sent her a smile of apology, hoping to ease the hardness in her expression. She looked up at Jace, and then hid her face in his chest.

That hurt. "Let's get out of here," I said.

"Oh, baby, I was so hoping that you would say that."

I didn't look at Arianna again as we left the floor and the club.

—◊◊◊—

A couple of hours later, I parked my car in front my apartment and stared at the patio doors. Driving home, I was hoping that Lewis would be asleep. The light I saw through the closed curtains told me that he wasn't, and I was going to have to tell the story I'd concocted in the shower at the motel.

The truth was that I had not gotten a shred of pleasure out of the encounter. I'd balanced myself on my knees and made all the appropriate noises while the man I'd picked up in the club humped me from behind, all the time wondering if Jace was giving it to Arianna in the same way, at the same time.

## A *Request for Closure*

I dropped my head into my hands. I didn't give a damn about Jace Barnes and I certainly didn't need to be sitting in a car trying to imagine him doing my friend. That kind of shit was sick.

I left the car. I already had my story; now all I had to do was tell it convincingly enough for Lewis to believe. "Hey," I said from the doorway.

"Where were you?" He had a frown his face, but his voice was calm.

"I went out with Ari for a drink and lost track of the time. Sorry," I said as I bent down to kiss his temple.

Lewis evaded me. "Then you *do* know what time it is."

"Yes, and I'll try not to let it happen again." I said those words knowing that it would happen again because I didn't know how to stop it. I didn't want to be like this but I couldn't help myself. It wasn't as if I really wanted any of those men. I screwed their brains out and when it was over, I always felt cheap, and dirty, and so guilty.

I hung my head, hoping Lewis wouldn't see my face. "I'm sorry," I said again. Then I ran to my bedroom and threw myself across the bed.

"Paige, honey. There's no reason for you to be crying like this. So you got home a little late. I'm not upset. I was worried. I thought you'd be here when I arrived this evening."

I heard his voice, but I had too many tears, too much pain, and too much sorrow to rein in my emotions. Now that the dam had burst, I didn't know if the water would ever stop flowing.

Lewis lifted me, sat down, and cradled me against his chest. "I'm sorry, Lewis, and I promise I won't do it again."

"Honey, it's okay. I'm not upset, and I don't have a problem if you and Arianna want to hang out together. Just let me know the next time or leave a note so I won't sit here worrying about you and Jessie. Right now, I need you to help me stow my things."

He dried my face and tried to kiss me. I did my best to elude him because I knew I was unworthy of this man. Lewis held my chin and planted his mouth on mine. I was unworthy, but this was the last night I would feel this way. Starting right this minute, I was going to do everything in my power to change.

*Jazmin*

"I'ma hit the pool, Jazzy. This Vegas heat is tearing a brotha up. Want to join me?"

"Nope." I took a sip of my colorful fruity drink. I had no idea what it was, but it was cold and pretty with its little blue umbrella, yellow pineapple, and red maraschino cherries sticking out of the top.

"Okay, I'll be back in a few."

"I'll be right here," I said, settling more comfortably in my lounge chair.

We'd flown into McCarran Airport with me trying to see as much of the Strip as I could from my tiny airplane window. I'd never been to Las Vegas and seeing all those lights reminded me of New Year's Eve in Times Square.

The airport was much smaller than I expected, given the number of people that supposedly come and go through this town, but I could feel the gambling fever in the air. Even in the airport, men and women occupied every slot machine, trying one last time to score that big hit before they had to go.

A limousine took us to the Tropicana, located at the southern end and one of the older hotels on the Strip. I walked through the door and into a tropical island filled with palm trees, tiki torches, and colorful bird motifs. Brick checked us into our room. On our way through the casino, he dropped twenty one-dollar coins in my hand and told me to try my luck. I stood in front of a slot machine and ten pulls later, hit for two hundred and fifty dollars. I tried to give the money to Brick but he wouldn't take it. We continued to the elevators and up to our room where we showered and went to dinner before attending the *Les Follies Bergere*, which Brick told me was the longest running show in Las Vegas.

This morning we'd breakfast from room service and we had been lounging by the pool ever since. Brick had promised to take me shopping later in the day, and that night our schedule included taking in a heavyweight championship fight at Caesar's Palace. I still hadn't met any of his teammates, their wives, or their girlfriends.

## A Request for Closure

I sipped from my drink, then set it on the table beside me, and adjusted my floppy straw hat. A girl could get used to this, I thought as I closed my eyes.

"Man, I ain't seen a rack like that since we were at the Playboy mansion a couple of months back."

"Don't you know it, my brotha. Baby girl is da bomb in that turquoise suit!"

"You ain't sayin' looking' but a word, man, 'cause I is looking' at something real good up in here."

I lifted the edge of my hat and squinted up at two of the tallest, finest brothas I'd ever seen. "Can I help the two of you?"

"Sistah, the only way you can help me is by telling me your room number."

"Go away."

"Now look-it what you done did, bro. You done got baby girl here all hot and bothered. Maybe she'll let me cool her off."

"This fine thing here ain't cooking' for no small fry like you. Sistah here looks like she needs a real man."

I shook my head in disgust when he moved his hand to his crotch.

"Man, you better keep your dick intact for that gal you're walking down the aisle tomorrow and let me handle this one. I got everything baby girl will ever need."

I was about to shut them both down and send them packing when Brick walked up drying himself with a white towel.

"Hey, it's the rookie. Whadup, blood?"

Brick sat in his chair. "Hey David. Hey Paul. What are you fellas up to?"

"Just enjoying the view, man," the one called David responded.

Brick glanced over at me before directing his eyes back at the two men. "Jazzy, this is David Bryant and Paul Danvers, two of my team-mates. Fellas, Jazmin Reed."

"I'll be dammed," Paul said. "She wit chu, Rookie?"

"You could say that."

I sat up and draped my arm across Brick's shoulders. "You could say that, but I *am* saying it."

"You got yourself one fine woman there, Rookie. Much respect, my brotha. Let's get out of here, Paul. I think I see something that might be a little more available over on the other side. Later, Rookie."

"Later," Brick responded.

I settled back in my chair again. "Why do they call you Rookie?"

Brick was still watching his teammates. "It's a tag they give all the first year players."

"Then it's not meant as an insult."

"Nope," he said, his eyes still on the two men. He finished drying off. "Let's get out of here, Jazzy. I'm ready to drop some cash in the casino."

————

That night, Brick waited until David and his fiancée, Gabriella, and Paul and his wife, Jonelle, left the car before he got out and assisted me from the black stretch limousine. He wore a three-piece black suit with a gold polyester shirt and I had on the green jersey matte. I adjusted the gold-colored shawl I'd found on our afternoon shopping trip over my elbows and took his hand.

In the car, there had been a lot of joking around about who would win the fight between Ken Norton, the current heavyweight champ, and Larry Holmes, who had been tagged the Easton Assassin. Outside of Muhammad Ali, what I knew about boxing could fit into a thimble and I wasn't really all that excited about watching two bruisers pound on each other.

When the six of us reached our seats, the rest of Brick's teammates were already there. They joked around, signed autographs, and passed around bottles of champagne as if they were drinking free water. The women with them were beautiful and as finely dressed as I was. However, most of them were quiet and didn't seem to notice the antics of the fun-loving bunch of overpaid ballplayers. Or if they did, they were most likely used to it by now.

Jonelle gripped my arm when I sat in my seat and discreetly pointed toward the entrance. When Rick James walked down the steps with his latest protégée Lady Tee, Teena Marie, I nearly fell off my chair. Decked out in a white jumpsuit, the man wore blood red, crystal studded, knee high, platform boots, and a matching gangsta-styled hat cocked to the side on his black braids.

Totally blown away, I had just leaned back in my seat when one of the players tapped Brick on the shoulder.

"Hey, Rookie. When you gonna introduce a brotha to this fine piece with you tonight?"

Brick exhaled and then reached into his pocket. He pulled out the blue velvet box. Before I knew it, he'd slipped the ring on my finger and turned around.

"Bill, this is my fiancée, Jazmin Reed. Jazz, Bill Walters." Then he grabbed my hand, the lights dimmed, and the announcer stepped into the center of the ring.

—⁓—

On Sunday evening, we walked onto concourse B at Stapleton Airport in Denver and a flashbulb went off in my face. I couldn't see anything as Brick gathered me to him and hustled us through the throng of people at the gate.

"Mr. Marks, tell us about her."

"When did the two of you meet?"

"When's the wedding, Mr. Marks?"

When my vision cleared, I chanced a peek and saw a large group of reporters with cameras pointed at us. They surged toward us, firing questions so fast, I didn't even hear half of them. Brick kept moving, using his body to shield me from the cameras.

"Vincent, over here!"

Brick hustled us toward a tall and balding white man, who then led us out of the airport and into a waiting limousine.

Once we'd settled and the car had taken off, the man looked at me. "I'm Walter," he said. "Walter Pike, Vincent's agent." Then he turned his icy blue stare on Brick. "Okay, Vincent. Let me hear it."

"Dammit, Walt. How'd they find out about this so fast?"

"They're reporters and, at the moment, you're news. I warned you when we signed that deal with the Nuggets that you'd have to be careful about what you did in public." He switched back to me, his expression so impassive, his face resembled stone. "This morning your picture was on the front page of the *News*, the *Post*, and the *Gazette*, along with the story of your life. Every newspaper subscriber in Colorado has read about your former modeling career and the accident that ended it. At this very moment, I can assure you that those reporters are trying to dig up every sordid detail of your life, assuming there are any, of course."

Brick was staring stoically at Walter. "Man, this is the pits!"

"Yes," Walter agreed. "It is. But you're a local celebrity now, Vincent, and headed toward much more if, as I believe, your ball handling skills prove to be worth the amount of money you're going to be paid. That means that you're public domain and the media is going to feed the public's desire to know." Walter let both of us chew on that statement for a moment before he continued. "Okay, here's how it's going to go. I've already called your publicist and she's scheduled a press for tomorrow afternoon. The two of you are going to show up and let these people see how in love you are. I will field the questions and give you a signal for those it is okay to answer."

"Brick," I said, tugging on the sleeve of his jacket. "I don't want to do a press conference."

"You have no choice, young lady. Once it became public knowledge that Vincent put a ring on your finger, you lost the right to make that decision."

I sat back in the seat. What had possessed this man to tell his teammates about us? I didn't even know he had the ring, especially since it was supposed to be sitting on my dresser until I chose to wear it. I thought about what Walter had said with an uneasy feeling that my life had just gotten real complicated.

# THE PAST

# FALL, 1979

# EASING INTO THE LOVE THANG

# Chapter 16

*Arianna*

In terms of time, it had been four months. In terms of amazement, I was still astounded. Every night Jace came home and I'd think to myself, what is this man doing in my house? At first, it felt like an intrusion, him with his uniforms, boots, books, and papers mixed in with my stuff, but then we'd drafted a routine where Jace pretty much did everything, except cook, and treated me like a queen. If anyone had predicted that one day I would live with a man and love it, I would have called them a liar. That wasn't my style, especially after growing up with my parents.

Being with Jace was different and it felt nice having someone truly care about me. Maybe it was that he'd kept his promise and had become my best friend. I did miss Jazmin and Paige, but Jace was the person I now shared everything with, and he was always there for me.

Jazmin and I had talked a few times, but she'd basically gone into seclusion. From what Jessie told me, I knew that Lewis had moved in with Paige. Other than a few glimpses of her at work, where we tried to avoid running into each other, I didn't know what was happening with her since I hadn't been anywhere near her apartment or she mine.

The phone on my desk rang and I hit the speaker button. "Yes, Ilene."

"Ms. Jackson, there is a man here who says he's looking for a beautiful woman to take home with him."

"Is he really tall and really dark?"

Ilene sighed. "Yeah, he's tall, and dark, and he's as handsome as sin."

"Ask him to tell you his name."

"He says he's Billy Dee Williams."

## A Request for Closure

"Tell him that I don't know a Billy Dee Williams, and that my man would be really angry if I went home with him."

"I'm handing him the phone so you can tell him that yourself."

"Are you ready to go, sweetheart?"

"I'll be down in a minute."

I forwarded the phone for the weekend, grabbed my purse, and practically ran out of that building. Jace was standing by the car; I stopped when he pulled a bouquet of yellow roses from behind his back.

I pointed and asked, "For me?"

"I don't know," he said, moving toward me and reaching into the front pocket of his uniform at the same time. "See, I was in that building a little while ago looking for a woman. She's about five six, has the biggest, brownest, prettiest eyes and a pair of breasts that make me drool. Oh, and did I mention that her lips are more luscious than the juiciest of berries and that her skin is as soft as silk, and she is the most gorgeous woman I've ever seen?"

He stopped and the twinkle in his eyes vanished, replaced by a veneer of seriousness that lined his face. "I don't know why she didn't tell me, but I recently found out that she had a birthday almost three months ago and these flowers and this," he flipped open the lid on a red velvet case, "are for her."

Sunlight glinted off the delicate chain bracelet nestled in pink cloth. "Oh, Jace."

He bent his knees until he was eye level with me. "Oh, Jace," he said, mimicking me. He handed me the flowers and latched the bracelet around my wrist. I hadn't purposely kept my birthday from Jace. It had been so long since I'd celebrated it that I'd forgotten that I'd had one. Jace twisted the bracelet around until I could see the fourteen-carat gold plate where he'd had the words *Jace's Property* engraved between two diamonds.

"You like?"

"I like."

Jace opened the car door. "First, we're going home so you can put those flowers in water. Then, we're going out for a belated birthday

148

dinner and when we get back, I'm going to take you to bed and make love to you all night long."

—◊◊◊—

Several afternoons later, I sat curled up on the couch watching a movie when Jace came out of the bedroom with something in his hand and his brow crinkled in thought.

"What's this?"

I looked at the paper. "The bill from Montgomery Ward."

"It says it's past due."

I glanced at the paper again. "Yes, it does."

"And that doesn't bother you?"

"Not in the least."

"Do you need money, Arianna?"

"Nope," I said, turning my attention back to the screen.

Jace turned off the television.

"Hey! I was watching that."

"I asked…if you needed money."

"And I told you, no."

"Then why haven't you paid this bill?"

"I haven't gotten around to it yet. I'll pay it. Don't worry about it."

"When?"

This man needed to find something else to do other than annoy me. "When what, Jace?"

"When are you going to pay this bill?"

"What difference does it make? It's my bill and I'll pay it when I'm ready."

He strode from the room. I got up and turned on the television. Ten minutes later, he was back and he clicked off the set on his way to the couch. When he sat down, he had more bills in his hands, which he began slamming down on the table one by one.

"Overdue! Past due! Overdue! Overdue!" He was breathing hard when he looked at me.

I cocked my brow. "Your point?"

"*When* are you going to pay these bills!"

"When I'm ready."

"*What* do you plan to use for money?"

"I have money," I said.

"Do you?" he said. Then he opened my checkbook and slammed it down, too. "You have sixteen dollars and fifty-eight cents! And that includes two dollars in cash! There is at least two hundred dollars' worth of bills here, Arianna Jackson!"

"How dare you go through my things! You had no right to do that, Alvin."

"I have every right! And I'm not having my woman walking around here broke."

For some reason, that comment hurt my feelings. "I'm not broke."

He pulled me to his chest. "Why won't you let me help you, Arianna?"

"I don't need any help."

"Yes, sweetheart, you do."

"No, I don't."

"Why are you being so stubborn about this? Instead of giving it back, why don't you just use the money I give you to pay these bills?"

"I don't want your money, Jace. I can take care of myself."

Jace sighed and squeezed me tight. "Okay, but this can't go on."

"I'll pay them, Jace. I will."

"I know you will, sweetheart. In the meantime, I'm going to take these off your hands." He gathered up the bills and rose from the couch. "If I hurry, I can get to Ward's before they close. I'm taking your car."

Oh, oh, I thought. "Um, Jace."

"What is it, baby girl?"

"You might want to take your car. Mine's just about out of gas."

I saw his jaw tense and muscles bunched beneath his shirt as Jace struggled to hold his temper. "No. I'll take yours."

Jace was quiet when he came home. He didn't seem to be angry, but rather in a somewhat thoughtful mood and his reflective gaze settled on me often. One would think that working in a finance department, I would have had a better handle on my own fiscal matters, and I don't know why I was so adamant about refusing his help. I knew I didn't want to start depending on Jace in the same way my mother had depended on my father. If she'd been more financially independent, she probably wouldn't have put up with his crap for so many years. With each passing day, Jace was becoming more important in my life, but I never wanted to find myself in the position of needing him.

After that day, my money problems disappeared. Jace never said anything else about it. Instead, he put money directly into my account and entered the amount in my checkbook. Except for the few dollars I occasionally asked for, he never gave me cash. He knew I'd slip that back into his wallet as I had been doing all along.

—∽∾∽—

*Paige*

I picked up a pair of socks from the bathroom floor, and then followed the trail of clothes into the bedroom. Lewis had stuff everywhere: on the floor, over the back of the chair, and hanging from the doorknob on the closet. Jermaine Jacob Lewis was a slob and this housework crap was for the birds. I dropped the things in my hands, sat on my bed, and pulled a joint out of the drawer on the nightstand.

In Lewis, I thought I'd found the man I had always wanted and I was doing my best to play the good little housewife. That shows how little I knew about myself or what I wanted. At the time I made that promise, I didn't know that Lewis was a homebody or that every single day would be the same as the one before.

At night, he came home and took out the garbage. If Jessie was in the house, he'd play with her for a while, then stretch out on the floor and turn on the stereo or the television. I'd come home and cook dinner.

## A Request for Closure

We'd eat, and while he put Jessie down for the night, I'd clean the kitchen and pick up around the house. Then we'd go to bed. On the weekends, it was grocery shopping, more cleaning the house, and endless laundry.

I was tired of picking up after Lewis and couldn't imagine doing it for the rest of my life. It reminded me too much of living with my mother. Only it was worse because I didn't have my friends.

Jazmin rarely left her apartment, and she didn't answer the phone or the door. I couldn't talk to Arianna either. I had seen her a few times in the parking lot, but whenever she noticed me, she quickly went up the side stairs to her apartment. Jessie still visited her, and while she hadn't said it, I knew that I was no longer welcome. That bothered me a lot, because I really missed talking to her.

Lewis came into the bedroom. "Hey," he said.

"Hey, baby. How was your day?"

"Okay, I guess. My unit's been assigned bivouac next week."

I raised my brow. If the boy was going to be in the field for seven days, he might want to have a little fun before he left. "Lewis, let's go to the club tonight. We haven't been out in months."

He untied his boots and tossed them to the middle of the floor. "Not tonight. I had a hell of a day and all I want to do is relax."

That's all you do every night, I thought, rising from the bed. I picked up the boots and set them side-by-side in the closet. "Please, Lewis. For a little while."

He began unbuttoning his shirt. "What's for dinner?"

*Oh, so now he was gonna ignore my ass?* "Did you hear what I said? I want to go out and I don't think it's too much to ask that my man take me!"

"Don't start, Paige." He stepped out of his pants and tossed them on the chair. "Where's Jessie?"

I blew out a breath. "Jessie's not here."

He went to the closet for his jeans and a white tee shirt, his standard after work attire. "You know, Paige, you really should keep better tabs on your daughter. Jessie's only five years old; you shouldn't let her wander around this complex as if she's grown. Something could happen to her."

Now, I just knew this man was not trying to tell me how to raise my child. "First of all, Jessie went to dinner with Jazmin and Brick. Second, Jessie's father lives in California and if he doesn't give a damn about her, why should you?"

"Paige, I know Jessie's not mine, but if I'm gonna live in this house, then I think I should have some say about the way things are run around here."

Jessie wasn't the issue. I was upset because I wanted to hit the streets and Lewis wouldn't take me. "Whateva, Lewis," I said, and then I left the room.

Dinner that night was cold cuts and chips because I was not about to spend my time cooking for a man who couldn't be bothered to take me out of the house.

All weekend we held stilted conversations and slept on opposite sides of the bed, and by the time Saturday melded into Monday morning, I was glad to see him go. I couldn't understand why Lewis wouldn't take me out when he knew it was important to me. I wasn't asking for something large and out of reach. This was such a small thing, and it was important, because I needed more than the drudgery of housework as my only entertainment. I needed to have some fun. That night, I dropped Jessie off at my mother's after work.

*You really shouldn't be doing this.*

Shut up, I responded silently to that voice in my head. I turned in the mirror, liking the way the hot and saucy red dress swirled around my body. Then I touched up my lipstick, grabbed my purse, and headed for the door.

"You're going to have a drink, and maybe one dance," I told myself, "and then you're bringing your hot-to-trot behind back home."

And that was the plan when I stepped through the doors of the Gallery, a new club that opened up across town. When I entered, I knew everything would be all right this time. I could have that drink and go home.

## A Request for Closure

This was not the Black Stallion, a hot room where the people I knew hung out. This joint was classy, from the raspberry carpet and gold railing lining a parquet dance floor to the white booths with cushioned seats. A large, silver disco ball spit out its colors on the crowd, which was rather large for a Monday night.

I couldn't really get into the music; the rock-'n-roll beat wasn't in me. Instead, I pressed through the bodies, and after making it to the bar, I ordered a glass of Chardonnay. I stayed where I was for a while and sipped from my glass. After gathering my strength to get through the sea of people again, I set my empty glass on the bar and began the struggle. A warm hand touched my elbow.

"Would you like another?"

The voice was deep and came from somewhere above me. I looked up to see where it was coming from. A black mustache topped a mouth of straight white teeth that sat in a face so striking, I think I forgot to breathe. He was dressed in black pants and a white shirt. His eyes were brown and he wore his black hair in a short Afro. He had to be at least six-foot four and over two hundred pounds.

"Yes, and thank you."

"Another white wine for the lady. Royal Crown Royal for me."

He handed me my glass, then led us out of the traffic jam. There were no seats, so we stood by the rail.

"My name's Ray. Raymond Steward. What's yours?"

"Paige Michaels."

"Paige. That's nice."

"Thank you."

"You here by yourself, Paige?"

"Yes," I said. "I needed a break."

"Me, too. I don't usually hang out in clubs and rock is definitely not my kind of music, but some of my colleagues convinced me to come." He glanced down at me. "And for once, I'm glad I did."

My heart jiggled, but only a little bit, because I was determined to be good. "What kind of work do you do?"

"I'm an architect. I work for Sloan Brothers. And you?"

"I'm a word processor with TMI; they're a defense contractor."

Ray nodded. "Do you like your job?"

"Not really, but it's a paycheck and my daughter needs to eat."

He suddenly looked distressed. "You're married, then."

"No. Divorced."

Someone jostled me from behind; Ray's arm ringed my waist.

"It's crowded in here tonight."

"Yes…it is."

The conversation halted as we sipped our drinks and watched the people on the floor. "Paige," he said after a few minutes. "I know this isn't our kind of music, but we could try to dance to it."

He set our glasses on a nearby table. We found a corner on the floor and actually danced for quite a while. Once I shut out the noise of the screaming guitars and concentrated on the beat of the drum, the music wasn't awful, exactly. Ray managed to find a rhythm, too.

Off the floor, he plied me with drinks and somewhere along the way, my white wine changed to rum and Coke, and we talked. On the floor, he held me close and all I could think about was how good it felt to be in the arms of this tall, mahogany brown man. Raymond had a broad chest, a narrow waist, and muscular arms. I pressed myself closer, felt a thick, hard bump at the base of my stomach and I knew that I was going to be in trouble.

By the time the club closed, I was so hot my skin felt clammy, but I tried to fight the feelings rising in my chest and between my legs. I needed to go home.

Raymond walked me to my car. "You going straight home?"

"Yes." That was the plan anyway.

"Where do you live?"

"I'm not telling you that."

"Okay. How about if I give you my address and you follow me home."

Why did that not surprise me? Yet I couldn't help being intrigued. Lewis seemed perfectly satisfied with the predictable routine of our relationship. I needed more, and I didn't want to think about Lewis tonight.

## A *Request for Closure*

Tonight, I wanted to think about Raymond Steward and how beautiful and desirable he made me feel.

Icy-hot sensations spread through my body; I gave up the fight. "Where do you live?"

He recited his address and a wave of dizziness washed over me. The man lived in the Pikes Peak Apartments—my apartment complex. I opened my car door, climbed inside, and rolled the window halfway down. "I'll follow you."

Driving to my apartment complex, I felt kind of reckless. This encounter had a potential for real danger, and I was courting disaster by sleeping with a man who lived so close to home, although I had no intention of ever giving him my address. No way was I going to lose Lewis over someone who would never mean anything more to me than a one-night stand.

Inside his apartment, Raymond took my hand and led me directly to the bedroom. There was no need for any chatter; we both knew why we were together. A few lead-in kisses and I undressed myself while he removed his clothes.

Raymond had an incredibly huge dick, long and thick, dark and smooth. Thinking about what he could do to me with that thing made my body tingle. I slowly drew my gaze upward as he approached the bed, committing to memory every hard muscle and angular plane making up his huge, muscle-packed form. Meeting his eyes, desire, raw and naked, flared and I slipped down on my back. The bedside lamp went out and large hands began soft caresses that had my mind spinning. For three hours, Raymond Steward hovered above me, bewitching my mind with a romantic verbal assault while guiding me on a pleasure-filled journey that left me gasping for breath and wanting more.

The next morning, I opened my eyes and knew immediately that something was different. Why didn't I feel dirty? Or guilty? I'd picked up a man I didn't know in a club, slept with him, and I felt good, and more alive than I'd felt in a long time.

That couldn't be right, and I waited for the condemnation that should have been reviling me. It didn't come, and ten minutes later, I rolled to my side. I felt no guilt or shame or any of those other emotions that usually made me hate myself for being so weak.

A large hand curved around my waist, and Raymond ran his tongue from the base of my neck to the lobe of my ear. "You were absolutely amazing, Paige, and I can't believe that I want you again." He pulled me flush with his body. "I know that we both have to go to work, but let's do it once more."

"Ray, we've been making love for most of the night. You can't possibly want me again."

He touched his lips to mine, then took my hand, and placed it over his crotch. Raymond Steward was rock hard. His lips worked more magic on my neck and face while his hands massaged my breasts. By the time his lips found mine again, I was too hot to care about anything.

# Chapter 17

*Jazmin*

Jazmin, we have to do this! I talked to Walter and the team publicist. Both of them said that if you don't attend this function with me, the press will start hounding us again. I know how much you hate that, Jazzy, so let's just do this thing and get it over with."

I shot Brick a withering glare and stomped out of the room. In the bedroom, I took a joint out of my dresser drawer and flopped down on the bed.

I was sick and tired of those reporters digging around in the minutiae of my life and printing everything they found, including the police record of the Macy's store incident. Not only had they printed a copy of the arrest warrant, they'd also amplified my role to that of a major gang lord out to take over the City of New York.

Everywhere I went, people followed. In the grocery store, women whispered behind my back. About a month ago, one of them actually ran up to me and yanked my hair. Then she turned to the others and yelled at the top of her lungs that it was real. Brick was so angry, he arranged to have my groceries delivered.

I could hardly open my front door without a flashbulb popping in my face or a reporter asking questions I didn't think they had any right to ask. Two months ago, I cussed one of them out, and then had to meet with the team's publicist and go through two weeks of sessions on how to deal with members of the media.

That pissed me off even more because taking those all day classes with that image consultant meant that I couldn't enroll in time for school. Because of Brick, I'd had to put my dream on hold, and at this rate, I wasn't sure if it would ever come true.

I thought all the hoopla was over until three weeks ago, when I called Arianna and Paige and asked both of them to go to the mall with me. I had intended for us to talk and get our friendship back on track, but we weren't inside the Citadel ten minutes before people came at us from all sides. Security broke up the mob and escorted us out to my car. That evening, Jace Barnes had shown up at my door. The man was furiously calm as he explained that he didn't want Arianna subjected to anything like that again. While he'd also said that he didn't have a problem with our friendship, except for a few phone calls, I haven't seen Arianna since.

But at least I still had my job. For some inexplicable reason, the store manager thought that all the notoriety surrounding Brick and me was good for business. Frankly, I was getting tired of having those women come in, stare at, and talk about me. They weren't buying anything and if I didn't need the money so badly, I'd have quit.

Brick sat on the bed. "Jazzy, I warned you this would happen."

*Yeah, but it was supposed to happen when I was ready, not because you got jealous of some dumb-ass jocks and went all cock-eyed in public.* "I don't want to go."

When I put the joint between my lips, he tried to snatch it out of my mouth.

"You know that you can't smoke that thing! You show up high at a public event and the media will have a field day."

I lit the joint, inhaled, and blew the smoke at him.

Brick rubbed the bridge of his nose. "Okay, Jazmin. I'm tired of fighting with you about this. If you don't want to go, then I won't go either."

"You have to go; you're part of the team."

His brows came together in a frown "Dammit, Jazmin! Why do we have to go through this every time we need to go somewhere? You know how important this fundraiser is, so get dressed; we're leaving in thirty minutes!"

## A Request for Closure

He left the room and I fell back on the bed. I knew I didn't really have a choice. If I didn't go, the rumor mill would go haywire and the media circus would start all over again.

—⟋⟍⟍⟋⟍—

On the ride home from the fundraiser, Brick poured champagne into two flutes and handed one to me. "See, that wasn't so bad, now was it?"

"No," I said, taking the glass. "Actually, it was kind of fun once I relaxed and started to enjoy myself. Jonelle and Gabriella gave me their phone numbers and told me to call if I ever needed to talk."

"You should talk to them, Jazzy. They've already been through this. David and Paul were first-rounders, too."

I laid my head on his shoulder. "I might," I said, although I knew it wasn't gonna happen. The only women I wanted to talk to were Paige and Arianna.

"Good," he said.

For a few minutes, we rode in silence. After the raucous celebration of the gala, the quiet and being alone with Brick felt nice.

"You know, Jazzy, we need to start looking for a house in Denver."

I stilled and the silence became a scream in my head. "Brick, we haven't even set a wedding date—"

"That's something else we need to do, so you can start planning the wedding. Camp starts next month and the season two weeks after that. Once that happens, my time won't be my own."

This thing with Brick was moving way too fast. Ever since he'd put that ring on my finger, he had been pushing me to set a date. Now he was talking weddings and houses, and I wasn't even sure I was in love with the boy. "Brick, what's the rush here? We've only been engaged for four months and since then I've barely had a minute to myself."

"I know it seems as if I'm rushing you, Jazzy, but I want to marry you and I want that to happen before the season starts."

*And that's the biggest problem with this relationship. It is and will always be about what you want.* "You know what, Vincent? I am not going to set a wedding date! I'm not going to look for a house in Denver! And I'm not going to make decisions about my life based on some timetable you have in your head. Since we met, this relationship has been about you and about what you want. Well, I have wants, too, and I not going to let you rush me into a marriage I'm not sure I even want!"

"But Jazzy—"

"No, Vincent. Either we slow this thing down and try to have a normal relationship like two normal people, or you can have this ring back right now." I was trying to pull the ring off my finger when his hand covered mine.

"No, Jazzy, don't take it off. Please." The kiss he placed on my lips felt so sweet, my heart swelled inside my chest. "Okay. We're going to do this your way. From now on, you call the shots."

I had expected an argument and for Brick to use his steamroller tactics to get me to do what he wanted. "Really?"

"Yeah. You're my dream girl, Jazzy, and I'm not going to lose you after waiting so long to find you."

"Thank you," I said, snuggling against him.

*You go, girl*, Mags said, and I closed my eyes.

Several weeks later, I heard my phone ringing as soon as I reached my apartment door. I hurried inside and snatched up the receiver, hoping that it was Brick, but knowing that it wasn't since he was probably in the locker room getting dressed.

"Hello, Jazmin. This is Gabriella Bryant, David's wife."

"Hi," I said, wondering why she was calling me.

"I know the game is starting soon, but I just wanted to call and invite you to a tea next Saturday. Now, we're holding it at my house and we'll be discussing the community projects the wives association will be getting involved in this year."

"But I'm not a wife.

Gabriella's laughter tinkled. "Oh, Jazmin, you are such a funny girl. The association is not just for those of us who are actually married to the players; it's for fiancées and girlfriends, as well. We all have to do our part in the community and to make our men look good."

"What time on Saturday?"

"Well, the tea starts at two and I'm so hoping that you'll be able to come. I know Vincent would want you to join us."

Gabriella's entire world revolved around David Bryant. It was too bad she didn't know that the man wasn't even on her planet. "Okay, Gabriella; I'll be there on Saturday."

I hung up the phone and went to my bedroom to change.

———

A short while later, I stood outside Paige's door listening to the music and laughter coming from inside. Tonight was the season opener and the Nuggets were playing the Lakers in California. Since I didn't want to watch it by myself, I'd called Paige and she'd agreed to throw together some snacks for us to munch on during the game. When I opened the door, I counted fifteen or so people spread around the living room.

Paige pulled me aside. "Lewis decided to invite a few of the guys from his unit and I rounded it out with some women."

"It's cool."

She was loading a platter with barbecued chicken and ribs. On the counter next to it sat a large bowl of potato salad, a pan of baked beans, and one of macaroni and cheese. Two cakes sat on the counter behind her, along with bottles of liquor and mixers. Paige had gone all out for this one.

"Need help?"

"Nope, I've got this under control. Why don't you fix a drink and go say hello to everyone."

I poured a vodka tonic and took a seat on the couch. It almost felt like old times, almost, because Arianna was missing.

———

*Arianna*

"Hey, baby girl!"

I closed the door and followed the sound of his voice. "Hey, your-self," I said, walking into the kitchen. "What are you doing here?"

"Making you some dinner. How was work?"

"Work was fine. Why?"

"Why what?"

"Why are you here instead of wherever it is you usually go on Wednesday night?"

"Had a change of plans."

Damn, I thought, because that meant I'd have to change my plans, too. Since we'd been together, Jace had always come home late on Wednesday evening, generally not arriving until ten or eleven. Sometimes he even stayed in the barracks. Wednesdays had become my opportunity to connect and hang out with the girls. It was also ladies night, and I was supposed to meet Monica at the club. The base had just brought in a new regiment of men. She wanted to check out the new brothers. I had planned to go along for company and perhaps to have a little fun. Since Jace was at home, perhaps I could have a different kind of fun.

"Why did you decide to cook?"

"Because I knew you'd be tired and I wanted you to relax tonight. Later, I thought we'd watch the game in case Brick gets to play tonight." He handed me a glass of iced tea and I lifted my head for his kiss. "Go and change. Dinner will be ready in a little while."

"Do you want some help?"

"Nope," he said with a grin. "I want you to sit on that couch and put up your feet."

After calling Monica, I changed into jeans and a top and then sat at the dining room table. I wanted to watch Jace in action. My heart tripped continually as I observed the bottom lip he gripped between his teeth while concentrating on stirring the spaghetti sauce or checking the pasta.

## A Request for Closure

Oh, no, I thought. When had I fallen in love with this man? Love! It was hard to comprehend, but for a few seconds I felt warm and good all over. Then doubt crept in and took over. I was so young and he was even younger. What did I know about love anyway? I knew that it made people vulnerable and that if vulnerable you got hurt. I'd seen that with my parents and it worried me. If I told Jace how I felt, would we end up hating one another, too?

I looked at him again and felt something so overwhelming it pushed the doubt from my mind. I didn't know what lay before us, and that made me anxious, but I also knew that I was going to take a chance on love with this man.

You're so good to me," I said to him over dinner.

"I'm supposed to be, I'm your man."

"Yeah, but...I don't know, Jace. You're so different from other men I've known. You're...well, you're different, that's all."

"Different good or different bad."

"Different good."

"So I guess that means you'll be keeping me, huh?"

"Yeah. I think I will."

"Good," he said, handing me my fork. Now eat before your food gets cold."

—⁂—

"Where have you been?"

I had just parked my car and climbed out. "The mall."

Paige laughed. "That's not what I'm asking and you know it. Did you see the game last night?"

"Yeah, Jace and I—"

I snapped my mouth closed. Except for a few glimpses, I hadn't seen Paige since the night she'd left the club with a man who wasn't Lewis. She looked cool and relaxed in the midday heat. My sweat glands started working overtime.

164

"What are you doing tonight?"

"Nothing," I said warily.

"If you get a few minutes, come on down to my apartment." She turned and walked away.

I went upstairs to my apartment running the exchange through my mind. Paige had chosen the game. I was simply abiding by her rules, so why was she suddenly speaking to me? I couldn't figure out what was going on with Paige, but when curiosity seized me and wouldn't let loose, I knew I had to find out. I grabbed my keys and went downstairs.

"Hey, girl," Paige said when I walked into the kitchen.

"Hi," I said, taking a seat at the table.

"So, how's it going?"

"Fine...I guess."

"I mean, with you and Jace."

My antenna rose. "Jace is fine."

She took out a bag of popcorn and a skillet. I rose and fixed two glasses of Pepsi. We didn't speak as she popped a bowl of popcorn and drenched it with butter.

"You cooking tonight?" She set the bowl on the table and took a seat.

"Nope."

"Me neither. After all that cooking I did yesterday, Lewis and Jessie can eat leftovers. I'm kickin' it tonight."

"Jace is taking me out—"

"Taking you out where?"

"You don't want to hear about that."

She sighed heavily. "Look, Arianna. When I found out about you and Jace, I was surprised. That's all. I apologize for the things I said to you and hope you can forgive me for acting like an ass that night in the club. Jace and I were never serious and, as he said, it was over a long time ago. Besides, I have Lewis."

*Really*, I thought with mistrust.

"Yes, really," she said in response to the disbelief that must have shown in my face. She stood and held out her arms. I left my chair and returned her hug.

## A *Request for Closure*

"I've missed you, Paige."

"I've missed you, too, Arianna."

"When you told me about Jace, I knew that I had to cut him loose. But I couldn't, because Jace makes me feel so wonderful and so special. I...I'm sorry, P."

"Ari, you don't have anything to be sorry about. I've seen how Jace looks at you. That boy cares for you, a lot. If he makes you happy, you do what you need to do to keep him, no matter what anyone thinks about it."

We returned to our chairs. "Now, where is Jace taking you for dinner?"

She smiled.

I smiled back, and over popcorn and Pepsi filled her in on everything that had happened between Jace and me since the last time we'd talked.

# Chapter 18

*Paige*

P aige Michaels."

"Is this the Paige Michaels who knows how to shake her rump to rock and use that same rump to rock a man's world?"

The voice was male, but I couldn't place it. "Who is this?"

"Royal Crown Royal and rock-'n-roll, baby."

"Raymond?"

"You got it, babe. How are you, Paige Michaels?"

No, no, no, I thought. "How did you find...how did you get this number, Raymond?"

"I've been thinking about you for weeks. Then I finally remembered the name of the defense contractor you mentioned the night we met. From there, the rest was easy. Will you have dinner with me tonight, Paige?"

"I'm sorry, but I can't."

"Why not?"

"I, um, I think I have to work late."

"I don't mind a late dinner, if I can share it with you."

I stifled a groan. His voice sounded so deep and so appealing, and then I forced myself out of that trance. "Raymond, I can't, and I'm running late for a meeting."

"Paige, wait!"

"No, I have to go."

My legs were shaking as I walked to the conference room. One-night stands were supposed to remain exactly what they were—one-night stands. They were not supposed to come back and haunt you later. I sat in my chair astounded and unable to believe that I'd given Raymond Steward enough information to track me down.

On one hand, it was very flattering to know that Raymond had that strong an interest in me, kind of made me feel all gooey inside. On the other, there was no way I could see Raymond Steward again...no matter how good the man was in the sack.

After the meeting, I gathered my things and rushed from the room. At my desk, the message light on my phone was blinking like a radar screen. I wanted to ignore it, but a call could have come from Jessie's daycare center, so I sucked up my courage and picked up the phone. There were six messages and every one of them was from Raymond. That rattled me even more, especially the last one that said that he wanted to meet me after work so that we could talk.

*Talk about what?* I had nothing to say to the man and another round between the sheets was out of the question. One day I was going to learn to keep my fast ass at home and out of other men's beds. At the end of the day, I rushed out of the building promising myself that Raymond Steward was my last one-night stand.

"Paige!"

I saw him, and I turned the other way.

"Paige, please stop!"

I stopped, exhaled, and turned around. "What are you doing here, Raymond?"

"I wanted to see you," he said, walking up. He stood close to me, so close I could feel the heat emanating from his body. Close enough for me to smell the fragrance of his cologne and too close for comfort.

I backed off a few steps. "I told you that I couldn't see you."

"No. You said that you couldn't have dinner with me tonight."

"Raymond, I can't see you again."

"Why not, Paige? Tell me why when we had such a great time together."

"We had sex together, Ray."

"No, we had great sex together but only after we'd connected on that dance floor. Have a drink with me and let's talk."

"Raymond," I said, rubbing my temples with my fingers. "I don't know how much plainer I can make this for you. I can't have a drink with you. I can't go to dinner with you, and I can't ever see you again. I'm sorry." I turned away and headed for the employee parking lot.

"Paige!"

I didn't acknowledge him.

"I'm not going to let you walk away from me. Paige, do you hear me? Paige!"

I waved him off and kept stepping.

—∿∿—

When I arrived at work the next day, a vase holding a dozen red roses sat on my desk. I read the card, and then I studied the flowers and tried to decide if I should keep them or throw them in the trash. I decided to keep them. Raymond called an hour later.

"Did you get my flowers?"

"Yes, they are very lovely, and thank you."

"Have dinner with me, Paige."

"No, Raymond. Goodbye."

When I came back from lunch on Thursday, a vase of yellow roses sat on my desk and one holding twelve pink ones. Raymond called at two.

"Did you get my flowers?"

"Yes, and thank you."

Raymond chuckled. "What, no 'they are very lovely' this time?"

"They are very lovely."

"Have dinner with me, Paige."

"No, Raymond. Goodbye."

The next day, I was sitting at my desk when Ilene walked up to her. "What's going on, Paige?"

"Nothing, why?"

"Wednesday you received a dozen red roses and yesterday two dozen more and today this came for you."

She held out a white box tied with a gold ribbon. I took the box. Ilene didn't move.

"Thank you," I said.

Ilene took the hint and headed back to the front desk.

"Raymond, what am I going to do with you?" I murmured as I untied the ribbon and pulled the lid off the box. Inside, I found a box of Godiva chocolates and a bottle of Chardonnay. Raymond called at nine.

"Did you get my present?"

"Yes, it is very nice, thank you."

"Have dinner with me, Paige."

"No, Raymond. Goodbye."

There was another and larger white box tied with a red ribbon on my desk when I returned from lunch. Inside, I found a small girl teddy bear dressed in red and a boy bear dressed in black pants and a white shirt. The boy bear had a tape cassette hanging around his neck. I dug deeper into the white tissue paper and found a tape recorder at the bottom of the box. I pulled it out, loaded the cassette, and lowered the volume. I didn't want anyone else to hear whatever was on the tape.

A few minutes later, I burst out laughing. It was Raymond. It sounded as if he were trying to sing one of those rock-'n-roll songs we'd danced to at the Gallery and he was doing a horrible job of it. I was still laughing when my phone rang ten minutes later.

"Did you get my present?"

"Yes," I said, trying to hold in my laughter. "It-it's interesting."

"Have dinner with me, Paige Michaels."

"Are you going to sing?"

"If I say no, will you say yes?"

"Yes."

Raymond exhaled. "Okay. Tomorrow night, my place at eight, and bring the wine."

—⁊⁊—

The next night, Lewis entered the bedroom. "If you can wait, I'll get dressed and go with you tonight."

My heart tripped and I examined Lewis in the mirror. I saw nothing that indicated that he knew the real deal and forced my heart to calm down. "Lewis, it's only going to be Arianna and me tonight. Besides, you said that you'd sit with Jessie."

"I'll drop Jessie off at your mother's."

"She won't be home this evening."

"Your sister can watch her then."

"She's going out tonight, too."

Lewis sighed in frustration. "Surely we can find someone to sit with Jessie for a couple of hours. You're always on me about going out. Tonight, when I want to go, we can't get a sitter."

"That's because you waited too late to tell me. Next time, we'll make plans in advance." I picked up my purse and left the bedroom before I said something that would tip him off. "I'm meeting Ari upstairs. See you later, baby."

I rushed up the stairs. "I need your help," I said as soon as Arianna opened the door.

"Come in."

"Hi, Jace."

"Hey," he said.

"Let's go into the bedroom," Arianna said. She closed the door behind us. "What's going on?"

"I need to borrow your car."

She grabbed the keys off the dresser and handed them to me. "You look good. Where are you off to?"

"Around the corner."

"You need my car to go around the corner?"

"Yes, and I can't explain now, but I'll fill you in later. Oh, and if you happen to see Lewis tonight, tell him you're meeting me at the club. Okay?"

"Why would I need to do that?"

"Tell you later, Ari, and thanks."

## A *Request for Closure*

I parked Arianna's car in a dark space under a tree and sat staring up at the building trying to figure out what was I doing there. Was it the sex? Certainly! With Raymond, it had been great. Then again, I did get it on a regular basis at home. The rush of living on the edge? Possibly. Seeing Raymond so close to home was definitely not a smart thing to do, but being smart had never been one of my strong points. Maybe it was because the boy was so persistent. Whatever it was, I was going to do this one last time, and then I wouldn't see Raymond Steward ever again.

Raymond was standing in the hallway when I arrived. The boy might have thought I wasn't coming or maybe he had a reason for being out there. Either way, it didn't matter. He was so fine my heart ceased to beat.

"Hi, Paige."

"Hi, Raymond."

"Girl, you look good enough eat."

"Thank you," I said, preening in a simple raspberry-colored dress that I'd perked up with some beads and matching earrings. He looked good, too, in his navy blue jacket and matching slacks.

"Have a seat," he said, leading me over to a brown sofa. "Where's the wine?"

"I think I forgot it," I said, shrugging my shoulders.

"Good thing I bought another bottle then. Make yourself comfortable and I'll be back with your wine."

Surveying the room, I could see that Raymond was a very Afrocentric brotha. Brown furniture, Kente cloth throw rugs, African masks, and statues filled the space. A tall, walnut bookcase filled with books sat next to the fireplace.

"Nice place," I said, taking the champagne flute he handed to me.

"Thanks, my sister helped me decorate. I only design the rooms. I have no idea what to put in them when they're done." Raymond templed his fingers, propped his chin on top and stared at me.

"What are you looking at?'

"A very lovely woman with something on her mind."

Yeah, there was something on my mind, like when we were going into the bedroom. "There is nothing on my mind, Ray, except wondering what's for dinner."

He heaved himself to his feet. "Coming right up. Why don't you head to the table while I get it?"

His dining room table was made of walnut. Gold edged his china, and he'd set out crystal glasses and cloth napkins. Raymond came out of the kitchen with a large crystal bowl of lettuce/tomato salad and a bottle of wine. The expression on his face was dismal when he sat across from me. "My sister was supposed to come over here and help me tonight," he said morosely. "But she got tied up at the office, and I can't cook. I threw this salad together at the last minute."

"It's okay, Raymond. I'm not all that hungry anyway."

After dinner, I helped clean the kitchen and we returned to the living room. Raymond went to the bookcase and returned to sit beside me on the couch. "You read much, Paige?"

*Not since they made me do it in high school.* "No, not really." I snuggled against his side and kissed his cheek. He glanced at me out of the corner of his eye.

"I do, and lately I've been into classic literature, especially books that were shrouded in controversy upon their publication. Last week, I finished a novel called, *The Invisible Man*, by Ralph Ellison. It's the story of a nameless, faceless, Southern black man and his struggle against conforming to the views of the white man and the invisibility he feels because of his race. It's a very deep book, but one I enjoyed."

"That's nice," I said, already bored with his conversation.

"Tonight, I thought I'd start a book with a lighter topic. It's another classic first published in 1928 and immediately declared obscene due its sexual content. D. H. Lawrence is the author. They published a cleaned up version in 1932, but this is a first run print."

"What's it called?"

"*Lady Chatterley's Lover.* I thought we'd read a couple of chapters tonight."

## A Request for Closure

Raymond kicked off his shoes; I followed suit. He patted his lap and once I had settled against his chest, he opened the book and began to read.

# Chapter 19

*Jazmin*

"Did you see me, Jazzy? Two assists and one rebound. I never thought coach would put me on the floor this soon."

"Yes, baby. I saw you."

Two nights ago, when the starter at the point guard position twisted his ankle, the coach had flagged Brick. They'd played the Boston Celtics and lost by ten points.

"Two days, Jazzy. Two days to relax and reconnect with my woman. I really missed you. Come here."

I scooted closer to him. "I missed you, too."

"You're just as beautiful as the last time I saw you." He kissed me, and then flopped back on the pillows. "Man, last night was incredible! When I heard my name and ran out on that floor, I can't even describe how I felt. My first ten minutes in the NBA. Do you have any idea how great that feels?"

Not really, but the boy had been going on about it for the last hour. I tried not to let it bother me, though. Brick was living his dream. I would live my dream one day, too. In the meantime, I needed to figure out this basketball stuff. I tuned him back in.

"Coach says I need to improve my jumper so I've been working on it with some of the other guys and it's really helped me a lot."

"Brick, I know what a rebound is, but what is an assist?"

"Jazzy, you have to remember this stuff when I tell it to you. Anyway, an assist is when one player passes the ball to another and it results—"

I kissed him.

"You're never going learn this game if you don't pay attention."

I kissed him again.

The pad of his thumb skimmed across my cheek. "Okay, Jazzy-girl. What do you want to talk about?"

"I think we've done enough talking."

"Oh, you do, do you?"

I pushed him back on the bed, and a few minutes later, Brick couldn't have explained what an assist was if his life depended on it.

Two hours later, he dropped the towel around his waist and went into the closet. He came out dressed in a pair of sweats and tied on some tennis shoes.

"I'ma run downstairs to see if Jace and Lewis want to hit the court for a while. I need to practice my jumper."

"Okay," I said, reaching for the ringing telephone. "Hello."

"Jazmin Reed?"

The man's voice sounded vaguely familiar. "Yes."

"Jazmin, you may not remember me, but—"

"Hold up. If this is about an interview, forget it!"

I hung up and was on my way to the bathroom when the phone rang again. "Look, I don't know how you got this number—"

"Jazmin, it's Michael Peters.

Somewhat dazed, I dropped to the bed.

"Jazmin?"

"M-Michael?"

"Good, you do remember me. Do you have any idea how long I've been trying to track you down?"

"No."

"I've been searching for you for a couple of years now, but after you had that accident, it was as if you disappeared off the face of the earth. Then a couple of months ago, I saw you and your fiancé on the cover of *Ebony*. How is Vincent, by the way? I know the Nuggets are expecting big things from him."

"Vincent is fine. Why are you calling me, Mike?"

He cleared his throat. "Oh, I know you must be busy, Jazz, and I don't want to hold you up. The reason for my call is that I wanted to let you know that I am no longer with Ford. I quit three years ago and started my own agency. Candice, Piper, and Alexandria have signed with me and I've had them working pretty steadily. We have bookings for Paris in the spring."

So, I thought when he stopped talking. "And?"

"And," he said, heaving a deep breath. "I wanted to know if you'd be interested in making the trip with us."

Okay…the man had completely lost me. "Why would I want to go to Paris, Michael?"

"Because Paris is the city of love, Jazmin. Everybody knows that."

"Flip Wilson, you're not."

"And you ain't no Cheryl Tiegs neither." We both laughed. "I've really missed that smart mouth of yours, Jazz. You were one of the best and I know you would have surpassed Naomi and Cheryl."

"Okay, Michael, enough with the flattery. What do you really want?"

"I told you. I want you to do the shows next spring."

"You're kidding?"

"Nah, I never kid about the business; you know me better than that. We're styling with the big boys now, Jazmin. I'm talking international runways, haute couture collections, and the top designers you've only dreamed of wearing."

"But my accident…I mean, I haven't walked—"

"Can you walk now?"

"Yes. But—"

"That's all I need to know. When can you come and see me in New York? We need to talk."

I spent the next few days convincing myself that Michael Peters was out of his mind. Modeling was a tough business. Clawing your way to the top took a lot of energy and a whole lot more fight. I was too old and I didn't have any fight or stamina left in me to go toe to toe with the competition.

*That's a load of bull,* Mags said. *You have the fight and you have the stamina. You're just scared, and living in this cow town has made you soft.*

I'm not scared.

## A Request for Closure

*Sure you are, girlie. If you're not, pick up the phone and prove me wrong.*

I don't have to prove anything. I like my life, exactly the way it is.

*More bullshit,* Mags said in a singsong voice. *If you like your life so much, then why are you sitting here thinking about becoming a model again?*

Shut up, Mags. I had enough to think about without her constant intrusion.

———

But Mags didn't shut up and the constant nagging had me so wound up that on Saturday, I drove to Denver in a daze. Firmly implanted in my mind were all of the things I knew could be possible if I were to decide to go with Michael to Paris. Countering those thoughts were all of the things I knew I'd have to give up. I had so much to think about, the very last thing I wanted was to spend my afternoon sitting in a room with a bunch of women I didn't know.

I checked the directions and made a right turn at the next light, which took me onto a street of stately brick homes. Gabriella had told me that she lived in the city of Cherry Creek. From what I could see, it was a neighborhood full of wealthy people. I pulled into the driveway, then drove around to the back of a two-story, Tudor-styled house where I parked my raggedy Pinto among the Mercedes, Jaguars, BMWs, and a couple of limousines.

"Hi," I said when Gabriella answered the door.

"Jazmin, I'm so glad you could drive up for our little meeting."

On several occasions, I'd asked the woman to call me Jazz. However, Gabriella Bryant was always so formal, as if she was part royalty and such requests were beneath her. She gave me the once-over and I saw the disappointment that followed. She was dressed in a two-piece, button-down, black and white jacket and skirt, nylons, and one-inch black pumps. Her hair looked as if she'd just stepped out of a salon and her makeup was flawless. I'd worn a colorful Bohemian top over some faded blue jeans, thrown my hair up into a bouncing ponytail, and my face was makeup free.

"Come in, Jazmin. The other ladies are already here."

We walked through a large and expensively decorated interior to a sunroom at the back of the house. All talking ceased when we entered and I stood self-consciously in the doorway while a room full of spectacularly dressed women appraised me. I sucked up my courage and moved to an empty space next to Jonelle Danvers on one of the two couches in the room.

Jonelle giggled softly as she leaned toward me. "Gabriella's pissed," she whispered. "Before you arrived, she was reminding everybody in the room that you were once a fashion model and saying how she couldn't wait to see what you'd be wearing today."

"Guess I disappointed her, huh?"

"No shit, Sherlock. Now I'm waiting to see how that snobbish, stiff ass gets herself out of this one."

I decided right then that I liked Jonelle Danvers, Jojo to those she considered friends. Girlfriend was a home girl from around the way.

I observed the embarrassed flush in Gabriella's face when she looked at me again. The girl should've said something if she wanted me to turn it out for this meeting. Gabriella glowered at the other women whispering in the room and cleared her throat, and my first meeting with the Denver Nuggets Wives Association began.

———∿∿∿———

When we broke for refreshments, Jonelle pulled me aside. "What do you think?"

"I think I'm going have a problem with this. First of all, I work most Saturdays and even if I didn't, I certainly don't want to be spending my time running up and down that damn highway every weekend."

"Yeah, I can understand that," Jonelle said. "Fortunately for me, Paul doesn't give a damn whether or not I associate with these women or do anything in the community. We've been married for ten years and my man likes his home and prefers to have me there."

Is that right? I thought back on my trip to Vegas.

Jonelle must have seen something in my face because she said, "Oh girl, I ain't even naïve. All the men look and appreciate, but Paul brings his ass home and makes sure that I know that all he did do was look, so I know all about the pool incident in Vegas. But I swear, if Gabriella had gushed David's name one more damn time I was gonna puke on the floor. She's so blinded by the money that she can't even see what going on right under her own nose." Jonelle discreetly nodded in the direction of Lucy Palmer, a tall and pretty girl with tan brown skin, black eyes, and a head full of black curls. She was the girlfriend of one of the other players. "That's been going on for over a year."

My eyes widened in surprise. "How do you know that, Jojo?"

"Paul told me," she said while surveying the women in the room. "And see Lorelei Taylor?"

I directed my eyes to a tall woman with alabaster skin, blue eyes, and a cloud of red hair. She was one of those women that men would classify as a FOXY mama.

"Lei was once a stripper and the team's publicist had to really work to clean up her image." Her eyes narrowed in the direction of our hostess. "And the high and mighty Gabriella Bryant was once paid twenty-five dollars to peel off her clothes in a porn film. Paul says she was desperate for money after she took her narrow ass to Hollywood and couldn't find enough work to feed herself."

Damn, I thought. Jojo had *all* the dirt. I wondered what she knew about Brick, and whether she would spill any of his shenanigans.

Jonelle took a sip from her tiny crystal punch cup and looked at me over the rim. "You don't have anything to worry about, Jazz. Vincent won't even leave the hotel when they're on the road. He and Paul and a few of the other players, who actually know how to act when they give their heart to a woman, play a lot of poker together."

I smiled. Yep, I thought. Jojo Danvers did have all the dirt.

"But I will tell you this, Jazz," she continued on a serious tip. "Being the wife of a professional baller is a lot of stress. Our men eat, sleep, and breathe basketball and only strong women can survive in their male dominated world. Adultery, sex, and drugs are part of the game, and a lot of these women have self-esteem issues because they haven't adjusted to the reality of always living in the shadow of their men. Dealing with a ball player's ego takes a lot out of a person."

"In that respect, Paul is no different than any of the rest of them. My job is to make sure his feet stay firmly planted on the ground. I constantly remind him that no matter how much money he makes or how many women throw themselves at him that there is nothing out there better than what he has at home. You can support your man, but you also need to find interests you can pursue that have nothing to do with basketball. I audition for parts and act in community theatre, and when he's at home and not playing, Paul helps me rehearse and attends my plays."

"It sounds like you have a good man, Jojo."

"I do," she said, a little smugly. "And I make sure he knows that I know that. That's why I'm about blow the gig so I can get home and fill our Jacuzzi, chill some champagne, and get into the skimpiest bathing suit I own."

"You have a Jacuzzi?"

"Yes, Paul had to have one. It helps ease the pain of his sore muscles. I like it too because it's a wonderful way to relax. Most of the players on the team have one; I expect Vincent will, too."

I drove home with my mind totally occupied with all of the things Jonelle Danvers had said and her advice on how to survive in Brick's world. That, along with the call from Michael, was a lot to think about.

# Chapter 20

*Arianna*

I entered my apartment after work and picked up the ringing telephone.

"What'd ya cook?"

"Hello to you, too, Mr. Man, and how was your day?"

"Sorry," he said, then, "hello, baby girl. My day was fine. How was yours?"

"My day was busy, but fine."

"What'd ya cook?"

"Jace, where are you?"

"At the barracks. What did you cook, Arianna?"

"Nothing. Why?"

"Get up, woman, and throw something on the stove. I'm on my way home and I'm bringing company."

"Not tonight, you're not. I'm tired and I was hoping you'd take me out to dinner."

"Oh, but baby girl, please."

"What's going on, Alvin?"

"Well, me and some of the fellas were in class and got to talking. Just guy stuff and one of the fellas started saying how much he liked his woman's cooking and that she was the best cook in the world, and I...well, I opened my big mouth and started bragging on you. So you see, you have to help me out here. I'll never live it down if you don't."

"If you got yourself into this, why should I help you out of it?"

"Because I love you, and I promise I'll take you out to dinner tomorrow if you'll do this one favor for me."

He loves me? This was the very first time Alvin Barnes had said those words. Must be the stress. "How many?"

"Just three, plus you and me."

"Hold a sec." I went to the kitchen, opened the freezer, and examined the contents. Chicken, fast and quick. I pulled out two birds and returned to the phone. "Chicken okay?"

"Will you fry it?"

"Yes."

"She said yes, and we're having fried chicken," he said, but not to me. "What else?" This he asked of me.

"Potatoes."

"Mashed?"

"Yes, and I'll make gravy, too."

He relayed the message. "What kind of vegetables?"

"Broccoli and corn."

"Broccoli and corn," he said to his companions. "No broccoli," he said to me. "Bill doesn't like it."

"You tell Bill to go to hell."

"Sweetheart, I can't do that."

"Then ask Bill if he likes peas."

"He does," Jace said, after apparent confirmation. "Baby girl, will you make some biscuits, too?"

"Yes, I will."

"All right! Thanks, sweetheart, I'll be there in a little while with the guys."

"Jace, please give me as much time as you can."

"Will do. Bye, sweetheart."

He hung up and I stared at the receiver. He loves me, I thought. Then I quickly hung up the telephone. I couldn't stand there grinning like an idiot. Jace was probably already in the car and I had chicken to fry! I didn't bother changing my clothes. I didn't have time. I grabbed an apron and got busy. Just as I figured, about thirty minutes later I heard the key in the lock and groaned. I was nowhere near having dinner prepared.

"Sweetheart," Jace called. "Where are you?"

"In the kitchen."

"Have a seat," he told his friends. "I'll grab some beers and be right back."

He came around the corner, tall and handsome in those fatigues. I lifted my head for his kiss, a lengthy caress that pulled a moan from my mouth.

"Need some help in here?"

"Nope," I said

He opened the refrigerator, grabbed three beers, and took my hand. "Come meet the guys."

In the living room, he handed out the beers. The men stood up to greet me. "Parker, you already know."

I smiled at Parker, a dark-skinned, medium build man with a crooked nose that had been busted in a bar fight in Philly. Personally, I thought he was a bit goofy and not very mature for his age, but the man was Jace's best friend."

Jace then pointed to a short stubby man with red hair and freckles on his nose. "That's Bill, and… Sorry, man, what's your name again?"

"Trevor Lawson."

"Trevor." Jace ushered me forward. "This is my lady, Arianna Jackson."

"Hello. Please make yourself at home. Dinner's not quite ready."

"That's okay," Trevor said. "According to Alvin, it's sure to be worth the wait."

I cut my eyes to Jace. "May I see you in the bedroom for a moment, please?"

"Sure," he said with a broad smile. "Be back shortly, guys. I need to get out of these clothes."

In the bedroom, I rounded on Jace. "Alvin, you don't know those two men. Do you?"

"Not exactly," he said, chuckling.

"I thought so."

"What tipped it off?"

"For one thing, you don't know their names. Second, I've never seen them before and I've met all of your friends. Third, no one who knows you would ever use your first name. Fourth—"

He cut me off with a kiss. "Enough!"

"Where'd they come from, Jace?"

He walked around the room taking off his clothes as he explained. "Okay, here's what really happened. I was sitting in class listening to these guys complaining about the food in the mess. I thought about you, and how you're always making sure I'm fed. I felt sorry for them. They haven't had a home-cooked meal since they've been here, so I invited them to dinner."

He stopped and his front teeth began to gnaw on his bottom lip. He never did that unless he was very nervous. "How angry are you?"

"Come here." He walked into my arms. "You…are a very nice man, Jace Barnes." His hands roamed my backside. When they slipped around my waist and started to lift me, I backed away. "Not now, we have guests."

"Oh, yeah." He dropped a kiss on my forehead. "I'm taking a shower. Tell them I'll be out in a few."

I returned to the living room. "Jace will be out as soon as he changes."

"Can I help?"

I looked at Trevor Lawson. He stood as tall as Jace and had a solid build. He also had a devastating smile and with his dimpled cheeks and thickly lashed dark eyes, the boy was definitely a looker. "Yes," I said. "You can set the table."

Trevor turned out to be a blessing. He set the table and when he completed that chore, he picked up a knife and began peeling potatoes. He also made two pitchers of iced tea, all the while engaging me in conversation. He was a good helper and a surprisingly entertaining man. My laughter evidently concerned Jace because he kept appearing in the doorway and each time his face bore a scowl.

The fifth or sixth time he came, I stood on tiptoe so that I could whisper in his ear. "Everything is fine, baby, and you can stop worrying.

No one can take your place." That seemed to pacify Jace and he stayed in the living room with his other guests until dinner was on the table.

—*◦◦◦*—

That night, Jace was particularly tender as he sent my body up in flames. I hardly had a chance to catch my breath before he was at it again. Finally satisfies, he rolled over to his back. I snuggled closer and laid my head on his chest.

"Thank you," he said, "for tonight."

"You're welcome." I closed my eyes and listened to the sound of his heartbeat. A long time of quiet passed, then...

"Arianna?"

"Yes, baby."

"I love you."

I didn't respond. I couldn't. Twice, and in the same day, this man had said that he loved me. Yes! I wanted to jump up and dance. Then, no, I thought. It couldn't possibly be true, and I began listing in my head all the reasons why I couldn't have heard what I thought I'd heard. My heart began to race. He had said the words and all I could do was pray that they were true.

He scooted down until his face was directly across from mine. "Why are you crying?"

"I'm not," I said.

His forefinger traced a trail of wetness on my face. "Yes, you are, baby girl. Now tell me why?"

"Because I love you, too."

Jace took me in his arms. "I knew it," he whispered heavily. "But Ari, why did it take you so long to tell me?"

"I don't know, Jace. I-I was afraid, I guess."

"But why? I've done everything I can think of to make you happy."

"And you have. It's just that when I think about my parents and how they ended up, I mean, I can't even imagine that the two of them were ever in love, but they must have been once, right?"

"Your parents don't have anything to do with us. What we have is special and there is nothing, baby girl, absolutely nothing you could do that would ever make what I feel for you turn to hate. You're my heart, Arianna, and you'll have my love forever."

"But Jace, what if something happens and you change your mind?"

"I'm never going to change my mind and I hope that you won't ever change yours about loving me." He settled us both in the bed. "No matter what," he sort of whispered under his breath.

I thought about that for a moment. "Jace, what does that mean?"

"Nothing," he said, hugging me tighter. "Go to sleep, baby girl. I'll see you in the morning."

I waited until Jace had fallen asleep. Then I left the bed, got my journal, and went into the living room. For the first time ever, I had something good to write in it. Alvin Jace Barnes loves me! Now how 'bout that!

---

*Paige*

Two weeks had passed since my first date with Raymond. That night, he'd read to me for over an hour; then he'd turned on some music and sat through four ass-kickings before throwing up his hands in defeat and declaring me the queen of backgammon. When he helped me to my feet, I thought we were finally heading to his bedroom. Raymond kissed me on the forehead; told me he'd enjoyed our evening, and escorted me to the door.

I had put myself at risk to be with him and all I'd gotten for my trouble was a salad, some funky reading from a book, and a damn board game. It took two days for me to calm down. However, after thinking about it, I had to admit that honestly I hadn't even missed the sex. I had enjoyed spending time with Raymond. Since then, I'd seen him at least four times and we hadn't gone anywhere near his bedroom.

I picked up the next section of my presentation and turned to my word processor screen. Too many female employees were quitting, mostly due to sexual harassment at the hands of former officers, who thought that they were gods. Sexual harassment in the workplace was a hot button issue in the women's rights movement and there was a push to get the Equal Rights Amendment passed by Congress. Unfortunately, the military held itself above the law in such matters. Since none of the others in my department were willing to put their careers at risk by volunteering to tackle the problem, my boss had assigned the task to the lone black employee in human resources—me. I had eagerly accepted the assignment because I would finally be able to show these bigoted bastards what I could do.

Twenty minutes later, I deleted the document and sat back in my chair. I didn't know what had made me think that I was going to be able to concentrate on this presentation when what I really wanted was to be with Raymond.

Arianna plopped into the chair next to my desk. "Hey," she said.

"Hey," I said.

"A new sandwich shop opened up on Cascade. Wanna go there for lunch?"

"I have an appointment." I was really seeing Raymond, but I wasn't ready to share that with Arianna or anyone else quite yet.

"Did you watch *Dallas* last Friday? Girl, that J.R. Ewing is something else. Can you believe what he—"

"Actually, I didn't get a chance to watch. I was out."

"Oh," Arianna said. A few seconds of quiet passed before she said, "Know something, Paige? You never did tell me why you needed my car to go around the corner a couple of weeks ago."

Arianna was correct; I hadn't told her. I'd meant to, but then I'd decided that Raymond was my special secret and one I wanted to savor for a while longer. "How is Mr. Barnes doing these days?"

Arianna quirked her lips. "Jace is fine, and you can change the subject if you want, but I'll find out who he is eventually."

"What makes you think it's a man?"

"Paige, you came to my house smelling all fine and dressed to the nines. You asked me to lie to Lewis, you have no clue what's happening on *Dallas*, and now you're gonna try to play it off like it wasn't for a man. Girlfriend, please. What's his name?"

"Raymond." My friends knew me too damn well. "Raymond Steward."

"What does Raymond Steward do for a living?"

"He's an architect, and Arianna, the man is so fine, I could sit and stare at him all day. He's intelligent and centered, too. But I think what I like best about him is that he treats me like a lady."

"You are a lady, Paige, so I don't know why you shouldn't expect to be treated like one."

"I don't know either." But I really did. For a while now, I'd been feeling the need to unburden myself and that little voice had been telling me that I could tell my friends anything and that they would continue to love me. However, like most folks, I had learned to tune out the sound of that voice.

Revealing the true me, even to my girls who I was sure, well, almost sure, wouldn't sit in judgment of me was scary. But now that inner voice was shouting at me, telling me to climb off that sturdy limb of secrecy and lies and let the chips fall where they may.

No way could I take that kind of plunge, but maybe I could test the waters a little. "Ari, remember last Christmas when I told you and Jazz that Pierce gave me this ankle bracelet?" I stuck out my leg to emphasize my point. "He didn't. I bought this for myself. Pierce gave me a blender. I spent over a year of my life with that man and that's all he could figure out to give me and he didn't even remember my birthday."

Confusion marred her face. "Why would you lie to us? We wouldn't have cared about something like that."

"I know," I said wearily, "but I cared. Men give the two of you presents all the time. Brick took Jazmin on a shopping spree and gave her a diamond ring after they spent one day together. Jace constantly brings you flowers for no reason, and that bracelet with his name on your wrist is diamonds and gold. I've been involved with a lot of men and not one of them, including Lewis, has ever thought to romance me the way Brick does Jazz or the way Jace romances you. And while I was always happy for you and for Jazmin, do you have any idea how it makes me feel?"

"Paige, I never thought about it. Otherwise—"

"Wait, I'm not finished." I pulled out my two bears and the tape recorder, along with the wine and candy. The flowers were long gone.

When I hit the play button on the recorder, Arianna's face scrunched into a frown.

"What is that?"

"Raymond trying to sing to me."

"I hate to say this, P., but it's a good thing that man's an architect because his singing leaves much to be desired."

"I think he sounds wonderful." I hit the stop button and I put my gifts back into my desk drawer. "I listen to that tape at least twice a day. He also sent me three dozen roses and you know what else? Ray reads to me."

"He reads to you?" Arianna was looking at me with real skepticism.

"Yes, girl. That's how our dates end. I curl up in Ray's lap and he reads to me."

Arianna sat up in the chair. "So, you think he could be the one?"

"I don't know, Ari. The first night I met him, it was my usual MO. We danced; we drank; and we ended up in his bedroom. Since then, he hasn't taken me to bed once. Do you think that means something?"

"I don't know; it might. What do you think?"

I considered that for a moment. "Ari, remember when you told me how special and wonderful Jace made you feel and that even though you knew you were risking our friendship, you couldn't give him up?"

"Yeah, I remember saying something like that," she murmured.

"That's how Raymond makes me feel. I mean, I know I have Lewis and that I should stop seeing Ray, but I can't. But then I don't want to give up Lewis either."

"I don't know what to tell you, P. You know I've always been a one man at a time woman. Even if I wanted more than one, Jace takes up so much of me, I don't think I'd have the energy. All I can say to you is be careful. Lewis is kind of laid back, but the man *is* living with you and I think that eventually he's going to want to know why you're leaving the crib at night."

I knew I needed to choose, but how could I when both men were equally good in their own way? This was getting to be too much. How had I let Raymond go from a simple one-night stand to being a real complication in my life?

However, I didn't think about that as I left the building and climbed inside Raymond's car or at the restaurant where we had lunch. Or on Saturday night when in the middle of a fierce debate of the author's intentions in writing the novel, Raymond had suddenly pulled me into his arms and kissed my mouth like a man dying of thirst. Or when he lifted me in his arms and took me into his bedroom where he took me on a two-hour excursion that left my mind reeling.

# THE PAST

# WINTER, 1979

# BUMPS IN THE ROAD

# Chapter 21

*Arianna*

On Thanksgiving morning, Jazmin arrived early, as she'd promised. Jace and I were hosting the holiday dinner and since Brick had a road game, she'd volunteered to help me cook. As I slid my turkey out of the oven, she placed her already done turkey on the table and began helping prepare the rest of the food. As we worked, I could tell she was preoccupied, but figured she was missing Brick.

"Arianna, what would you say if I told you that I was thinking about modeling again?"

"I would say go for it." I was pouring pumpkin pie mix into shells and I assumed she was talking about doing something at the department store where she worked.

"But I'm so old."

"Jazz, you're twenty-five. By most standards, that's not considered anywhere near old."

"In the modeling world it is, but when I sent Michael my picture, he said that he thought I still looked pretty much the same as I did when I was nineteen."

"Who is Michael?"

"Michael Peters. He's the reason I started modeling in the first place. He has his own agency now and he wants me to come to New York to talk about getting into the business again."

New York? "What about Brick?"

Jazmin walked out of the kitchen and sat at the dining room table. "Brick's the reason I can't go."

I joined her. "You love him, don't you?"

She shook her head in denial, and then covered her face with her hands. "Yes," she said, through her fingers. "I don't even know how it happened, Ari. Six months ago, I hated this place and I was seriously thinking about moving back home, and then I met Vincent and nothing's been the same since."

I know exactly what you mean, I thought. "Have you told him how you feel?"

"No," she said in exasperation. "I'm afraid to tell him. Arianna, Mommy just got married for the sixth time and now she's back in New York. Not one of her marriages has lasted longer than three years. I've always told myself that I wasn't anything like my mother, that when I got married it would be for life. But what if it turns out that I'm exactly like her, Ari? I didn't want to fall in love with Vincent because I don't think I know what it takes to hold on to a man."

"You are not anything like the General. For one thing, you're a lot nicer person, no matter how bad ass you think you are." She chuckled. "Jazmin, up until a few weeks ago, I was standing exactly where you are now. I wasn't sure how or when it happened either, but I fell in love with Jace and I was afraid to tell him, too. I don't know," I said, leaving my chair to finish my pies. "I think it was because of my parents. I mean, it only makes sense that they must have been in love once, but I don't think two people ever ended up hating each other more. I was afraid, and honestly, I'm still afraid that Jace and I will end up like the two of them. I try not to think about that, though. I love Jace and I told him. But this has to be your decision and only you will know when the time is right."

"But *how* will I know when the time is right?"

"Jazz, I don't know a thing more about love than you do. I'm feeling my way through this and trying to take tiny steps so that if something happens, hopefully I won't be too tangled up to find an exit."

"I thought you said that you loved Jace. If that's true, then why would you be looking for a reason to leave him?"

"I do love Jace. But his love is so intense sometimes it's a little stifling and in the back of my mind, there is this little voice warning me to be careful. Jace hasn't said it in words, but I know he wants nothing less than total and complete devotion from me, and he knows I'm trying to hold back on him. Lately, he's been pressuring me to quit my job. I'm not going to, because I'm trying to hang on to something of me so that I won't be totally dependent on him. But the longer I'm with him, the quieter the voice gets, and day by day, I feel myself giving more and more of me to Jace."

"Wow, Ari, that's too deep for me to even think about at this point. It was only a few days ago that I even knew that I loved Vincent Marks. Now I gotta work up the courage to tell him."

"I know, and you will. Quite honestly, I'm fighting a losing battle. Jace has already won the war and he knows it; he's just waiting for me to acknowledge his victory."

Jazmin chuckled. "If that man doesn't have an ego the size of Texas, I don't know who does."

"Guess you haven't taken a real good look at Vincent Marks, then."

"Yeah, I have," she sort of mumbled. "He and Jace seem to have a lot in common when it comes to that."

"Yeah, they do seem to, don't they?"

Jazmin started to respond, but Paige and Jessica swept into my apartment to help us finish the cooking.

Later that afternoon, there were so many people in my apartment that I thought the seams would split. The noise, the loud music, and the laugher had given me a headache, but Jace was happy playing host to our guests.

"Baby girl? Can you lift a couple of beers from the fridge for me?"

"Yep," I said, and headed for the kitchen. I got the two beers, turned around, and came face to face with Trevor Lawson.

"Hello, Arianna."

"Hello."

"I wanted to thank you again for the dinner. It was the best meal I've eaten since I left home."

"You're welcome. Would you move please? Jace is waiting on these."

Trevor moved, but he came in my direction and before I could react, he'd covered my mouth with his.

## A Request for Closure

I stared at the floor. "You shouldn't have done that, Trevor."

"I couldn't help myself and I'm not going to apologize. I think you're a beautiful woman and I also believe that you're a beautiful person, too. I only wish that I'd met you first." Trevor stepped even closer and I moved back until I hit the wall.

"Please don't," I said, evading another of his kisses.

He placed his hands on the wall behind me. "Arianna, I understand that you're Jace's woman now. My assignment here was temporary, but in a few months, I'm coming back to Colorado and you should know that I'm going to do everything I can to take his place."

I didn't know what this man was thinking to come up in my house and say this kind of stuff to me, and I didn't stick around to hear anymore. I ducked under Trevor's arm and left the kitchen. I took the beers to Jace. He pulled me down on his lap and examined my face. Then he kissed my lips so hard they felt bruised when we parted. When the last of our guests left that night, Jace left, too.

——————

The change in Alvin Barnes happened overnight; at least it seemed that way to me. The next day, Jace was gone when I woke up and he didn't return until late that night. As the week progressed, a distance developed between us and widened with each passing day.

His spontaneous kisses and hugs stopped; his daily calls to the office dwindled from five or six to one. He stopped coming home directly after work, and when he did finally make it in, I could tell that he'd been drinking. If I said anything about it, Jace would sling an insult that was intended to hurt. It did.

I didn't understand how Jace could treat me so badly when the passion in our bed was still there as hot and exhilarating as it had always been. Only there was no longer any talking and cuddling afterwards. Jace took what he needed from my body, then moved away from me and went to sleep. In the space of a few days, we'd lost our ability to communicate and I began to see shades of my parents in the two of us.

The following week, he became even more surly and moody. Since I couldn't talk to him about it, I wrote in my journal. I spent hours writing and reviewing our relationship, looking for something that I might have done to set our current situation in motion.

I refused to consider the possibility that Jace was trying to end our relationship. I was in too deep and the man had sole possession of my heart. If Jace ever left me, I wasn't sure what I would do, but I knew that the pain of losing him would hurt worse than any I'd ever felt in my life.

By the third week, I'd had enough. Jace hadn't come home all weekend, hadn't called, and I didn't care what the problem was anymore. If the boy wanted to leave, I'd help him pack his bags. Not feeling well, that night I curled up with a blanket and a pillow on the couch. I was on my way to dreamland when the front door suddenly swung open and crashed against the wall. Jace entered and slammed the door. I jumped up and backed away as he stalked across the floor. I'd never been so scared in my life.

"Jace, what's wrong!"

He stopped in front of me. "How long have you been seeing him, Arianna!"

I dropped to the chair behind me. "I don't know what you're talking about."

His hand curled into a fist. My mother's face flashed before my eyes and I tensed. His hand didn't move and when I tried to rise, he dropped to his knees and laid his head in my lap.

"What did he do that I haven't done for you, Arianna? Tell me and I promise I'll do it."

"Alvin, what are you talking about?"

He pushed himself to his feet. "Trevor," he mumbled, shrugging out of his wet trench coat.

"Trevor? Trevor Lawson?"

## A Request for Closure

Jace went to the couch and fell down. "I saw that Nigga pushing up on you and if the two of you think it's going down like that, then both of you are crazy!"

"Jace, Trevor is a lonely man who stole a kiss. It meant nothing, at least not to me."

He leveled a glare at me. "I'm not a fool, Arianna, so don't try to play me like one. That jive ass Nigga stepped up in my house and dissed me in front of my lady. That muthafucka's checked if he comes anywhere near you again."

I opened my mouth but nothing came out. Alvin Barnes was the biggest idiot walking the face of the earth. Finally, I found my voice. "Is that what this has been about, Alvin? You've been treating me like shit over some man I didn't even know until you brought him in this house."

Jace acted as if he didn't hear that. "I've been looking for that Nigga since Thanksgiving. I found out tonight that he shipped out." He grabbed my arm and pulled me over to the couch. "He's gone, Arianna, and I'm letting you know right now that it better not happen again!"

"I can't control what these men do, Alvin, and you should know me well enough to know that I could never be with two men at the same time." When I stood, he pulled me back down. "Let me up. I need to go to the bathroom." He followed. I closed the door and turned the lock.

I sat on top of the toilet lid. Is this how it had started with my parents? Some trifling misunderstanding that had blown up to the point where neither of them even knew what they were fighting about anymore?

Jace rattled the knob. "Sweetheart? Baby girl, I'm sorry for how I treated you." He rattled the knob. "Arianna, open the door."

I didn't want to talk to him. I didn't want to see him, and I didn't want to do this anymore; not with Jace, not with anyone. I folded my arms on the counter and laid my aching head down. I must have fallen asleep because when I opened my eyes, Jace was holding me. His kisses on my face nearly smothered me and the more I struggled, the tighter he held on. "I'm sorry," he kept saying. I didn't want to hear it and the more he said it, the angrier I got.

"Arianna, I'm sorry. Please forgive me, sweetheart."

He lifted me, took us into the bedroom, and sat on the end of the bed. His hands released the top button on my blouse. I stilled their movement. He placed his lips on mine.

"I need you to forgive me," he whispered while teasing his lips along my mouth.

I began to thaw.

Jace took advantage and lowered me to the bed. His hands began their roving; his mouth its journey. Soon my shirt and bra were gone. I tried to resist him, but too many months of loving this man had trained my body to respond. What he'd done—his treatment of me—no longer mattered. The only thing that mattered was that Jace cool the heat his lips and hands had ignited.

—*∞*—

*Jazmin*

I was supposed to be studying but I kept glancing at the clock on the nightstand. Brick should have been back in Colorado by now and I was waiting for the phone to ring. Tomorrow night, they were playing the Knicks at McNichols Arena, and I would be in the stands with the other wives, fiancées, and girlfriends.

I'd spent the entire week thinking, thinking so much my brain hurt. Talking to Arianna and Jonelle, but mostly Arianna, had really helped me put things in perspective. Jonelle knew what it took to be the wife of a professional sports athlete, and while I valued that information, Arianna knew me, and she understood my anxiety about Brick because she shared the same fear about Jace. For Arianna, love had been something to avoid; for me, it had been a roll in the hay and a kiss goodbye. Both of us had grown up in violent households with no role models to teach us anything about love and neither of us really knew what constituted a healthy relationship.

My girl had taken the leap anyway. Arianna had told Jace that she loved him and she was happy. Tomorrow night, as soon that buzzer sounded ending the game, I was to going find Vincent Marks and claim my happiness, too.

"Jazzy! I'm home!"

I threw my textbook down and ran out of the bedroom.

"Stop," Brick said. "It's been a long trip and I want to look at you, girl."

He'd been gone for ten days and I let him look his fill while I did the same. "I thought you were staying in Denver tonight because of the game tomorrow. Don't you have to report for practice in the morning?"

He crossed the room. "Yeah, but I didn't want to go one more night without you, Jazzy. I came to get you. There's a car waiting downstairs."

I didn't even have to think about that. "Let me pack a bag and I'll be ready to go."

—⁓—

We'd been in the limousine for about thirty minutes when Brick finally let me up for air. He poured a glass of champagne and handed it to me. "Jazzy, I want to throw a party."

I took the glass and Brick put his arms around me again. "A party, why?"

"I need a break and I want to have some fun before we gear up for the rest of the season. You know how much I love playing ball, but I'm with the team every single day. If we're not practicing, then we're in an arena with thousands of people screaming at us."

That kind of made sense. "When do you want to have this party?"

"Let me see. We have six games before the end of the year, but I'm off on Christmas and our last game is on the twenty-ninth. I'm thinking about New Year's Eve. I'm sure I can get one of the hotels to rent out a ballroom and they can cater it, too. It's kind of late notice, but if I take care of everything else, can you get Paige and Arianna to help you make some calls?"

"I can do that. What about your teammates? Do you want me to call them, too?"

"Nope. I see those fellas every day. But I will talk to David and Paul."

"Brick, I need to tell you something."

"What, Jazzy-girl?"

I took a deep breath. It was now or never. "I don't have a problem with throwing a party and I think it's great that we'll be celebrating New Year's together." My heart started racing and I had to stop. How in the world had Arianna gotten through this?

*Just tell him*, Mags said.

I stared at the tinted panel in front of me. "Brick, I love you and I think this party should also be our official engagement party."

I never should have said anything, I thought, when several minutes ticked off the clock and Brick didn't respond.

"You forgot to say…more than life itself, Jazmin Reed."

I swiveled my head. "What?"

He sat forward and ran both hands over his face. "You didn't look me in the eye and you forgot to say that you love me more than life itself."

"Brick," I said, moving back into his open arms.

He turned on one of the overhead lights. "Let me hear it again, Jazzy-girl."

This time I looked deeply into his eyes, so deep that I felt as if I could see into his soul. "Vincent Marks, I love you more than life itself and I want our party to also be a celebration of our official engagement."

Brick hugged me tight. "Thank you, Jazmin. I love you more than life itself, too. And you'll have my heart forever."

For a few minutes, we held on to each other. Then Brick kissed me and sat back.

"Now that that's out of the way, we need to get back to discussing the plans for our party…unless you have a problem with that."

"No. I don't have a problem with that."

# Chapter 22

*Paige*

W hen are you going to open up to me, Paige? We've been seeing each other for weeks and I don't know any more about you than when we first met."

I set my wineglass on the table and tried not to appear nervous. Raymond was badgering me for information that I couldn't give him. "Raymond, you know I have a daughter, you know what I do for a living, and you know that I like you. What else do you need to know?"

"How old are you, Paige?"

"Twenty-three."

"What is your daughter's name?"

"Jessica, and she's five."

"Where is Jessica's father?"

"In California?"

"Does she ever see him?"

"No. Are we through playing twenty-one questions now?"

"Why can't I meet Jessica?"

I did like him, but Raymond was getting way more serious about this relationship than I was at this point, because I was still at an impasse over who I wanted more: him or Lewis. "Because."

"Because why, Paige? Jessica is a part of you, and I want to know everything about you."

"Jessie is young and very impressionable. I don't bring men to my house because I don't want my daughter to get attached to someone who may not be around very long."

He sat back and exhaled. "Is that what you think, Paige? That I won't be around long?"

I scrutinized his face. "I don't know, will you?"

"I don't know where this relationship is going, Paige. I do know that I've been sensing hesitation on your part. It's almost as if you don't trust me, as if you don't want me to know anything about you. I don't believe I've done anything that should make you feel that way about me and I've been more than open with you."

Raymond had been open with me. He was twenty-nine. His birthday was in March and he liked to travel, play basketball and tennis. He was an avid reader and a chess master. He'd grown up in St. Louis and had attended the University of New Mexico's school of architecture and planning. He'd never been married, had no children, and had been seriously involved with only two other women.

His parents still lived in St. Louis and his only sister was married with two children and lived in Colorado Springs. He was intelligent, handsome, and knew how to drive a woman wild in the bedroom. Any woman would be lucky to have Raymond Steward in her life. I was not that woman.

I pushed back my chair and stood. "Raymond, I've enjoyed the time we've spent together, but why don't we end this now?"

He stood, too. "No, Paige. I told you once that I wouldn't let you walk away from me. All I'm asking is that you talk to me and tell me about yourself."

"Don't you get it yet? I can't."

"Are you married, Paige?"

"No, Raymond." Two times one is two, I thought, trying to locate my purse through the blur in my eyes.

He embraced me. "Precious, just talk to me."

I looked up and Raymond chuckled. "Don't laugh at me," I murmured.

"But your face looks like a fudge-striped cookie." He chuckled again as he pulled a handkerchief from his pocket and wiped the mascara from my cheeks. "I'm sorry, Paige. Here, let's go to the couch." Raymond sat me down. "I'll be right back, and don't you dare try to leave."

I knew this was my chance to end this farce. Raymond was a decent man and he deserved to be with a decent woman who would be a lot more honest and forthright with him than I ever could. I knew I had to get out of his life, and yet I sat there on that couch.

"Paige, would you like more wine or something else?"

"Um, something else." I left the couch and stood in the kitchen doorway. "Rum and coke, if it isn't too much trouble."

"Nothing is too much trouble for you, precious. But aren't you supposed to be on the couch where I left you with specific instructions not to move?"

I tried to laugh at that. "Yes, but something you should know about me is that I have a really bad stubborn streak and I don't like people telling me what to do."

Raymond crossed the floor and hugged me so tight it lifted me off my feet. "See, that wasn't so hard, was it?"

"No, it wasn't."

"Okay. I'm not going to push you anymore tonight. When you feel up to sharing something else, let me know. Deal?"

"Deal," I said.

"Why don't you go and get our book. I'll be out in a minute."

I returned to the living room. I pulled *Lady Chatterley's Lover* from the shelf and sat on the couch to wait for Raymond. I took the glass from his hand when he returned. "What are we going to read when we finish this book? We're on the last two chapters."

"I don't know yet, precious, but I'll find something for us."

"I think I'd like to choose the next one, Ray."

"That's fine with me," he said as I made myself comfortable in his lap. I guess I had already made up my mind about Raymond. I needed to give him up, but I also knew there was no way that I could. The book I had in mind was a lengthy novel and a classic I would get nothing out of except the thrill of hearing his voice. It wasn't one he had because I'd already checked. By my calculations, Leo Tolstoy's *War and Peace* would take Raymond and me well into another year together.

—❧—

Lewis's car pulled up outside and Jessica ran out of the house. I watched the two of them through the open patio door. She lifted her arms and he picked her up. He wiped away the crocodile tears running down her face.

"What's the matter, sunshine?"

"Paige says I can't help decorate the Christmas tree."

"How come?"

"She said it's her tree…and it's ugly."

Lewis rubbed her back soothingly. "Oh, it can't be that bad."

"It is. It's ugly! There's no lights on it."

"No lights?" His brow wrinkled. "What did she put on it?"

"Ugly red bows."

"What else?"

"Nothing! Just ugly red bows."

Lewis slid the screen open, walked inside, and set Jessie down. "You've got to be kidding."

"See," Jessie said, pointing. "I told you it was ugly."

"Why don't you go outside and play," I said, turning to Lewis. "What do you think?"

He walked around the tree very slowly, taking time to view it from every possible angle. "I agree with Jessie. This thing is ugly."

"Well, I don't care what either of you think," I said with a huff. "I like it."

"You can't be serious, P. Where are the lights?"

I began picking up the boxes. "There are no lights."

He followed me into the kitchen. "What about the colored balls? The tinsel?"

"We ain't having none of that either. This is my tree. I wanted red bows and that's what I got."

"Surely you can put one string of lights on it for Jessie."

"No. I think it's pretty the way it is."

"Christmas is for kids, Paige! What's Jessie supposed to do with that thing?"

"She can look at it."

## A Request for Closure

"This is pathetic, Paige, and I'm not going to let you do this." He went over to Jessie. "Sunshine, go outside and play for a little while."

She sniffed. "But the Christmas tree—"

Lewis hugged her to him. "Don't you worry about the tree. Daddy's going to take care of it."

Daddy? My heart jumped in my chest. When had their relationship developed into a father-daughter union? Where was I when it happened? But I already knew. While I was out trippin' with Raymond, Lewis had been at home with Jessie.

"Can I go see Auntie Ari and Uncle Jace?"

"Yes," he said, kissing her cheek.

"Okay," she said, happy again. Jessie skipped to the door. "I love you, Lewis. Bye, Paige."

As soon as the door closed, Lewis went over to the tree and started yanking off the red bows and tossing them on the floor.

"What do you think you're doing!"

I grabbed his arm; he shook me off. When I came at him again, Lewis picked me up and dumped me on the couch.

He bent over me. "I am sick and tired of this shit, Paige Michaels, and it's time you grew up! Jessica is the child in this house, not you! You can't always have everything your way and I'm putting my foot down on this one. We're going to decorate this tree the way my daughter wants it decorated, and I don't give a damn how you feel about it!"

"You are not going to tell me what to do in my own house, Jermaine Lewis, and I certainly never gave you permission to tell my daughter that you're her daddy!"

"I don't need your permission. Jessie has been calling me Daddy for months, something you might have noticed if you were ever in this house! When she asked me if I would be her daddy, I told her yes, because Jessica needs someone around here who acts like an adult. Not a mother who only cares about herself and what she wants."

That accusation drew me up short. "I love my daughter, Lewis."

He sat beside me. "I never said you didn't, but you leave this house at least two nights a week and every weekend while I'm at home with Jessie. What did you think would happen?"

"I don't know. I guess I never thought about it."

He drew me into his arms. "Paige, I love you, but if we're going to be a family, I really need you to work with me and Jessie on this."

My head jerked up. "You love me?"

"Stay here; I'll be right back."

Lewis loved me? The words I had never heard from anyone except my daughter rolled around in my head. He'd said it, but I was having a hard time believing because deep down I knew that I didn't deserve his love.

I was selfish, and I did want to have everything my own way. And I didn't understand what was so wrong with that. I mean, wasn't that the way it was supposed to work when you moved out on your own and paid your own way? I took care of my daughter. Jessie had a roof over her head, food to eat, and she seemed to be doing just fine.

"I was going to wait to give this to you, but I want you to have it now."

I took the gaily-wrapped box. "What is it?"

"Your Christmas present," he said, sitting beside me again.

I pulled the gold ribbon, set the box on the table, and ripped off the bright red paper. When I opened the box, there was another box inside. "What is this, Lewis? A joke?"

"No, open that one."

I removed the paper and found another box. "Lewis, how many of these are there?"

"I guess we'll know when you open the last one."

The sixth box was very small and Lewis took it from my hand. He tore off the paper, flipped the lid, and held it out in the palm of his hand.

The pear-shaped diamond sparkled; I felt faint.

"Paige, when Jessica asked me to be her daddy, I didn't really know how I felt about becoming a father. I told myself that I wasn't ready, that I had a lot of things to accomplish before I became anybody's father. On the other hand, I love that little girl and it would make me very happy if I could be in her life forever."

"You want to be Jessie's father?"

"Yes, and I want to be her mother's husband, too." Lewis slipped from the couch and knelt in front of me. "Paige Michaels, I love you. Will you please marry me?"

I stared at him, unable to comprehend what the man had said. Then it finally penetrated my brain. Jermaine Jacob Lewis had asked me to marry him!

"Yes," I screamed, right before I tackled him to the floor. I showered his face with kisses until Lewis caught my head between his hands. He kissed me long and hard before bumping me off his body. He seemed so pleased with himself.

"You want me to put this thing on you or not?"

Lewis took my quaking hand and slipped the ring on my finger. This was what I wanted. What I'd always wanted—a man who would love me enough to marry me and be a father to my daughter. I jumped on Lewis again. When we finally left the floor and headed for the bedroom, the boy wasn't wearing a stitch of clothing.

# Chapter 23

*Jazmin*

To celebrate New Year's Eve, Brick found a hotel in Manitou Springs, a picturesque, mountain town that sat at the foot of Pikes Peak. He'd booked all of the rooms, reasoning that he didn't want anyone driving home drunk and had arranged a full day of activities for January 1, including a trip up the mountain on the Pikes Peak Cog Railway.

That night, the ballroom held a festive air; colorful streamers and balloons hung from the ceiling. A local band played their rendition of the Funkedelics, "One Nation Under a Groove," and many of Brick's one hundred and fifty close and personal friends were into their own groove on the dance floor. Others helped themselves from the platters of food set out on buffet tables along one of the walls, while some held up the bar on the other side of the room. The rest were socializing at round, white-clothed tables covered with confetti, hats and blowers, and silver buckets holding champagne. The party was jammin' and I scanned the room for my man, easily spotting him in a forest green tux signing a napkin for one of the guests.

I adjusted the shoulder pads on my gown and headed back to our table. The dress was jet black and made of jersey silk. It had long fitted sleeves, and a serious toga wrap, piped in green, draped over my left shoulder. I'd styled my hair into a French twist with curling strands framing my face. Except for my ring and the diamond studs Brick had given to me for Christmas, I wore no other jewelry.

Strong arms surrounded my waist. "We did good, Jazzy-girl."

Brick kissed the side of my mouth, taking it fully when I rested against him and twisted my head to reach him.

## A Request for Closure

"You two need to take that shit up to your room," Paige said with a chuckle.

Girlfriend was looking seriously tough in a hot pink, floor-length gown made of a fine crepe covered in sheer pink chiffon that exposed her shoulders. I'd lent her my rhinestone jewelry and styled her hair into finger waves. Sitting next to her, Lewis wore a standard black tux with a pink rosebud in the lapel.

"Leave them alone, P." Arianna said, looking as sultry and tempting as any sex siren, and clearly distracted as she returned the smile sent by the man at the table next to us. "Brick and Jazz are in love and there is nothing wrong with them showing how they feel about each other."

Jace wore a midnight blue tux, and the fierce expression on his face clearly indicated his irritation with Arianna, which was understandable since Arianna had been silently getting her flirt on with the man at the next table all night. She wore a vibrant, fire engine red gown that fell low in the back, dipped to reveal the surface of her breasts in the front, and was held in place only by the thinnest of spaghetti straps. Her hair was a mass of curls, and she wore gold hoops in her ears, her gold bracelet, and a marquis diamond, her Christmas present from Jace, around her neck.

My heart jumped when Jace grabbed her arm and though I knew he thought he was whispering, anger made his voice louder than he intended.

"I don't know what you think you're doing, Arianna Jackson, but I'm telling you right now, it had better stop!"

Disgust filled the glare she leveled at him. "You've got your nerve, Alvin Barnes. I'm not doing anything that you don't do."

This was about to turn ugly and I didn't want to see it go there, not between those two. They were supposed to be an example of how love was supposed to be, at least for me.

"Arianna, Jace. Come on, y'all, this is supposed to be a party."

The next thing I knew, Jace had jerked Arianna against his body, and only Brick's hand on my arm and the slight shake of his head kept me from moving.

"Stay out of it, Jazzy. It's between the two of them."

212

"That man practically has his dick out like he's ready to screw you on the table, Arianna. I'm your man and you'd better start acting as if you know that!"

She leaned back. "First of all, you're going to stop telling me what to do. I'm tired of it, Alvin, and of your jealousy."

The other couple at the table excused themselves and headed for the dance floor.

Seeing the astonished expression on everyone's face, Jace stood and pulled Arianna from the chair. I held my breath, waiting for him to lose his cool entirely.

"Let's dance," he said, and taking her hand, he led her off to the floor.

I looked at Paige; she answered with a shrug.

I sat and peeked up at Brick. "Baby, would you be so kind as to bring me a vodka tonic.

"No problem, Jazzy. You want anything, Paige?"

"I was just about to ask Lewis for a white wine."

He stood up. "Got it, honey. Be right back."

I waited until they were out of earshot. "What is Arianna doing?"

"She's pissed at Jace."

"Why?"

"Apparently, he hit the roof when she showed him the dress and ordered her to take it back to the store."

"No, he didn't."

"Yes, he did," she said. "Now I think Ari's trying to show him that he can't boss her around."

I rolled my eyes. "That's some silly shit she's pulling, and all I can say is that the girl better cool it. I don't think Jace Barnes is going to stand for much more of this."

"I think it's between the two of them. Jace needs to get his jealousy in check. If he doesn't, he's going to lose Arianna because our girl's gonna walk."

I sat back and observed the two of them. Jace had his face right in Arianna's, but my girl was giving it right back to him. Which was cool, I thought. The two of them could argue until the moon turned blue as long as Jace Barnes didn't put his hands on her. If he did, the man had better have an up-to-date life insurance policy, 'cause Paige and I would never sit still and allow nothin' like that to go down.

However, I did breathe a little easier when Jace kissed Arianna and pulled her close. I hoped that meant that all was right between them again. As much in love as I knew Jace and Arianna were, if those two couldn't make it, Brick and I didn't stand a chance.

Brick handed me my drink and a glass of champagne. "It's almost time," he said, taking my hand, and we joined the rest of the eager crowd counting the seconds until the official start of the new year.

Paige

"You and Jace okay?"

Arianna and I were on our way to the ladies' room. She seemed fine, but I needed to know for sure.

Her shoulders lifted in a nonchalant shrug. "We're fine, and he's already apologized for acting like a total jerk in front of everybody."

I chuckled. "He did make an ass of himself, didn't he? Then again, you were egging him on a little bit."

"I know, but I'm tired of his jealous displays, P. And I was trying to show Jace that I was with him because I wanted to be with him, not because I had to be with him."

"The man loves you, Arianna."

"And that's supposed to make up for his behavior?" She folded her arms over her chest. "It's so ridiculous, P. I've been living with Jace Barnes for months. The man has to know that I love him. I don't understand where his jealousy comes from, and tonight I told him that if he didn't check it, he wouldn't have anything to be jealous about because I was going to be done."

Listening to Arianna voice the same sentiment that I had earlier was a little haunting. "Hopefully he got the message this time."

"I hope so, because I'm not putting up with it anymore."

"Yeah, right. Like you're going to walk on Alvin Barnes. That man has you heart, body, and soul. You aren't going anywhere, Ari."

"You're probably right about that, too. I do love Jace, and other than these temporary bouts of insanity, the man is incredible. However, he needs to understand that I won't put up with his jealous temper anymore, and I *do* mean that."

"I hear you, girl. But I also know Jace Barnes and...well, you be careful, Ari."

"Don't worry, I will," she said, pushing on the door of the bathroom. "Paige?"

I whirled around. No, no, no, I thought. What is he doing here? When Raymond moved in my direction, I quickly hid my hands behind my back.

Arianna touched my arm. "Is that Ray?" Her voice sounded as if she were in awe.

"Yes," I whispered.

"He's very handsome."

"I know. I need to talk to him."

"But Paige, Lewis is here. What are you going to tell him?"

"I don't know yet. But go on, I'll meet you in the bathroom in a minute." When she entered, I slipped my ring from my finger and into my purse. Then I quickly headed for Raymond. "Hi," I said when I reached him.

"Happy New Year, precious. You look lovely this evening."

"Happy New Year and thank you."

A silence rose between us while we stared at each other. Raymond's attire was almost entirely black, black three-piece suit, black shirt, and black shoes, but the tie around his neck was startling white as well as the carnation he wore in the lapel. Because I'd accepted Lewis's proposal, I hadn't seen Raymond in two weeks. Seeing him now, my heart beat so fast I thought it would break through my chest.

"I didn't know you'd be here, Paige. When Brick called about this party—"

A curtain of panic fell over me. "You know Vincent Marks?"

"Vincent and I shared a dorm room at college."

No, no, no, I thought. This could not happen. Sleeping with Raymond was one thing, but knowing the same people was out of the question. Now it was too, too close to home.

"I tried to get in touch with you all week," he said. "I wanted to give you your Christmas present and ask if you'd attend this thing with me." Then he looked somewhat downhearted. "How was your Christmas, Paige?"

"It was wonderful, and yours?"

"I had dinner with my sister and her family. It was okay, but it could have been better."

"That's nice." I knew where he was going and it was a conversation I didn't want to have. I stepped around him. "Have a good time, Ray."

He put his hand on my arm. "I wanted to spend Christmas and ring in New Year's with you, precious."

"I have to get back, Ray."

He stood so close that I could feel the heat of his body. "I know. I saw him. Is he the reason you're so distant with me?"

I didn't have an answer. What was I supposed to tell this gorgeous, generous, and patient man? I couldn't tell him that while I was sleeping with him, the man I was going to marry was sitting at home with my child waiting for me.

"Come outside with me for a minute."

"No. I have to go."

"This will only take a minute, Paige. You owe me that at least."

He was right, except that I owed him much more. At the very least, I owed him an explanation. Only I wasn't sure I would be able to give him one. "Okay," I said.

Raymond took my arm. Outside the club, he pulled me to him and I couldn't stop myself from returning his quiet kiss. He started to lift his mouth from mine, but as if unable to stop kissing me, he increased the pressure on my lips and I opened my mouth. Raymond plunged his tongue inside and the duel he initiated was so intimate and so passionate the core of my being flooded with longing. I wanted this man. I needed this man, and in that moment, I didn't care about anyone or anything else.

He dragged his mouth away, pulled me deeper into his embrace, and pressed my head to his chest. "Precious, please. You have to tell me what's going here." Raymond sounded breathless.

I wanted to cry. How could I explain anything to Raymond, when I didn't even know myself? I was wearing one man's ring and I wanted another so much my heart hurt.

Raymond pushed back from me. "How serious are you about him, Paige?"

I didn't answer; I couldn't.

"Precious, please talk to me. I have to know before I get into this any deeper than I already am."

I hung my head. "I don't know."

Raymond sighed in frustration. "Okay, Paige. But my heart is on the line here. I can't and I won't continue to invest my feelings in you when you aren't willing to do the same with me."

"B-but, Raymond—"

He held up his hand. "No buts, Paige. Until you can come to me, free from whatever it is that's holding you back, I don't want to see you anymore."

This time, Raymond was the one who walked away and all I could do was stand there. One times one is one, I thought, watching him leave and feeling more miserable than I'd ever felt in my life.

———

*Jazmin*

About the middle of January, I went to my door and froze when I saw who was on the other side.

"Hello, Jazmin."

"W-what are you doing here?"

"Shut your mouth, Jazz, and invite me in."

217

## A Request for Closure

"Of course," I said, stepping back. "But Michael, what are you doing here?"

He unwound the red scarf around his neck and shrugged out of a black, snow-covered mohair coat. He handed both to me. Underneath, he sported a pair of black corduroy pants and a black wool, turtleneck sweater. "It's cold as a witch's behind out there. According to my pilot, you guys are having a blizzard."

"Yes, I know," I said, closing the door. "That's why I'm here in my house like any other sane person would be."

Michael moved to the couch. He was a tall, slender-built man with an athletically toned frame. "Aren't you going to offer me something to drink, Jazmin? I need something to warm these bones of mine."

"Would you like a cup of cocoa?"

Michael's eyebrows rose. "Girl, who are you talking to? What the fuck am I supposed to do with a cup of cocoa?"

"You might try drinking it."

Michael looked at me as if I'd gone stupid. "Come on, Jazz. Quit messin' around and share that vodka that I know you have stashed somewhere in this place. Nice digs, by the way."

I didn't bother to respond and went into the kitchen. I could hardly believe that Michael Peters was here, in the flesh, sitting in my living room. I'd called him two months ago about the fashion show and he'd seemed to accept my decision. At least he hadn't come back with his usual flap.

This gig had to be big for him to jump on a plane and fly into a blizzard to see me. I returned to the living room and handed him a tall glass of ice and the bottle of vodka. He poured the glass full and took a generous swallow.

"All right," he said on a deep sigh. "I'm feeling better already. Y'all got enough snow in this state to kick a grown man's ass. All I need now is some herb and I'll be good as new."

I went into the bedroom and brought him a joint, then sat on the opposite side of the couch. "Dammit, Mike! Are you going to tell me the reason you're here sometime today?"

His lids drifted down to hood his eyes. "Girl, you need to chill and quit ridin' this brotha's back. By the way, I see that you still have that sexy swag when you move. Once a model, always a model, I say." He tossed a smug smile at me and lit up.

With his curly blonde hair and blue-gray eyes, there wasn't a chance in hell that Michael Peters could be mistaken for anything other than what he was: a very handsome, white dude. He grew up in Brooklyn, in the Brownsville projects because his parents, who'd been passionately involved in the civil rights movement long before the sixties revved things up, had refused to leave when the rest of the whites abandoned the neighborhood faster than the blacks and Latinos could move in.

"Number one, you're cool and everything, Michael Peters, but you ain't no brotha. Number two, why are you here?" He offered the joint; I waved it away.

"Cool. More for me." He leaned forward with his arms on his thighs. "I'm here to change your mind about doing the show."

"What are you, hard of hearing all of a sudden? I told you that I'm not doing that show. So, if that's the only reason you're here, you can jet now."

"Come on, Jazz. Don't tear a brotha down before I've had a chance to build myself up. I heard you *say* that you didn't want to come to Paris, but I didn't quite catch the rhyme or the rationale."

"Then catch this." I held out my hand.

"Nice, but this can't be the only reason."

"True. The other is Vincent. Going with you would take me out of the country for at least two months. And it's not just the fall/winter collections in Paris; it's Milan and London and Toronto and New York."

"That's it?" Michael said, his voice full of incredulity. "You're gonna blow me off because your sports jock boyfriend might miss your ass for a minute! Damn, Jazz, I thought the two of us were tighter than that."

"We are tight, Mike, and I can never repay you for everything you did for me back in the day. But I'm not a model anymore, haven't been for a while, and I think I want to try something different. That something different is Brick."

## A Request for Closure

"What if I upped the ante to three thousand?" My face remained passive. "Five thousand then! Damn, girl, but you're twisting a brotha's arm. Now you've got me digging into my personal piggybank."

Michael was serious and my cheeks heated from the excitement; I wasn't Iman, Naomi, or Cheryl. My name was Jazz and this was a lot of money per show to be turning down, especially when my checking account had a lot fewer zeros in it.

As quickly as that thought came, another replaced it almost immediately. Having Brick Marks in my life was worth more than any amount of money. "I'm sorry, Michael, but the answer is still no. I can't believe you flew all the way here to offer me more money to do this show."

Michael left the couch and paced the floor. The joint dangled from his mouth as he ran both hands through his unruly curls. "Okay, Jazz. Here's the real deal. One of the designers specifically asked for you."

Though it wouldn't make a difference, I couldn't help wanting to know. "Who?"

"Dario."

"Dario! Are you talking about Dario Pantaka…the Dario Pantaka who, six years ago, set the world of fashion on its head…that Dario Pantaka?"

His lip inched up. "That would be the one."

"Michael, you've got to be kidding me!"

"I tried to tell the man that you were off the circuit, but Dario's hard-headed and won't listen."

"But how does he know about me when I haven't been on a runway in years?"

"Seems he saw you in a show a few years back and was so impressed with the way you moved that he designed his latest line with you in mind. I'm under orders to do whatever it takes to get you to Paris. Come on, babe. I gave you your break and I stood by your side throughout your entire career, short though it may have been. Jazz, you gotta help a brotha out here!"

Talk about twisting arms. Michael Peters was a master at it. Now he was calling in favors, and he'd thrown in Dario as an incentive to get me

220

to bite—Dario, the man who'd taken lace and leather and done things no one had thought possible. I glanced at Michael again, only to see that he'd pushed out his lips and was giving me his most pathetic puppy dog look. How could I turn him down when he'd been such a huge part of my success in New York? Then again, Brick had become a huge part of my life now, and I knew that he would never go for something like this. I blew out a deep breath. "Okay, Michael. I'll think about this again and—"

Michael came across the room and hugged me tight. "Thanks, Jazz. I knew I could count on my girl to have my back." He clapped his hands together. "Okay, we need to get you to New York—gotta get some comp cards done and some current head and body shots so they can throw them up on the wall and get your sizes to Dario."

"Wait a minute, Mike. I am not saying yes. I need to talk to Vincent and see where his head is about my doing something like this. The answer could still be no."

"I'm not worried about that, Jazz. You can convince a man to do anything; you always could. Just make sure you're in New York by the eighth."

"Michael, don't you dare commit me to doing any of these shows until you hear from me." He smiled slyly. "Michael, I mean it!"

"Got it, babe," he said, returning to the couch. "So, tell me—what is it that you like about this state so much that it makes you want to stay here instead of coming home?"

———

"You talk to him yet?"

"No, Michael. I told you that Brick is on the road and he won't be back in town until tonight."

"You know, Jazmin," he said, "there's this really cool invention that a lot of folks are into nowadays. It's called a telephone. Pick one up and call the brotha!"

## A *Request for Closure*

"I'm not doing that. This is a conversation I need to have with Brick in person." Michael had called every day since he'd left Colorado a week ago. It was a ploy to make sure that he stayed in the forefront of my mind. He needn't have bothered because I had been thinking of nothing else.

"I need an answer by the end of the week. I can't be waiting on you forever."

"Then don't wait."

"Come on, Jazz. Don't be like that."

"Michael, I'll call you when I've made a decision."

I hung up and sat for a minute. I really wanted to do this gig.

*Yeah, right,* Mags said. *You're not even trying to do this gig, girlie. If you did, you'd miss pretty boy Brick Marks way too much.*

I would miss Brick, terribly. Then again, basketball constantly took him away from me so it shouldn't make that much of a difference if I weren't here for a couple of months. Taking this job would mean that I would be able to pay for the rest of my schooling. It also meant that I would be able to put a substantial chunk of dough in the bank for my salon, things reiterated by Arianna and Paige who both thought that I should take advantage of the opportunity.

I got up and went back into the kitchen where I had been in the middle of preparing Brick's favorite dishes. The boy loved baked chicken and collard greens with a bowl of mashed potatoes and gravy on the side, and if cornbread came with it, Brick was in food heaven. I checked the bird, and then headed for my bedroom. If I was going to convince Brick to agree to this, I needed to find something soft and inviting to wear, but not too inviting or I'd never get the boy to listen to me.

A few hours later, Brick popped the last piece of cornbread into his mouth. "Jazzy-girl, that meal was slammin'. I'm going to be in the gym for days working work off these calories."

"Do you want anything else...more chicken, greens, or are you ready for dessert now?"

Brick studied me across the table. "I'm full, Jazzy. I couldn't eat another bite."

222

He dumped his napkin on the table and left his chair. When he stopped behind me, I tried to keep my heart from jiggling.

"Are you sure, 'cause there's peach cobbler in the kitchen."

"Yep. The meal was fine and so is the company. You're looking hot in that tube top and skirt, and I love it when you wear your hair like this. The candles are a nice touch, too." He took my hand and tugged me out of my chair. "Let's sit on the couch and snuggle, Jazzy, and you can tell me what it is you've been dying to talk to me about all night."

This man was so perceptive it amazed me. Here I thought I had played it cool all evening and Brick had read my act as soon as he entered the house.

"Brick," I said when we'd settled on the couch. "What would you say if I told you that I have an opportunity to model again?"

"I would say that's great, Jazmin, but I would like to know more about this opportunity."

I ruffled my fingers through my hair and tried to contain my excitement. "I can hardly believe this myself, but Michael wants to take me to Europe, Paris actually. He said that Dario Pantaka specifically requested me because he saw me in a show years ago and now the man's designed an entire line of clothes around me!"

"Who is Michael and who is Dario Pantaka?"

"Michael's an agent and the person who got me started in modeling. He used to work for Ford, but now he has his own agency and he wants me to go to Paris with him. Me! Can you believe that, Brick!"

"You're really excited about this, aren't you?"

"Yes. Dario is one of the top designers in the world. The man's clothes are hot and every model would give anything to be chosen to show off his collection."

"Then I think you should do it."

I stopped grinning like a nitwit. "There is a downside to this, though."

"And that would be?"

"I have to book a flight that will get me to New York by the eighth and I won't be home for about two months."

## A Request for Closure

I peeked at him. Brick was thinking about what I'd said, and I was anxious for his reaction.

"Two months?"

"Yeah. I need to get to New York for some photo shoots. We'd leave for Paris from there."

"The eighth, but that's only two weeks from today, Jazzy."

"I know. What do you think now?"

"I'd still have to support you, Jazmin. I want you to have everything your heart desires; and if this is something you want to do, then I'm behind you one hundred percent. But what about the wedding?"

I hadn't spared one thought for that wedding since Michael Peters stepped up in my house. I'd been too ecstatic over the prospect of going to Europe. "I'll concentrate on nothing but you and the wedding when I get back."

"Promise, Jazzy?"

"I promise, Brick."

"Okay then, Jazzy-girl. You go and do your thing. I'll be here when you come back home."

# Chapter 24

*Paige*

I'm telling Daddy!" Jessie screamed the words at me right before she ran out of the kitchen.

She slammed the door to her bedroom and I fought with myself not to go after her and whip her little butt. Jessie had wrecked the kitchen. She'd spilled flour all over the counter and small handprints marked the cabinet doors. Eggs she'd dropped spattered the floor and there was milk running down the side of the counter. I knew I shouldn't have yelled at her; she had been trying to do something nice for Lewis, and honestly, I hadn't been in the best of moods since Brick and Jazmin's New Year's Eve party.

It's going to be okay, I told myself for the hundredth or thousandth time. It had to be, and I had to make myself believe it. Otherwise, I might as well wither up and die. For the past month, I'd moved through life with all the enthusiasm of a slug. I was the shell of myself, a ghost walking around in a dark shadow, seeing life, but not really participating, and in the process, I had made life a living hell for Lewis and for Jessie.

And all of this was because of Raymond Steward. I missed Ray, and at this point, I was willing to do and say almost anything, if only he would see me again. I'd already called him so many times that I'd stopped counting and I did my best to mask the pain I felt each time he rejected me—as soon as Raymond heard my voice, he hung up the phone.

Two weeks ago, I'd showed up at his job. Raymond had taken one look at me and had gone back inside the building. Last Saturday, he wouldn't even open his door when I tried to tell him that I'd brought the next book for us. He'd told me to leave and walked away. I had stood there for ten minutes, even though I knew that he wasn't coming back. Talk about humiliating yourself for a man.

Lewis didn't know what to make of any of it and kept asking me what was wrong, if I was mad at him, if he could do anything to make it better. Now that was a question my seriously bruised ego couldn't answer.

I walked out of the kitchen and a whirlwind in the form of Jessie breezed by me. She'd heard Lewis pull up and wanted to get to him so that she could tell her side of the story first and gain his sympathy. I clucked my tongue against the roof of my mouth and went to sit on the couch.

"Hey, sunshine," he said to her when he entered.

"Daddy, Paige yelled at me again, and I didn't even do nothing."

"Do anything," he said as he picked her up.

I pointed to the kitchen.

"Did you make that mess in there, Jessie?"

She ducked her chin. "Mmm, hmmm."

"I don't think you should have done that, because now someone has to clean it up."

Her lips trembled. "But I was making a cake for you."

"A cake for me! Boy, I bet that would have tasted so good."

"Yeah," she said quietly. "And then Paige yelled at me and sent me to my room. Was I bad, Daddy?"

"No, sunshine. You weren't bad and that was a nice thing to try to do for me. But the next time, you should ask Mommy to help and then there won't be a mess."

"I'm sorry, Daddy. Will you help me clean it?"

"Yes, but first I want to talk to your mother. I'll come and get you when we're done."

He set her down and Jessie went back to her room. Their whole conversation made me want to throw up. Lewis clean the kitchen? Now that was joke. If that kitchen got cleaned, I was going to be the one doing it, because as far as I could tell, Jermaine Lewis had never scrubbed a dish in his life.

He dropped down beside me. "What's wrong, Paige?"

226

"Nothing."

"Something has to be wrong. You've been stomping around this house and coming down on Jessie and me for no reason I can think of since New Year's. When I ask, you don't seem to have a reason either."

Tears stung my eyes and I blinked them back. "I'm sorry."

"Don't be sorry; just tell me what's wrong. I can't help unless I know."

"Nothing's wrong."

Lewis sighed and stood. "I'm going to change and get Jessie. Then we'll get started cleaning up that kitchen. You in the mood to go out to dinner?"

I brightened a bit at that suggestion. It would certainly be a change from the norm and maybe I'd be able to get myself together enough to stop ragging on my family. "Yes, and I'll clean the kitchen, if you'll help Jessie get dressed."

"Okay," he said, and left the room.

Lewis had immediately jumped on that deal, just as I knew he would. He had no problem dealing with Jessie, but except for taking out the garbage, the man didn't do anything that anyone could possibly construe as housework.

I went into the kitchen again, looked at the mess, and burst into tears.

—⟶⟵—

"What's wrong with you?"

I bustled by Arianna and went to the couch. "I can't get Raymond to listen to me. He won't take my calls or answer his door."

"P, what did you expect? You've been playing two ends against the middle and the rope finally snapped."

That touched a nerve and my attitude soared up the scale. "What do you know about it anyway, Arianna Jackson?"

"I know it was a bad situation that I hoped would work out for you."

I crossed my arms. "It has worked out. I'm happily engaged to a wonderful man."

"If that's true, then what's the problem?"

Agitated, I rubbed my temples with both hands. "I want Ray!"

She took a seat in the chair and for several long moments, Arianna stared at me. Observing her, I got the distinct impression that she'd reached her limit with me and my man troubles.

Finally, she heaved a sigh. "You know what, Paige," she said calmly, evenly. "You can't have Ray!"

My head snapped back from the force of her fury, but Arianna was not finished.

"He's made it clear that he isn't interested in being involved with you anymore. And you know what else? Ever since I've known you, you've been trippin' behind these men, and in and out of their beds, and I don't understand why you can't be like the rest of us and be satisfied with one. You had a good thing with Lewis, and you started messing around with Raymond. You had a good thing with Raymond, and you chose Lewis. Now that you have Lewis, you want Raymond. This is not a soap opera, Paige, and we're certainly not on some damn movie set. You're messing with *real* lives, and with *real* men. You need to be a *real* woman and make up your mind about what you want and who you want it with!"

I knew that Arianna was pissed, but damn, she didn't have to come down on me like that. I needed advice, not a lecture, and I sat there fuming in the wake of her attack, trying to think of a way to throw her words right back in her face. I couldn't, because I knew what I was doing wasn't cool. I was playing with fire, and it was a blaze of my own making.

The anger drained from my body. "But what if I can't choose between them?"

"You'd better choose, and you'd better do it soon or I can assure you that you're going to lose both of them. No man or woman likes being played, Paige, and I'm not surprised that Raymond won't talk to you. Shit, you're lucky I'm still talking to you."

I took that as a sign that it was time to lighten the mood. "Yeah, right," I said with a chuckle. "I ain't in love with your ass."

Arianna didn't even crack a smile. "True, but who are you in love with? Lewis or is it Raymond? Frankly, if I was either one of them, I wouldn't want your trifling behind."

Now she had pissed me off again. "You can go to hell, Arianna!"

"Mmm hmm. You're mad because you don't like hearing the truth, but you'd better put the truth out there, and soon, or you're going to wind up alone…again."

"My friend, you may refer to my previous statement and go straight to hell."

Arianna moved to the couch. "Paige, I *am* your friend and that's why I'm trying to tell you what you need to hear. You can't keep running back and forth between Lewis and Raymond. It's not fair to them and more importantly…it's not fair to you."

"I know, Ari. It's just that they are both good men and in their own way, they both give me what I need. If I could somehow meld the two of them together, I wouldn't have this problem because then I'd have the best of both worlds."

Arianna didn't respond, but her face told me that she was gearing up to tear into me again. I'd gotten the message the first time and I didn't need to hear the repetition. "Where is your man this afternoon?"

"Jace pulled weekends this month." She glanced at the clock. "Actually, he should have been home by now, but he's probably stuck somewhere cussing up a storm because of this snow."

"It is pretty bad out there. I hope he's okay."

"Jace is fine, and you'd do better to spend those worry coins on yourself. It's time for you to get your stuff together, Paige, and make some hard decisions on what you're going to do about the men you've got dangling on hold." She reached for the ringing telephone. "Here, it's Lewis."

The front door opened and Jace walked in. Arianna immediately went over to him. She helped him remove his coat and then tilted her head back to receive his kiss. I don't think Jace even saw me, and when they walked into their bedroom, I knew that he had become the sole focus of her attention.

## A *Request for Closure*

A deep voice calling my name pulled me back to the phone. "No," I said to Lewis. "Just make something for the two of you. I'll be down later."

I hung up the telephone. I remember thinking months ago that Arianna knew something about men and relationships that I didn't know. I had no idea how long they were going to be in that bedroom, but I wasn't leaving until I found out what that something was. Though muted, the noises coming behind the door were a little disconcerting so I left the couch and turned on the television.

Forty-five minutes or so later, the bedroom door opened and they came out of the room. Earlier, Arianna had worn a ponytail neatly pulled back from her face. Now her hair was a chaotic riot of curls around her head. Her lips were plushy and full and she was gazing up at Jace with dreamy contentment. Both of them wore robes.

"Hey," I said sitting up.

I thought Jace was going to leap out of his skin when he heard my voice. Arianna's eyes widened as comprehension dawned.

"P! I forgot you were here!"

"Obviously," I said, trying not to smile.

Jace, who seemed to have regained some of his composure, moved behind Arianna and wrapped his arms around her as if he were trying to shield her or himself. "How long have you been here, Paige?"

"I was here when you walked in the door."

Arianna's face flushed with embarrassment. "Excuse us, please," she said, grabbing Jace by the hand and tugging him back into the bedroom.

As the afternoon changed over into evening, I sat with my mouth slightly askew as Jace pampered Arianna. He asked and she told him what she wanted for dinner. I couldn't believe it when he cooked it, served both of us, *and* cleaned the kitchen.

"Lewis would never do any of those things," I told her as the two of us made ourselves comfortable in the living room.

"Yes, but would Raymond?"

Until we claimed to have had enough, Jace kept our wineglasses filled, rolled joints, and kept the music soft and light while we sat and talked. When he finally sat down, pulled Arianna's feet into his lap, and began to massage them, my jaw dropped.

When Jace excused himself to go into the bedroom, I couldn't keep the envy out of my voice. "How did you train him to do all of that, Arianna?"

"I didn't train Jace. He came that way."

"No, he didn't."

"Yes, he did. Jace cooks all the time and he cleans, and he takes care of me. As you well know, it's not all peaches and cream, but he gives me what I need and I try to do the same for him. Jace is a one-of-a-kind…for me. Who is your one-of-a-kind, P? And what are you going to do about it?"

———

*Jazmin*

"Once again, we have Jazmin and this time she graces us wearing one of Dario's finest creations yet. Thousands of tiny Asian silkworms worked tirelessly to create…"

I returned Piper's confident wink as she passed by wearing a silky gown of pale pink and yellow. The stylist had sprayed and crimped her red hair into a spindly creation that resembled the branches of a tree. Then I lifted my head higher and hit the walk for my turn in the spotlight. I strutted to the end of the runway, swished my hips to the beat of a classic rock song, then executed a dramatic turn and made my way back to the stage.

I turned again and stood preening in the popping flashes of light until Dario came onto the stage. He lifted my hand and brought me forward and the clapping grew louder. Someone handed him several bouquets of red roses. He laid the flowers in my arms and stepped back as the explosive applause of the audience echoed around us. The rest of the models joined us and after several prolonged bows from Dario, the show was over.

## A Request for Closure

Backstage, I exchanged the flowers for a glass of champagne one of the assistants held out and crossed to the racks where another assistant waited to help me out of the outfit I'd presented on stage. She pulled down the zipper on the back of the dress and took my glass while I shimmied out of the gold, silver, and silk frock. I handed over the garment and took my glass, then headed for the makeup tables so that I could have the heavy mask of cosmetics cleaned from my face.

This had been my routine for the last three months and for the most part, I'd been having the time of my life. Everything fascinated me: the chaos and constant buzz of activity backstage, the beautiful models and temperamental designers, the spectacular clothes I wore, if only for a few minutes, and most of all, the adoration and sometimes hysterical appreciation from the audience.

Because of Dario's fame and his constant reference to me as his top model, my name had been popping up in print on a regular basis. I had thought being the focus of all of that media attention would bother me, but I was wrong.

Fashion was a world of extravagance. It was a world of elegance and glamour, and on the international level much larger and grander than anything I'd ever experienced in New York. Having my picture splashed on the pages of a fashion magazine wearing a fabulous gown was so much different from having reporters lurking and scraping up the grime of my life to plaster in the local newspaper. For too many years, I'd forgotten how it felt to be a part of this world, and if not for Michael, I would have never known how much I'd missed it when I'd had to leave it all behind years ago. Michael was sure that international stardom was just around the corner, but I wasn't sure that it was a place I would be able to go.

—∞—

I looked around at the elaborately dressed people packing the room and sighed. Two hours ago, all I'd wanted was to go back to the hotel and crash. Somehow, I'd let the other models talk me into accompanying them for another night of non-stop, last-until-dawn parties that usually followed a successful show. This party was our third stop and it was a star-studded affair where the fashion elite mingled with celebrities of every entertainment discipline and local politicians in a free-for-all of booze, drugs, and sex.

I returned the wave Piper threw from across the room. We had been roommates for the entire tour. She was from Wisconsin and had that fresh face farm appeal. She was engaged to her high school sweetheart and we'd talked a lot about weddings in general and our own in particular. I also liked Alexandria and Candice. However, none of them could replace Arianna and Paige. I really missed my girls. Most of all, I missed Brick. Two months had dragged into three and from what I could gather through our frequent phone conversations, he was not a happy man.

The basketball season was over for him. The Nuggets had finished second from the bottom in the Western Conference. Brick wanted me back in Colorado and planning our wedding as I'd promised when he'd agreed to let me try my wings at this modeling gig again. Every time we spoke, it was as if a war raged inside me. I wasn't sure if my yearning to be home with Brick and my friends would win out over the glamorous appeal of the life I led now.

Even if I had wanted to go home, I couldn't. I was making mad cash and lured by the money and the thought of how much I had already stashed away for my salon, I had committed myself to finishing out the season. It would be another two months before I returned to Colorado.

When Miko Gallegos parked on a stool beside me, I tried not to grimace. Miko was a booking agent for a top international modeling agency and his sole mission in life seemed to be convincing me to stay in Europe so that he could take over and manage my career.

"Great show tonight," he said, staring into the room.

"Thanks," I said, and then waited for his next move.

Miko ordered a drink and another vodka tonic for me. "When are you going to ditch that hack and take me up on my offer?"

## A Request for Closure

I accepted my drink from the bartender and took a long sip before responding. "I've told you several times that Michael is and always will be my agent for as long as I'm in the business, Miko."

"I'm not convinced that staying with Michael is the best thing you can do for your career. What's he paying you per show?"

"I don't believe that's any of your business."

"Right," Miko agreed. "What if I told you that I've been authorized to offer you double anything he's paying you?"

It was common practice to try to steal models from other agencies. Michael was probably working the room doing the very thing Miko was trying to do. "You don't know what Michael's paying me."

"Doesn't matter. I'll double any offer he's made or will make, plus you have my assurance that you will be our top star, which means top bookings and every major show. And to seal the deal, we'll even throw in a fully-furnished, luxury penthouse suite in any European city you choose to live."

Now that was an offer almost too good to refuse, which I was about to do when I saw Michael.

"I wonder how it is that I knew that when I found Jazmin, I'd find the persistent, if not Machiavellian, Miko Gallegos right by her side."

A red stain flushed Miko's already ruddy cheeks, but he rallied quickly and rose from the stool to shake Michael's hand. "Well, if it isn't the bodacious Michael Peters. How are you, man? Find any other ladies as lovely as Jazmin to join that ignominious agency of yours back in the States?"

I listened to the banter between the two men and tried not to laugh. As glamorous as fashion presented itself to be, it was as cutthroat as any other business.

A guileful smile tinged with animosity curved Michael's lips. "Not yet, Miko, but rest assured that I am steady on the job. Spotting talent of Jazmin's caliber is an art form. It takes time, patience, and an eye for extraordinary beauty. For some of us, it's a natural ability. In your case, there is some literature I can recommend that may help you hone your skills in this area."

Miko's mouth dropped open. Michael's last insult had cut deep and pulling the shreds of his tattered dignity together, he first glanced in my general direction. "Jazmin, as always, it was a pleasure." He nodded at Michael. "Mr. Peters."

Michael laughed when Miko stalked off. Then he turned to me and helped me from the stool. "Let's go, Jazz. The others are waiting for us by the door."

# THE PAST

# SPRING, 1980

# A MOMENT FOR TRUTH

# Chapter 25

*Arianna*

J ace turned twenty-one on April twenty-fifth. I took him to a restaurant
chosen for its romantic ambience. The wine steward popped the cork
on the bottle of champagne and I slid his present across the table. I
winked at Jace. "It's okay to fill his glass. Today, he's legal, and that," I said
when he opened the gift, "says that you're mine."

He laughed when he read the inscription, 'Arianna's Property,' sten-
ciled on the plate, but quickly hooked the 14k ID bracelet around his
wrist. After dinner, we stopped at the Stallion. We were early and the
place was pretty empty. Not that it mattered because we didn't plan to stay
that long.

The waitress delivered our drinks and I was laughing at something
Jace said when a woman approached our table. Her hair was wound up
in a knot on top of her head. She wore a white blouse with a bow tied
from the decorative flaps on the front, a black skirt that fell to about an
inch above her knees, and black pumps. She wasn't very tall, but she was
very pretty—not gorgeous or beautiful, just pretty.

I don't know why I had a weird sense about this woman, but I did. As
soon as he saw her, Jace stiffened in his chair.

"What's wrong, baby?"

He didn't respond, and when the woman stopped at our table, he
stared straight ahead.

"Hello," I said.

"He'll never be free."

"I beg your pardon?"

Jace scraped his chair back and leaped to his feet. He grabbed the
woman by the arm and yanked her away from our table.

## A Request for Closure

She struggled against his hold. "He'll never be free, bitch, because I'll never let him go!"

I sat there with my mouth wide open trying to ignore confirmation of what my mind already knew to be true. Jace had been sleeping around and she'd busted up his game.

He returned to our table and tried to take me in his arms. "I'm sorry, Arianna. That never should have happened."

I pulled back. "Who is she?"

He didn't respond.

"Is *she* the reason you don't come home on Wednesdays?"

He still didn't answer and I saw red.

"Dammit, Alvin. Answer me! Who is she?"

I saw the muscle working in his cheek right before his jaw clamped down. Then he looked me in the eye and said, "My wife."

"Wife!" The word exploded in my head, its sound echoing like a gunshot fired in a canyon. I suddenly felt faint, but I didn't fall out. I wanted to scream, but I didn't do that either. What I did do was calmly rise to my feet, pick up my purse, and walk out of that club.

I stood outside the Stallion trying to clear my blurred vision. I heard the howl of a brisk wind in the dark, felt the numbing chill of its breeze through the hole Jace had blasted in my heart. Standing there, I took in deep gulps of air, hoping it would stop the searing pain.

Then I heard footsteps. I knew they belonged to Jace. I ran for the car, pulling out my set of keys so they would be ready when I got there. He called my name, but I climbed inside and started the engine. The Firebird roared to life. In the rearview mirror, I saw Jace as I backed out of the parking space. He threw up his hands in a gesture meant to make me stop. I hit the gas and headed for the street.

Before I knew it, I was at home stumbling up the stairs to my apartment. I was shaking so much it took several tries before I could fit the key into the lock. Inside, I went directly to the bathroom, undressed, and stepped into the shower. I turned the water to hot and scrubbed my body hard, but it wasn't enough to get the feel of his hands off me. I stepped out, pulled the curtain back, and ran a tub full of hot water. I got in and

240

closed my eyes. I didn't think about Jace, the woman he claimed was his wife, or anything that had happened after I met him. I sat in that tub for over an hour, stunned, and hurt beyond anything I could ever imagine.

Several hours later, the front door opened. I was sitting in bed hurting so badly all I could do was stare at the blank page in my journal. Jace entered the bedroom. His eyes met mine, and then he began removing his clothes. The ensuing silence filled with tension and was more ominous than anything I'd ever felt. I waited until he'd hung up his clothes and approached the bed.

"What do you think you're doing?"

His eyes filled with uncertainty. That lasted only a couple of seconds before the expression on his face hardened. "Going to bed."

I willed my mind to keep it together. "Not here, you're not. You want to go to bed…then go home and sleep with your wife!"

Fury leaped into his face. For a brief moment, I thought he was going to yank me out of that bed. Then Jace sat on the edge, his back facing me.

"Don't let her do this to us, Arianna. I swear, she means nothing to me."

"Seems to me you should have thought about that before you married her."

I turned off the light; Jace left the room.

An hour or so later, he awakened me with kisses all over my face. I tried to push him away, but his arms moved around me like a band of steel, trapping me against his chest.

"I love you," he said, punctuating the words with kisses. "Listen to me, baby girl. I love you. P-please don't let her destroy us."

"There is no us," I said, turning my face away.

Jace turned it back. "There is an us," he declared furiously. "That woman has ruined everything good in my life but she's not going to ruin this! It's not going to happen. I won't let it!"

"It's too late, Jace. Everything's gone."

"It's not too late!" When I chanced a glance at him, a volatile storm raged in his face. "I love you and I don't care what I have to do to keep you. She's not going to ruin this! And you're not either!" I didn't respond.

I couldn't. "Ari," he said, softly. "Don't give up on me now. I love you and nothing, not Debra and not you will ever make me give you up."

He released me, moved to his side of the bed, and tugged me against his body. "Go to sleep, baby girl. We'll talk about this in the morning."

Sleep? Talk? No way was I having that discussion with him, and all night I lay awake waiting for his arms to relax so that I could get up. However, every time I tried to move, his arms became even tauter. That told me he wasn't asleep either and that for that night I wasn't going anywhere.

———

*Paige*

"Raymond, please don't hang up!"

"What do you want, Paige?"

"I'm sorry."

"You're sorry. Is that it?"

Think, I told myself, because now that I had the boy on the phone, my brain had shut down.

"I have to go. I have a project meeting in five minutes."

"Wait! I need to see you, Ray. Can I come over tonight?"

"No."

That one word was hard to take and I couldn't hold back my tears. "Ray, please…I-I just want to talk."

His breathing became heavier. "Precious, please don't cry," he said.

He was trying his best to resist. Through the receiver, I could almost feel the fight he waged.

"All right," he said after a minute or two. "I'll be home at seven."

"Thank you, Ray."

"Don't thank me, and stop crying. All right?'

"All right," I said sniffling.

———

242

It was almost seven o'clock. I'd been sitting outside Raymond's apartment with my back braced against the wall and my head on my knees for over thirty minutes. I was trying to figure out something to talk to him about so that he wouldn't toss me out of his crib.

"You waiting on anyone in particular?"

I could have sat on that floor forever memorizing every nuance of his features. The shaggy sway of his one raised brow; the hard line of his jaw; the cinnamon glow buried under the surface of his skin; the perfect curve and plumpness of his lips; and the fluid movement of the hand he held out to me.

As soon as I was on my feet, Raymond snatched his hand away as if he couldn't bear to touch me and I waited nervously while he reached into his pocket for his keys and opened the door. I didn't follow him inside; after his last rejection, I felt I needed an invitation.

He looked back. "Are you coming in or what?" I entered and closed the door. "Have a seat, Paige." I sat on the couch. Raymond seated himself across the room. "Why are you here?"

My hands flexed with a need to touch him. I put them under my butt to stop their movement. "I wanted to say…" I stood up and paced the floor.

His eyes narrowed as they followed me. "If you have something to say, then you need to say it. I have a busy evening ahead of me."

"Ray, this is so hard for me."

He didn't respond, but anxiety entered his gaze when I moved toward him. Leaning down, I took his face in my hands. He stiffened in the chair when I pressed my mouth against his.

"Baby," I said on a breath.

I had no choice but to move back when he stood up. "I thought you said that you wanted to talk."

My heart began to thump. I could talk to Arianna and to Jazmin. They were my friends, and no matter what they thought about my behavior, they would always be my friends. With men, it was different and the only language I learned that they understood had nothing to do with verbal communication.

## A Request for Closure

I popped the top button on my blouse.

"Don't, Paige. I'm not taking you to bed."

I released another button.

"No, Paige. This game you're playing is tired. I want a woman who wants to share my life. I made a mistake in thinking that woman was you."

I winced. His words were sharper than a knife, but I ignored the tear that ran down my cheek. Sticking out my chin, I popped the last button on my shirt and pushed out my chest, giving Raymond a closer view of the fruit I'd dressed up in a red lacy bra for him. I held out my arms and he quickly came to me.

"No, precious," he said, re-buttoning my shirt. "Not this time. You've talked to me with your body long enough. Tonight, I want you to talk to me with your heart."

He led me to the couch and sat us both down. Raymond slouched back and threw his arm over his eyes. I rubbed my hand over the large bump in his pants, then grabbed his manhood in a firm squeeze.

He sprang upright and gripped my wrist. "I meant what I said, Paige. We are not sleeping together tonight!" He exhaled. "Look, the only reason I let you come over here was because you said you wanted to talk. So, get to talking or please leave."

"Why are you making this so hard for me?"

"Lady, you have no concept of the meaning of the word. Do you have any idea how hard it's been for me to live with the fact that since the moment I met you, you've been playing me for a fool?"

"It wasn't like that."

"Then what was it like? I've asked you repeatedly if you were married."

"I'm not married! Lewis is…" Lewis is what? I asked myself. "Lewis is just a man I've been seeing," I finally said.

"Like you were seeing me? I wonder if Lewis knows how fickle your affections are. I certainly didn't. Tell me something, Paige. Did you pick him up in a club, too, and how many other men are you just seeing? Or do you scrounge the clubs on the spur of the moment, picking up any man who is willing to take you to bed?"

His words cut deep; taunting, angry words that were so true the utter shame of my sluttish ways beamed into my soul, so nasty and polluted my entire being felt defiled. I covered my face with both hands, uncaring of the tears that leaked through my fingers. I couldn't look at Raymond; I didn't want him to see me. I wanted to die, I felt so horribly, horribly bad.

"It wasn't like that with you, Ray," I whispered.

"Hmmm. I wonder," he said. "Then why were you in that club that night, Paige? We were the only dark spots in the entire place. I was there because some colleagues invited me along for a night out. Why were you there? Could it have possibly been because you were looking to test a dick of a lighter color?"

I leaped up from the couch. "Stop it, Raymond!"

He jumped up, too. "I'm not going to stop until you tell the truth! I want to hear you admit that you never cared anything about me! That I meant nothing more to you than a good fuck, which you then went home to compare by sleeping with another man!"

"All right!" I screamed. "I'm a slut! Is that what you want to hear, Raymond? Well, now you've heard me say it! I'm a connoisseur of one-night stands. I pick up men, strip my clothes, and let them have their way with my body." I dropped to the couch. "Are you satisfied now?"

"Why, Paige?"

"I don't know."

He sat beside me and tried to pull me into his arms. I pushed him away.

"I'm a whore, Raymond."

"No, you're not, Paige."

"I am! I did it with you. I've done it with countless other men. I'm sorry, Raymond. I should have never agreed to see you again. I never get involved with the men I pick up, and I should never have let myself become involved with you."

"But you did, precious. Why do you think that was?"

I stared at the bookcase. "I don't know."

# A Request for Closure

Raymond pulled me to him again and this time I didn't resist, but I lay against his side stiff as a board, afraid that at any moment he would throw me out of his home.

"Know something, Paige? You say those three words more than any person I know, and they are an automatic response for any question asked of you. However, I believe that you do know, and we're going to sit here until you work out the reason or the courage to tell me."

So we sat there, him silent, and me staring at that bookcase. Emotionally drained, I closed my eyes and tried to find comfort in the feel of his arms around me. My deepest secret of all I'd never shared with anyone. Well, no one other than my mother and that psychiatrist, who'd thought she'd traced the problem to the absence of my father in my life and that she'd, successfully, helped me learn the difference between fact and fantasy.

Since neither of them had believed me and I was too scared to tell anyone else, I'd shoved the despicable incident to the back of my mind. Then I'd layered it with enough denial so that I could almost believe that it had happened to someone else. Tonight, Raymond had peeled away those layers. But there was no way I could tell this man that one of my mother's boyfriends had raped me when I was eight years old or how worthless and unloved I felt when after telling her, she'd called me a liar.

"Want something to drink?"

"No."

"Sure? I know I have a bottle of wine around here somewhere."

"Okay," I said, and he left the couch.

I sat there for a few more minutes before I went to the door of the kitchen. "Raymond, I know why I kept seeing you when I'd never done that before."

He set the corkscrew on the counter and crossed to me. "Why, Paige?"

I cleared my throat. His stare was piercing and I didn't deserve him or any of the emotions I saw in his gaze. "Because you're the first man to treat me as if I was more than a body." He didn't say anything so I continued. "After that first night, I wasn't going to see you again. If you'll remember, I tried to tell you that, but you wouldn't let it go. I don't know. It made me feel good about myself, and I haven't picked up anyone since you."

Without a word, Raymond went back to the counter. He opened the wine and picked up the glasses. I trailed him back to the living room and sat on the couch.

He poured the wine and handed me my glass. "Tell me about yourself, Paige."

"What do you want to know?"

"Everything."

# Chapter 26

*Arianna*

Seven anxiety-filled nights had come and gone since I'd learned the truth about Jace's marital status. Seven nights, in which I'd had little sleep because I didn't want to be in the bed with him. The morning after Jace's birthday, I asked him to leave. He'd indignantly refused, and I hadn't spoken a word to him since.

When I opened my eyes on Saturday morning, Jace wasn't in the bed. I heard him though and his whistling told me that he was in the kitchen. I took a shower, and after dressing, I grabbed my purse and keys.

He was waiting in the living room. "Sweetheart, I made your breakfast." I rolled my eyes. He held out his hand. "Please."

I ignored the hand and walked to the table. He'd fixed breakfast all right, and it included all of my favorites. The aroma wafting up from the plate of sausage in the middle of the table made my stomach rumble. The scrambled eggs were sunshine yellow and fluffy. Jace had already put pats of butter in the middle of the grits. There was a tower of brown toast sitting next to a platter of watermelon slices that looked ripe and full of sweet juice. Jace seated me and went back into the kitchen. I pushed back my chair and left the house.

Standing by my car, a panicky feeling hit me and I couldn't figure out why I had come outside.

"If you're going to the store, give me a minute. I need to go, too."

I guess I must have looked as bad as I felt when Paige walked up because the expression on her face changed to one of concern. "What's wrong with you?"

"Jace is married."

"What do you mean, Jace is married?"

"You know what I mean. He's married, as in he has a wife."

Paige continued to stare at me as if she'd heard, but had not processed what I'd told her. Then her eyes widened in astonishment and her face mirrored the bewilderment I know must have shown in mine. "Wait a minute. You mean, he's married and he didn't tell you?"

Too choked up with tears to speak, I nodded.

"Oh, my God," she said, and before another second passed, she was around that car hugging me.

"Did you know?" I mumbled against her chest.

"No, sweetie. I didn't know. If I had, you can be sure I would have told you. Let's go into the house."

I pushed away from her. "Why?"

"We need to talk."

"No, I have to go."

"But where are you going?"

"I don't know," I said. When I saw Jace on the stairs, I hurriedly climbed inside my car and drove away.

—*◦◦◦*—

My mind was in trauma mode and as I drove, I felt it slip into overload. Turmoil had my mind so twisted that I could hardly think and keeping up with the morning traffic took concentration I didn't have. I could keep driving and risk an accident or find somewhere to pull over until I could get it together. Up ahead, I saw a park and eased my car to the curb.

As soon as I stepped on the grass, a calmness settled over me. It's peaceful here, I thought, letting my eyes take in the beauty of another of the parks Colorado spent so much money maintaining. The area was a large rectangle—a green grassland with colorful flowers and a man-made lake. There was a baseball game going on. I walked across the grass, sat in the bleachers, and shut out the sounds of happiness around me.

## A Request for Closure

It was peaceful, and because I so needed it, I let the tranquil setting envelope and push everything else from my mind.

I sat in those bleachers until all around me was pitch black. No matter how hot it gets during the day in Colorado, coolness comes with the night. Feeling the sudden chill, I finally rose from the bench and walked back to my car.

I didn't want to go home. Jace was there and I didn't have the strength to deal with him. I was trying to figure out another place to go when the name Chandler Houston popped into my mind. I found a telephone booth, parked, and turned on the overhead light. Then I took out my address book and a dime.

—⁓—

Chandler was standing on his porch when I pulled into his driveway. I'd had no idea how much I needed his hug until after he'd pulled me into the warmth of his embrace. We entered the house and went into the great room. He poured a light burgundy into the two crystal glasses already sitting on the table and handed one to me. I downed the contents practically in one gulp and Chandler re-filled my glass. When I finished that one and held the glass out for more, he removed it from my hand. Then he sat beside me, pulled me into his arms, and cradled me against his chest.

He never said anything and he asked nothing of me. For a long while, he just held me and I held on to him, soaking up the comfort I needed. I had no idea how much time had passed when Chandler's warm kiss woke me from a dreamless sleep.

His eyes crinkled at the corners when he smiled. "You hungry, sugar?"

I sat up and stretched. "Not really, Chad."

"Well, I am, so why don't we go into the kitchen and you can keep me company while I fix myself something to eat. Bring the wine."

I sat on a padded stool at a tiled counter as Chandler turned to the refrigerator and took out two steaks, fresh broccoli, and a loaf of French bread. In exchange for a glass of wine, he handed me a small bag of potatoes and peeler and I set to work while he took out a cutting board and began chopping onions. We ate our meal at the counter, laughing as we reminisced about the times we'd shared. I helped him clean the kitchen and we returned to the living room. Back on the couch, Chandler handed me a seven and seven and lowered himself beside me.

"Okay, sugar, tell me why you're really here."

A wall of hurt welled up inside my chest, but rather than answer his question, I set my drink on the table and reached for him. Chandler Houston loved me. Tonight, I wanted to bask in that love, and when our mouths came together, I returned his passion kiss for kiss.

"Come upstairs with me, Arianna."

It took a few seconds for my brain to register his request. Chandler had been my first lover and my introduction to the world of sexual enjoyment had been so sweet, unfulfilling, but sweet. But maybe tonight it would be different. "All right," I said, allowing him to guide me up from the couch.

Walking up the stairs, I began having second thoughts. Then I decided to hell with it. Maybe in some small way I thought I'd be getting back at Jace for all the lies. Whatever the motivation, I was going to do this.

Chandler opened the door to a large and nicely furnished bedroom. It was not his. He led me over to the bed.

"Arianna," he said, sitting beside me. "You have no idea how happy you made me when I picked up my phone and heard your voice. You also have no idea how hard it's going to be for me to leave this room, go to my own and sleep, knowing that you are down the hall from me. Nevertheless, that's exactly what I'm going to do, Ari. And I hope I won't come to regret this decision.

"Chandler," I murmured, touching my lips to his. "You don't have to leave."

He sighed. "Yes, sugar. I do. I don't know what he did to hurt you so deeply, but it must have been something monumental if it has driven you into my arms. I love you, Arianna, and more often than you can possibly imagine, I spend my nights dreaming of making love to you. It's not going to happen tonight. I don't want you this way, Ari. When I take you into my bed again, it won't be because you are trying to get back at another man."

Shamed, I bowed my head. Why couldn't I have fallen in love with Chandler? After all, how hard could it be to love someone who already loved you?

He left and returned a few minutes later with a pair of his pajamas. He laid them on the bed and after touching a gentle kiss to my forehead, he left again. I glanced at the telephone on the nightstand. I knew that Jace was sitting at home worried about me and I should call to let him know that I was okay, but I couldn't make myself do it. I needed to be away from Jace, even if it was only for one night.

I took a hot shower, dressed in the pajamas, and crawled into bed. I closed my eyes, and rather than pray for Jace and me, I asked God to send Chandler a good woman to love and care for him, someone who wouldn't do to him what Jace Barnes had done to me.

—〰〰〰—

The next morning, I went home. The front door flung open before my key hit the lock and Jace snatched me into the house. Before I could react, he had me pinned against the closed door.

"Where have you been!"

"None of your business!"

His hands pressed my shoulders into the hard wood. I'd seen him angry many times, but that had been mild compared to the fury in his face now.

"Then make it my business! I sat on that couch all night waiting for you to come home and that was the very last time that's gonna happen.

You understand me, girl? I ain't putting up with this shit from you, Arianna. You want to be mad at me? Fine! Be mad! But at night, your ass better be in this house! Now, where have you been?"

"I don't have to tell you anything."

Jace put his face right into mine. I don't think there was enough space for air to get between us.

"I hope the two of you had a great time," he snarled, "because that muthafucka's dead!" He grabbed my arm, pulled me to the bathroom, and shoved me inside. "Take a bath!"

I turned around and crossed my arms. "No thanks. I already had a shower."

"Take another one!"

I swallowed and then threw back my head. "No."

Jace was in the bathroom like a flash. His arm encircled my waist and he dragged me to the tub and somehow holding on to me while I fought him, managed to turn on the faucets. The next thing I knew I was in that tub. I sat down. I had to; the sandals on my feet had heels and I would have fallen and broken my neck if I hadn't.

Defeated, I hung my head and cried. "I hate you," I whispered.

Jace sighed and knelt beside the tub. "I know," he said, removing my shoes. He took off my clothes and pushed in the stopper. He reached for a cloth and the soap and started scrubbing my body.

"I hate you, Jace."

"Believe me, baby girl, I know."

I cried all through that bath and repeatedly told Jace that I hated him. He washed every place on my body several times, including my hair, before he seemed satisfied. Out of the tub, he dried me off, sat me on the toilet, then got out the blow dryer. In the bedroom, he dressed me in a nightgown and put me to bed. He walked to the door.

"Jace?"

He turned around, and all I could think was how much I loved him. "I didn't sleep with anybody last night, but I hate you...and I'll never forgive you for what you've done to me."

## A Request for Closure

He inhaled sharply as if I'd struck him. "You're tired. Go to sleep, baby girl." He left the room and closed the door behind him.

# Chapter 27

*Paige*

"Is Daddy going to the zoo with us?"

This was the fifth time Jessie had asked that question and I gritted my teeth to keep from yelling at my daughter. Now that I was seeing Raymond again, the gloom that had veiled my life had lifted and everything had pretty much returned to normal. I was happier than I'd been in months. However, there was a dark spot marring my euphoria, and it was Arianna. I hadn't talked to her since the day she'd told me about Jace. She brushed me off at work and he blocked my access at her front door. That I didn't like at all, and I had called Jazmin in Milan, hoping she could give me some pointers on how to help our friend. Jazmin had been as shocked as I was about Jace. Since Milan is eight hours ahead, she'd been on her way out to do a show and hadn't had time to talk. I had to figure out a way to talk to Arianna. However, today I had another problem, and that was my daughter.

For the past hour, I had been trying to get Jessica dressed for her first meeting with Raymond, only she didn't know that. She wasn't doing anything out of the ordinary, but I was nervous enough already and not in the mood to deal with any more of her antics. She'd dawdled over breakfast, taken thirty minutes to find her dress shoes, and wouldn't sit still when I tried to comb her hair. Now I was attempting to change her dress after she'd spilled milk down the front of the first one. We were late; I still had to get dressed, and I was quickly running out of patience.

Jessie pulled on my robe. "Paige! Is Daddy going to the zoo with us?"

## A *Request for Closure*

"No, Jessie. Lewis is at work and he won't be home until later. Now, will you please hold your arms up so that I can put this dress on you?"

"No!" Jessie snatched the dress out of my hands and wiggled away. She threw it on the floor. She stared at me with defiant eyes, her lips pushed out in a pout. "I want to go to the zoo later with Daddy!"

That's it! I had reached my limit and it was time to deal with my obstinate daughter. One times one is one, I thought as I walked toward Jessica and her eyes widened in fright. When I reached her, I picked her up and sat on the bed with Jessie on my lap.

"Listen to me, little girl, and listen good. We are not going to the zoo later; we are going now. You are going to cooperate while I get you dressed and then you are going to go into the living room and sit on the couch until Mommy is ready to go. If you get off that couch before I tell you to, I am going to whip your butt. Do you understand me, Jessica Michaels?"

Jessie nodded her head and climbed off my lap. She went to get her dress and slowly made her way back to me. Watching her, I wondered, as I often did, how a high-yellow man and a tan-colored woman had created a chocolate-skinned baby with long, curly brown hair and heart-stopping features that would one day drive men wild.

It wasn't Jessie's fault that I was so nervous or that she had a flutter-headed mother. She loved Lewis, but because of Raymond's insistence and my inability to deny him any longer, I was about to bring another man into her life.

When she stood in front of me but out of reach, I held out my arms. "Come here, Jessie."

With hesitation, she moved forward and when she was near enough, I pulled her to me. "Mommy loves you," I said, kissing her cheek.

"I love you, too, Mommy," she said, and then she handed me the dress.

---

Jessie took my hand as we approached Raymond. He wore a pair of tan slacks that he'd paired with a dark green polo shirt. When he saw us, his radiant smile reached out to us, but he was smart enough to wait for us to come to him.

"Who's that?" Jessie asked.

"A special friend of Mommy's. His name is Raymond and he wants to go to the zoo with us today."

Jessie stopped. She tugged on my hand, forcing me to stop, too. "I don't know him." Her wary eyes focused on Raymond. "Daddy said I couldn't talk to strangers anymore."

"Jessie, Raymond is not a stranger because Mommy knows him and he has been waiting a long time to meet you."

I knew she was confused, but she took my hand and followed obediently as we crossed the short distance to where Raymond stood.

"Hi," he said to me. Then he crouched down to Jessie's level. "Hello, Jessica. My name is Raymond and I am very happy to meet you."

Jessie half-hid herself behind my legs. I couldn't believe it. I had been trying to teach Jessie about strangers for years. Apparently, Lewis had succeeded where I had not. I reached for Jessie and brought her forward.

"It's okay to say hello to Mr. Steward, Jessie. He's a nice man."

"Your mommy's right, Jessie. I am a nice man and I'd like to be your friend. In fact, I have a present for you. Would you like to see it?"

Jessie nodded, but she didn't look at Raymond until he pulled one of his hands from behind his back and held out a box that contained a very pretty doll.

"She has on a blue dress, just like me."

"Yes, she does," Raymond told her. "I saw her in a store and figured that maybe if you could be my friend, you could be her friend, too."

Jessie took the box from Raymond and stared adoringly at the doll. "Thank you," she said shyly.

Raymond stood. "She's absolutely gorgeous, Paige, just like her mother."

---

## A Request for Closure

*Arianna*

I was lying on the bed fighting sleep when I reached for the ringing telephone and placed the receiver at my ear in time to hear Jace shout, "Forget this number! You come near my woman again and I'll kill you!"

I replaced the receiver. A minute or so later, the bedroom door creaked opened. Jace called my name. I didn't answer, and the door closed again.

For three weeks, I had been trying to sort through my confusion, and though I'd been ignoring him, Jace was as attentive to my needs as always. We slept on opposite sides of the bed and he didn't press me for any affection, but he had become more diligent about knowing my whereabouts every minute of the day. He was like a shadow I couldn't get rid of. He drove me to work, called to check on me several times a day, and picked me up. Everywhere I went, Jace went, too.

Even worse were the dreams—dreams filled with faces of the church people I'd known circling around me with eyes full of righteous indignation. They kept me awake at night and in a constant state of stress while I wrestled with my conscience over what to do about Jace.

Tired as hell, but more tired of thinking about Jace, I left the bed. In the living room, I sat on the couch. "Who was on the phone?"

"Nobody, and he'd better not call here again!" As suddenly as the anger came, it vanished. "Ready to eat?"

"I want to know who called my house."

"This is not *your* house, Arianna! This is *our* home! You are not going to disrespect me by having other men call here, and any that come through that door are dead men."

"You're not going to kill anybody, Alvin. And just so we understand each other, I will invite anyone I please to come into *my* home because if memory serves me correctly, your name doesn't appear anywhere on the lease."

"That lease will be changed tomorrow!"

"Why, Jace?"

His face radiated sadness when he knelt in front of me. "Sweetheart, I know I hurt you really bad and I'm sorry; but you have to give me a chance. I can make this up to you, if you'll let me try."

"Why?"

"I love you."

"You can keep your love. I don't want it. I want to know why you lied to me."

"I didn't lie."

I shoved him away. "You did lie! You deliberately set out to make me fall in love with you. You've been here for a year, and yet you never said one word about your wife. How many people know you're married, Alvin?" I threw up my hands in frustration when he didn't answer. "I'll bet everybody knew. Everyone, except me! Do you know what kind of fool that makes me out to be?"

He blew out a deep breath. "Baby girl, I'm sorry I hurt you. I also know that nothing I say is going to make this any better for you, but I love you and no matter what you do or say, I'm not leaving."

"Yes, you are leaving. In fact, I want you out of here tonight!"

"Ari, listen—"

"No, you listen! What do you take me for, Alvin Barnes? A complete idiot? If I listened to anything you had to say now, that's what I'd be. I want you to pack your things and get your lying, cheating ass out of my house tonight!"

His hand shot out, grabbed the front of my robe, and yanked me forward. "I have never cheated on you, Arianna Yevette Jackson, and tonight you're going to shut your mouth and listen to me!"

In the living room, Jace alternately sat and paced the floor. I watched him, furious that he thought he could tell me what to do. I knew I needed to get away from Jace, but before I could move, he sat beside me.

"Ari...Debra and I haven't been together in two years, and I am going to divorce her, only right now, I can't. Things are...there are things involved and I'd rather not go into them because they have nothing to do with us."

"You'd better go into them because so far I'm not buying what you're trying to sell."

"I said I'm going to divorce her! Isn't it enough for you to know that?"

"No, it isn't! Spill it, Alvin. All of it! Or get your shit and get out of my house."

"She has my daughter," he murmured.

I know I heard what he'd said. Only the words floated around my brain like a mixed-up puzzle and my mind was too busy fighting the disillusionment to process his words. "What did you say?"

"Debra has my daughter. The only time I get to see Lauren now is on Wednesdays. If I divorce Debra, I won't even have that because she's already told me that I'll never see my child again."

The last shred of my tolerance fell by the wayside and I got up and went into my bedroom. Jace had handed me another bitter pill, and like life sometimes, it was hard swallow.

"I knew you'd react like this! That's why I didn't tell you!"

I tossed him a withering glare.

His arms surrounded me and pulled me back against his body. "Don't you see what's happening, Arianna? We have a good thing and you're letting her break us up."

I removed his arms. "No, Jace. This is about you and me. Or rather what I thought was you and me."

"She has everything to do with it. None of this started until you found out about her."

"And that's the point. I had to *find* out about her. If I hadn't, you wouldn't have ever told me."

"That's not true. You would've had to know sometime. I would—"

"When, Alvin? Oh, it doesn't matter. All I want to know is why you chose to play this game with me."

"This is not a game!"

My hands curled into tight fists. "Yes! It is! You've been playing with me since we met. I just don't understand why. What was it, Alvin? Was I an easy mark? You didn't even sleep with me that first night. I doubt you've done that with any other woman. What was that about? And why are you still here?"

"I'm here because I love you and I want you to love me."

"I want to know why you did this, Alvin Barnes, and I want to hear the truth. For once in your life, tell the damn truth."

"Okay," he sighed. "Okay." He waved his hand at the bed. "But first, will you please sit down?"

I sat, folded my hands in my lap, and waited for him to start talking.

"The night we met…in the club…it was not the first time I'd seen you and it was not the first time you'd seen me. I knew who you were all along."

I must have looked surprised because he said, "Paige."

I nodded, but remained silent.

"I never saw you at her apartment and I didn't know the two of you were friends until the day I came home from—"

He stopped, examined my face, and decided to start his story elsewhere. "Paige and I hooked up one night shortly after I'd moved out on Debra for cheating on me. Earlier that evening, I had asked for a divorce and she'd laughed in my face. I was angry and depressed and I went to the club to get drunk. I met Paige a few weeks earlier and that night, *she* approached me."

The more he talked, the madder I got. "So you're saying that this was all Paige's fault."

"No, Arianna. I want you to know all of it so we can put this behind us and move on with our life."

"Go on."

"I knew that Paige was seeing other guys, so there was never any chance of the two of us getting serious. It was only for a couple of months and that stopped when she hooked up with Pierce Reynolds. Then they started throwing those weekend parties. Since I didn't have anything better to do, I went to some of them.

"That's when I saw you for the first time. You were walking across the parking lot and all I could do was stare. I came back that next weekend and waited for you to come out of that building, and when you did, I

261

honked my horn. You didn't even turn around. So, I kept coming back, and I even tried to talk to you a couple of times and you wouldn't stop."

I was frowning. "I don't remember any of this."

He cut a glance at me. "I know. Anyway, that night in the club, I watched you search for your friends knowing that you weren't going to find them. Earlier that evening, you'd told me no three times when I asked you to dance but then you danced with every other man in the room."

"That's not true, Jace."

"It sure seemed like it to me. I'd been trying to get your attention for months and you barely acknowledged that I existed. That night, I guess I decided that I'd had enough. So, I bought a couple of drinks and went over to have a talk with your friends." He came and sat beside me. "I'm telling you this because I need you to understand how I felt, Arianna. I had to fight off other women, but couldn't make an impression on the one that I wanted.

"And the reason I didn't sleep with you that night was because you'd been drinking. You looked so tempting in that nightgown I could hardly wait to take you to bed. That was when I decided to wait. At the club, I kept getting in your face waiting for you to say something until it dawned on me that you weren't pretending. You really had no idea who I was, and it had taken so long to get you to notice me, I wanted to make sure that when I made love to you that you remembered it was me."

*I don't believe this shit*, I thought. "So, this whole thing was a setup!"

"No, Ari. I created an opportunity and used it to my advantage. I spent that whole week in the field thinking about you. I was so out of it that if one of the guys hadn't yanked me to ground, I would have taken a bullet. I knew then I was in love with you. When I got here and you were so angry, I knew it was because you had to feel something for me and I figured I'd better stake my claim before you changed your mind." He kissed me lightly on the lips. It was so sweet and so tender that I wanted to cry. "Baby girl, can we go to bed?" he whispered against my mouth. "I really need you to touch me tonight."

# Chapter 28

*Jazmin*

Frothing bubbles swirled around my neck as I sat soaking in a large, slipper-shaped, claw-footed tub. The pumping adrenaline I'd felt during the show that evening was gone, having been seeped from my bones in the steam of a hot milk and honey bath. In the other room, I could hear Candice, Alex, and Piper discussing their planned night out in the streets of New York City, but my mind wasn't on their conversation. I was thinking about Arianna.

I'd tried to call her. Jace had answered the phone and it had taken everything in me not to cuss him all the way out. I left a message. I don't know if he gave it to her, though, because according to Paige, she only saw Arianna at work and the girl wasn't talking. After several more telephone calls produced the same results, I suspected that Jace was screening her calls.

Next week that would change. Though fashion was a year-round business, for me the season was over, and I was going home. One of the first things on my agenda was to see Arianna, Jace Barnes be damned.

"We're leaving, Jazz."

"Okay, Piper. Have a good time tonight."

She peeked around the bathroom door. "Are you sure you don't want to go with us? This is our last week together, and we don't mind waiting if you've changed your mind."

"No thanks. When I get out of this tub, I'm hitting the sack. Last night's shindig wore these old bones of mine to a nub. But after a good night's sleep, I'll be ready to hit the streets again tomorrow."

## A Request for Closure

Piper laughed. "I certainly hope that my bones look as good as yours do when I get to be your age, Jazz. See ya sometime in the morning, old lady."

I flicked water off my fingers at her and Piper hurriedly closed the door. I soaped a Loofah sponge and scrubbed my arms and legs. I could vaguely hear them talking in the room as they prepared for their night out. Then I heard the door to the room open and shut as they left. I relaxed back in the tub and closed my eyes.

A couple of minutes later, the bathroom door opened again. "I thought you guys had left. What do you want now?"

"You can start with a welcome kiss and we'll see where it goes from there."

My eyes popped open and water and suds flew everywhere as I slipped and slid all over that tub trying to get into an upright position. When I finally managed to grab hold of the edge, I stared at Vincent Marks as if he were some sort of apparition. His soft chuckle confirmed that he was no ghost.

Brick crossed to the tub, clasped his hands around my head, and pressed his mouth to mine. I wrapped my arms around his back and our lips never parted when he rose to a standing position, bringing me with him and out of the water. The kiss, in which we tried to devour each other's lips, lasted several minutes, and by the time it ended, Brick was almost as wet as I was.

He set me on my feet, but did not release his hold. "How you doing, Jazzy-girl? Did you miss me?" Before I could respond, his hand drew my head forward. "Never mind," he whispered right before his lips crashed against mine again and he lifted me in his arms.

Two hours later, Brick moved off to the side and released a deep and sated sigh. The man had been ardent, almost savage in his lovemaking. His first excursion had been quick, with him laying me on the bed, unzipping his pants, and plying me with a frenzy of long and deep strokes that had taken the edge off his hunger, or so he'd said when it was over and he'd stood to undress. When Brick returned, his pace had

264

slowed considerably and the pleasurable touches of his hands and lips were still making the rounds in my heart.

"Whew," he said as he folded his arms beneath his head and stretched out. "Now you can tell me how much you missed me, Jazzy-girl."

I twirled a lock of his hair around my finger. "I have missed you, Brick. You have no idea how much. What I can't figure out, though, is why you're here when I told you that I was coming home next week."

His lips tilted upward. "Got that message and ignored it when I decided to come and get my woman. Wanted to make sure that you got back to Colorado with no diversions this time."

"I *was* coming home, Brick."

"I know that, Jazzy. I just wanted to make sure, that's all." He suddenly left the bed. "I'm hungry. What kind of room service they got in this place?"

The place was the Carlyle, home away from home for the world's elite and a dominant fixture in the Upper East Side skyline since 1931. Throughout the tour, Michael Peters had ensured that his models had the best of everything. We'd flown first class into every city, stayed in the most opulent hotels, dined in the finest restaurants, and had always had a limousine at our disposal.

The tower suite I shared with Piper overlooked Central Park, had two king-size bedrooms, a living room, a kitchen, and a grand piano that neither of us played. The furnishings and décor filling the room revealed a refined European elegance that included dozens of vases of fresh cut flowers. If I didn't know it was a hotel, I would have thought I was staying in someone's private home.

"Oh, I think you'll be able to find something or we can go downstairs in a little while. But come over here for a minute, I want to talk to you."

Brick turned from a breathtaking view of the New York skyline. He plopped down on the bed and brushed a lock of my hair over my shoulder. "What do you want to talk about, Jazzy?"

"First of all, you, And how you're feeling now that the season is over."

## A Request for Closure

"Except for missing you, I feel great. But I have to tell you, Jazzy, playing in the NBA is a lot different from playing at the collegiate level. These guys are serious. This is their livelihood and they don't mess around. I thought the transition would be easy, but having to play three or four games a week, and keeping my body in shape so that I would stay healthy through the season sure was tough on a brotha. And not having you there to ease the aches and pains didn't help either."

"I know, but next week, we'll be home and our lives can get back to normal."

"Yeah," he said as he kissed me. Then he stretched out on the bed. "The team didn't do so well this year, but I managed to get a lot of playing time under my belt and everything's intact. And to make sure I stay healthy, I'm going to participate in the conditioning program during the off-season. But I won't start that until after we're married and come back home from our honeymoon."

The wedding again. The whole time I was away, I had missed Brick, but unless he mentioned it, I hadn't given one thought to the wedding or the promise I'd made to him. "Uh, Brick, I was wondering—"

"No, Jazmin," he said, apparently thinking he knew what was on my mind. "No more postponements and no more excuses. You promised me five months ago that we were going to get married and when we get home you're going to plan our wedding."

"Brick, what I wanted to know was if you knew what was happening with Arianna?"

"Oh…I haven't been home that long, but Jace caught up with me on the court a couple of weeks ago and we did talk. I had no idea that Jace had a wife. Did you?"

"Hardly. If I had known, I would have made sure that Arianna knew about it long before now."

"The man's torn up over this, Jazzy."

I didn't give a damn about Alvin Barnes or his feelings. "Have you seen Arianna?"

"Nope. Haven't seen her, but I'm sure she's okay."

I reared back. "Alvin Barnes has been lying to Arianna since the day they met. If it was you, I'm very sure that I would not be okay. Neither would you by the time I finished kicking your ass."

Brick tugged me down on top of him. "But it's not us, Jazzy. I know Arianna is your friend and how much you care about her, but despite the mess he's made of things, Jace cares about Arianna, too, and he's very sorry about what's happened between them."

Again, Brick was giving me that male perspective. I hadn't seen Arianna, but I knew that the pain she must be feeling had to be almost unbearable. I should have been there when she needed me the most.

However, when Brick put his mouth on my breast, I lay back on the bed and told myself not to think about it any more. Next week would be soon enough to figure it all out, and by next week, I would be back home and able to help Arianna.

Brick was my man and he'd come all the way to New York to be with me. Tonight, I needed to concentrate on that, and the wonderfully erotic things he was again doing to my body.

# THE PAST
# SUMMER, 1980
# THE CROSSROADS

# Chapter 29

*Arianna*

I guess when you're in love you can excuse almost anything, and because I needed to justify what I was doing, I found myself making excuses that loving Jace was not wrong. It was all her fault. She'd driven him away and now she wanted to deny Jace access to his child because he didn't want her anymore.

Jace had filed for divorce and Debra had taken Lauren to New York. After doing so, she'd threatened to send Lauren out of the state if Jace or any of his family came near her. He was worried out of his mind. I tried to be supportive, but the stress was tearing me apart.

Other than work, he'd been keeping me inside that apartment and away from my friends. Jace pleaded with me to love him again, begged for a second chance, and when coupled with his lips and hands, his voice was loud. However, it was not loud enough to drown out the condemnation of the other voices hounding me night and day.

"Dinner's ready, Arianna, and tonight I want you to eat it."

I flipped a page in the magazine I wasn't reading. "I'm not hungry."

"Ari, you haven't had a decent meal in weeks. You have to eat, baby girl."

"I said, I'm not hungry!"

The seat beside me dipped with his weight. "What's wrong, sweetheart?"

"Nothing."

"Yes there is. So talk to me."

"Jace, I'm fine…a little tired maybe."

"Tired, huh?"

"Yeah. A little, I guess."

## A Request for Closure

"Maybe you should go lie down."

"I'm not that kind of tired."

"What kind of tired are you?"

I didn't respond.

He lifted my hand. "Don't shut me out, baby girl. You used to talk to me about everything. Now you don't talk to me at all, unless you have to. I don't like this, Ari. I want it the way it used to be between us."

"We can't go backward, Jace. We have to go forward and whatever happens...happens."

"Whatever happens, happens," he repeated. Jace frowned. "What does that mean?"

"It means exactly what I said."

"Oh." He rested his head on my shoulder. "I spoke to Samuel today."

Samuel was Jace's lawyer, but I was not in the mood to hear anything about his divorce proceedings. "Jace, not now."

"I've given this a lot of thought, Ari, and you need to hear this. I called Samuel because I want full custody of my daughter."

I twisted my head. "You plan to have your daughter live with you?"

"No. I plan to have her live with *us*. Debra is crazy and Lauren needs to be around a woman who will be a good influence on her."

"Jace, I'm not ready to be a mother."

"Sure you are, and you'll be great."

"You're not listening to me, Alvin. I don't *want* to be a mother."

"Arianna, Lauren is my daughter. I can't and I won't leave her with those people. Marrying me means accepting her, too."

I didn't respond because if I did, Jace was not going to like what I had to say, and the fight that had been on a hiatus for weeks would erupt.

"Ari, this is important and I need to know how you feel."

I tossed the magazine on the table. "I'm tired, Jace. I think I will lie down for a while."

—⁓—

*Go to him. He needs you.*
*Tell him to take his problems and get out.*
*Go to him.*

The debate raging inside my mind was driving me nuts. In my head, I wanted Jace out of my life, but my heart kept pulling me in a different direction. What I really wanted was for everything to go back the way it was…before Debra…before Lauren…before, when it had only been Jace and me. I wanted the impossible. We could never get back what we'd had.

Jace sat on the bed and burrowed his hands underneath me. I returned his kisses, but only because I needed them so badly. "Are you ready to eat now?"

I sought his mouth and tried to communicate what I needed. He gripped me tightly and sighed as if he'd been waiting for me to wake up and come back to him. I lowered us to the bed and soon we had removed our clothes.

Then we made love the way we used to—no limit…full passion…with nothing held back, and relished in the pleasure we gave to each other.

—◦◦◦—

"Barnes is married."

"Why are you calling me, Russell?"

"Alvin Barnes is married and I assumed that you didn't know. Now you do and you can give him up."

"Why would you assume anything?"

"You mean you're not going to give him up? Even after what I just told you?"

"That's none of your business."

"Why would you want to be with a man who is unfaithful to his marriage vows, Arianna? Jace Barnes does not love you. I do! He has a wife. I don't, and it's time to end this ridiculous fling you're having with him! It can't go anywhere. The man's already married!"

## A Request for Closure

"Thank you for the information, Russell. I'm hanging up now."

"He's an adulterer, Arianna! Maybe you didn't know before, but you know now. If you continue to see him, then you're no better than he is!"

Despite my outward appearance of calm, the call from Russell did a number on me. Alvin Jace Barnes *was* an adulterer and I was nothing more than a harlot that preyed on unavailable men. His accusations stayed uppermost on my mind for the rest of the day. By the time I arrived home, I had worked myself into battle mode.

"You bastard," I yelled as soon as Jace walked through the door. "Do you know what I went through today because of you?"

Shock replaced his smile. "Baby girl, what is it? What happened?"

I responded by striking out and my hand landed against the side of his face. Jace forced my arms behind my back. I fought to free myself.

"Stop it, Arianna!"

"Let me go!"

"Not until you calm down."

We engaged in a stare down until Jace increased the pressure on my arms enough to achieve my defeat. My head hit his chest and I burst into tears. Jace walked us to the couch and sat with me on his lap.

"Why did you have to marry her?"

"Debra bothered you today?" Incredulity filled his voice. I shook my head no. "Then who? Stop crying and talk to me, Arianna. No one messes with my woman and gets away with it. Do you understand?" I nodded. "Now, tell me who it was and I'll take care of it."

I wiped my face. "No. It's okay."

"It's not okay! I want to know who upset you and you're going to tell me."

"I can't."

"You can and you will, so start talking, girl."

"Leave it alone, Alvin. There's nothing you can do."

I got off his lap and headed for the kitchen. Jace stalked behind me.

"I'm trying to help, but you want to shut me down. I'm sick of this, Arianna, and I'm not coming in here and having you attack me ever again. Now, who was it?"

"Nobody! Just leave me alone."

"I will when you tell me what I want to know!"

The pressure that had been building inside me exploded. "All right," I hissed. "You want to know, I'll tell you. It's you! You're the one who did this to me and I'm not letting you get away with it anymore. Get out, Alvin Barnes! Get out of my house! Get out of my life! I don't want you anymore!"

I'd finally said it, the thing I had wanted to say for a long time, but was too scared to voice, because I knew that once said, Jace would act on it. All water under the bridge now. I'd said I didn't want him and it was over. I lay back on the bed. I knew he hadn't left. I also knew he would come to me; he always did. I dozed off, and when I awoke, the bedroom was dark and though I couldn't see him, I knew he was there.

"Arianna?" His voice sounded hoarse. "Ari?"

"Yes, Jace."

"Arianna, don't do this. Please don't send me away. I hate that I hurt you this badly. I love you...so much that it hurts me sometimes. I'm sorry for what's happened, but I can't change it. If I could, I would. I'd do anything for you, sweetheart. You know that. I don't want to leave, so tell me how to fix this, Ari. Tell me what to do so that you'll be happy with me again. Please!"

"Jace, come here."

"No! Tell me how to fix this and I'll do it. Then it'll be okay again."

I snapped on the lamp and a jolt rocked my body. Gone was the self-assured man who'd come into my life and taken it over. Jace looked totally crushed and defeated. I reached out my hand. "Baby, come to me."

I saw the confusion in his eyes. He wanted to come, but he was unsure. "It's okay, Jace, or would you rather I came over there?"

Several agonizing minutes passed while Jace tried to make up his mind. I was going to wait him out, but when I sat up, he started moving forward slowly. He stopped at the edge of the bed, letting it become the reason he could come no nearer.

I rose to my knees and held out my arms. "Please."

## A Request for Closure

His steps were tentative, but they finally brought him around the bed. He wouldn't touch me, so I touched him, everywhere I could. A tear rolled down his cheek. I brushed it away with my fingers and continued to caress his face until his hands stilled my movements.

"I don't want to lose you, Arianna. I swear I don't. I'm going to fix this. Somehow, I'm going to make everything right again."

"It's okay, my darling, and I'm sorry I hurt you. I didn't mean what I said and I don't want you to think about it anymore. We'll fix this together. Okay?" He didn't answer. "Jace, I love you and we'll get through this together. I promise."

"Together," he repeated. He laid his head on my chest. "I love you, Arianna."

"I love you, Jace. No matter what, I will always love you."

"We're going to beat this thing, sweetheart. And as soon as it's over, I'm going to make you my wife."

We stretched out on the bed and spent the night holding each other until morning's light.

—⁂—

### Paige

"Dinner's ready, Jessie. Go and wash your hands."

She didn't answer and I stepped out of the kitchen. Jessie was outside waiting for Lewis to get out of the car. He picked her up and entered the house.

"Hey."

"Hey," I said. "You're home early but that's good because now you can have dinner with us."

"Smells good. What did you fix?"

"Tuna casserole. Jessie's having hot dogs."

"Mmm," he toned, smiling at Jessie. "Mommy made both of our favorites. Let's go wash up for dinner."

At the table, Lewis blessed the food, and then dipped into the casserole while I added the fixings to Jessie's hot dog and salad to her plate. I passed Lewis my plate and filled her cup with milk.

"Which dressing do you want, Jessie?"

She glanced at the three bottles sitting on the table, and then at me. I had seen that look many times while growing up and it had always had the power to make me cringe. My mother was a master at cutting people down to size with a mere glance, which was where my daughter had learned it.

Only Jessie had paired hers with the impudence she'd been displaying ever since we'd returned home. My daughter was challenging me and she was doing it because she knew there was nothing I would do or say about it.

The trip to the zoo had gone so well that I'd decided that it was okay for Raymond and Jessie to get to know each other. Since that outing, he'd taken us horseback riding, to a children's concert, and today to Santa's Workshop in Manitou Springs.

Jessie had been riding the merry-go-round when Raymond had suddenly touched his lips to mine. It was an impulsive move, and one we both regretted as soon as we realized that Jessica had witnessed the kiss. My naturally forward daughter had asked Raymond why he'd kissed her mommy. He'd immediately grown flustered and I had told Jessie that special friends sometimes showed affection for one another.

Apparently she had not bought into the explanation and her behavior since we'd been home had bordered on insolence. I'd already stopped myself several times from doling out the punishment she deserved. I couldn't punish Jessie. She was a child and I had made the decision to place my daughter in the middle of my mess.

"Which one are you going to have, Daddy?"

Lewis picked up the French dressing. "Your favorite," he said, screwing off the cap and topping both of their salads.

"Guess what I did today, Daddy?"

"What, sunshine?"

"I went to see Santa Claus and I had my picture taken on a train."

## A Request for Closure

"Drink your milk, Jessie."

She gave me that look again. "I don't want it. I don't like milk."

"Yes, you do."

"No, I don't!"

I picked up her cup and practically forced it into her hand. "You do so like milk, and you'd better drink every last drop."

"Paige," Lewis said intervening. "If she doesn't want the milk, why are you trying to make her drink it?"

The words I wanted to spout at him clogged in my throat. This wasn't his fault either. I took the cup from Jessie and set it on the table. "You're right," I said. "Jessie, if you don't want the milk, then you don't have to drink it."

Apparently satisfied with her victory, Jessie began eating her dinner.

—◦✿◦—

That night, I sat in the bathtub feeling nervous and jumpy. Jessie had stubbornly insisted that Lewis help get her ready for bed, and while there had been no further incidents with her after dinner, only God knew what she was telling him now. Why did life have to be so complicated? Why couldn't it be simple, uncluttered, and tranquil?

A year ago, Arianna, Jazmin, and I didn't have any cares in the world. Now all of our lives were drenched in turmoil. I'd finally cornered Arianna at work and told her that she needed to get away from Jace. I tried to tell her that I didn't think it was fair of him to saddle her with his wife, his child, and his unending quest for a divorce. Only she wasn't trying to hear anything I had to say. I wasn't sure what was going on with Jazmin, but she'd told me that she was thinking about signing up for another season. When I jokingly reminded her that Brick was waiting on her to come home and plan their wedding, she had pretty much told me to mind my own business.

And me...my turmoil was of my own making. As much as I wanted to choose between them, Lewis and Raymond both provided something that

I needed. Moreover, Lewis had become the father Jessie needed in her life. So, rather than give up one for the other, I had decided to keep them both. Except for the occasional nightmare about it all blowing up in my face one day, I had been handling the stress and doing a fairly good job of juggling my time between the two of them.

Lewis walked into the bathroom. I covertly examined his face for a hint of something that might not be right. He was smiling as he sat on the side of the tub.

"Jessie sure had a good time today. My little girl talked so much I didn't think she would ever go to sleep."

"She had a very active day."

"So I gathered. Want me to wash your back?"

I held up the cloth. He took it and kneeled by the tub. He seemed thoughtful as he soaped the cloth and swirled the rag over my skin. "I have been wondering about something though."

My heart stilled. "What's that?"

"I was wondering if you'd let me know ahead of time when you plan an outing with Jessie so that I can go, too."

I exhaled. "Of course. I would have told you today, but by the time I decided to go, you had already left for work. You've been working a lot lately, Lewis."

"I know. And I know that I've been neglecting you and Jessie, but the new rotation went into effect today and I'm off weekend duty for a while, so I'll have more time to spend with the two of you." He dipped the rag into the water and rinsed the soap from my back.

"Really." I took the cloth he held out.

"Yep," he said, rising to his feet. "So why don't we plan something fun to do with Jessie next weekend."

"Okay," I said, rubbing the washcloth across my chest.

Lewis stared, his gaze glazed and concentrated on my breasts. "How long are you going to be in that tub?"

"Not long. I'm almost finished."

"Good. I'll be in the bedroom waiting."

# Chapter 30

*Jazmin*

Who knew how much being away from a place could change a person's attitude about it? I know I didn't. Traveling the world had been exciting, this past week in New York, especially sharing it with Brick, even more so. But I never expected the keen sense of well-being that hit me when the plane touched down in Colorado Springs.

At the same time, I hated that the plane had landed. It was too soon. Already I missed Michael, the other models, and the life I had left behind. That morning, we'd shared a tearful parting. Still upset that he hadn't been able to convince me to stay, Michael had given me a clipped goodbye and walked off with others toward the international gates and a plane that would take them to Brazil. Watching them leave, I'd felt sorry for myself. I wanted so much to go with them, but I had chosen Brick over my career, and for the second time in my life, my days of walking the runway were over.

When the last passenger left the first class compartment, I rose from my seat and adjusted a long, turquoise silk scarf around my hair and neck. I shrugged into the jacket of an off white, vintage Jacquard suit and clapped on a pair of dark Hollywood-style sunglasses.

"You ready yet, Jazzy-girl?" Brick had dressed comfortably in a pair of black walking shorts and a red, open collar shirt. He was staring at me with his lips pursed in amusement and smirkish-looking glint in his eyes.

I flipped the ends of the scarf over my shoulders and grabbed my Louis Vuitton clutch. "Yes. Let's go."

At the complex, Paige was waiting when I stepped from the car. I returned her almost choking hug of welcome and a similar one from

Jessie. Grabbing my arm, she led me over to her apartment and opened the patio doors. I stepped inside and the shouts of 'welcome back' were almost as deafening as the loud bass beat of Ray, Goodman & Brown's "Special Lady" blasting from the stereo.

Before I could recover from that jolt, people surrounded me on all sides. All were wearing summer gear. Here I stood, dressed like a 1940s screen legend and feeling woefully out of place among my friends and others who didn't feel the need to dress to impress. I twisted my head to locate Paige, who stood in the doorway with a huge grin on her face. At the very first opportunity, I was going to kill her.

I replenished my drink and leaned back against one of the counters in the kitchen. An hour ago, I'd slipped up to my apartment where I had exchanged my fashion model duds for a white cotton top and a pair of blue jean shorts. Now I didn't feel so out of place.

"Where is Arianna? I stopped by her apartment and no one answered."

Paige shrugged her shoulders and set the bowl in her hands on the counter. "Jace took her to see his lawyer this morning. I guess they haven't made it back yet. But I told her about the party and I know she's planning to be here."

"You mean to tell me that Ari is still with Alvin Barnes?" Paige filled a glass with wine and motioned for me to follow her.

In her room, we sat on the bed. Dressed in a hot pink vest and paler pink linen shorts, she looked cool and composed, while I was so antsy I could barely sit still. Paige pulled a joint out of a drawer in the nightstand and lit up. I waved it away when she held it out to me.

"Come on, P. Tell me what's going on. Why is Arianna still with Jace?"

"Because she loves him," she said, blowing out smoke. "At least, that's what she told me when I asked."

An unladylike snort left my mouth. "Loves him? Alvin Barnes is a liar and he's married. How can she stay with a man like that?"

"Beats me, but there's more."

"What *more* could there possibly be, Paige?"

## A Request for Closure

"He has a child."

"What!"

"Jace has a daughter and his wife won't divorce him."

I jumped to my feet. "Has Arianna Jackson lost her fucking mind! That girl can have any man she wants and I want to know why she still wants him!"

"I already told you. She loves Jace. She also told me that he wants her to go off the pill so that they can have a child together. And the reason they went to see his lawyer—"

"Stop!" I looked around for something to hit, then forced myself to calm down. "I know Ari's not seriously considering getting pregnant, P. And if she is—I mean, what in the hell is the matter with her?"

"I've already told you twice."

"Well, don't tell me again!" I sat back on the bed, shaking my head. "This is unreal."

"I know. With all of that religious brainwashing Arianna went through growing up, she would be the last person I would have thought would end up sleeping with a married man."

"It's not as if she knew and deliberately chose to do this, P. If anyone is at fault, it's him."

"Whateva," she said. "All I know is that as much as I like men, I would never mess around with one who's married."

Paige had always been self-absorbed, and normally I would have let her comment slide. However, today her inability to empathize with Ari's situation and her attitude about it struck the wrong chord in me. "With the number of men that you've fucked, how do you know that you already haven't?" I saw the surprised hurt that crossed her face and sighed. "Paige, I'm sorry I said that and you know that I love you, but this stuff with Arianna is really upsetting to me."

"It's all right, Jazz. I know you didn't mean anything by it."

"I have to talk to her."

"It won't do any good. I've been trying to get Ari to see the light ever since she broke the news."

"I have to try."

282

"I know. So did I."

I thought about that for a moment. For all of her apparent indifference, Paige was worried about Arianna, and she was waiting for me to come up with the plan. At the moment, I didn't have one. This thing Arianna had with Jace was strong, possibly stronger than anything I could say or do to break it. But I had to find a way to make Arianna realize that she needed to free herself of his hold over her.

"So, tell me. Why did Jace take Arianna to see his lawyer?"

———

Arianna arrived later that afternoon. Unlike my expectations, she looked nothing short of radiant. She wore a white sundress and sandals, and did appear to be thinner, but other than that, everything about Arianna was the same, except that perhaps she looked a little more knowledgeable about life. I cornered her and before she could turn to Jace, hustled her from the room.

"Hey, girl," I said, giving her the biggest hug I knew how to give.

"Jazmin," she said when I released her. Her smile was so serene that it bordered on angelic. "You have no idea how much I missed you."

And I had no idea how much I'd missed, I thought, thinking about all of the things that Paige had told me. "I missed you, too, Ari. How are you holding up?"

She appeared not to understand the question if the blank expression on her face was any indication. "What do you mean?"

"You know what I mean. I don't have to spell it out for you."

"Oh, you want to know how I'm holding up now that I know that Jace is married."

"That's exactly what I want to know and I also want to know why you're still with him."

"Jazz, I shouldn't have to spell *that* out for you. I told you a long time ago that I loved Jace."

"But Arianna, he's married to another woman and—"

## A Request for Closure

"Jace doesn't love Debra. He wants a divorce, but she's trying to use his child to hold on to him. But Jace is working it out and as soon as his divorce is final, he wants to marry me."

"Don't you think that he should have told you all of that before he got involved with you, Arianna?"

I could tell that what I'd said bothered her. Then she smiled that sickeningly sweet smile again. "Yes, he should have, but Jace also explained why he didn't and I'm okay with it."

"But are you okay with him?"

"I love him, Jazmin."

If I had been here when all this went down, I know that I could have convinced Arianna that staying with Jace was not in her best interest. I tried once more to break through her wall of resistance.

"You deserve better than Jace Barnes! He doesn't love you and he's only using—"

"Jace *does* love me, and to prove it, he added me to his life insurance policy today. Jace is trying to take care of me, Jazmin, and that makes me happy. I'm also happy that you've finally come home, and I love you, but please don't try to spoil this for me."

Sounded to me as if Jace Barnes was trying to bribe Arianna into staying with him, but after a quick survey of her face, I knew that I couldn't say that to her. Instead, I pulled my friend into my arms and hugged her again.

Despite Paige's warning that it would do no good, I had tried, and I had failed just as she had.

—◈—

*Arianna*

"I've always wanted to do that."

Jace and I were watching one of those cops versus the bad guys, action thrillers he loved so much.

"What?"

284

"Be a cop."

"You, a cop? The man who keeps us supplied with top of the line weed. A cop? Right," I said.

"I'm not kiddin', Ari. I've wanted to be a policeman since I was six years old."

"You have?"

"Yep."

"Why am I just hearing about this now?"

"I guess watching the movie made me think about it."

"If you wanted to be a policeman, why didn't you pursue it?"

"Had to get married."

"You *had* to get married?"

"Yep. Debra was pregnant and I joined the army to support my daughter."

"Oh." I laced my arm through his. "Jace, when you married Debra, did you love her?"

He chuckled. "Now why do you want to know something like that?"

"I just do. Did you love her, Jace?"

"No, sweetheart. I didn't love Debra. I married her because it was the right thing to do." His fingers tipped my chin upward and he looked me in the eye. "Are you sure you want to hear about this?"

I pressed my body closer to him. "Yes. I'm sure."

"Okay, but remember you asked, so don't you dare try to go off on me."

"I won't," I assured him. The look on his face clearly said he didn't believe that. "I promise I won't get mad, Jace. So tell me."

"All right. Debra and I went to high school together. She wasn't crazy then like she is now, and it wasn't a big deal. I mean, we weren't boyfriend or girlfriend or anything, but I ended up taking her to the prom and...well, let's just say we didn't go straight home afterwards."

"Couldn't keep those pants zipped, huh?" I said teasingly.

"Yeah. Something like that. Anyway, about a month after graduation, Debra told me she was pregnant and I married her. End of story, sweetheart. But you know what?"

## A Request for Closure

"What?"

"I sure wish I had kept my pants closed, at least until I met you. If it had been you, and not Debra, I bet you wouldn't have let me anywhere near your panties that night."

"Oh, I don't know. You are kinda cute and all."

Jace laughed loudly. "You didn't have sex in high school. I'll bet you were a prude and a tease. How many guys did you piss off back then?"

"None."

"You were a cheerleader and I remember ours. The guys used to say they were some hot little numbers."

"Yeah, right. I'll bet your knowledge came first hand."

"What do you mean by that?"

"Don't try to play the innocent with me, Jace Barnes. By the time you and I met, your knowledge of sexual pleasure was in the ozone layer. While I, on the other hand, had no experience whatsoever."

"What do you call those three guys who had their hands all over you before we met?"

I raised my brows. "What three guys?"

"The ones you told me about that—"

"I have no idea what you are talking about, Jace Barnes. No one touched me before you."

He pulled my leg into his lap. "I remember that conversation and you told me that you had sex with three guys before me. Now, are you going to tell the truth?" He trailed his finger up the sole of my foot. "Or do I have to torture you?"

"Don't, Jace. Please."

"Tell the truth," he said adding more fingers.

"There was one, Jace, and that's it. There weren't any others."

"You're lying. I distinctly remember you telling me three."

"Okay, I'll tell the truth, but you have to let me up first."

As soon as he did, I jumped up and backed away. "I lied! There was nobody until I met you, Jace Barnes." Then I ran for the bedroom and tried to close the door on him. He easily shoved it open and stalked me

286

until my legs hit the back of the bed. "All right. There might have been two," I said to appease the wicked glint in his eyes.

"Nope," he said, gripping me by the waist and lowering me to the bed. "It's too late now. You lied and now you're going to pay."

———

"Jace, you can still be a cop," I said from the floor where I sat between his legs while he used the blow dryer on my hair after our detours to the bed and a shower. Now that I knew his heart's desire, I was unwilling to let the conversation slide.

"What?" he yelled over the noise.

"Ouch," I said, rubbing the spot where he'd encountered a tangle. "That hurt, Jace."

He turned off the dryer. "Would you move your hand and sit still?"

"I said, you can still be a cop, if you want to."

"Where's the hair brush? You got the hair brush down there?"

"Alvin Barnes, will you listen to me?"

"I am listening, but I need the hair brush." He shoved me in the back. "Move."

"Here," I said, handing it to him. "Why don't you want to talk about this?"

"Ari, being a cop was a childhood fantasy. There's no point talking about it 'cause it'll never happen." His fingers fluffed my hair and massaged my scalp. "What do you want me to do with this stuff?"

"Brush it back into a ponytail," I said. "If it's a fantasy, then you must not have wanted it too badly."

"I did want it, and I still do, but life didn't turn out that way."

"Life is what you make it, Jace. If you really want to be a cop, then you'll do it."

He snapped the rubber band into place. "I'm done." He helped me up from the floor. "You really think I can do it?"

"Yes. I do. Don't let an opportunity to pursue your dream slip away."

## A Request for Closure

He picked up the hair products and dryer. "Well, it's something to think about anyway and I'm going to need to decide soon. My stint with Uncle Sam is almost up."

Stunned, I watched him walk from the room. I knew I needed to go after him and ask the question, but I couldn't move. When he returned, he sat down and pulled me into his arms.

"When, Jace?"

"When what?"

"When is your tour here over?"

"In a couple of months. They were in the barracks today trying to convince people to reenlist. I still have a few weeks to decide though."

"What are you going to do?"

"Thinking 'bout being a cop."

"That's not funny, Jace. Are you going to reenlist or not?"

"I haven't decided what I'm going to do, but I'm sick of the army. If I reenlist, we'll have to move. I want to go home."

"To New York?"

"That's where home is. Why are you worried? It doesn't matter what I do, you're going with me."

"Jace, if you reenlist, you could end up anywhere."

"Not just me, baby girl—we. We're getting married, remember?"

I loved Alvin Barnes. I truly did, but reenlistment meant reassignment. If I went with him, I'd have to give up everything: my home, my friends, and my job. I was sure I could get another job, but until that happened, I would be totally dependent on Jace.

If he didn't reenlist, it meant moving anyway, because Jace wanted to go home and with a messy divorce hanging over his head, he was in no position to take me anywhere. It was then that I realized I was not ready to handle any of the changes our relationship was about to undergo.

I slid my eyes towards him. He was so good to me, and I loved him with all my heart, but instead of saying that, I grabbed on to the only lifeline I could find. "Jace, you never asked me to marry you."

He sat up immediately. "Sure, I did."

288

"No. You didn't. You *told* me we were getting married. You never asked me what I wanted."

"If that's all that's bothering you, baby girl, I'll ask you now."

"You can't."

"Sure I can. Arianna Jackson, will you marry me?"

I smoothed my hand over his ebony cheek. "Jace, you can't ask me that. You're already married."

I think it finally dawned on him exactly what I was saying because he suddenly yanked me into his arms.

"I'm not going to let you do this to us, Arianna. We've been through too much. I need you. We have to get married."

"Jace," I said, hating that I couldn't stop myself from hurting him. "We can't."

"Yes we can. Maybe not now, but as soon as my divorce come through. Dammit, Arianna! You promised me!"

"Jace, listen—"

"No! I'm not listening to you anymore, Arianna Yevette Jackson, soon to be Barnes." He stood up and glared down at me. "You promised me that we would be together. We're getting married and when my tour here is over, we're moving to New York!"

Jace left the room before I could respond.

# Chapter 31

*Jazmin*

W hat about this one, Jazz? It's a pretty mint green, and I like the way the leaf pattern trails up the sleeve. I'm not sure what material they used for it though. Oh wait, says here that it's—
"

"Belgian lace," I said, glancing at the picture. It was a beautiful dress and a style that would suit both Arianna and Paige, who was also sitting at my dining room table perusing bridal magazines and catalogs. I picked up my glass and went into the kitchen. I pulled a bottle of vodka from the cabinet. "You two want anything?"

Arianna glanced at the clock. "No thanks," she said.

"It's a little early for me," Paige said, still rooting through the pile of magazines on the table.

I shrugged, mixed my drink, and returned to the table.

"That's your second one this morning," Arianna said.

Actually, it was my third. I'd had one to stave off the wedding bell blues before they'd arrived. I fired a glare at her. "Who are you, my mother?"

Her face remained impassive as she held my hostile gaze. "No, just a friend making an observation."

"Well, you can keep your damn observations to yourself."

"She's concerned, Jazz, and frankly, so am I. You didn't used to start drinking at ten o'clock in the morning and you don't seem to have any interest in planning your own wedding. We've been at this for weeks and you have yet to make any decisions about what you want." She laid her hand on my arm. "What's wrong, Jazmin?"

"Nothing's wrong." I picked up a magazine and began flipping the pages.

"Yes, there is," Arianna said. "And I think I know what it is. You don't want to marry Brick."

I slammed the magazine closed. "I *do* want to marry Brick!" I left the table again, and flopped down on the couch in the living room. "I-I just don't want to marry him right now."

The two of them came and flanked me on both sides.

Arianna lifted my hand. "How come, Jazz?"

"I don't know," I said rather irritably.

"I think you do, and I also think you're in the same place with Brick as I am with Jace."

I started to deny what she'd said, but then my curiosity took over. "What do you mean by that?"

Arianna sighed. "Do you love Brick?"

"Yes," I said a little uneasily because I wasn't sure where the girl was going with the question.

"I love Jace, too. Right now, he has a lot of problems and I don't think they are going to be as easily resolved as he thinks they are. I know Jace loves me, but he's asking me to give up my life to become embroiled in his, and I'm not sure if my love for him is strong enough for me to do that. Ever since I found out that Jace is married, our relationship has been about him—his problems, his wants, and what he wants me to do. Lately, I've been asking myself how what I want fits into all of this. But I'm not trying to compare you and Brick with Jace and me."

She might not be comparing, but the comparison was there, nonetheless. Like hers with Jace, my relationship with Brick had been all about him: his career, his lifestyle, and his wants. Doing the tour with Michael had made me remember that I had wants and needs, too. "But I love him, Arianna. Brick wants this wedding. If I don't marry him, I know I'll lose him."

Paige circled her arm around my shoulders. "But what do you want, Jazmin?"

## A Request for Closure

*Now that's a question I've been dying to ask myself,* Mags said. *What do you want, girl?*

"I want Brick and I want to marry him," I said, blinking away the water misting my eyes. "But I also want to model, and one day, when I have enough money, I want to open my beauty salon."

"Then that's what you should do," Paige stated with confidence.

"Think so, huh? Well, unfortunately, I can't have everything I want. During basketball season, Brick and I barely saw each other. My being a model halfway around the world only added stress to our relationship, and since I can't have everything I want, I guess I'd better get back to planning this wedding."

—————

"Jazzy-girl, where are you?"

"In here," I called, sitting up on the bed. I had lain down for a nap after my class that afternoon. The emotional strain of trying to plan a wedding I didn't really want, plowing my way through an exam I hadn't studied for, plus all the vodka I'd consumed had left my head reeling.

"Well, get out here, where I can see you, girl."

I came around the corner. Brick had left for Denver early that morning for a conditioning session with the team. He still had on his team jersey and gym shoes. His hair flowed around his face and his eyes were alight with love. He also had a long and overly large box in his arms as he crossed to meet me.

I rose on my toes for his kiss. "What's that?"

"Don't know, but it's for you. The manager said you were out when it came and he gave it to me when he saw me in the parking lot."

Brick set the box on the table. "By the way, the closing is scheduled for Friday afternoon. Since I have another session with the team, we can drive up together and spend the weekend."

*It's now or never, and let's not go with the never this time,* Mags said.

"I can't go to Denver on Friday, Brick. I have a class."

"Jazmin, we have changed the date of this closing twice because of your schedule, and the only reason they've continued to hold this house for us is because I play ball for the city. But I'm not canceling this closing again, so you'll have to skip school on Friday."

He left the room, which was good because I didn't want to have another argument with him over that house. I was more interested in the box.

I ripped off the brown paper, folded back the flaps, and then stood to lift the black, plastic bag inside. I carefully laid the bag on the couch, pulled down the zipper, and nearly lost my footing.

The dress was a Givenchy original, an off the shoulder, snow-white satin gown with a sweetheart neckline and a bodice decorated with a delicate pattern of tiny freshwater pearls. Transparent silk chiffon over-laid the full skirt, and the color was so soft and so subtle that you could hardly tell that it was mint green. I also found a flowing cathedral train edged in the same green and a pair of white satin slippers tucked into the bag.

My vision turned blurry. The gown was beautiful, and the wedding dress that I had described to Piper. Hearing the shower, I quickly repacked the gown and set the box back on the table. I sat down, opened the envelope, and pulled out the note and picture inside.

*Jazz,*

*This gift is from all of us, along with our wish for your happiness on your wedding day and in your new life with Vincent. We thought we'd send it early in case alterations are necessary. With the dress, I am also sending an apology for my behavior in New York. You had a brotha's back and helped me out when I needed you, and I acted like a jackass in return for that favor. But you know I love you, girl, and I miss you a lot. Be happy, Jazmin. Enclosed is my itinerary for the next six months. If you get a minute, drop a brotha a line every now and then and let me know how you're doing.*

*Michael*

In the picture, Michael stood amid Piper, Alexandria, and Candice and all held drinks in their hands. Carnival in Rio de Janeiro had been the theme of the party, if their colorful, skimpy costumes and elaborate headdresses were any indication. On the back, it simply said, "Wish you were here." I flipped to the picture again and couldn't help thinking about how much I so wanted to be there with them.

"You cook anything today, Jazzy? I'm starved."

Brick had showered and changed into another pair of sweats. Again, I thought about how lucky I was to have him. However, the photo in my hands pulled my gaze away. "There's a meatloaf in the refrigerator," I said absently while staring at the picture.

He plopped down beside me. "What's in the box?"

"My wedding dress. It's a gift from Michael, Piper, Alexandria, and Candice."

"Really," he said, his brows arching with interest.

I blocked him when he reached for the box. "It's bad luck for the groom to see the bride's dress before the ceremony."

"No it isn't, Jazzy. It's bad luck for the groom to see the bride before the ceremony."

"Brick, you cannot see my dress."

"Just a peek...a tiny one."

"No," I said as I stood.

I hefted the box and as cumbersome as it was, took it into the bedroom. When I returned, Brick was still on the couch with the picture and Michael's itinerary in his hand.

I went into the kitchen. "I'm putting the meatloaf into the oven and some potatoes. Dinner should be ready in about an hour."

He appeared in the doorway. "Know what, Jazzy? I'll take a pass on the meatloaf for another time. Tonight, I'm taking you out to eat."

—⁓⁓—

Brick took us to La Petite Maison, a totally charming and elegantly appointed little cottage located on West Colorado Avenue. The restaurant had opened only a couple of years earlier, but had become our favorite place to eat. He liked the restaurant because of its quiet, romantic atmosphere and excellent service. While the romantic air was cool, I came for the crème brûlée; a rich custard that was silky smooth and so delicious it made my mouth water thinking about it.

During dinner, Brick talked about his day and the rigorous training he'd undergone, to which I had responded with the appropriate remarks or questions, but my mind was on Michael and the others and what they were doing at that moment.

I was waiting for my dessert when Brick sat back and leveled a studied stare on me.

"You make any decisions about the wedding today, Jazzy? September thirtieth will be here before we know it."

"We looked through a bunch of magazines and catalogs, and I'm still waiting for a couple of the designers to send me their lists. But now that my dress is taken care of, the rest should be easy."

"What about the flowers, the cake, the invitations, and the other arrangements?" His stare was intense.

"I'm still working on all that."

"Hmmm," he toned.

"Brick, you know that I've doubled up on my classes and it's been hard to keep up and do all of this…this wedding stuff at the same time."

"That's why you have a wedding planner and my mother and your mother to help you, Jazmin. All you have to do is tell them what you want."

I didn't say anything.

"And since you can't seem to find the time to do that, I'm wondering if you want a wedding at all."

"I want a wedding, Brick." Just not right now.

"Hmmm," he toned again. "If that's true, Jazzy-girl, then perhaps it's me that you've decided you don't want."

Alarm bells tinkled in my head. "That's a silly thing to say. Of course I want you."

Brick banged his fist down on the table. The other couples in the dining room looked in our direction. Noticing the stares, he went through an almost physical struggle to calm his emotions. Fury reigned in his face, and when he spoke again, his voice was an impassioned whisper. "Then why won't you help plan this wedding, Jazmin Reed! And why are you so evasive whenever I ask you anything about it!"

I reached for his hand. He snatched it back. Hurt, I folded mine in my lap. "Baby, I'm doing the best that I can."

"Are you?"

The waiter set my dessert in front of me but the thought of eating the mushy custard turned my stomach. "Brick, can we leave now? I'm not feeling too well all of a sudden."

———⁂———

Brick didn't speak in the car and wanting to erase the scowl on his face, I searched my mind for something positive that I could say about the wedding. I couldn't come up with anything and I didn't want to argue with Brick about this anymore. I just needed to tell him how I felt and be done with it. Having decided that, I spent the remainder of the drive trying to think of a way to tell the man I loved that I couldn't marry him...at least not now. Though I'd made my decision, something kept niggling at me, something I couldn't quite put my finger on and it bothered me for the rest of the ride home.

As soon as we entered the house, Brick stalked off to the bedroom. I slipped my shawl from my shoulders and went to sit on the couch. When he didn't come back, I went into the bedroom. Brick was sitting on the bed and he'd taken my wedding gown out of the box. He'd spread the gown on the bed and he was rubbing the material between his fingers.

"Know something, Jazzy? I don't know who wrote it, but there is this ancient proverb I heard once and it reminds me of you." He held out his hand. I went over and he pulled me down on his lap. "If you love it, set it free. If it returns, it is yours forever. If not, then it never was. I don't know why, but that old adage makes me think of a beautiful butterfly."

His hands gripped my waist and pulled me closer. "Since the day I first saw you, all I've wanted was for you to be mine, Jazmin."

I laid my head on his chest. "I am yours, Brick."

He kissed the top of my head. "And I'm yours, Jazzy-girl. But the timing for us was not right then, and lately, I've been thinking that the timing is not right for us now."

I sat up. "Brick—"

"So, I've decided to set you free, Jazmin Reed, and when you leave to join Michael and the others on the tour, I'll be waiting and praying that one day, you'll come back to me."

*He's giving you an out,* Mags said. *Take it!*

And I could have taken it. It would have been so easy. Instead, I tuned Magnolia out and turned her off for good. I didn't need her butting into my business any longer because I suddenly knew what had been bothering me.

All along, I had thought that our relationship had been about Brick. In reality, our relationship had been about me. From the moment he'd stepped into my life, everything Brick had done, everything he had said, and everything that had been under his control had all been for me. The ring he'd purchased and set on my dresser. The support he'd given me through my struggle with school. How easily he'd agreed to let me go to Europe. He'd done all of that for me and he'd done it all because Vincent Marks truly loved me.

All he'd asked in return was for me to be his wife.

If I couldn't do that one thing for him, how could I tell this man that I loved him? And I did love Brick, with all my heart, and it was time to put his needs ahead of mine for a change. "Vincent Marks, you are the sweetest man in the whole world and I don't deserve you. But my days as a model are over. You and I are going to get married and live the rest of our lives together."

He tweaked my nose. "I know that, Jazzy," he said, with his usual confidence. "I know, too, that one day you will come back to me. Right now, you're going to Europe, and you are going to become the superstar you were always meant to be."

## A Request for Closure

"I *do* love you, Brick."

"I know that, too, Jazzy-girl." He bumped me off his lap and rose to his feet. "There is one thing I'd like you to do for me though."

"What's that?"

"Would you put on the gown, so that I can see how beautiful you would have looked on our wedding day?"

# Chapter 32

*Paige*

S top it, Raymond!" I removed his hands from my waist and pointed at the counter. "Get over there and get busy."

"But you taste way better than anything you're putting in that pot."

We were in Raymond's kitchen where I was attempting to teach him how to make spaghetti. Then at least he'd know how to prepare something the next time he invited someone for dinner. Only Raymond was not cooperating. All he seemed interested in was kissing me on the neck and rubbing up against my backside.

I grabbed the front of his shirt and pulled him to me. "You're supposed to be chopping the onions I'm going to need to put in this spaghetti sauce in a very few minutes."

"I know that," he said, and kissed me on the nose.

"You have the attention span of a two-year-old, Raymond Steward. How in the world do you get anything done at work?"

"I'm working right now—working on you and trying to get you to work on me. Come with me, I need to show you something in the bedroom real quick."

"I already know what you want to show me."

"No you don't, because I haven't showed you yet."

I squeezed the front of his pants. "Oh, I know."

Raymond groaned and turned off the stove. Taking my hand, he led me through the house to the bedroom. An hour later, we were back in the kitchen. After having some of his hyperactive energy ridden out of him, this time Raymond was more than willing to help get the meal completed. I watched him work and wondered how I was lucky enough to have a man like Raymond Steward in my life.

Since the night of my emotional confessional, I'd been trying to figure out a way to end my engagement. Lewis was a wonderful man and he loved my daughter. Two hearts would be shattered and I was having a hard time accepting my culpability in causing this mess. But Raymond had asked for the chance to prove that he was the one man who could be enough for me. I had agreed. Finally, I had made my choice.

"I'm going to set the table and in a few minutes we can eat." I left the kitchen with plates, napkins, and utensils. "What's this?" I was looking at the blueprints spread on the table.

"The plans for my house."

"You're building a house!" I couldn't keep the excitement from my voice. "Where?"

"In St. Louis."

That answer didn't translate well. "Ray, if you live here, why are you building a house in St. Louis?"

He came out of the kitchen. "I was going to talk to you after dinner about this, but we can do it now." He pointed to the blueprints with pride. "I've been envisioning this house for years, Paige. The first time I saw it was in a dream. I was eighteen, and when I woke up, I knew what I wanted to do with my life. I've been saving for years because I also knew that one day I'd have the opportunity to build my dream home."

"But in St. Louis, Ray? I don't understand."

"A couple of days ago, I was offered a promotion to a director level position. Sloan Brothers is based in St. Louis and the position is in the home office."

"Oh, I see." Although I didn't really see at all. Or maybe I didn't want to see.

"I accepted the job, Paige."

Dazed, I sat in the nearest chair. Two times two is four, I thought, trying to work through the shock his news had caused. "And you're leaving, right? When?"

"In two weeks."

"Two weeks," I whispered to myself. "But we've only finished ten chapters of *War and Peace*."

He smiled as one might when indulging a child. "Is that all you have to say, precious?"

No, I had a lot more to say. Only I didn't know how to voice what was on my mind, which was to ask him to please take me with him and be the one who didn't leave me behind. However, Raymond's plans not only for his house but for me as well were already crystal clear. "Would you mind if we had dinner another night?"

"But the spaghetti…it's not done yet."

I went to the couch and grabbed my purse. "All you have to do is mix the onion with the hamburger, let it fry until the hamburger is done and mix it with the sauce."

"Paige, don't go. Let's eat our dinner and talk about it."

I rose on my toes to kiss him. "Congratulations on your promotion, Raymond. Good luck in St. Louis." I hurried to the door.

I was almost to my car when he grabbed my arm. He pulled me to his chest and brought his mouth down on mine. I held on to him and returned the kiss with all of the passion I could, because it would be the last one that I ever shared with him.

When the kiss ended, Raymond wouldn't release me. "I love you, Paige and I'm building the house for—"

"There's no need to explain. I understand perfectly." I pulled back from his arms.

"I love you, Paige!"

I climbed inside my car. "Goodbye, Raymond."

He was still talking when I started the engine, and after backing out of the space, I couldn't help taking one last look. Raymond stood there, looking confused and frustrated at the same time. I wanted to stop and go back to him. I wanted to beg him not to leave, or if not that, then to take Jessie and me with him. The reality was that despite everything he'd said to me, Raymond, like all of the other men who'd passed through my life, was going to leave me behind, too.

## A *Request for Closure*

So, I didn't stop, and driving away from him, I told myself that it didn't matter, that I still had Lewis. That thought provided no comfort at all, because no matter what happened, I would always remember the first man in my life who had ever romanced me and treated me as if I were something special, and the only man who had ever taken root in my heart.

I couldn't go straight home. I needed to compose myself before Lewis saw me and wanted to know what was wrong. Knowing that I wouldn't be able to tell him, I drove around for a little while, and when I felt I'd sufficiently pulled myself together, I headed back to the Pikes Peak apartment complex and to my family.

———✺———

The disillusionment I felt over Raymond was nothing compared to the shock I experienced when I entered the bedroom and found Lewis packing his suitcase.

One times one is one, I thought, as I placed a hand on my chest and tried to stop the frantic beating of my heart. "Lewis?" He didn't say anything. He didn't have to; his face said it all. The man was incensed. "What are you doing, Lewis?"

"I'm packing," he said tersely. "By the way, Jessie is upstairs at Arianna's."

I ignored what he'd said about Jessie, and although my mind told me that I knew, my heart told me to ask anyway. "I can see that. What I don't understand is why."

Lewis kept throwing his clothes into that suitcase. I stepped in front of him.

"Lewis?"

"Oh, you understand all right, Paige!" Then he shoved me out of the way and went back to packing his clothes.

I did understand. I didn't know how he had found out, but somehow he had. I went into the living room, sat on the couch, and began rebuilding the wall that had shielded my heart since the age of eight. But for every brick I put in place, two came crumbling down.

When Lewis entered the room with his suitcase, the last brick fell in a cloud of dust and my shattered heart lay in the ruins. "How did you find out?"

Lewis laughed. It sounded dry, without humor, and full of hurt. He bent over the rack where our combined albums were stored and began sorting his from the stack. "Now that's an interesting story," he said. "Earlier tonight, I went outside to call Jessie in for dinner and when she didn't answer, I knew she'd again gone beyond the boundaries I set for her. I was wandering the complex looking for her, and that's when I saw you. How long has it been going on, Paige?"

Lewis knew about Raymond and he was leaving so there was no point in giving him the details. On the other hand, Raymond was leaving, too, and I was about to be alone again, so what did it matter anymore? "For a while now," I finally answered.

"That's what I figured." He glanced at my left hand. "Where's your ring?"

I went to the kitchen table and picked up my purse. I held the ring out. Lewis didn't move.

"Don't you want it back?"

His jaw clenched and his eyes closed. I could see his inner struggle to hold himself together. A few moments later, his eyes snapped open and they were blazing. "No! You keep it. I don't want anything that will remind me of you! Maybe you should let Raymond Steward know that you have it, so that he won't spend his money unnecessarily."

Lewis took his albums out to the car. Two times two is four. Three times three is nine. He entered again and went to the hall closet. "How did you know?"

"How did I know what?"

"His name, Lewis. How did you find out his name?"

Lewis leveled a smirk at me. "I could tell you it was Jessie, and though she confirmed it, actually it was you."

## A *Request for Closure*

"Me!" I stood up and moved toward him, but stopped when I saw the warning glare in his eyes.

He slung his coat over his arm, and then did a visual check of the apartment for anything he'd left. "The day you went to Santa's Workshop, Jessie told me that she'd had a good time with her friend, Ray. I figured another kid had gone with the two of you. Later that night, you murmured his name in your sleep. I still didn't make the connection, until tonight when Jessie walked up and asked me if I wanted to meet her special friend, Raymond Steward." Lewis blew out a breath. "I always knew you were selfish, Paige, but how could you make my daughter a part of this, too?"

He stalked out the door. I ran behind him. "Lewis, what about Jessie? What am I supposed to tell her?"

He stared at the ground. "Tell Jessica that I love her and that she will always be my little girl."

Then he climbed in his car and drove away.

Stunned, I stood in the parking lot long after the red of the tail lights on the TransAm disappeared down the street. Finally shivering with cold, I went back inside my apartment and directly to my bedroom, where I threw myself across the bed. Reaching up, I gathered Lewis's pillow and placed it under my head. I pressed my nose into its softness and inhaled his scent, and I wished him back, knowing all the time that no amount of wishing was going to bring him back. In two weeks, Raymond would leave, too, and no matter how hard I wished, it wouldn't bring him back either.

A short while later, something soft rubbed against my cheek and I opened my eyes. Jessie had crawled up on the bed next to me. She sat with her legs folded Indian-style, smiling at me with wide, bright eyes. I stared back and it hit me so suddenly that I blinked.

All of my life, I had been looking for someone to be there for me, someone to help me through my ups and downs, and to love me for who I was and not for who they thought that I should be.

Though she'd never known her father, Jessie had been with me through the divorce. She'd been there through countless other men.

Lewis was gone and Jessie was still there. When Raymond Steward left, Jessie would still be there. Jessica was the one person who had always loved me unconditionally, and she was the one person who would always be there.

"Where's Daddy?"

Instead of answering, I tugged Jessie into my arms and silently vowed that from this day forward, I was going to be there for my daughter. Later, when I wasn't so exhausted and had a chance to figure it out myself, I would explain to her about Lewis. Right now, I just wanted hold on tightly to my baby.

# Chapter 33

*Arianna*

"What am I supposed to do while you and Debra are making like husband and wife?"

Jace had not signed up for reenlistment, and in less than four weeks, he was leaving for home. Lauren was back in New York and was fine, according to his mother. Upon her return, however, Debra had filed a counter suit...and she'd nailed Jace for infidelity. I wasn't involved, but to strengthen his custody case, Samuel had advised Jace to move back in with Debra.

Jace adamantly refused that option, then found he couldn't really refute the advice. He wouldn't have to stay long, only until Debra dropped her suit. Even so, Jace wanted me with him, and I wanted us to be together. So I sat with him that night and tried to reason in my mind how we could make this work.

"You can stay with my mother."

"And do what, Alvin? Besides that, how would your mother feel about me coming into her home, knowing her son has a wife?"

"Mom knows what is going on with Debra."

"But think about the position you'd place her in...place me in. You can't possibly think that Debra is going to let you get away with that."

"Debra doesn't have to know."

"What are you planning to do, sneak around? I'm not moving to New York to live like that. I'd rather stay here and when this is over you can send for me."

"How can you ask me to do that when you know I want you with me?"

"Right now, it's the only thing that makes sense. You go to New York and get your divorce. I'll stay here and keep my job. That way, you won't be distracted trying to find a way to support both of us and deal with Debra at the same time."

"Okay, Ari. If we do this your way and I send for you, will you come?" I guess I must have waited a heartbeat too long to answer because Jace suddenly got angry. "You won't come, Arianna! I know you won't. I'm not leaving you here. When I go, you go!"

"Getting angry is not going to help. We're trying to find a solution here."

"I'm trying to find a solution. You're trying to convince me to leave here without you. Once I'm gone, you'll forget about me and find someone else. That's it, isn't it?"

"I'm not going to dignify that with an answer."

"That's because it's the truth!"

I stood up. "Why don't we discuss this another time, Jace? When you're more rational."

He followed me into the bedroom. "I'm rational now, and all I want to know is if you'll come when I send for you."

I wanted so badly to tell him yes, but I couldn't. "May I have some time to think about this, please?"

"How much time?"

"Jace, this is a big decision for me. New York is your home. Mine is here, and I'm the one who has to give up everything. I won't know anyone in New York City."

"You'll know me."

"What about my job? And my friends?"

"I've already said you're not going to work, and you'll make new friends."

"Jace, I *have* to work. You're getting out of the army. What are we supposed to do for money?"

"I'll get a job!"

"I thought you were going to be a policeman."

## A Request for Closure

"I don't want to discuss this anymore, Arianna. You're going to New York."

I reached for his hand. "Jace, please. You said I could think about it."

"Arianna, I know you're scared and this stuff with Debra isn't helping, is it?" He sat on the bed and lifted me into his lap. His kisses were warm, and soft, and so full of love I couldn't help responding. "I love you, Arianna. Please come with me. Now, not later. What will it take to convince you? Do you want me to beg? Is that what you want?"

"No, Jace."

"Then say yes, baby girl." He tugged my blouse over my head and pushed up my bra. Jace knew my body well and between his lips and his hands, it was only a matter of minutes before he had me reeling in ecstasy. Jace mounted me. "Come with me, baby girl," he repeatedly whispered in my ear while thrusting himself into my body.

"Jace," I moaned.

"Come with me," he repeated, and before it was over, I had given Jace the answer he wanted to hear.

"You'll never regret this, sweetheart. I'm promising you right now that everything will be all right. You won't change your mind again, will you?"

"No, I'll come to New York."

"And you'll leave with me. When I go, you go."

"Yes, if that's what you want."

"That's all I want, sweetheart."

Soft kisses rained down on my face. What Jace didn't know was that I was already regretting my answer. It didn't feel right. I felt as if he'd manipulated me into doing what he wanted. In his eyes, however, all I saw was his love, and I tried to let that convince me that I'd made the right decision.

"What are you doing?"

"Checking over these reports for payroll." I set the papers aside when Paige sat in the chair beside my desk.

"I handed in my resignation."

"What! Why!"

"Because I'm moving to Denver."

"Get out of here. You aren't moving to Denver. You just took that job to head up the word processing center."

"I'm not kidding, Ari. I *am* moving to Denver. I got a job. And guess what else."

"What?"

"I'll be making almost ten thousand more a year than I'm getting now."

I studied her for a couple of seconds. She was serious. "That's great, Paige." I stood up to give her a hug, then plopped back down in my chair. "God, I wish I was going with you."

"You do?" she said, looking more than surprised.

"Yeah. If I went to Denver with you, it would sure save wear and tear on my heart."

"Jace is still leaving, huh?"

I nodded. "Yeah."

"And you're not going with him?"

"I told him that I would, Paige, but how can I? Everything's so complicated. Jace is going back to live with Debra. He says it's only until he can convince her to give him the divorce. What am I supposed to do while he's doing that? I love Jace, but I can't see myself sitting in New York caught up in that mess. What if this divorce takes years…or never comes through? Then where would I be?"

"Girl, I don't know." We both sat silent for a few moments before Paige sat up. "Listen, Ari. Why don't you come to Denver with me? I found a job. I know you can, too."

"I don't know. Maybe I will. When are you moving?"

"Next week."

"Next week! That's so soon, P."

"I know. They want me to start as soon as possible and I've already turned in my resignation."

"P, you're not doing this because of what happened with Raymond and Lewis, are you?"

"No, Arianna! I'm doing this for me...and for Jessie. I am sick to death of Colorado Springs and the men that live in this town. Jazmin got out and I'm getting out, too."

"I hear you, girl."

Paige stood up. "I need to get back downstairs. You think about what I said, Arianna, and if you decide you want to make the move to Denver, too, give me a call."

"You know I'll help with the packing. When are you going to start?"

"I've already started."

"Then I'll be down tonight."

That night, Jace talked about his plans for us when we arrived in New York. I didn't mention anything about Paige, her plans to move to Denver, or that I was considering going with her. But I was.

A week before we were scheduled to leave, I changed my mind for the last time. I wanted to go with Jace, and some days I actually thought that I could. However, I was scared, not of Jace or that he didn't love me. I was afraid of leaving the security of my home and going off with a man who was not free to be mine. If Jace weren't married, I wouldn't have hesitated to pack my things.

For now, it was best if I stayed here and when Jace had his divorce, he could send for me and I'd come running. I didn't tell Jace of my decision. He was so adamant that I would be with him when he left, I knew he'd never accept it, and I didn't want to spend our last week together arguing.

So, I kept my mouth shut and gave him all the love I had to give. Alone, I cried tears of heartbreak. I was able to keep up the I until the night Jace came home earlier than expected and caught me in the middle of one of my crying jags. He didn't say anything as he rushed over and held me until I finally pulled myself together.

"I'm sorry, baby. I don't know what came over me."

Jace rubbed the last of the water from my face. "I do. You've decided not to go with me." He smiled sadly. "I could convince you to change your mind, you know."

"But you won't."

Wanda Y. Thomas

"No, baby girl. I won't. Not this time."

"I'm sorry, Jace. I tried. I really did."

"I know you did, sweetheart. This is all too much for you. I guess I was hoping you'd go with me anyway. It's okay, Arianna. I know you love me. I've asked an awful lot of you and I understand why you're afraid to take a chance with me now, but promise me this. When I have my divorce and I send for you, will you come to me?" I nodded against his chest. Jace raised my face. "Say the words, Arianna. I need to hear you say the words."

"When your divorce is final and you send for me, I will come to you, Jace Barnes, no matter how long it takes."

"Okay. That's all I can hope for right now. And don't you let any other man take my place. You're mine, Ari, now and forever, and I'll send for you as soon as I can. I promise."

That he'd accepted my decision so easily made me love him even more. When all this craziness was behind him, I could go to him and everything would be all right.

———

Two months after Jace left, I was still writing in my journal. Letting him go without me had been the hardest thing I'd ever done. Even though I'd almost changed my mind at the last minute and jumped in that Firebird with him, I'd gotten through it. I'd watched him drive away with my heart aching and tears in my eyes. He called every night, and while I still believed in him and in his promise to me, Jace had moved on to the next phase of his life. And being away from his constant pressure had given me a clearer perspective.

Jazmin was having a ball in Europe and she wasn't coming home anytime soon. Paige was doing well in Denver. She liked her new job and she had gone on a man hiatus, according to her. I was the only one stuck in the same place and I needed to change that.

## A Request for Closure

I closed the journal and went to retrieve the others that I kept in a box in the back of the closet. Beginning with the first, I spent the day reading them from cover to cover. Then I threw away all but the last two, the ones that chronicled my relationship with Jace. Sitting there thinking about my life, I decided that other than shopping, I had no love of finance. What I really liked was writing, and reading those journals had shown me that I might have a natural talent.

I got up and readied myself for bed. Tomorrow, I would contact Paige about moving to Denver, and once I landed a job, I would enroll in some writing courses. When Jace sent for me, he'd find me waiting, but it wouldn't be in the same place as where he'd left me.

# THE REUNION – PART II

## COLORADO SPRINGS, COLORADO

## SUMMER, 1999

# Chapter 34

*Friday Night*

Paige, try to call her husband again. It's almost seven and Ari knows we're sitting here waiting on her. Something must have happened or she would have called by now."

"You're right." Paige picked up the phone and quickly dialed the number she'd already dialed four times that day. "This is Paige Michaels," she said when Freddie answered. "Is Arianna there?"

His heartbeat stopped. This was the ninth time the phone had rung that day. Earlier, he hadn't answered because he was upset and hurt that Arianna had actually boarded that plane. This time he'd answered because he'd needed to hear her voice and to tell her how sorry he was for the things he'd said.

"Is Arianna here? She called eight hours ago and told me she was there. What's going on, Paige? Where is Arianna? Where's my wife!"

"Wait, Freddie, wait! I don't mean to upset you, but I haven't seen Arianna. I thought she might have changed her mind about coming. If she's here, then I'm sure she's on her way, so don't panic. I'll—"

"Don't panic? You call here and tell me that my wife is missing, and then try to tell me not to panic. Well, it's too late for that!" Freddie dropped into the armchair behind him. *Oh, honey,* he thought. *I didn't mean to upset you like this.*

Paige heard what she thought were quiet sobs and she began to panic, too. "Freddie! What happened between you and Arianna? Freddie! Answer me!"

Jazmin snatched the phone. "Freddie, this is Jazmin Miller. Freddie?"

On his end, Freddie exhaled. "I'm sorry, Paige. But I—"

## A Request for Closure

"This isn't Paige, it's Jazmin. I need to know what happened between you and Arianna."

*What happened,* he thought, *was that I drove my wife away.* "When Ari called me this morning, I said some things to her that I didn't mean."

"What *things,* Freddie?"

At first, he wasn't going to answer. What he'd said to his wife was their intimate business. Now Arianna was missing and it was entirely his fault. "I told her...I told Arianna that I didn't want her to come back."

"Why in the world would you tell her something like that?"

Freddie knew why but it was hard for him to admit that jealousy and anger had formed the words he'd spoken to his wife. "I didn't mean it and only said it because I was upset. I love my wife and if Arianna ever left me..." Freddie took a deep breath and let it out slowly. "I'm coming out there to find Ari. When I do, I'm bringing my wife home where she belongs."

"If I were you, I'd want to do the same thing. But as her husband, I'm sure that you know how sensitive Arianna is and that it hurt her deeply when you told her not to come home. She's probably somewhere brooding about it. Once she figures things out, she'll call or show up here. And there's always the possibility that she might be on her way home right now."

Paige slumped against the counter. There was nothing more important to Arianna than her family, and she couldn't let Arianna lose her marriage because of something she'd done, no matter how good the intentions. Paige went to her purse and pulled out her cell phone.

"But what if something's happened to her? What if—"

"Nothing has happened to her!" Jazmin paced the floor. "What you should do is stay by the phone in case Ari calls you first, and I'll keep you informed of what's happening on our end."

Freddie knew he had to do something and that something was catching the next flight to Colorado. Only it wouldn't leave until tomorrow and he could drive there just as fast. Then again, if Arianna was on her way home, he needed to be here when she arrived. "All right," he finally said. "I'll wait until I hear back from you."

Jazmin smiled in spite of the situation. "And Frederick Lane, you can stop being jealous of Alvin Barnes. You are the only man in Arianna's heart and the most important person in her life. She tells me that every time we talk."

"Thank you, Jazmin. I'd better hang up now, in case Ari's is trying to get through to me. Goodbye."

"Bye, Freddie." Jazmin hung up the telephone and dropped her head to her hands. Life was just too damn complicated. Then she stood and rolled her shoulders. When she saw Paige on the phone, she went into the kitchen. She needed a drink.

"He's on his way."

"Freddie is staying in Kansas…in case Arianna calls or shows up. I absolutely cannot believe that man threw Ari out of her home. God, men are such bastards sometimes." Jazmin drained her glass.

"I'm not talking about Freddie. I called Jace and he's on his way."

"You called Alvin Barnes to come over here. Paige, why would you do that? Arianna is not going to want to see Jace. She's going to want her husband."

"I didn't know what else to do."

Jazmin slammed the glass down on the counter. "Dammit, Paige! Why did you do this? Arianna had a good life and she was happy. Was it worth it, P? Arianna is supposed to be your friend. You didn't have to do this, not after all this time."

Paige crossed her arms over her stomach. "Ari *is* my friend and I'm not carrying out some grudge against her. I know she loves Freddie. I just wanted her to resolve things with Jace so that she could be free of the man, not lose her family over him."

"I guess that didn't work out, now did it?"

Jazmin left the kitchen and went to the room Paige had shown her earlier. Her marriage was about as fucked up as it could get, so Paige's telegram had played no part in destroying her life. But to do something like this to Arianna, to take away everything that Ari loved like this—Well, it wasn't right, and Jazmin wasn't sure if she would ever be able to forgive Paige Michaels this time.

Paige was on her way to talk to Jazmin when the front door opened.

"Is she here yet?"

"Not yet." When Raymond opened his arms, Paige laid her head on his chest. "God, I wish I'd never sent that telegram."

"It will be all right, precious. I'm here now and I'll take care of everything."

—◦◦◦—

"Jace!" Paige hugged him around the neck so tightly he had to back up a few steps to keep his balance. "I'm so glad to see you!"

He set her away. "You're still looking good, Paige."

"You are too." She grabbed his hand and pulled him inside.

"Has Ari made it here yet?"

Her exuberance died. "No, and before you ask she hasn't called either."

Worry replaced his smile. "What are we doing about that?"

"We were just discussing what our next move should be. You must be Jace Barnes."

Jace looked at the tall man standing behind Paige. "I am, but my friends call me Al."

"Raymond Steward," he replied, moving around Paige. "My friends call me Ray. Good to finally meet you, man."

"Good to meet you, too, brotha." Jace pumped the extended hand. Then he narrowed his eyes at the woman standing at the end of the hallway. "Jazmin Reed?"

She smiled. She'd come out to see what all the commotion was about and maybe with the hope that she'd finally see Brick. "Actually, it's Jazmin Reed-Miller now. How are you, Mr. Barnes?"

Jace dipped his chin and his lips tilted in a mischievous grin. "Mr. Barnes," he said, mimicking her austere tone. "Like you don't know somebody. Girl, you'd better get over here and give me a hug."

Freddie dialed Arianna's cell phone. When the message service answered for the fourth time, he let loose with a loud expletive and slammed down the telephone. That woke his son and Freddie headed for the nursery. An hour later, he was sitting in Arianna's rocking chair when the ringing telephone woke him. He put James into his crib, pulled up the cover, and ran to his bedroom.

"Arianna!"

"No, Frederick, this is your mother. And why you are yelling into this telephone?"

"I'm sorry," he said, ruffling his fingers through his hair. "I was hoping you were Ari."

"Hoping? Arianna hasn't called to check in with you yet? Her plane left at five o'clock this morning. Surely she's arrived in Colorado Springs by now."

Freddie sat heavily on the bed. "She did call, Mom, and I said some things that upset her and her friends haven't seen her."

"Oh, Frederick. I told you to let go of this thing you've been carrying about that man a long time ago. Arianna gave you three sons and she has stood beside you throughout your marriage. She's not going anywhere, Freddie."

"I know, but I was so angry when she left."

"You told her to go! At least that what she said to me when we talked the other day. Arianna doesn't want to see that man and she was waiting for you to ask her not to go." Madeline exhaled. "What am I going to do with my two children? But more importantly, what are you going to do about your wife?"

"I don't know, Mom. Wait until Ari calls me, I guess."

"You guess? You mean to tell me that you're going to sit here while your wife is in Colorado with another man! I thought I raised you better than that, Frederick Allan Lane."

"But the boys—"

"Can come and stay with their grandparents, but then you know that. What are you afraid of, Frederick?"

He closed his eyes and forced himself to voice the fear he'd carried for over seventeen long years. "I guess I'm afraid that now that Arianna has heard from Jace Barnes, she doesn't want me anymore."

———⌘———

## A Request for Closure

The volume of the conversation escalated and Paige closed her eyes. They'd been at this for over an hour with the discussion ranging from starting a search to calling the police, and they were no closer to a resolution than when they'd started. A knock sounded on the door and she rose to answer it, wishing with all her heart that she'd minded her own business. Opening the door, Paige stared at the woman in front of her.

"I need to use your phone."

"Arianna!"

The other three people in the room froze, and then they were all in the doorway.

Raymond grabbed the suitcase. Paige pulled Arianna into the house. "Where were you?"

"Are you all right, baby girl?"

"I'm fine."

"We were so worried," Jazmin said, "and Freddie is frantic. It was all I could do to convince him to stay in Kansas. Come with me, we need to talk."

"But I have to call Freddie."

"In a minute." Jazmin picked up the phone then led the way down the hall to a bedroom. "Before you call home, I want you to know that everything's okay. Freddie's deeply sorry for the things he said to you."

"Did he say that, Jazmin?"

"Yes, he did, and you needed to know before you dialed." Jazmin gave her quick hug. "That's it, girl. Now, call and talk to your husband."

A few minutes later, Arianna hung up. It was ten o'clock in Delphos, Kansas. Where was her husband?

―⌇⌇―

The phone rang and Jace looked toward the noisy instrument. Her snub earlier had stung, but he'd written it off to the stress of the evening and had been waiting politely for Arianna to get off the phone. He stood and picked up her suitcase.

Jazmin stepped in front of him. "Leave her alone, Jace. Ari's been through enough today."

He blew out a weary breath. "I'm going to talk to Arianna."

"Why don't you give her some time to settle down," Raymond suggested.

"Too much time has passed already." Jace turned for the hallway.

"Jace."

He glanced over his shoulder at Paige.

"Ari's been hurt enough, not only today but in her life. Don't you go in there and give her any more pain."

He nodded and left the room.

———

Jace poked his head around the door. "I have your suitcase, baby girl, and I'm coming in."

Arianna put up her hand. "I don't want to see you."

He entered and closed the door behind him. "Why not, Arianna? It's been a long time and I've been so looking forward to seeing you again."

The expression on her face changed to alarm and Jace stopped in the middle of the floor. He hadn't fooled himself into thinking that they would share a holly-jolly reunion, but they had once loved each other, and in his mind, that should count for something. While his mind worked on another approach, Jace completed a visual inventory.

Her face showed no signs of aging and her body was fuller and more curvaceous. She was more beautiful than he remembered and it was a struggle for Jace to remain where he stood when all he wanted was to take Arianna in his arms and hold her there forever.

He took a tentative step forward. "Baby girl, I—"

"Don't call me that. I am forty-five years old and have three babies of my own."

He moved to the end of the bed. "I'm sorry, Ari. I'm not trying to upset you, but no matter how old you get or how many babies you have, you will always be my baby girl, here." Jace pointed at his head. "And here," he said, pointing at his heart. "So, if I forget and slip up, I'm asking you now to forgive me. Okay?"

"What do you want?"

"Mind if I sit down?"

Arianna surveyed the room. The only place he could sit was on the bed. Knowing that dredged up memories that she quickly squashed. "No." She got off the bed; and kept going.

Jace moved to stop her. "We need to talk."

"Alvin, there's not a thing that you can tell me that I want to hear at this late date."

"I'm sorry that I didn't keep my promise to you, Arianna. I wanted to send for you, but I couldn't."

At one time, she had wanted nothing more than for Jace to explain. Now, she didn't care. "Thank you for the apology. Would you please leave now?"

"Don't you want to know why, Ari?"

"No, Jace. I don't."

Life had a way of balancing the scales. While it had been difficult for him to accept, in the long run, it was for the best that they had separated. Incited by his insecurities over a cheating wife, he'd become a master manipulator—something a high profile shooting followed by required sessions with the department therapist had pointed out to Jace. It was a skill that served him well as a detective now, but he'd used it back then to keep Arianna tied to him. All he wanted was a chance to offer a heartfelt apology for the things he had done to her. Arianna was going to make this as difficult as possible for him. Truthfully, he'd expected nothing less. "Okay, baby girl. We'll talk later."

---

Jazmin heard rustling outside the door and bounced to her feet. This time it had to be Vincent Marks.

"Mom, I'm here!"

Paige ran out of the kitchen and Jazmin plopped back down.

"Jessie! Why didn't you call? I told you that Raymond would pick you up at the airport."

"I got here okay."

Paige's eyes filled with love. "Yes, you did."

Jessie crossed to Jace and kissed him on the cheek. "Thanks for coming, Uncle Jace."

"You're welcome," he said.

"Hey, Stepdad. You taking care of my momma?"

"Sure am, pumpkin. Stand back so I can take a look at you."

Large brown eyes, densely lashed and set in a dark oval face, stared back at him. Long, curly tresses hung over her shoulders. At five feet, ten inches, Jessica had a willowy figure shaped by generous womanly curves.

Jessie glanced at Jazmin. "What's crack-a-lacking, Auntie Jazz?" Jessie laughed at the look of surprise on Jazmin's face. "Oh wait a minute," she said. "I need to use terminology y'all know. Whadup? What's shak-in'? What's hap-pen-in', Auntie Jazz?"

Jazmin couldn't help chuckling. She hadn't seen Jessie, a first-year law student at Stanford University since she'd brought her to New York as a college graduation present three months ago. "Get over here, girl, and quit acting so stupid."

"Where Auntie Ari?"

"Probably asleep. She went to bed thirty minutes ago."

Jessie's face fell. "But Mom, you know I'm not staying here tonight. I just stopped in to say hello to everybody, especially Auntie Ari."

"I said that Ari went to bed. You'll have to see her in the morning."

An hour later, Jessie left and Paige stretched her arms over her head. "Know what, y'all? It's been a long day and we have an even longer one tomorrow. I think we all need to get some sleep."

# Chapter 35

*Saturday Morning*

The next morning, Arianna was up with the sun and on the phone attempting to reach Freddie. Back home, he normally put in two good hours getting the early morning chores out of the way before she and the boys even opened their eyes.

Their home sat on land adjacent to her in-laws and since it was Saturday, Arianna knew that her boys were at their grandparents for their weekly pancake breakfast. Freddie, who loved being a farmer, was probably out in the barn.

Disappointed again, Arianna hung up. She filled a cup with coffee and took it with her outside to the patio. The sun felt warm on her face. The air smelled clean and fresh, reminding her of home and of her family. She'd been away for one day and already she missed the routine of the life that she'd come to love.

Her lips turned downward when she thought about Jace. He'd finally come back and he'd apologized. For Arianna, that was enough. She shaded her eyes with her hand and made a decision. She'd stay for the wedding because she'd promised Paige. Then she was going home to save her marriage. She entered the house and went back to the phone. When Freddie didn't answer, she dialed her in-laws.

"Mama, it's Ari. Is Freddie there?"

"Arianna! We were so worried about you. Are you all right, Daughter?"

"I'm fine, Mama. Is Freddie there? I really need to talk to him."

"He's not here, Ari. He had to make a trip into town. Why don't you leave the number where you are with me and I'll make sure he calls you when he returns."

Arianna rattled off the number and spoke briefly to her sons before hanging up the phone.

"Good morning. I see you've already made coffee."

"Morning, P."

Paige reached into a cabinet for a cup. "How are you doing this morning?"

"I'm fine, or at least I will be when I talk to Freddie."

Paige poured her coffee, added cream, and sat at the kitchen table. "You didn't talk to him last night?"

"He didn't answer, which is odd since it was so late." Arianna looked at Paige with sad eyes, but couldn't voice the words that hammered at her heart. Her husband didn't want to talk to her. "Freddie likes to work the horses early on Saturday." She shrugged. "You know, before the sun gets too hot."

"I understand." Paige took a sip from her cup. "When we lived here all those years ago, I never would have imagined that you would wind up as a housewife living on a farm in Kansas and also be a best selling novelist. Or that Jazz would be a world famous model and the owner of a chain of exclusive salons."

"Well, I figured Jazz would own her salons one day; it was all she used to talk about. But don't forget yourself on that list of accomplishments. Michaels' Executive Services has coached some of the top corporate leaders in the nation and that consulting business of yours makes money hand over fist. I'd say that we all exceeded any dreams we may have had when we were twenty-something. We've grown up, Paige."

"That's for sure," Jazmin said as she entered the room. "Morning, y'all."

"Morning, Jazz. For someone who used to be one of the top models in the world, you still look like hell in the morning."

"Forget you, P."

"How did you sleep?"

"Like a log, Ari. All that stress you provided last night wore me out. But I see one of you has made the coffee, thank goodness."

Arianna turned back to Paige. "So tell us, how did you and Raymond hook up after all this time?"

"Actually, it was Jessie. In fact, she's been the catalyst behind all of this."

Jazmin joined them at the table. "What do you mean?"

"What I mean is that I was a child when I had Jessie and I wasn't raising my daughter in the best of environments. Everything happening around Jessie affected her more than I knew."

"Jessie's fine, Paige," Arianna said. "She's a wonderful young woman and she has you to thank for that."

"No," Paige said quietly. "She had the two of you, and for a while she had Lewis. Anyway, after I explained to her about Lewis leaving, Jessie seemed to be okay with it. Then Raymond moved to St. Louis. You left for Europe, Jazmin, and Brick moved to Denver. Jace left for New York, and though you did eventually move in with us, Jessie was away from you for several months, Arianna. It wasn't until years later that Jessie told me that she felt as if all of the people she loved, that her family had abandoned her."

"Oh, Paige, I'm sorry."

"It's not your fault, Ari, and Jessie took matters into her own hands. Though she didn't have a chance to get to Lewis for his, she did get phone numbers from all of the others. When we moved to Denver, she called Brick, and she called Jace, and she called Raymond to let them know where she was, and she's been in contact with all of them ever since."

"But what does that have to do with you and Raymond?"

"Hold up, Jazz, I'm getting to that." Paige left the table to refill her cup. When she sat back down, she said, "Six months ago, Jessie called me from school. She had broken up with her boyfriend and she was very upset. I told Jessie that she would hurt for a little while, but that eventually she would find true love with the man that she was supposed to love for the rest of her life. She asked me why I'd never found true love. I told her I had. When she asked me who the man was, I told her Raymond Steward."

"I knew it," Arianna whispered almost to herself.

"Raymond told me that he loved me. At the time, I didn't believe him because he was leaving me like all of the others and I wanted to be the one who walked away that time. Anyway, about two weeks after talking to Jessie, Raymond showed up at my front door with roses and a bottle of wine. The rest, as they say, is history."

"I should put your story in a novel."

"You do, and I'll sue you, Arianna Lane. I'm not trying to have my life put in anybody's book."

"But think of all the money we'd make. I should write about you, too, Jazz."

Jazmin pushed up from the table. "I'm going to take a shower, and just so we're clear on this, I'm with P. If I see even a hint of my life in one of your books, I'll sue your ass, too."

Arianna chuckled, but stopped when she glanced at the phone.

Paige touched her arm. "I'm sorry for what's happened, Ari. I never meant to cause trouble between you and Freddie."

"I know. It's just that Freddie thinks I still have feelings for Jace, and he couldn't be more wrong. I love my husband and I'm not going to lose him over something I should have put to rest twenty years ago." She rose to her feet. "I think I'll try to call him again."

Paige gave her a shaky smile. "I think maybe you should."

———⟨∽∿∽⟩———

*Saturday Afternoon*

Jace watched Arianna hang up the phone and leave the room. He followed. He'd been trying to talk to her all day and she'd adroitly avoided being anywhere around him.

At the door to her bedroom, Arianna suddenly whirled around. "Leave me alone, Alvin!"

"Arianna, please. I just want to talk, and the sooner we do that, the sooner I'll leave you alone."

She turned away and prayed for strength. Until she let him say whatever he'd come to tell her, Jace would continue to nag her. Arianna opened the door. "Okay, Jace. I'm ready to talk now."

Arianna sat on the bed. Before he could join her, she pointed at the dresser. "You can stand over there."

## A Request for Closure

A little disappointed, but willing to concede to her wishes, Jace crossed to the dresser. Leaning back, he crossed his arms over his chest, a chest, Arianna noted, that had spread wider and gotten thicker over the years. Since she was looking anyway, she noted the other changes time had wrought on Alvin Barnes. His hair, while still full of waves, had grayed to salt and pepper. There were crinkles at the corners of his eyes. Other than that, his face and skin were ebony smooth and Jace still radiated the confidence that had been so much of his persona. Time had been kind to Jace and Arianna had half a mind to tell him, but quelled the urge almost as quickly as it came.

Jace chewed on his bottom lip and clenched his hands into fists before pushing them into his pockets to hide his nervousness. He loved this woman and it shouldn't be this hard to find something to say to her, but it felt awkward between them, like they were two opposites on a blind date going nowhere fast.

Other women found him attractive, if their constant advances meant anything. But only one had ever held his heart, and that one was inspecting him as if he was a lab specimen smeared on a Petri dish. Had it been anyone other than Arianna, he might have held up under the scrutiny. However, it was Arianna, and Jace Barnes couldn't take it any more. He sucked in a deep breath and diverted his eyes from her unblinking stare. The silence grew even more uncomfortable as he searched his brain for something that would crack Arianna's frosty demeanor. This was ridiculous. Now that he had her attention, surely he could think of something to say. He swallowed and then said the first thing that came into his head.

"How have you been, Ari?"

"After twenty years, I can't imagine why you would care how I've been."

Anxiety crossed his face. "I care, baby girl. I've never stopped caring about you."

She stood up. "I've been fine, Jace. If there's nothing else, I have things to do."

He blocked her path. "Sit down, Arianna." She still had that stubborn streak, he noted, when she crossed her arms in defiance. "Please," he said, waving his hand to aid his request.

She crinkled her nose, but did as he'd asked. He quickly took a place beside her, and immediately regretted the move when a light floral scent twitched at his nose. Jace inhaled, and then fought off the urge to bury his face in her hair.

"Regardless of what you think, I do have feelings for you. One of the things I wanted to tell you is that I have purchased and read all of your books. You're a talented writer, Arianna, and I want you to know that I'm proud of you."

Arianna heard the sincerity in his voice and stared straight ahead as she battled to hold her resolve. "So is my husband. How is *your* wife, Alvin?"

Not expecting that response, he blinked. "What wife, Arianna?"

She looked him in the eye. "Debra."

Jace didn't want to answer, preferring to forget that period in his life. However, Arianna was talking to him, and since Debra was the reason they were not together, she deserved to know the truth. "Debra and I divorced over nineteen years ago."

Rocked by his answer, she could only stutter, "But I thought, I-I—" She stopped to steady her nerves and her voice. "If that's true, then why didn't you send for me?" As soon as the words left her mouth, Arianna wanted to call them back. It no longer mattered.

Jace picked up her hand, pleased when she didn't pull away. "Baby girl, I didn't send for you because I was in no shape to take care of you."

His explanation would make no difference, but Jace was here, so she might as well get the answers denied her for so long. "Why, Jace?"

He stood in front of her, staring at the floor. "She wasn't mine, Arianna."

Confusion marred her features. "Who wasn't yours, Jace?"

"Lauren!" His voice sounded ruthless and hard, but the anguish she saw in his face pulled at her heart. "Lauren," he repeated in a much softer tone. "As soon as I arrived in New York, I knew that I couldn't live there without you. I told Samuel that I wanted full custody of my daughter and an immediate divorce. When Debra received the papers, she did an about face and told me that I could have my divorce on one condition. That condition was that I give up all rights and claims to Lauren." Jace walked to the dresser.

## A Request for Closure

"Of course I told her no, and that's when she told me that Lauren wasn't my child, and after blood tests proved her claim, I fell apart, Ari. I didn't have you. I didn't have my daughter, and I didn't know what to do."

All kinds of thoughts ran though Arianna's mind, but dumbfounded, she could find no words to utter in response.

When she didn't say anything, Jace continued, "Then I learned that I was accepted into the police academy. At first, I wasn't going to go, but I remembered what you'd told me about pursuing my dream. My plan was to complete the program, get my badge, and then come get you. But before I could graduate Jessie mentioned in one of our conversations that you were dating someone a-and…" His voice trailed away and Jace blew out a deep breath.

Arianna stood on shaky legs. "And what, Jace?"

He turned to face her again. "I was a married man when I left Colorado and I had no right to ask for your promise to wait for me. And as much as I loved you, Arianna, I realized that you deserved a chance to find happiness with someone else. It was the least I could do after what I put you through."

In the silence that followed, Jace spent several long moments staring at Arianna. When he held out his arms and she saw the plea in his eyes, she had no choice but to go to him.

"I'm so sorry that happened to you, Jace."

He pulled her close and rested his cheek on top of her hair. "I'm the one who's sorry, Arianna. I married the wrong woman and supported a little girl who wasn't mine for four years. And because I did that, I lost the only woman I've ever loved."

—∽∿∽—

"Auntie Jazz, what are you doing? Paige doesn't want those roses in her bouquet. Those are for the other bouquets, yours, and Auntie Ari's."

Her eyes flashing fire, Jazmin threw down the flowers and rose from her chair. "Know what, Jessie? I'm done with this. Paige should have let the wedding planner do these flowers."

"But Auntie Jazz. The bouquets need to be finished by tonight and I don't know where Auntie Ari went. You have to help!"

*I know where Auntie Ari went*, Jazmin thought, her anger rising like the tide. Auntie Ari was in the bedroom doing who knew what with a man who wasn't her husband. Then she pushed out a breath. It wasn't Arianna's fault that Brick hadn't yet put in an appearance. She wanted to know where the man was and she was getting tired of waiting for an answer.

"Look who I found outside!"

With joy shaking her entire body, Jazmin turned to look. Then she realized that she didn't know the very handsome and very large man who'd entered the apartment. She stood when Paige hustled him over to the couch.

"Jazmin, you don't know this man because you'd already left by the time Arianna and I moved to Denver."

"I know him," Jessie said, leaving the table to join the group.

Staring at her, Freddie tried to jog his memory. "Jessica Michaels?" He chuckled. "Don't tell me that you're the same Jessica Michaels that used to get all up in my business when she was seven years old."

Jessie rewarded him with a beatific smile. "The one and the same, Mr. Lane."

My God, Jazmin thought. This is Arianna's husband! The man was stunning! She watched Freddie and Jessie exchange a quick hug, and then she thought, My God, this is Arianna's husband! "Excuse me," she said, slowly backing out of the room.

"Hold up, Jazz," Paige said. "I want to introduce you to Freddie."

"In a minute," Jazmin said, and then she quickly disappeared down the hallway.

Freddie stared after her. "What was that about?"

"I don't know," Paige said. "She's been acting strange all weekend. Would you like something to drink?"

"I would," he answered. "But first, I need to see my wife."

Listening to the conversation in the living room, Jazmin stood outside the door to Arianna's bedroom. Should she knock or just go in? Jazmin decided to do both.

## A Request for Closure

Now why did it not surprise her to see Arianna in the arms of her former lover? Jazmin pushed off the thought. She needed to get this over with before Paige took it into her head to bring Freddie Lane back there.

"Arianna, you need to go into the living room!"

"Why?" Arianna asked, but her eyes were on Jace.

"Arianna!" Jazmin grabbed her by the arm and pulled her away from Jace. "You need to get out of here right now," she whispered through barely parted lips. "Your husband is in the living room and he's looking for you!"

Brows furrowed, Jace watched Arianna hurry from the room. "What's going on, Jazmin? Who's here for Arianna?"

Jazmin was furious. She'd never understood the power that Jace held over Arianna. The girl was happily married, and yet it had taken him one day to get her back into his arms. In their youth, she'd thought that Jace Barncs was a bastard, and apparently, the man hadn't changed. "I don't know why you're here, Jace, or what you're trying to do. But Ari's husband is here now and whatever you were thinking was going to happen between you and Arianna is over!"

His jaw clenched tight, but Jace held his temper. He had to because seeing Arianna and attending Paige's wedding were not the only reasons he'd come back to Colorado.

"Freddie?"

He turned, and in the next millisecond had Arianna lifted into the air and his lips melded to hers in a kiss so hot, Paige felt the scorch of their love.

One of his hands caressed the side of her face. "Honey, I'm sorry that I hurt you, and I'm here to ask you to forgive me. I love you, Arianna Lane, more than I can ever tell you or show you. But I swear I will spend the rest of my life telling you and showing you, if you'll come home with me."

"You came for me, Freddie."

"I love you, Arianna. You're my life. I won you from him once and I'm going to fight to keep you from going back to him."

"I'm not going anywhere, Freddie. How can I when everything I love is in Kansas, except you because you're here with me now?"

# Wanda Y. Thomas

"You still love me?" He sounded so incredulous Arianna had to kiss him. After all of the years they had shared together, he was still so insecure about her feelings for him.

"Frederick Allan Lane, what do I have to do to convince you that you have all of my love?"

A throat cleared and he glanced over her shoulder at Paige. She pointed to the two people who had come into the room. Freddie let Arianna slide down to the floor.

She took his hand. "Freddie, I'd like you to meet Jazmin Miller and, um, Alvin Barnes. Jazz and Jace, my husband, Frederick Lane."

"I'm so happy to meet you, Jazmin." Freddie pulled her into his arms and squeezed her tight. "Thanks for your help yesterday."

"You're welcome, Freddie, and you're as handsome as Arianna said you were."

He glanced at his wife, saw the anxious tinge in her eyes, and extended his hand to Jace. "Hello, Alvin. It's good to meet you, as well."

Jace was studying Arianna. The glow in her face told him that she was happy and that she truly loved this man, and it was a love that far surpassed anything she'd ever felt for him. In some small way, knowing that compensated for the fact that he couldn't be with her. He shook the hand Freddie offered. "Glad to meet you, too, Freddie. You have a good woman. Take care of her and keep her happy."

"I know, and don't worry, I plan to."

# Chapter 36

R ay, do you remember that doll you gave me the first time we met?"

"I sure do. I bought her because I was afraid that you wouldn't like me and I had to do something to help me get over my anxiety."

"I still have her."

Jazmin heaved a sigh. All day, she'd tried to keep her spirits up even though each minute that ticked off the clock broke her heart a little more. Gathered in the living room, they were eating pizza and reminiscing over old times. All of the players were there, except one, and Jazmin had reached the end of her patience. Jace was on the phone and she waited until he'd ended his call and returned to his chair, before saying, "Okay, Paige. We're all here, now why all the secrecy about this marriage?"

"The secrecy is not about my marriage, Jazmin. It's about yours."

Jazmin's head snapped back. "Mine? What are you talking about?"

"Did you know that William was married before he married you?"

"Yes, Jessie, I did. Why?"

Jessie passed the ball to Jace.

"Where did the two of you get your marriage license?"

Jazmin tsked her tongue in exasperation. "New York, but I don't see how that's any of your business."

Crossing to her, Jessie laid her hand on Jazmin's shoulder. "Auntie Jazz, don't get mad. This is important. What did William tell you about his first wife? I mean…before he married you?"

Jazmin examined the faces of everyone in the room. All except Arianna, Freddie, and Jessie diligently avoided making eye contact with her. She looked down at her hands. "William's first wife's name was Rachel. They met in college and she died very young. That's all I know. Why are you asking these questions?"

"Before we answer that," Jace said, "I have one more. Where did your marriage ceremony to William take place?"

Agitated, Jazmin stood and walked to the patio doors. Jace and Jessie knew something about her marriage, but for the life of her, Jazmin couldn't figure out what. "William and I were married in Oak Bluffs, Massachusetts."

"Whose idea was that?" Jace asked.

"William's. His family owns a summer cottage and he told me that he'd always wanted to get married there."

When she turned around, Paige stood in front of her with a drink. "Jazz...sweetie, you need to sit down." She handed the glass to Jazmin and led her back over to the chair. "Go ahead and tell her, Jessie."

"Auntie Jazz, William's first wife is not dead like he told you. She's alive and living in a mental institution in Elmira, New York."

"She's been there since 1989, and as far as I have been able to determine, prior to her marriage to William there was nothing wrong with Rachel Miller," Jace interjected. "And when Jessie asked me to check it out, I found no record of their divorce...or of your marriage."

Thunderstruck, Jazmin almost slipped off the chair. Sharp pants of air left her mouth and she quickly lifted her glass to hide her agitation. What they were saying could not possibly be true. There had to be a record! "I signed my marriage license, and so did William, and so did the judge who married us. And William provided a copy of the death certificate when we picked up the license."

Jace reached inside his black jacket. "Is this the death certificate?"

Jazmin took the paper. It had been ten years, but she was sure it was a copy of the document William had shown the clerk. "Yes."

"It's a fake, Jazmin, and you and William were never married, at least not legally. A marriage license obtained in the state of New York is only valid if you use it in the state of New York. William apparently knew that, which is why he made sure your wedding ceremony took place out of state."

"But a judge performed our ceremony."

"If William Miller could find someone to fake a death certificate, I'm sure he had no problem finding someone to perform a fake marriage ceremony. I've been a detective for fifteen years and I've arrested people who've tried to get away with it. There is no record of a marriage that took place between you and William Miller, Jazmin, in New York or anywhere else."

Jazmin refused to believe the things she was hearing. She had to. If she didn't, it meant that she'd wasted the last ten years of her life. Ten years that William Miller had stolen from her! She leaped to her feet. She had to get out of there.

Jessie grabbed her arm. "Auntie Jazz, are you all right?"

"No, I'm not all right!" She shook Jessie off. "I'm going back to New York to kill that lying, no good bastard!" Then she fell back into her chair and dropped her head into her hands. For ten years, she'd been living in hell with a man who wasn't even her husband. "Why?" she murmured.

"None of us can tell you why, but there's a lot more that you need to know. For years, William has been filing fraudulent tax returns. On one, he claimed Rachel Miller as his wife. On the other—"

"Jace!" Arianna signaled that he should stop.

"But I can fill you in on the rest later."

Tears stung the back her eyes but Jazmin refused to let them fall. "How did you all know…I mean, why did you start checking into this, Jace?"

"Because Jessie asked me to."

"Let me tell her, Uncle Jace." Jessie circled her arms around Jazmin's shoulders from behind. "Remember when I came to visit you in New York?"

That was as far as Jessie got because Paige went to answer the knock at door and Vincent Marks diverted everyone's attention when he swept into the room. He looked at Jace, who nodded. Without acknowledging the others, he headed directly for Jazmin.

"Jazzy-girl, I'm here now, and I'm telling you that everything is going to be all right." Taking her hand, Brick tugged her from the chair, took the seat, and resettled Jazmin on his lap. "Has she heard all of it?"

"Not yet," Paige said.

Jazmin's trembling body jolted upward. "I don't want to hear any more."

Brick squeezed her around her waist. "You need to hear all of it, Jazmin, and then you and I will talk about what happens next."

Jazmin didn't respond and Jessie continued her story.

"My first four days with Auntie Jazz were a lot of fun. We did a lot of shopping and Auntie Jazz took me to a Broadway play. Then her husband came home early from a business trip. I don't know what it was about him, but I didn't like him and I could tell that he didn't like me. He and Auntie Jazz argued a lot, and one night, I thought I heard her cry out, like he was hitting her or something.

"Later, I got hungry and left my room. The door to William's study was open and he was on the phone. At first, I tried not to listen, but the lawyer in me rose to the surface, especially when I heard William say that his wife was dead and that he had a death certificate to prove it.

"A minute or two later, I heard him say, 'I will be at the sanitarium tomorrow. Have Rachel ready when I arrive because I'm not going to wait around this time.' When I got home, I called Uncle Jace and Uncle Brick and told them what happened. The rest you already know."

—◁∽▷—

Releasing Jazmin, Brick left the bed. He'd hoped to arrive sooner; he'd wanted to be the one to break the news to her. However, his flight from New York had landed only twenty minutes ago. He'd expected her to be upset, ranting and raving, or cussing up a storm, and while he'd never seen her cry, perhaps he'd even expected tears.

## A Request for Closure

Jazmin was doing none of those things. She simply sat on the bed, staring at the floor, and she'd been sitting in the same position for the last thirty minutes. Though he couldn't see her face, Brick knew she was in the process of shutting down.

That he would not let happen. That rat of a man wasn't worth it. "Jazzy-girl, I know you're feeling pretty low right now, but would you please look at me. I need to see that beautiful face of yours."

She wanted to look at Brick; she'd been waiting two whole days just to see him again. He was the reason she'd come back to Colorado, but Jazmin couldn't make herself do it. "You knew about William, too."

Her voice was extremely soft, not like his Jazzy's voice at all. "After Jessie called us, Jace began looking into William's background. It wasn't until a few weeks ago that he was able to put it all together."

"Jace told me that my marriage to William is a sham."

"Did he say anything else?"

"Isn't that enough! I spent ten years of my life with that…that son of a—"

When Jazmin jumped to her feet and marched the floor, Brick took off his jacket and threw it on the bed. "Rest assured that tonight he paid for every one of those years in spades, Jazzy. Men who hit women are pussies. I made sure William understood that or at least he will when he gets out of the hospital. And right before I arrived here, Jace placed a call and IRS agents are swarming his office at this very minute."

Jazmin hurried to his side. "Brick, what did you—"

She stopped and gulped in air. Nothing about Brick Marks had changed, except his hair. It no longer swung around his shoulders, but the much shorter style was more befitting his age. He was still long and lithe, his dark skin smooth, and the light still danced in the depths of his black eyes. "You're still gorgeous," she whispered.

His lips curved upward in a sensual smile. "So are you, Jazzy-girl. So are you."

And then she was in his arms, and Brick was kissing her, and the fire that she'd banked but that she had never allowed to die flared into a

338

roaring blaze. Her breasts ached to feel the stroke of his hands. Her panties were wet from the flow of her desire for this man.

Before she knew it, their clothes were gone and she was on the bed lying in his arms, and to Jazmin Reed, minus the Miller, at that moment, nothing else mattered. Not William, or what he'd done to her, nothing except Vincent Bernard Marks.

---

*Sunday Afternoon*

The two black horses snorted as the carriage came to a stop in front of a massive structure. Jazmin took in the mishmash of spirals, arcs, and peaks and felt the creeps flow through her.

A French priest had commissioned Miramont Castle in 1895, and since 1976, the Manitou Springs Historical Society had been restoring the four-level house with fourteen thousand square feet of living space to its former Victorian splendor. Among the forty-six rooms inside the house were a grand staircase, a sixteen-sided room, a drawing room with a gold ceiling, and a massive two hundred-ton sandstone fireplace. The chapel where the wedding would take place had eight walls. Now a museum open to the public, the castle, according to legend, was haunted.

"Why did you pick this place again, P?"

Paige rose from her seat and adjusted the garment bag holding her gown over her arm in preparation to leave the carriage. "I didn't. Raymond did, because he was fascinated by the nine distinct architectural styles used in the castle's construction."

Jazmin was still looking up as the coachmen helped the women from the carriage. By the time she blinked and took his hand, the others had reached the entrance. Jazmin forced herself to walk and not run up the steps, telling herself that she didn't believe in ghostly tales or wandering spirits. Then again, did anyone really know for sure? Jazmin wasn't about to find out because she had no intention of being by herself anywhere in the castle.

———∽∾∽———

All manner of thought ran through Jace's mind when Arianna stepped out of the dressing room wearing a deep peach, ankle length gown of silk. Spaghetti straps crossed her shoulders and back, and matching pumps adorned her feet.

Unable to stand still, he hurried to her side. "You look gorgeous, baby girl."

"Thank you, Mr. Man." She straightened the peach rose bud in his lapel, and then purposely dragged her hand down the front of his chest.

"You're still a flirt, Arianna Lane," he said, handing her the clutch bouquet of cream-colored orchids and peach blush roses.

"Freddie tells me the same thing," she said.

Jace tugged back the cuff of his shirt, revealing the ID bracelet Arianna had given to him years ago. "Except for cleaning, I've never taken this off. And I never will."

She stared up at him with a look of wonder. "Why, Jace?"

He brushed a curl back from her cheek. "Because for as long as I live, the words on this bracelet will always be true."

Jace presented his arm and together they moved to the doorway and began their walk down the carpeted aisle.

As soon as he saw his wife, Freddie surged to his feet, his heart thumping in his chest, his gaze glued to her softly swaying hips. They had gotten married in a judge's chambers. She had worn a blue business suit; his had been tan. They rarely had a reason to dress up, but there had to be some reasons even in Kansas and Freddie vowed to find them.

Jazmin came out of the room and Brick didn't even try to hide his feelings. He planted a light kiss on her mouth. "You're a knockout, Jazzy-girl."

"Thank you," she said. Her dress was also peach with a floral patterned bodice and a Tarzan shoulder strap.

"You know that as soon as we get that mess in New York straightened out, we're next."

She took her bouquet and they stepped up to the doorway. "I know, and I don't have a problem with that."

Jessie came out of the room wearing a dress with a shirred empire bodice edged with white ribbon and rosettes made of Italian chiffon. Her escort was Raymond's nephew, Jeffery—a man who towered over Jessie by a good six inches.

Jeffery was single, childless, and had followed in his uncle's footsteps. He currently worked as a junior architect for Sloan Brothers. Jessie examined the tall, muscular body, and then tossed him a dimpled smile. Jeffery swallowed hard and although his knees turned to jelly, he managed to present his arm and somehow escort Jessie to the front of the chapel without tripping over his size twelve feet.

Paige stepped up to the doorway. Her gown was a pure silk mermaid sheath of diamond white with a dramatically scooped neckline and edges trimmed in Japanese freshwater pearls. A ring of baby's breath circled her head and she wore no veil. Since there was no one to give her away, she and Raymond had decided to walk down the aisle together. Tonight, the wedding party would celebrate with an early dinner and a relaxed evening of friendship. Tomorrow, her friends would return to their homes, Jessie would go back to school, and she and Raymond would leave for a two-week honeymoon in Paris.

Her eyes sought his. He appeared nervous as he handed her the bouquet of cascading white Casablanca lilies and white tea roses.

She squeezed his arm. "It's going to be all right, baby. We've waited a long time to do this."

Raymond exhaled and quickly pulled himself together. "Yes, we have, precious. Too long, so let's get ourselves down that aisle and do this thing."

# Chapter 37

H ere, Jessie." Arianna set her glass on the dresser. "Take this shawl in case it gets cool."

"Yeah," Jazmin said. "And no matter what he says, do not let Jeffery talk you into doing anything on the first date."

Jessie rolled her eyes. Her aunts and her mother were starting to bug her.

"And make sure he brings you home at a decent hour. The two of you don't need to be out in those streets until all hours of the night."

"The club closes at two, Paige."

"When you dance with him, make sure he keeps his hands on your waist," Jazmin chimed in. "If he tries to put them anywhere else, you sock him, right in the nose."

The four women looked at each other and broke out laughing.

"I love all of you, but y'all act like I'm a baby or something. I know how to handle myself. Besides, shouldn't y'all be out there with your men?" *Instead of in here all up in my business*, she thought, but would never say aloud.

Paige crossed to Jessie and looped a lock of hair behind her ear. "*Our* men are perfectly fine in the living room. They have their dominoes and their beer. And no matter how old you get, Jessica Michaels, you will always be my baby."

Jessie exhaled. "Okay, I'm ready."

"Just remember what we told you, okay?"

"Okay, Auntie Jazz."

"Do you have your cell phone?"

"Yes, Mo-ther!"

Jessie returned the hugs from Paige and Jazmin, then crossed to Arianna, who opened her arms. "I really like this one, Auntie Ari. I sure hope that he likes me."

"He likes you, Jessie."

"Really?"

"Really. Jeffery spent the entire day sneaking peeks at you."

"I know; I saw him, too. Know who he reminds of?"

"No, who?"

"Uncle Jace, and the way he used to look at you all the time."

Arianna hugged Jessie tighter. "Then you have nothing at all to worry about, Jessica."

"What are the two of you whispering about?"

Arianna released Jessie. "Nothing, Jazz. Just girl talk."

When Jessie left, Paige glanced at her two friends. "Think she heard anything we said?"

"Oh, she heard all right," Jazmin said with a laugh. "The question is, will she listen?"

"She'll listen," Arianna said. Jessie has a good head on her shoulders, and she has us."

"That's more than we had." Paige crinkled her brow in thought. "I remember wanting to leave my mother's house more than anything in the world, but when I finally stepped out, the world threw rocks and boulders in my path."

Jazmin picked up her vodka tonic. "I know what you mean. When I left the General's house, I felt as if I'd jumped into the ocean and sunk to the bottom. I knew I couldn't stay down there, but all I could do was flap my arms and pray that I reached the surface."

"And then you met Vincent Marks, and he lifted you up, and Paige met Raymond and he did the same thing for her."

Jazmin peered at her closely. "And what about you, Ari? Are you still in love with Jace?"

Arianna walked over to the dresser and lifted her eyes to meet those of her friends in the mirror. "Being with Jace taught me a lot about love and life. Mostly, I learned that I am a survivor and that I am not like my mother, totally dependent on a man and pissed off because I have no other options. But no, I don't love Jace. He's part of my past. Freddie is my present and my future." Arianna grabbed her drink and returned to the bed. "I had a lot of questions that I carried around with me for too many years. Now I have the answers and I'm at peace with Jace and the past we shared. When you go home, are you going to be okay?"

"Like you, I'm a survivor, too, Arianna—always have been. I learned a long time ago that when life knocks you down, you'd better get up or a steamroller may come along and flatten you. Honestly, if I ever see William Miller again, I think I'll kill him. But coming back here reunited me with Brick. He's flying home with me tomorrow and the first thing we plan to do is get the rest of my things and find a place to live. Since my marriage wasn't legal, I'm sure I'll be very busy for a while separating my life from William's."

"But I thought Brick was going to star in that soap," Paige said. "In California."

"He was, but he's decided to turn down the part." She shrugged her shoulders. "Says he wants to try his luck on the stage. I think he's doing it for me, so that I can stay New York."

"He's doing it because he loves you, Jazmin. Brick has always loved you."

"I know, Ari, and that's why as soon as it can be arranged, I'm going to marry that man like I should have in the first place. Now what about you, Mrs. Raymond Steward? How does it feel to finally be a married woman again?"

"It feels good." Paige examined the rings sparkling on her finger. "You know, for a long time, I thought it was the being married part that mattered. And the two of you know how many men I went through all because I wanted a man to walk me down that aisle. But I learned that it's the *particular* man you marry that really counts." She sighed. "I've thought about this a lot over the years. The three of us were a mess back then. We were lost souls who didn't have a clue as to what we were doing, so we stumbled through life and hoped for the best."

"But we were lucky because we stumbled into each other," Arianna said.

"That's true," Jazmin said, sitting up. "Okay, since we all have our glass, I have a toast." She raised hers. "The first is to Paige. My wish is that you and Raymond share happiness, peace, and love for the rest of your lives. The second is for the three of us. We shared a lot as young girls and we grew apart as we matured into the women we are today. Here's to making sure that we never let that happen again."

"Hear, hear," all three said as they clinked glasses and drank.

Paige surveyed the smiling faces of her friends. Other than her marriage to Raymond, she hadn't really been sure what would happen that weekend, but after a rocky start, it had turned out for the best after all.

Now that Arianna had the answers she'd needed, Paige felt sure that their friendship would blossom into what it had once been, and that her friend was back in her life to stay. Once she'd learned about the true state of Jazmin's marriage, Paige's only goal had been to get her friend out of a situation that Jazmin had refused to acknowledge was bad. In doing that, Jazmin had reunited with Brick, the man Paige had known that her friend truly loved all along.

In another life, she'd thought that she needed a man to be happy. While she would love to reclaim those years of being without him, walking away from Raymond was the best thing she could have done for herself. She'd never needed a man to make her happy or to take care of her or her child. Once she'd learned that she could be fine by herself, God led her back to Raymond Steward.

"I have one more toast," Paige said, raising her glass into the air again. "And this one is to closure."

# Group Discussion Questions:

1. Did your mother or someone else in your life teach you about love and the relationships shared between men and women? If yes, did/does it help you in your relationships as an adult? If no, would it have helped?

2. While reading ARFC, were you able to identify the motivating factors behind the behavior and actions of Paige, Jazmin, and Arianna? Discuss what motivated each of the women.

3. Some of the decisions Jazmin, Paige, and Arianna made were the result of childhood trauma. How do you think the experiences of your childhood affect your life today?

4. Was Freddie justified in his feelings of insecurity regarding Arianna's love for him?

5. Given his issues, was Freddie right to let Arianna return to Colorado? Why or why not?

6. Paige fell in love with two men at the same time. Do you think that she really loved Lewis? What about Raymond? Have you ever been in love with two people at the same time? How did you handle your situation?

7. After months of living with Jace, Arianna is shocked to learn that he is married. Discuss your thoughts on how she handled the situation. What would you have done in her place? Do you know anyone who's had an affair with a married man or woman? Did that person know that the other person was married?

8. Jazmin chose her career over love. What would you have done in her situation? What do you think about Brick's decision to let her go?

9. The youngest person in this story had the most influence over the adults in her life. Discuss Jessie and the effect the adults in her life had on her. What type of woman do you think Jessie would be today?

10. After her confession, what do you think about Raymond's decision to continue his involvement with Paige?

11. William was an abusive husband. Why do you think Jazmin stayed with him for so long?

12. What would you do if you learned after ten years that your marriage was a sham?

13. Which character in ARFC did you identify with the most and why?

14. Of Arianna, Paige, and Jazmin, whose story touched you the most? Why?

15. Of the five (5) men—Jace, Frederick, Brick, Lewis, and Raymond—would you chose any as a romantic partner? Why or why not?

16. Should Paige have interfered in the lives of her friends? If you knew that your brother, sister, best friend, daughter, son was involved in an abusive relationship, what would you do?

# About the Author

In 1994, God led **Wanda Y. Thomas** to the dusty desert and Decadent City of Las Vegas. "Though God may have had a hand in it," says Wanda, "It was actually a home shopping network, which relocated about 100 people from across the country to Las Vegas, and then laid us all off within a month." That experience and the lessons learned prompted Wanda to review the goals on her *Life's List*, and to pursue the one that said: *write a book and get it published*. Wanda is an awarded-winning author of five full-length romance novels and a novella. She is the Vice President of Affiliate Relations for a cable television programming network and lives in Calabasas, California with her son. To learn more about Wanda and her books, please visit her website at www.wandaythomas.com or write to her at wanda@wandaythomas.com.